"*I need to tell you,*" Prince Thabiso said between kisses, "*who I am.*"

Who I *really* am, he added silently.

"I know who you are," Ledi said. She pulled off her t-shirt, revealing a soft, worn-looking gray bra cupping her silky brown breasts. "You're the guy who learned to cook for me. The guy who's made me laugh harder than I have in a long time. The guy who—" She whispered the rest in his ear.

He chuckled and ran a fingertip over the lace that edged her bra. "I love that you speak so freely."

"Only with you. I feel like my entire life has been me trying to keep everything together, but right now I want to fall apart."

He could see the want in her eyes. "I must tell you something, Ledi."

But how could he?

By Alyssa Cole

A PRINCESS IN THEORY

~RELUCTANT ROYALS~

ALYSSA COLE

AVONBOOKS

An Imprint of HarperCollinsPublishers

Excerpt from *A Duke by Default* copyright © 2018 by Alyssa Cole.

A PRINCESS IN THEORY. Copyright © 2018 by Alyssa Cole. All rights reserved. Printed in the United States of America. No part of this book may be used or reproduced in any manner whatsoever without written permission except in the case of brief quotations embodied in critical articles and reviews. For information, address Harper-Collins Publishers, 195 Broadway, New York, NY 10007.

First Avon Books mass market printing: March 2018

Print Edition ISBN: 978-0-06-268554-4
Digital Edition ISBN: 978-0-06-268555-1

Cover design by Nadine Badalaty
Cover photographs by Michael Frost Photography; © trait2lumiere/
Getty Images (stairs)
Cover dress designed by Nicole Simpson (adorned by Nicole)

Avon, Avon & logo, and Avon Books & logo are registered trademarks of HarperCollins Publishers in the United States of America and other countries.
HarperCollins is a registered trademark of HarperCollins Publishers in the United States of America and other countries.

FIRST EDITION

18 19 20 21 22   QGM   10 9 8 7 6 5 4 3 2 1

*For all the people who were told
they couldn't be princesses:
you always were one.*

A
PRINCESS
IN THEORY

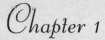

Chapter 1

Sender: LikotsiAdelele@KingdomOfThesolo.the
Subject: Salutations from the Royal Family of
  Thesolo

Dear Ms. Smith,

I hope that my letter finds you well. I, Likotsi
Adelele, assistant to His Royal Highness, have sought
you out high and low over the last few months, at
the behest of the most exalted—and most curious—
Prince Thabiso. He has tasked me with finding his
betrothed, and I believe I have succeeded: it is you.
Because our prince is magnanimous, kind, and understanding, he is willing to cleanse the festering wounds
of the past and allow them to heal. In order to aid in
this process, please send the following verifications
of identity: a scan of your license, passport, or other
form of ID; up to date medical records—

Sender: LikotsiAdelele@KingdomOfThesolo.the
Subject: RE: RE: RE: RE: Salutations from the Royal
　　Family of Thesolo

Hello again, dear Ms. Smith,

They say persistence is a virtue, and I consider myself most virtuous, as I have now written several times without acknowledgment, and yet I press on. It is the will of the prince that he meets the woman chosen by the goddess Ingoka to be his bride, and I am charged with bringing his will into fruition. It occurs to me that perhaps you fear repercussions for the headstrong and thoughtless actions of your mother and father, but fear not. All will be well . . . if you are indeed the woman chosen to be the future queen of Thesolo. I am quite sure you are the woman he is searching for. But, I must, MUST, have some proof of identity before we proceed any further. I will not expose the prince to perfidy. So, I beseech you to (a) respond and (b) provide me with—

Sender: LikotsiAdelele@KingdomOfThesolo.the
Subject: FWD: RE: RE: RE: RE: RE: RE: RE: RE: RE:
　　Salutations from the Royal Family of Thesolo

To the most kind, most gentle Ms. Smith,

Perhaps you have not received the electronic missives I've sent over the past few weeks (see below)? I cannot believe that you've read my heartfelt pleas and ignored them. If you are worried that the people of Thesolo have forsaken you for your malfeasance, fear not. Despite the rupture in trust caused by your parents' selfishness, the contract of marriage, made before goddess and government of our people, still stands. As I stated in my previous emails (see below, if you did not scroll down at my first urging), although I believe you to be the rightful recipient of this email, before I can introduce you to Prince Thabiso after this long absence, I will need more information. Please provide a scan of your license, passport, or other form of ID; your current address; social security number—

I really don't have time for this," Naledi muttered, the soothing hum of various expensive laboratory equipment masking the aggravation in her tone.

She deleted the email with a jab at the trash can icon on the screen of her phone.

The first couple of emails had been amusing, a welcome distraction from the rest of her inbox, which was primarily comprised of calendar reminders about study sessions, student loan payment nudges, data sets to be solved, and other evidence of grad school life. The emails had become less entertaining as the subject lines grew more urgent and it became clear that this wasn't a random occurrence: somewhere in the world, a scammer had zeroed in on *her*. The knowledge was disturbing to someone as private as Ledi and triggered a sense of helplessness all too familiar for a woman who'd been bounced through strangers' homes for most of her childhood.

Ignoring the emails hadn't worked: the spammer had redoubled their efforts, undeterred by Ledi's lack of response. She'd considered blocking messages from the sender, but it seemed scarier *not* knowing if she was receiving disturbing emails.

Ledi pushed her safety goggles up onto her thick

curls, which she'd smoothed back and pulled into a puff ponytail, and mentally reviewed her to-do list. She'd already created the media needed for experiments, prepared slides, and input data that morning, so she'd actually be able to get some studying in.

She hefted her copy of *Modern Epidemiology* from out of the backpack at her feet and slid it onto her desk. Balancing her lab assistant job, waitressing, and grad school hadn't seemed overly ambitious at first— Ledi had been juggling jobs and school since she was thirteen. But as tension gripped the back of her neck at the thought of finals and experiments and what the hell the future held, she wondered if maybe she hadn't bitten off more than she could chew.

She'd been lucky in that she'd transitioned from foster care to adulthood better than some people she'd been in the system with, but luck wasn't a statistically significant factor in planning her future. Making money, on the other hand, was a proven course of action, and having multiple sources of income was a safety net she couldn't live without. She didn't have family to turn to when times got rough, and one mistake at work or school could have a domino effect on the life plans she had so carefully been setting up.

"Hey, Naledi."

Brian, the postdoc, was suddenly hovering over her shoulder.

Brian was super fun to work with: on her first day, she'd introduced herself, and he'd asked her to take out the trash more frequently—he'd thought she was the cleaning woman. He often stopped to explain basic concepts to Ledi—and Ledi alone—during lab meetings, while asking Kevin, the newbie, for his advice on how things should be run.

So fun, that Brian.

She turned to face him. His dark hair was sticking out every which way and his face was unshaven. He looked stressed-out, which wasn't unusual but generally didn't bode well for her.

"Hi Brian," she said, trying to find the pleasant but deferential tone that seemed to edify him. She hated that she couldn't just talk to him like a normal human, but apparently there was *something* about her that had led him to tell Dr. Taketami—the lab's Primary Investigator, and thus Ledi's boss—that she was "giving him attitude."

Ledi couldn't afford to be labeled as a problem.

She'd wanted to be a scientist since her fourth-grade teacher had handed her a battered copy of *National Geographic*. Ledi had been fascinated with the cover: a close-up shot of a woman with dark skin, just like hers, peering into a microscope. That scientist had been trying to cure a mysterious disease, and Ledi had gleaned from the image not only that she wanted to do the same thing but also that she *could*.

She hadn't foreseen all the other variables that went into life as a woman in STEM: politicians who treated her profession with contempt and threatened her future—and the world's. Fellow scientists like Brian, who thought that women in the lab were their personal assistants instead of their equals.

"How are you this morning?" she asked him in the tone she'd heard secretaries on old syndicated TV shows use to placate their sexist bosses. Brian smiled; he'd watched the same reruns it seemed.

"Actually, I'm a little behind in my work after getting back from the Keystone conference." That was when Naledi noticed the sheaf of papers in his hands.

This motherfucker, she thought.

"Oh what a shame," she said.

"There's this grant application that has to go out and we're kind of screwed if we lose this funding. Since you don't have much to do . . ."

"How do you know I don't have much to do?" she asked in the same polite tone, unable to repress the question.

Brian cleared his throat. "Well, you're just sitting here."

"Kevin is just sitting here, too. He's clearly watching a movie on his phone," she said, tilting her head toward her lab mate across the room, who was laughing at whatever he was streaming. Her voice was still calm and polite, but she saw Brian's brows drawing together in annoyance.

"Look, we all have to do grunt work sometimes. It comes with the territory. Do you think you're somehow exempt from putting in the work?"

Ledi sucked in a breath. She worked hard—so much harder than she should have had to, really. That was the problem. When you worked twice as hard all the time, working at the average rate was slacking off.

"No," she said quietly. "I don't think that."

Why did I even say anything?

She'd learned early on that challenging the people who held power over you made you undesirable, and undesirability meant gathering all of your things into a black plastic trash bag and being sent back to the group home. She swallowed against the brief wave of nausea and remembered the workshop for women in STEM she'd taken. She had to lay down her boundaries or people would assume she had none.

"I have no problem paying my dues, but this is the fourth grant you've asked me to help with," she said. "And let me guess, it's due this week?"

Brian nodded stiffly.

"Kevin has never done one of these for you before," she said gently, though she was tired of being gentle. She was just plain tired.

"All the more reason for you to do it," Brian insisted. "You won't make beginner's mistakes."

And there it was; if she continued any further she'd be pushing, and as much as she'd heard about leaning in, when Ledi pushed she was usually met with a brick wall exerting equal and opposite force. She should have just taken the forms with a smile and kept her mouth shut.

"Sure. I'll get right on it. Sorry."

She put her textbook away and took the papers, somehow managing not to crumple them into a ball, and Brian walked off without saying thanks.

Ledi took a deep, centering breath.

Asshole postdocs are temporary, but scientific discoveries are forever.

When she opened her eyes, Trishna, her lab mate and a fellow Public Health student, was watching her from across the work table. Her long, dark hair was pulled back and her safety goggles magnified the annoyance in her eyes.

"He's such a jerk," Trishna said, and Ledi allowed herself a brief moment of camaraderie before shrugging it off.

"It's not a big deal," she said brightly. She smiled at Trishna and hoped her expression wasn't as murdery as she felt.

"It is a big deal. Fuck Brian," Trishna said. Then her brows lifted behind her goggles. "He's probably jealous of your practicum with Dr. Kreillig's Disease Task Force this summer, you know. It sounds so badass. Task force! Like that meme with the dude with sunglasses. 'I'm here to cure diseases and chew bubble gum, and I'm all out of bubble gum.'"

Trishna grabbed two test tubes and pointed them menacingly around the lab.

Ledi might have laughed if Trishna hadn't brought up yet another one of her bumper crop of problems. She shuffled through the grant papers Brian had just left her without really looking at them. "Yeah. I'm looking forward to learning a lot this summer."

What she wanted to say was that her advisor Dr. Kreillig had stopped responding to her emails and phone calls and she actually had no idea what was happening with her summer fieldwork, but sharing that kind of info would have been un-Ledi-like.

"The task force seems to have a great dynamic," she added for effect. If you said inane things with a smile people couldn't tell they were being stonewalled. "They did a great job containing the recent outbreak of Legionnaires' disease."

Being outwardly friendly while keeping people at a distance was second nature to Ledi. She thought of it as her social phospholipid bilayer: flexible, dynamic, and designed to keep the important parts of herself separate from a possibly dangerous outside environment. It had been working for the prokaryotes for eons, and it would suffice for a broke grad school student, which was only slightly higher on the evolutionary scale.

"When are you starting?" Trishna asked.

"Still waiting to hear back about that. Dr. Kreillig is pretty busy." Both of those things were generally true.

"Ooo, maybe he's busy with some kind of epidemic?" Trishna offered helpfully. "Apparently, last year when cases of Zika started to pop up, he was MIA for a few days."

Ledi wouldn't wish an outbreak on anyone, but that might explain why it'd been over a week since she'd heard from him. A week felt like forever when her practicum, her resulting thesis, and perhaps the path her entire career would take were on the line. If only Dr. Kreillig were as motivated as her Nigerian—or Thesoloian, to be more accurate—scammer, she wouldn't be in this situation.

"What about you?" Ledi asked, changing the topic.

"Eh, I leave for Maine the week after exams."

Ledi's phone vibrated and she saw a text from her friend Portia pop up on the screen.

> We're having an opening at the gallery where I'm interning tomorrow night. Free wine and cheese! You love free wine and cheese! ☺

Ledi loved free food and drink of all kinds, but if she went to this opening she'd have to squeeze into the trendy art gallery with a hundred other like-minded people to obtain it. She'd also likely have to deal with drunk Portia. Drunk Portia was not on Ledi's miles-long to-do list.

> That sounds fun, but I have to work at the Institute until nine tomorrow. ☹

> **Aw, boo. Maybe we can meet for drinks after?** 👆

> Maybe!

Maybe not. Portia was her best friend, but Ledi was too exhausted to deal with alcohol-fueled hijinks. She wanted a glass of wine after a long day so she could unwind, not as a prelude to a night of debauchery.

She didn't have anything against debauchery, but she had no time for it—or for the spike of anxiety each time Portia flagged down a waitress or headed back to the bar.

Portia was the perfect example of why Ledi's social cell membrane existed. Once someone slipped through, Ledi couldn't help but worry over them, and worrying had no concrete results in the real world except draining her much-needed energy.

> Oh, did you check your MyGeneScreen results? I'm 83% African and 17% European. I have to break it to my mom that we are not, in fact, descended from a Cherokee princess.

> **Yikes. Hold off on that conversation though. You know I don't believe in the accuracy of these tests.**

Portia had received a couple of the DNA test packs from some promotional event for social media movers and shakers, and had given one to Ledi. Ledi had been momentarily seduced by the possibility of knowing more about her background, but when the email announcing her results had arrived, she'd deleted it.

What did it matter? She was 100 percent New Yorker and that was all she needed to know. Sure, the genetic database linked you with possible relatives but . . .

But what? She had survived a not so great childhood, she was on her way to being a pretty damn great epidemiologist, and she didn't need any scientifically shoddy data to introduce more confounding factors into her life.

She was fine.

"Everything going okay with the grant stuff?" Brian called across the lab. "You understand everything?"

He gave her a thumbs-up that was somehow a question. She wanted to reply with her own one-finger salute, but instead she gave him a wide, fake smile.

"Everything's under control!" she said brightly, and wished it was true.

Chapter 2

*L*edi cursed the spam filter gods, again, as she stepped into her cramped Inwood studio apartment later the next evening. She also cursed herself for forgetting to throw out the trash before sleepwalking to the university library that morning—her place smelled like the cheap Chinese takeout that she'd eaten two nights before.

She dropped her backpack on the floor and pulled the tied-off plastic bag emblazoned with an enthusiastic THANK YOU! from her doorknob. The sounds of her neighbors' lives echoed in the hallway along with her footsteps as she headed for the trash compactor: Mrs. Garcia across the hall, the widowed retiree who DVRed her telenovelas and watched them at top volume every night when she got home from her volunteer work; Jayden and Ben, the children in 7 C, who always seemed to be laughing maniacally about something; Boca, the parrot that cursed in Lithuanian every time someone passed the door of 7 H.

She could also smell her neighbors—dinners prepared in the style of at least four continents, plus the hazy contribution of the hipster stoner who had moved in a few weeks before.

The trash compactor room took all the communal smells, then fermented and magnified them. She held her breath as she entered the small room, used her sleeve to open the bacteria-covered trap door to the chute, and dropped in the remains of her egg foo yung. Her phone vibrated in her pocket and, in a flash of irritation, Ledi considered tossing it in, too. That would be a temporary solution to her annoying spammer problem, however, and she'd worked much too hard for the phone to consider it disposable.

She'd lucked into a rent-controlled apartment right out of high school, and her part-time job at the Institute's upscale dining hall paid a great hourly wage for waitressing work, but the phone had still been a big chunk of her budget. A chunk that could have gone toward paying off the remainder of her undergrad loans, or at least some of the interest. She'd had a good rate locked in, but then her loan had been sold to some random company intent on fleecing every sucker who hadn't been able to pay for their college education on the spot. The thought of all the money she owed and would owe to various government entities made her want to put the phone safely down and jump into the compactor chute herself.

And who would really notice if you did, except for bill collectors? And Portia?

She headed back to her apartment, scrubbed her hands in the sink of her tiny bathroom, and then collapsed onto her futon.

She winced. *I really need to get some memory foam in my life.*

She had enough money saved to make the futon upgrade, but her brain rejected the expenditure, placing it on a pedestal as something the future Ledi, who had enough money to make such purchases without triple-checking her bank account balance beforehand, could buy. Ledi didn't know how much money would be enough, but she was sure she was nowhere near that goal.

She stretched and closed her eyes against thoughts of money and her uncertain future. Her body ached from hours on her feet waitressing at the Institute, and her brain was mush from studying and trying not to worry about her practicum.

She'd told herself not to get too excited when Kreillig had offered her the summer internship because excitement was just another name for expectation, and expectations were the fastest route to disappointment. But then she'd read a blog post on *girlswithglasses.com* about minimizing your accomplishments. It had asked readers to leave their latest accomplishment in the comments, and under the guise of web community semi-anonymity, she'd posted *I GOT A FUCKING AWESOME INTERNSHIP!!* She'd reveled in the likes and encouragement from fellow commenters, but now she felt like she was paying for it with the torture of waiting for Kreillig's response.

And then there was the spammer who thought Ledi was delusional enough to believe she was princess material . . .

Frustrated squeaking from the corner of her apartment broke through her daze, and she sprang out of bed, spurred by the quick, sharp guilt of disappointing someone—or something—dependent on her for survival.

"Sorry! Shit, you must be starving!" She hurried to the small cage near the room's sole window, which provided a spectacular view of the brick wall of the adjacent building. It wasn't much to look at, but Gram-P and Gram-N had once been destined to become slides under some researcher's microscope, so she was pretty certain they appreciated it.

The two white lab mice hopped up excitedly, their small pink hands pressing against the glass as she approached. It was a Friday, which meant she'd brought them some high-fat chow from the lab.

"Yup. It's the good stuff," she said, grabbing the sandwich bag from her backpack and dropping the pellets through the mesh at the top of the cage. They squeaked appreciatively and ran to gather their meal.

"What do you guys think?" she asked, leaning on the wall beside the windowsill.

Two sets of beady pink eyes looked up at her. Gram-P stopped chewing the pellet he held in his paws, as if waiting for her to go on.

"Do I look like princess material to you?"

Gram-N turned his back to hunt for more chow, and Ledi had to agree with him.

She didn't know why the Thesoloian scammers

had decided to target her, of all people. She looked around her tiny apartment. Clean but obviously secondhand furniture she'd acquired from Goodwill stores and curbs on garbage night. Postcards and cheap prints she'd framed to give some personality to her living area, and one really nice painting that had been a gift from Portia. Like most of her life, her interior decoration had been borne of other people's scraps. The scammers obviously needed to refine their search criteria.

Or maybe they were right on target.

The selfishness of your parents . . . She hadn't thought about her parents in so long, but the emails from this Likotsi had made her start to wonder again. She'd almost replied, *almost*, then reminded herself that this was how they lured people in. Maybe there was some database of kids who had aged out of foster care without being adopted or reunited with family members that these assholes were trawling for victims.

Ledi took a deep breath around the jumble of emotions coalescing in her chest, a sensation she hadn't felt since she was seventeen and sitting in her college dorm room, watching parents of every kind move their kids in. She'd lied and said her parents had already left when people asked where they were; it was easier than dealing with the pitying looks she got when she told the truth. Several of her undergrad classmates had graduated thinking her parents were alive. It hadn't mattered; those people had been part of the outside environment of college life.

Ledi pushed away the aggravating thoughts.

The emails were more than mere annoyances. They were a reminder of what she had lost. She was an adult now, making her way in the world and doing a damn good job at it, but part of her would always be the four-year-old hiding in the closet of an unfamiliar foster home unable to process that she'd never see her parents again.

She remembered her father's dark skin and the way his smile seemed like it made the world turn. She remembered that her mother smelled of flowers and cocoa butter, and the way it felt to be squeezed tightly in her arms. But that was it, apart from a few shards of memories that sometimes came in dreams and splintered if she grasped them too tightly. She didn't know who they were, or who *she* was, and each one of the emails reminded her of the heart of the matter: she was alone.

Gram-P squeaked and hurried to the side of the cage closest to her. He pressed his paw against it, as if sensing her sadness. She gave the glass an appreciative stroke with a fingertip and sighed.

It doesn't get more pathetic than this, Ledi thought, pushing off of the windowsill and taking the few short steps that carried her to the kitchenette. *Being comforted by* Mus musculus.

Her phone vibrated but she ignored it, knowing it was either another annoying email or Portia texting to see if she'd changed her mind about meeting for drinks. Both possibilities held the same appeal for her, since Portia still considered *The Hangover* her template for a fun night out.

Ledi glanced at the phone, the glow from the screen catching her attention. Maybe she should go out. She hadn't done anything fun in a while, and hanging with her best friend was healthier than talking to mice. But the thought of fake banter with strangers at a bar, or worse, Portia asking her what was wrong, made the decision for her. Talking about what was happening with Kreillig and with her spammer would make it too real, and Portia would of course try to fix things because Portia was invested in fixing everything that wasn't herself.

Ledi reached for the freezer. She'd spend the night with Ben and Jerry, who didn't ask questions and stayed off the sauce unless you were talking rum raisin. They wouldn't drag her into any shenanigans, and they certainly wouldn't judge her for indulging in the childish fantasy that maybe, just maybe, the scammer from Thesolo was telling her the truth.

LEDI AWOKE FROM dreams of Bonferroni correction rates to the sound of jackhammering. Her alarm hadn't gone off yet, meaning it was way too early or too late for any kind of construction to be happening. She could call 311 to complain, but they wouldn't do anything anyway. It was the placebo pill of emergency numbers. She pulled the pillow over her head.

The sound started up again just as she was drifting to sleep, and she realized it wasn't outside. The pounding was coming from inside the house, so to speak.

"Ledi! I have to use the bathroom!" a familiar voice called outside her front door.

Oh fuck.

Portia. At Ledi's door in the middle of the night instead of at her own Brooklyn apartment. *Again.*

Dammit. There goes my REM sleep.

She was so tired that she almost cried at the loss of precious sleep. She could pretend she wasn't home, but doing that would have two possible outcomes: (1) one of her neighbors would be woken up instead, possibly resulting in a scene; (2) Portia would wander off, leaving Ledi to worry whether she'd made it home okay. Both outcomes resulted in loss of sleep, so opening the door would save her time and energy, and maybe a visit to the ER.

That's what friends are for, right?

She crawled out of bed and undid the column of locks on the door. The distinct odor of old Irish pub smacked her in the nostrils when she opened the door, and she scrunched her nose.

"Are you okay?" she asked out of habit. It was the same thing she replied first thing in the morning after waking up to drunk texts. Portia looked okay, though; better than okay.

One day Ledi would do a case study on how her friend was always so pulled together, even at her hot messiest. Portia's slim-fitting ivory pants only sported a few stains, and her tailored brown blouse was just wrinkled enough to be fashionable. Her earrings, necklace, and bracelets were a mix of refined classic and chunky boho chic that suited her perfectly. Her rust-gold ringlets were popping, her edges were flourishing, and her light brown skin was clear and smooth, apart from a smattering of freckles.

The only thing off was her eyes. They were full of the wariness that often arose after a few drinks, even when she was supposedly having fun. It was something that Ledi hadn't been able to understand in all their years of friendship. She hadn't been able to persuade Portia to talk to someone whose job it was to understand, either.

"I'm fine. I hope I'm not bothering you," Portia said in a soft, only slightly slurred voice as she squinted into Ledi's studio. "I just hadn't seen you in a while, and I got worried when I was texting and calling and you didn't respond. The after party wasn't too far from here—well the after-after party, which was just me and the artist at his apartment—so I decided to stop by and see if you were still alive."

Portia grinned and shrugged, and a bit of Ledi's annoyance dissolved. A tiny bit. A microscopic bit. Ledi *had* been too busy to meet up for the last few weeks, despite Portia's persistent requests for dinner, drinks, and invitations to various artsy events. And Portia had been worried—no one besides her had really worried about Ledi since she'd transitioned from foster care to living on her own. But showing up drunk on a friend's doorstep in the middle of the night wasn't cool, even if it was well-intentioned; and this wasn't the first, or even the fifth time it had happened.

Ledi had talked to Portia both as a friend and as a soon-to-be health care professional. During each discussion, a chastened Portia promised to take it easy with the partying and a frustrated Ledi explained that she wouldn't keep dealing with drunken hijinks; both of them swallowed the lies easily because what was the alternative?

"Ledi?" There was the slightest twinge of panic in her friend's voice.

Ledi sighed.

"It's the middle of the night, so, yes, you're bothering me. But since you came to make sure I didn't get serial killed, it's okay I guess," Ledi said, stepping aside to let her in.

It's not okay.

Portia stumbled into the apartment, making a sharp right to maneuver herself into the bathroom that had seemingly been built for a contortionist.

Ledi walked over to her tiny kitchen. She filled a bottle with water and dropped in an effervescent multivitamin that would help stave off a hangover. She stood for a moment, watching the bubbles through the clear plastic and listening as her toiletries were knocked off of their shelves in the bathroom. The weight of a question she tried not to ask herself too often settled over her.

Wouldn't it be nice if someone took care of me, instead? In her experience, unless they were getting a paycheck, no one was interested in that particular task.

The toilet flushed and there was the crash of something hitting the tile floor. Ledi cringed.

"I also wanted to make sure you were okay, after the whole Clarence thing," Portia continued their conversation seamlessly as she stepped out, rubbing her hands on her pants. She pulled out her sleek phone, which was at least three generations ahead of Ledi's and double the size. "I have to replace your candle. I'll order one now and it'll arrive tomorrow. And you really need to get some new hand towels. I'll add those to the order."

Ledi blinked.

Candle? Okay, that's what the breaking glass had been. Towels? The ones she had were fine. Clarence? She'd already put that short-lived relationship out of her mind; an ill-timed pop-up text from his side piece had revealed his true nature. A few weeks of freedom from his boring finance industry stories had proven what a blessing Melissa *"I'm naked and waiting"* S. had been.

"Um, thanks? But Clarence is history. He's been filed away in the Annals of the Journal of New York City Fuckboys." She handed Portia the bottle. "Along with ninety-five percent of your hookups."

"Good." Portia ignored the poke about her own dating life and instead flopped onto the futon and began scrolling on her phone while sipping from the bottle. "Should we kill him? I'd help you hide the body. You know my family owns land all over the northeast. Oh, look at these hand towels with little microscopes on them!"

She held up her phone toward Ledi.

"No need to kill Clarence—having to live with himself is punishment enough," Ledi said, and then leaned down to examine the phone. "And the towels are cute but I can buy my own."

"Why? I said I would pay for them. And we should still shank him," Portia said around a yawn.

Ledi shook her head. Portia *might* kill for her, but she would do it with some kind of fancy steak knife from Tiffany's or wherever rich people shopped for cutlery, not a crude shank. Or if she did use a shank, it would be some artisanal weapon she'd crafted at one of her workshops, made with salvaged beach glass or something.

Portia was a perpetual student, trying anything that interested her, then moving on when the next thing caught her fancy. She could afford to coast, choosing where and how seriously to pursue her studies on a whim. Ledi tried not to resent that, and mostly succeeded. Portia hadn't asked to be Richie Rich any more than Ledi had asked to be a Little Orphan Annie.

Ledi climbed into the bed beside Portia, jerking a portion of her blanket from under her friend. She could sleep for a little while longer. She'd be having biostats for breakfast with her study group, and then a long shift at the Institute awaited her, with more studying capping off her night—and more grinding her teeth about her internship if Kreillig didn't get back to her.

"Ledi?" Portia tugged the blanket out from beneath her and pushed it toward Ledi.

"What's up?"

"I didn't really bother you, did I?"

Ledi was still annoyed, and she didn't want to encourage bad habits, but part of her was glad Portia had stopped by. She'd been consumed with school and work, and she'd forgotten how good it was to interact with someone who had nothing to do with either.

"No. You didn't."

Portia responded with light snores; she was already asleep.

Ledi sighed and stared up into the darkness; she was wide-awake. She hadn't given much thought to her most recent break up, but now she wondered why Portia had worried Clarence would return—Ledi had never expected him to hang around to begin with. She was like a faulty piece of Velcro; people tried to stick to her, but there was something intrinsically wrong in her design. Twenty plus years of data, starting from that first foster family, supported that hypothesis. Hell, Portia's late-night drunk visits were worrisome, but Ledi was still shocked each time that her friend cared enough to stop by.

Is that why you put up with it?

Ledi shifted on the futon, rolling away from the uncomfortable thought but not quickly enough to evade another one: it'd been a relief when she'd found out about Clarence's cheating—he'd proven her Velcro hypothesis correct. And when he'd shrugged and said, "It's not like you love me," he hadn't been mistaken. Her social cell membrane had kept her heart intact.

Still . . . she wondered what it would be like to let

someone in. Not Clarence, who'd been a Break Glass In Case of Emergency kind of boyfriend, but someone who might actually prove her hypothesis wrong.

That would be terrifying.

Ledi tossed and turned, as if wriggling free from the thoughts that threatened to bind her, and Portia grumbled on the other side of the bed.

She was fine on her own. She always had been. And if no good guy ever made it past her barriers? Well, that'd be fine, too.

Just fine.

She stared at the ceiling, willing herself to sleep. Her brain had other ideas, taking her on a guided tour of all the work she had to complete and explaining how inability to do so would result in complete and utter failure. Finally, like a rat on a wheel going full tilt, she exhausted herself with all the ways she could fail and the repercussions of each possibility, and began to slide into sleep.

Oh god, yesss, this is so much better than sex, who needs a man? she thought as she was tugged into the sweet darkness of slumber—and then her phone vibrated.

She groaned into her pillow, her body heavy with fatigue, and reached for the phone.

Sender: LikotsiAdelele@KingdomOfThesolo.the
Subject: Time Is of the Essence

Ms. Smith,

I know that you have received my messages—I can see that they have been read. I do not know why you ignore my attempts at contact. It is imperative that you respond at once or—

"Motherfucker," she growled.

This time she didn't delete the email. They wanted a response? She'd comply.

Sender: N.Smith@webmail.com
Subject: Re: Time is of the essence

FUCK. OFF.

Chapter 3

"Your Highness—"

Thabiso opened his eyes, his position on the massage table ensuring that his personal assistant's Italian leather loafers were in his direct line of sight. They were hours into the flight to New York City, but he was sure that if he looked up, Likotsi would still be sporting her tailored suit jacket, vest, and tie, and her shirt would still be as crisp as if it had been freshly ironed. He had long ago resigned himself to never being best dressed in the palace.

He didn't look up, though. He closed his eyes and concentrated on the masseuse's nimble hands working his body. Her fingertips pressed into his muscles, which were still tight after three days of stressful trade meetings in Liechtenbourg. Her work was an exercise in futility, given the additional meetings that awaited him in New York, but Thabiso took pleasure where he could. The tabloids that conjectured on the daily lives of royalty would be sorely disappointed if they knew that Africa's most eligible bachelor spent most of his time stressed about work and trying to get a quick dose of relief, like most mere mortals.

"Sire?" Likotsi pressed.

Thabiso sniffed in aggravation. He had wanted just this brief moment of repose before their wheels touched the ground and the onslaught resumed. He was tempted to press his hands against his ears and scream like he had when he was a child—his tantrums had been legendary, and the king and queen had often remarked that he was lucky he was the sole heir to the crown with the way he tried their patience.

They remarked on his being the sole heir often.

No pressure.

The sound of one loafer tapping against the carpeted floor added an agitating backbeat to the relaxing music the masseuse was playing. Thabiso knew what that tap meant: Likotsi had something important to tell him. Perhaps something to do with the African Union trade agreement.

They make fools of us with this offer, Prince Thabiso. We must decline it!

Or maybe there had been another skirmish with the South African farmers who had been encroaching on Thesoloian lands.

If the crown will not protect our lands, we'll be forced to protect ourselves, Your Highness.

There was also the corporation that wanted to mine Thesolo for the rare earth minerals needed for their cell phone screens and hybrid cars. With the way they pressed, one might think those items were more important than the ecological future of a small African kingdom.

This will be very lucrative for Thesolo's coffers, Your Highness. I am the finance minister and I know more of these matters than you. Trust me.

Or, most worryingly, perhaps his parents had finally made good on the threat to find him a bride since he wasn't taking serious measures to further the Moshoeshoe royal line.

"Son, you have put off this duty for far too long. Our subjects are worried about the future of the kingdom and there are whispers of bad omens."

It seemed that everyone wanted or needed something from him, and the number of people who saw him as both provider AND protector was ever increasing. It was like quicksand, his responsibility; it had been sucking him down bit by bit from the moment he was born. Sometimes Thabiso was certain the pressure would crush him. He was a prince who would be a king, and there was no retiring, no respite, from his duty to his people.

He so badly wanted a respite. That option wasn't available to only sons, though. Thabiso pushed against the resentment that had started to grow like an insidious weed in the more shadowy corners of his mind. Resentment of his parents for not bearing more children, of his people for expecting him to be more like a mythical prince than a flesh and blood one. Everyone had forgotten there was a Thabiso following the word Prince, so much so that sometimes he forgot, too.

"My prince?"

He could evade his responsibilities no longer.

He lifted his head from the massage table to meet Likotsi's eyes. Instead of being dimmed with worry, they were wide and bright. In her hands, she clutched the sleek tablet she used to coordinate every aspect of Thabiso's life, from dental appointments to dating to drafting political accords.

"There is news," she said. She tugged at her tie, a cardinal sin and a tic that showed just how excited she was.

His curiosity was piqued.

"That's quite enough, Trudy," he barked over his shoulder to the masseuse. She bowed and slipped away to the service area of the private jet, likely to gossip with the steward.

"That was Melinda," Likotsi corrected. "Trudy was fired two weeks ago after you had an unfortunate reaction to her massage oil mix en route to Kenya. You nearly had her banished from the kingdom, if you'll recall."

"What I recall is the rash that plagued me throughout the meetings in Nairobi," Thabiso said irritably. "I had to have make-or-break policy discussions with the heads of major nations while trying not to rub my buttocks against my seat for relief. Trudy was lucky I didn't have her thrown into a dungeon."

Likotsi waved her tablet back and forth. "I have important news to share, unless you wish to continue discussing this grave injustice?"

Thabiso scowled at her mockery but deigned to let it pass. Likotsi knew very well just how much she could push him, and it was further than most. In part because he admired her, but also because he wouldn't survive a week without her and they both knew it.

Your grandfather fought off colonizers with his bare hands and you can't function without an assistant, Ingoka wept.

"What is it? More directives from the finance ministers? More unrest from my subjects about whether I dress too much like a Westerner or smile too little or smile too much?" Thabiso swung his legs over the edge of the massage table and sat upright, trying to look dignified while wearing nothing but his boxer briefs and scented oil. Complaining about what was part and parcel of his exalted position wasn't exactly dignified either, but he was exhausted.

Likotsi glanced up at him, concern in her eyes. "Are you quite sure you're all right?"

"Yes." He was a prince. Of course he was all right. He had to be. "Get on with it."

Likotsi nodded, and her worried expression quickly changed to one of self-satisfaction. "The palace department of culture and international relations recently told me that they'd received a hit from that genetics testing site, one of the few off-Continent matches, and I grew suspicious. Using my formidable internet skills, I was able to narrow down the area to North America." Likotsi paused a moment, as if to bask in incoming praise. Thabiso stared at her, and she sighed and continued. "Two countries out of the entire world made my search much easier, sire. And, perhaps it wasn't entirely aboveboard, but I obtained the user's log-in name for the genetics site and found a match on a web forum for nerds. HeLaHoop is quite active on a site called GirlsWithGlasses. HeLaHoop, aka Naledi Smith, née Naledi Ajoua, has an IP address in New York City . . ."

Naledi Ajoua.

He was starting to feel something other than agitation: Excitement. He hadn't felt that emotion in some time. Being groomed to lead a kingdom generally lent itself to emotions like frustration, anger, and panic, if one really cared for one's subjects.

Thabiso cared quite a bit.

His fingertips pressed into the underside of the massage table. "You told me you had some information, but you hadn't updated me about this development."

"Well, I didn't want to get your hopes up. And until . . . five minutes ago, there was nothing new to report." With a click of her heels and nod of her closely shaved head, Likotsi began to crow as if she were announcing before the Thesoloian court. "She has finally responded, Your Majesty! Your missing matrimonial match! Your beleaguered betrothed beauty— "

Thabiso grabbed the tablet before Likotsi could continue with her horrific attempts at alliteration.

"Prince—"

"Shh!" Thabiso made a shooing gesture in Likotsi's direction. His head was suddenly strangely light and his body heavy.

Since he was a boy, he'd heard tales of his bride-to-be and the wicked, selfish parents who had stolen her away. Each nanny had placed his or her own twist on the tale, and some had even conjectured about their inevitable reconciliation.

"The will of the Goddess cannot be denied, my Prince! Do not fret!"

A photo of their betrothal ceremony had hung in the palace living quarters, two chubby-cheeked toddlers dressed in brightly patterned garments, flowered garlands crowning their heads. Her eyes radiated with happiness as she played with the petals surrounding them, and he gazed at her with earnest adoration. Unfortunately, he hadn't mustered that emotion for any of the other women who had come into his life since then. He'd had friends, and he'd had lovers, but no one who'd made him feel like that besotted younger version of himself, preserved for posterity.

Their story had become his own personal fairy tale, or like the Mills & Boons romances he'd sneaked from the queen's library as a teen. And like those fairy tales, he'd put Naledi out of his head as the realities of adulthood had set in. And then a few weeks ago, he had come across that photo again, and in the midst of budget planning, wheeling and dealing ministers, and pressure from his parents, a longing had opened in him like a fissure. It had surprised him—the desperate, childish hope that was unbecoming of any man descended of the Moshoeshoe warriors. But it had been there all the same. And the only way to get rid of such a foolish hope was to snuff it out. He'd needed to find her before he could achieve that goal, and now Likotsi had.

Would she be like one of the silly girls his parents kept presenting him with, women programmed like automatons eager to prove how subservient they could be? Or like the women he wined and dined while traveling, so blinded by proximity to power that they never noticed there was a prince beneath the crown?

Your objective was to rid yourself of this weakness, not indulge it. If she's a twit, all the better.

"Your Highness," Likotsi said, hand moving toward the tablet as if she wanted to snatch it away. "I'm sorry, but in my excitement I failed to relay that her response was less than optimal. I believe that her parents have poisoned her against you. There can be no other explanation for this crass response to my perfectly polite messages."

"Hmm." Thabiso scrubbed his thumb over the screen, and his betrothed's words slid into sight.

FUCK. OFF.

The smile that tugged his cheeks upward wasn't controllable, and the laugh that followed was ridiculous. Royalty shouldn't laugh like a hyena from a bush story; his deportment teacher would reprimand him. But he read the two words out loud and laughed until tears streamed from his eyes and caught in his beard.

As a child, he'd imagined Naledi in some tower far

away, being held by an evil sorcerer. He'd imagined she'd needed saving and he would be the one to do it. *FUCK. OFF.*

Oh no, Naledi didn't need his help at all.

"Prince?" Likotsi's loafer was tapping again. "I don't know what spurred this attempt to find your betrothed, but now that she has responded, how would you like to proceed in light of this . . . unsavoriness?"

Likotsi's nose scrunched as if she smelled burned mealie pap. That was okay because Thabiso had always liked the burned part of the corn meal porridge; perhaps because it was one of the few imperfections that made it through the many quality filters surrounding a prince who was the sole heir to a kingdom.

"It seems that this Naledi may have been worth the wait. I would like to meet her. Now."

Likotsi glanced pointedly out the window of the jet, then back at Thabiso.

"Well, I don't expect you to summon her thirty thousand feet into the sky," Thabiso said. "When we land in New York City, have her brought to me immediately."

Likotsi raised her brows. "Well, that would be considered kidnapping in the US, Highness. You *are* protected by diplomatic immunity, but perhaps we could save that perk for a more important matter. We can ask her to come to you, but given her response I'm not sure that she will."

An unfamiliar annoyance pulsed through Thabiso. He wanted something, and it wasn't guaranteed he would have it. That was rare, indeed, and it whet his desire to a sharp edge.

"Fine. Then I will go to her."

Likotsi gasped, but when Thabiso looked at her she had schooled her face back to bland acceptance.

"Whatever you think is appropriate," she said. "I don't have a home address yet, but I believe I've located her place of employ. It seems that she might be"—another wrinkle of the nose—"a waitress. What a life her parents' thoughtlessness has condemned her to! In Thesolo, she would have lived a life of luxury! Her hands would be as smooth and soft as—"

"Likotsi!"

She flinched and straightened her tie. "My apologies."

"You said you could locate her—get on with it. I could use a diversion on this trip, and I believe I've found it."

"Yes, sire."

Thabiso sat still on the massage table, any relaxation Melinda's work had provided forgotten. His muscles were taut with excitement—and fear? No, that wasn't it. It was the same sensation he got before making an important speech or having to make a decision that would impact his people for generations.

"I'm nervous," he muttered to himself.

Life had been nothing but a series of mundane duties for so long—even the occasional trip to a hot new club or date with a Nollywood starlet had become just another part of his job. He hadn't been this nervous about a woman since his first time making love, but he'd had *some* idea of what to expect then. Naledi was a mystery, and perhaps a mistake. Part of being a good prince meant he avoided mistakes at all cost, but this time . . .

He didn't expect a happily ever after like in the slim white romance books of his youth. He expected excitement, and it looked like Naledi could provide just that.

Chapter 4

*L*edi, I know you're busy but—"

She whipped around and glared at Dan, also affectionately known as "fuck-my-life Dan" and "Shit-I-have-a-shift-with-that-asshole-Dan Dan" to her and her coworkers at the Institute's dining hall. Ledi was regretting having agreed to work in the weeks leading up to finals, and his presence wasn't helping.

When she'd walked into the Institute's kitchen, he'd been dramatically scribbling in his Moleskine with his shiny Montblanc. Of course, he'd had to share the profound spoken word poem he'd written, entitled "Macchiato Mama." And now he wanted more of her attention.

"I. Am. Busy."

Her words came out sharp as the steak knives on the plates she balanced on her forearms.

She was already covering four tables to his one. The group of astrophysicists was keeping her on her toes with their requests for detailed explanations of every dish on next week's special tasting menu. The mathematicians lingering across the dining room kept forgetting to eat their food as they debated some theorem or another—Ledi had already been chewed out by Yves, the Swiss chef, for bringing their meals back to be reheated twice. As if she *wanted* to destroy the textural integrity of his precious swordfish.

Even better, all of the guests had to be out of the dining room within the next half hour so she could finish prepping for a VIP event that night. A new employee was supposed to come in and shadow her, which would have been great if she had been working with someone besides Dan. Dan, who couldn't manage the simplest task without having to come back for reinstruction several times.

"I was setting up for the event and I think I'm having a quarter-life crisis," he said. She thought he was joking until she saw his expression. He was completely earnest and also looking at her as if she was his therapist instead of his coworker.

Fuck my life.

"Dan." She exhaled slowly and tried to think of a response to this bullshit. "The life expectancy of the average American male is seventy-eight, and you're thirty something, so this would be closer to a midlife crisis."

"Shit." Dan's eyes went wide. "You're absolutely right."

Ledi's forearms were strong, but the large cuts of fish and fine dining ware were heavy. She hadn't dropped a plate since she'd first started waitressing in high school, and if Dan made her break her streak she'd significantly reduce his life span.

"Is there anything else?" she asked, voice strained. Her arms were beginning to feel shaky.

"It's just . . . I didn't think this would be so hard," he said, plucking at the wrinkled tuxedo shirt that all servers at the Institute dining hall had to wear. "Unfolding tables, carrying trays of dishes, cleaning up after these *people*. I mean, aren't they supposed to be geniuses? They're slobs. I thought this job would be easy."

This motherfucker, she thought.

"This job is easy, actually," she said, trying to not to let her frustration show. She needed to manage whatever meltdown he was having and get through the rest of the night. "It's physically demanding, and sometimes emotionally, but unlike the work they're doing out there, it's not rocket science."

Dan's mouth sagged into a grimace. "I thought this gig would really help me get into the mindset of the hero of my novel. You know, getting my hands dirty. But everyone is always expecting me to do something for them." He glanced at her, as if he pitied her. "I know you wouldn't understand anything about creativity, but this place is killing my muse."

Only the knowledge that Yves would fillet her if she asked him to make another swordfish steak prevented her from flinging one of her plates into his face. She was used to people thinking she wasn't capable of comprehending things, but it was the pity in Dan's voice that grated on her. She didn't need anyone's pity. And the patrons could be a bit odd, but they were actually changing the world, while Dan scribbled lines about "eyes like spots of caramel."

Yves pecked out from his office. "If I have to reheat that fish one more time," he growled, and made a slitting motion across his neck. Ledi wondered how people had ever mistaken the Swiss for a peace-loving people. They had invented those knives and they knew how to use them.

She took a deep breath and remembered that this was a job that paid her well and provided insurance to part-time workers. Dan wasn't worth losing her access to low co-pays.

"Just give me a minute and we can talk this through, okay?"

He nodded but his gaze was past her, as if he was still mulling his napkin-folding-induced crisis.

She hurried the food to the mathematicians, making it to the table just as her arms were ready to give out, with a gentle reminder that they needed to actually eat it this time. They nodded and dug in without looking up at her, but as she headed back to the kitchen one of the astrophysicists flagged her down, asking her to bring him some more of the kale that had been used as garnish on his plate so he could demonstrate a wormhole theory.

"It's in the curl of the leaf, you see," Dr. Zietara began, and launched into a complex explanation of matter folding in on itself. Ledi couldn't grasp everything he was saying, but it was still fascinating. It was moments like this that reminded her why she loved working at the Institute—great minds had to eat, and sometimes they shared some of their greatness within earshot. She appreciated that he made eye contact with her, including her in the conversation—researchers in her own field sometimes gazed past her when explaining things, as if assuming she wouldn't understand—but then she remembered all the work looming ahead.

"The dining room is actually closing soon, sir," she said when he finally took a breath.

"Excellent!" he replied, taking more paperwork out of his backpack and dropping it decisively on the table. "We can work in peace once those ridiculous mathematicians leave."

He and his colleagues glared across the dining room.

Ledi groaned and hurried back to the kitchen. The kitchen that was much too quiet. There should have been the clang of metal as Dan moved tables out from the back storage room or at least the sound of the expensive Italian espresso machine as he freeloaded yet another cappuccino.

"Dan?"

The end of her question ended in a yelp as she stepped on something slippery and almost lost her footing. She looked down to see an abandoned tuxedo shirt beneath her sensible work shoe. Of course he couldn't just quit like a normal human being, or wait until after his shift. He had to make an artistic statement. He was probably walking shirtless to freedom and planning to use that as the final triumphant scene of his novel.

Fuck.

Just like that, the calm she had been struggling to maintain began to crack. An unusual pressure beat at her sinuses as each individual task on her to-do list seemed to multiply before her eyes like a norovirus.

Dan had left her to set up and wait on a party of forty people—alone. She had hours of studying ahead of her when she got home or she'd fail her bench exams and her first year of grad school would be an expensive bust. Her thesis was floundering and her advisor was MIA and her awesome summer practicum was uncertain. And she just knew that the mathematicians were going to ask her to reheat their fish again.

"Fuuuuck," she exhaled.

The doors leading from the dining room opened and Ledi tried to pull her features into a smile. It was probably Dr. Zietara coming to check in on his kale.

But instead of a peeved researcher standing in the doorway, there was the finest man Ledi had ever seen outside of a social media thirst trap pic. For a split second she was hit with the sensation of greeting an old friend after a long absence, but she was mistaken: she didn't know this guy.

He was tall, with the broad-shouldered, well-defined V of a body that announced swimming was part of his workout regimen. He wore a forest green T-shirt and straight-legged black jeans that fit snugly, but not enough to advertise his eggplant emoji. She would have thought the pants were tailored, but who would waste money on tailored jeans?

His skin was a rich, dark brown, slightly darker than her own, with hair that was shaved on the sides and twisted into short, perfect dreads on the top. A well-maintained beard framed his lush lips and highlighted the sharp angles of his wide jaw instead of hiding them.

That beard made her fingers itch to stroke it, or to grab her smartphone and photograph it for posterity. She wasn't as good at social media as Portia, but she'd rack up a million likes within the day, for sure, if not some kind of award for heroism on behalf of male-attracted humanity.

"Um," she said. Her general reaction to men she met in her daily life was indifference or tolerance, at best, but something about this man sent her thoughts spinning far, far away from lab work or serving or studying. The only data she was currently interested in collecting was the exact tensile pressure of his beard against her inner thigh, and the shift in mass of his body on top of hers.

He cleared his throat and she realized she'd been crouching and staring up at him with an intensity that might have made him fear for his well-being. She doubted it was a new experience for him, but it was for her, and her face heated in embarrassment.

She kicked Dan's discarded shirt under the metal table and pulled herself up straight. "Can I help you, sir?"

It felt strange to address someone near her age so formally, but at the Institute you never knew who was a VIP. The most important researcher often came to the dining room in his bathrobe and nothing else. Besides, he had an air of authority about him.

"There's a man outside who says he's in need of kale? He's quite insistent."

Oh—he had an accent, too. Kind of British, but with something else just as charming layered over it.

"Kale?" Somewhere in the back of Ledi's mind, a connection was sparking, but all pathways were currently occupied trying to process whatever was going on with the hot guy in front of her.

He smiled, the kind of smile that made little crinkles around the corner of his eyes, and Ledi felt it all throughout her body.

"Yes," he said, in that deep, accented voice. "Kale. A leafy green, quite good in a moroko mash, but I imagine you don't serve that here. Maybe you do, though? I haven't had a chance to familiarize myself with the menu."

Familiarize? Menu? Ledi's scattered deductive reasoning skills slowly pulled the pieces together.

This was the new hire. She felt a brief pang of regret as her beard vs thighs fantasies collapsed like one of Yves's soufflés. Now that she knew she'd be training him, he was firmly in the coworker zone.

"Oh, you're already helping customers? That's great, showing initiative," she said. Her brain had registered that he fell into a group labeled "Nope," but all of her cylinders still weren't firing. She was trying to sound bright and in charge, but her vocabulary center was stuck on "Damn, he fine," making forming sentences a bit difficult. "Um. Here."

Ledi grabbed a fistful of kale from the chopping board on the counter and shoved it toward him. He looked from the greens to her face and back again, his brow furrowed in obvious judgment.

"You're right, I should be wearing gloves," she said. "I of all people should be enforcing that. Public Health! Germs are the enemy!"

She was fairly certain that the look he gave her as she dropped the kale onto the cutting board and snapped a latex glove onto her right hand was the same one she doled out to subway preachers with questionable knowledge of Biblical texts ranting about the apocalypse.

"No, that's not it at all," he said, shaking his head, and everything clicked into place for her. How had she made such a silly mistake?

"Oh, right!"

She turned and grabbed a small, round bread plate, slapped a thin paper doily on it, and then placed the kale on top, giving it a few gentle spruces before it went off to be used as an educational aid.

"Nice catch. Presentation is always important," she said as she handed it over to him. "I'm usually more on the ball, but it's been a long day. A long week. Month!" She reined herself in. "You seem to have some experience already, so you can take this over to the table, okay? Remind them that the dining room will be closed to members in twenty minutes and they have to leave. I'll go get you a tuxedo shirt to change into, then we can start training."

She made finger guns and a little tongue-clicking noise at him before she could stop herself.

What the hell. Where did that come from?

She turned and speed-walked away, seeking refuge in the walk-in fridge. She was sure steam was rising from her face—and that wasn't the only thing that needed cooling.

You're an adult, Ledi chided herself. *Just because the finest, most lickable man you've ever seen in real life is going to be working next to you all night is no reason to start acting like some classic '90s movie character.*

The problem wasn't just that he was attractive; hot guys were a dime a dozen in New York City. It was that she was attracted *to* him. And it wasn't just physical; for a moment she'd had the ridiculous feeling that she knew him. Had felt a connection that was as improbable as it was impossible . . . It would be hard to forget a man like that.

She felt a brief surge of panic; it was just her luck that the new guy had some kind of viral effect on her—her social cell membrane had collapsed. Her defenses were down, and she still had the whole rest of the evening to get through.

She was in deep shit.

She dropped her chin to her chest and let out a loud groan of mortification.

The door to the walk-in opened and Yves stuck his head in, his silver eyebrows raised in curiosity.

"Everything all right?" His gaze darted suspiciously around the small space.

"Don't ask," she muttered, sliding out past him.

"I keep count of the zucchini!" he called after her.

Chapter 5

Thabiso stood in the middle of the orderly stainless steel kitchen holding the plate of kale, staring at the space Naledi had occupied before giving him an order and rushing off.

This was the woman who should have been his bride, whose destiny had been entwined with his by religious divination and royal decree. The woman whose family had broken their promise and brought dishonor on themselves and on the priestesses who had fasted and sweated and prayed for days before choosing Naledi as the future queen. She should have been bowing down and begging forgiveness; instead she had thrown greens at him and ordered him about as if he were a peasant and not a prince.

His people would be incensed, his parents aghast. Thabiso was intrigued.

Naledi.

Her eyes were large, the deep brown irises fringed with long, long lashes. Her skin was a smooth, radiant brown that gave her an aura of innocence, as if she'd yet to encounter anything in this life trying enough to crease her brow in worry. Her mouth was another tale entirely. Wide, lush lips that left any thoughts of innocence far behind even though they were bare of makeup. Her accent was not quite like the New York accent from films he'd seen, but captivating all the same.

She was more beautiful than the photos Likotsi had poached from her barely used social media accounts. She'd been reserved in the photos—the pictures hadn't captured her energy. There was a solid air about her; she seemed like someone you could trust to get a job done.

Then why was she here, and not in Thesolo as her betrothal demanded?

He could have just asked her that, point-blank, but something had stopped him. It was the way she had looked at him. There had been heat in those lovely eyes of hers as her tongue swiped over her luscious bottom lip, but more importantly, there had been no sign of recognition. He had been slightly annoyed as he'd watched and waited for a reaction from her and realized none was forthcoming. He had imagined dozens of variations on their reunion—her apologizing, at the very least, had been a recurring theme. There had been no kale in any of them. But the way she had looked at him as if he were just another man was like a magic door opening up beside the one he'd thought was his only way forward.

She doesn't know who I am.

Thabiso was used to being regarded as HIS ROYAL HIGHNESS, was bored of it really, but the thread of lust that had spun taut between them like a strand from Fate's loom had been inspired by him and him alone. Thabiso had wanted to tug at the thread, pull her closer until she was in his arms. And he wanted to enjoy just a bit more of her time before he became Prince Thabiso and she became another Thesoloian project to be managed. Because that was what any talk of betrothal and marriage would be for him: work.

There was something else that had held him back: her eyes. The aura of joy and happiness from her childhood photo was gone. She'd been friendly, but there was a wariness to her that gave him pause. He had been trained to read body language, an invaluable skill when negotiational prowess could decide the future of millions of people, and she was as cagey as any diplomat he'd ever encountered. But in the moment when he'd first caught sight of her, she'd been vulnerable. Frustrated. A woman at the end of her rope.

Thabiso had often wondered how his life had been impacted by her absence—he'd spent a lifetime being told what could have been if his betrothed hadn't disappeared—but what had her life been like without him? Without Thesolo?

He'd meant to sweep into her mundane job and dazzle her, a task made easy when you were royalty, but nothing had gone as planned since he'd walked into the building.

When a riverbed takes a sharp curve, the water follows.

Thabiso looked down at the kale, then turned and walked out of the double doors toward the table of rude people who had assumed he was a waiter. Naledi had believed this as well. Was there something about him that exuded a sense of servility? He had thought his shirt becoming, but perhaps he would have to tell Likotsi to retire it.

Thabiso dropped the plate onto the table with a loud ceramic *thunk*.

The man who had requested it took it up in his hand without even looking at him, continuing to converse with his compatriots. He had just been waited on by royalty and couldn't even manage a nod of gratitude?

Son of a two-legged antelope . . .

Thabiso waited a moment longer for the recognition owed to him, and then snatched the kale back.

"I beg your pardon," the man said, clearly confused as he finally turned his gaze toward Thabiso.

"Your pardon is denied. I just performed a task for you. The correct thing to say in this situation is 'Thank you.'" Thabiso imbued each word with the disdain learned from years of etiquette lessons.

The man sputtered, eyes wide behind his glasses, then stammered out a thanks. Thabiso returned the kale to him.

"You are welcome." He clapped his hands together. "Now, you must leave this place, as I've been informed that there is work to be done for a later event. I give you permission to take this plate with you, as it's obviously of inferior quality and will not be missed."

The man and his group of friends quickly gathered their things and shuffled out. He crossed his arms over his chest and watched them go.

Do I ever thank my servants?

He couldn't remember explicitly doing so. His servants had always been there, like the photos of ancestors on the walls and the furniture handed down for generations. Surely, they didn't feel affronted when he waved or beckoned without a word. He was a prince, after all. He had expectations that commoners couldn't be expected to understand.

A familiar censuring tap on his shoulder reminded him of Likotsi's presence. "If I may be so bold, Your Highness—what, exactly, are you doing?"

"I'm working," Thabiso said. He was feeling rather pleased with himself. Not only was he an excellent negotiator and a shrewd businessman, but having completed the tasks assigned him, he was well on his way to becoming a master waiter, too. The goddess really did shine on all of his undertakings. "It appears I have acquired a job."

Likotsi's mouth gaped in dismay and she shook her head. "No. No, Sire. You have a job. Princeing. And you also have a business dinner with the Omega Corporation in two hours."

Thabiso had thought he would show up, make Naledi rue the day her family had slunk out of Thesolo like minks, and then continue with his trip. But she hadn't known who he was. And he wanted to know more about the intriguing, if somewhat strange, beauty.

Thabiso shrugged. "Omega can wait."

Likotsi's mouth went tight. "The finance ministers made very clear how important this meeting is."

The finance ministers sent me here to sell our country's well-being to the highest bidder. But he couldn't tell her that; she knew his most intimate details, but not that he'd agreed to allow the minerals to be extracted from beneath peoples' ancestral lands. There would be relocation, paid for of course, but it still didn't sit well with him.

"The people will understand that the well-being of a nation comes first, Prince Thabiso."

Sometimes a prince had to do unsavory things. And sometimes plans changed.

"The goddess has presented me with the chance to know Naledi, and I cannot pass it up for Omega Corp."

"Is that what you wanted, sire? To . . . *know* her?"

Thabiso hadn't thought so. What had he wanted when he tasked Likotsi with finding her? A reckoning? An outlet for his frustrations? Something, anything, other than the thousand worries that beat at his shoulders like the noonday sun? It didn't matter. Now that he had seen Naledi, he wanted to know her. It may have been a whim, but that was his wont, and it was the very least owed to him.

"Naledi has mistaken me for a new coworker. Can you think of a better chance for me to learn about her, and why she left, than to observe her from the same lowly level she occupies? If I tell her who I am, as planned, she would immediately change her behavior and we might never learn the truth."

He was being selfish, and for a very simple reason. He'd never had someone ask him to do something simple like deliver a dish of food; no one would ask such a thing of a prince—not unless they wanted to be shamed. The demands usually made of him were much more strenuous and always came with a price, no matter how deferential the person was when they asked. Naledi had ordered him to do something without blinking, without a hint of brownnosing, and he found that he wanted her to do it again.

Likotsi drew herself back in horror. "You wish to engage in deception! By Ingoka, goddess of truth and virtue, I cannot allow it."

Thabiso dropped his gaze to the ground, not because he was ashamed but because he had long ago learned how to bypass his assistant's innate sense of honor. He caught her eye and grinned at her, then glanced around the room conspiratorially.

"Why Likotsi . . . don't you wish to solve the mystery of the missing matrimonial match? To discover why her parents abandoned their lives, friends, and family? Why they fled from their duties and her birthright?"

"Well . . . yes." Some of the stiffness went out of Likotsi's shoulders.

"And do you think if I tell her who I am, she'll just reveal that secret? Especially in light of her response to your email campaign?"

Likotsi paused, pursed her lips. "Perhaps not."

"Then it is settled. I can get close to her through this job and find out her secrets. It will be an undercover adventure, like in the Suncatcher novels of our youth!"

Just then, a lanky young man walked into the dining room, his hoodie and faded jeans indicating he was a student. He hesitated and, seeing no one else around, turned to Thabiso and Likotsi.

"Hey. I'm Jamal. I'm supposed to start working here this afternoon? Sorry I'm late. My train was stuck in a tunnel for like forty-five minutes. You know how it is."

Ah. The source of their misunderstanding—and the man who had allowed him to gain closer access to his betrothed. The priestesses often said that Ingoka took many forms to shepherd believers onto their true path. Thabiso took such sayings with a grain of salt, but perhaps Jamal was one of these shepherds.

"The position has already been filled, Jamal," Thabiso declared. "But you will be reimbursed for making your way here. Likotsi, please pay him for his troubles." He glanced at the kitchen doors, through which Naledi could emerge at any moment. "Outside."

"Wait. Hold up!" Jamal said, taking a step forward in protest. "You can't just go back on your word. I need this job, man."

The pleading in the man's voice took Thabiso by surprise—who would be so upset over the loss of such trivial work? But then Thabiso remembered the charts about joblessness in American youth that he had studied; jobs were not plentiful in this country, and colleges were not free or affordable as they were in civilized nations like Thesolo.

"Give him fifteen thousand dollars," Thabiso said, his gaze still on the kitchen. "Twenty. Just do it away from here."

Jamal stood still, mouth wide-open. The hands he'd thrown up in annoyance dropped to his sides and smacked against his jeans. "That isn't funny." His brow creased. "You serious?"

"You question my honor?" Thabiso asked, slitting his gaze toward Jamal.

"People don't go around slinging cash like this. Is this a joke or . . ."

"If you want the money, follow Likotsi and she will give it to you."

Thabiso could tell Likotsi didn't approve of this expenditure. "Your Hi—"

"I've spent more on shoes and you've said nothing. Get the young man his money and I will see you at the hotel tonight."

She gave a brusque nod and made for the exit with Jamal quick on her heels.

"Thank you?" he called out over his shoulder.

Thabiso headed back to the kitchen, to Naledi. He'd been training to run an entire country for most of his life. How hard could serving dinner be?

Chapter 6

$\mathcal{S}$erving was hell.

Thabiso had thought he was fit and had stamina, but he was drenched in sweat, he'd pulled something in his back while attempting to lift a heavy tray, and he was ready to throw in the towel on this little scheme.

Perhaps I didn't think this through.

The initial setting up had gone well. He knew what a proper place setting looked like—the fastest way to expose one's gaucheness was to pick up the wrong utensil, and all fine dining setting configurations had been drilled into him. He'd basked in Naledi's praise as he'd swiftly laid down silverware as she put out the glassware. They'd worked smoothly, in tandem. Her arm had kept brushing against his as she reached past him to place a wineglass here or a bread plate there—he'd never realized how much grace there was in such work—and it had felt like some kind of choreographed dance.

She hadn't said much about herself as they'd worked, and had politely rebuffed any attempt at chitchat related to her personal life. He didn't know where she lived, where she'd grown up, what school she went to, or whether she was dating anyone, but he learned all about the history of the Institute and the scientific advances that had taken place there.

"The people who eat here can be kind of strange, but some of them have made incredible discoveries in their research," she'd said, something like awe in her voice. "Years of study and focus—obsession—on one crazy specific thing, all for the nearly impossible goal of changing the world."

"Is that what you want to do?" he'd asked. "Change the world?"

She'd lost a bit of her enthusiasm then. "I don't know if I'll ever be in a position to do that, with my work. Besides, in this work, you're usually reliant on someone else with money or power, and I've seen how they operate—cutting the funding of important research, or trying to make money instead of helping people. It's like they forget that out of everyone in the world, they've been trusted to do what's right."

She'd gazed at him with clear emotion in her eyes, then a few blinks and it was gone. Not gone—hidden.

"Do you think it's easy, having such power?" he'd asked. He was truly curious, and it was perhaps the first time he could get an honest answer without having his royal title taken into account.

Ledi had laughed. "Easy? That depends. If you want to use your power to exploit people and gain personal wealth, then yes it's pretty easy. But if you want to change the world for the better . . ."

"Not so easy," he'd said. He knew that to be true. He'd thought of the countless meetings where his initiatives were shot down, called wastes of money. He had the same education, more, than his ministers, but he was the Playboy PanAfrique, after all. Sometimes he still pushed for things. But more often than not, he gave in. Giving in was easier, and he wondered if it wasn't worse than exploiting. That was at least taking action; he'd grown complacent.

She'd shrugged, clearly done with the conversation. "I'm going to go fill the water pitchers while you finish up here."

It was when the guests had arrived that everything went downhill. There had been no further getting to know his betrothed—from that point on Thabiso was simply trying to survive.

He had been to countless catered events; they made up a good portion of his meals when he was away from Thesolo, and at home when they had functions for visiting dignitaries. He knew the drill from the guest side: mingle, have a drink or two, then everyone is seated, and the food is brought out course by course. Thabiso had never thought about the logistics of this, though. It had just worked, in the same way that his watch ticked along without him thinking of the gears. The gears were quite important, it turned out.

Plating up food correctly and serving it to the right person without error was not quite as simple as he'd imagined. Ledi and her chef, a grumpy Swiss guy who reminded Thabiso of his former headmaster, had already prepared the salads, so it had just been a matter of carrying out large, oval trays of them and handing out the plates. After the first tray Thabiso tried to heft onto his shoulder went crashing to the ground, Ledi had flashed him an understanding smile and handed him two plates; one for each hand.

"I'll carry the trays tonight," she said. "Just grab plates from mine and things will go smoother."

Things did not go smoother.

Thabiso managed to elbow one attendee in the ear

and learned that "get it yourself" was not an acceptable answer when a guest asked for something, even if you were clearly busy.

Next, they'd had to help the chef do up the dinner plates, which had been another exercise in humiliation. He'd thought he had an eye for design but while Naledi's plates had looked like dishes from a trendy restaurant, Thabiso couldn't get his vegetables to cooperate and his plates were smudged and splattered with sauces and jus.

Is this what happens in the kitchen at every function I've attended? he'd asked himself. He'd never given much thought to how dish after dish came from the kitchen, perfectly presented. It had just always been so, no matter where he traveled. It seemed impossible that so much work went into making a plate of food that was about to be masticated look like a piece of artwork.

He'd also failed on the serving front. Naledi whirled through the crowd of people who planted themselves in her path like stubborn donkeys, tray balanced on hands that seemed too small and wrists too thin to support its weight. His own hands shook as he lowered plates to tables, and he'd slid a portion of salmon in a butter thyme reduction right into a guest's lap.

Naledi refilled water from a pitcher with one hand and poured wine with another, without spilling a drop. The front of Thabiso's shirt was splashed with a middling pinot noir.

Worst of all, the interest and respect that had flashed in her eyes earlier in the night had all but disappeared, replaced with disappointment and fatigue.

"Oh my!" A woman shouted as an ice cube bounced off the rim of her glass and into her cleavage as he refilled her cup.

Thabiso debated what to do. He'd removed the salmon from the man's lap earlier. Was he supposed to retrieve the ice? Naledi slid in front of him before he could act, smoothly grabbing the pitcher and filling the woman's glass without incident.

"I'm sorry, ma'am. Here's a fresh napkin for you to dry off with." She turned to him with a grimace distorting those lovely lips. He knew he was making her job harder, but it galled to see her look at him like he was a worm that had slithered to the surface during a heavy rain.

"Jamal, can you come with me for a minute?" she said, placing a hand on his arm and guiding him back into the kitchen. Her touch felt good, even though he knew what was coming. If anyone in his employ had made even one of the errors he'd made, they would have been out of a job and likely banned from working anywhere else in the kingdom once word of their ineptitude spread.

Ineptitude? If that was the word springing to his mind, what must she think of him?

The back of his neck tingled with warmth. What was this sensation that made him want to hide his deficiencies away where Naledi couldn't see them? He passed a stainless steel fridge and his hunched shoulders and deferential expression shocked him. He recognized what he was feeling then; he'd seen it in so many people he'd dismissed from his presence over the years. It was shame.

He was a Moshoeshoe. Shame was not supposed to be in his range of emotions. Would she dare to point out his weaknesses, this woman who had abandoned her duties and denied him the path laid down for him by the goddess? Everything in him bristled, ready to lash out at her in a preemptive strike. Let her try to belittle him. He'd tell her how she demeaned herself like a common peasant. He'd tell her exactly what orifice she could place any of her critiques of him. He was a prince, damn it.

Her hand lingered on his arm, warm through the material of the cheap tuxedo shirt, then slipped away. She looked up at him, brow wrinkled, but instead of a reprimand, Naledi gave a fatigued laugh, the sound almost drowned out by the noise of an oven vent. It wasn't fake or forced or condescending. In fact, it was comforting.

She grabbed a cupcake from a picked-over dessert tray and handed it to him.

"Are we allowed to eat this?" he asked. "Is this not stealing?"

"It'll go in the garbage if we don't eat it. I try to take leftovers and give them to the homeless when I can. It's technically illegal, but I hate seeing good food thrown away."

"Oh." Thabiso never gave much thought to waste. He was used to having too much to eat, to taking a few bites and waiting for the plate to be taken away and the next dish to arrive. He took a bite of the cupcake.

"So, I'm starting to think maybe you lied on your résumé," she said as she chewed.

Actually, I only lied about my identity. I'm sure Jamal's résumé is correct.

"It seems I am not fit to complete the tasks you have given me," he said. His body was suddenly tense—his response had unwittingly echoed the one he'd given his mother just the week before.

"Whether you believe you are capable or not does not matter my son. You are the heir to the throne. The sole heir."

That had been a less encouraging response than Thabiso would have liked.

"It's okay. Shit happens," Naledi said.

"No," he said. His fist closed around the cupcake and a few crumbs dropped to the floor. "You do not understand. Failure is not an option for me. I should be able to do this easily, and yet I have done nothing but make a mess. You have lost your confidence in me."

My people will lose their confidence in me.

"Look, stop stressing yourself out, okay? It's not that deep." She took a bite of her cupcake. "I'm in grad school right now. For epidemiology."

"You wish to help people with skin problems?" he asked, glad that she was finally opening up to him. "Yours is quite beautiful, so—"

She sighed. "No, that's dermatology. Epidemiology is a public health field. I study infectious diseases."

"Why?" he asked quickly. This was the first thing she was purposefully revealing and he didn't want to lose the opportunity.

"When disease strikes, it's always the most vulnerable populations that are hit hardest. I want to do research that helps make the world safer for them."

She said it like it was a simple thing. Thabiso's grandest wishes were to be left to his own devices for just a few hours and to have a good glass of scotch, in that specific order. He had been born with the task of saving his people; Ledi had too, according to the priestesses, but she didn't know that.

"So you do want to save the world," he said. "That is quite honorable."

"It's a job," she said, smoothly dodging his praise. "But that's not my point. So I'm a research assistant in a lab, too, when I'm not working here. I've been doing this since undergrad, and the first lab I ever worked at was studying the spread of venereal diseases. One day, after pulling three all-nighters in a row to study, I was asked by one of my postdocs to transfer some samples of gonorrhea. I was totally out of it and dropped the samples all over myself while not wearing protective gear."

"Oh," Thabiso said. Americans were known for oversharing, but he didn't know why she chose this particular moment to disclose such personal information to him. It was odd, but admirable he supposed.

"I'm sorry to hear that. I know these diseases carry a stigma, but it is nothing to be ashamed of." He'd been giving that speech to teenagers since he was a teenager himself and the face of Thesolo's youth sexual health education campaign. It had been his first initiative, back when he hadn't been completely weighed down by his role.

Naledi gave him a strange look. "It wasn't contagious, Jamal, though I appreciate your support. I didn't know that, though. I freaked out and activated the emergency shower, getting water everywhere in the process. I shorted out the centrifuge and ruined experiments that had been weeks and months in the making."

Thabiso suppressed a smirk, imagining the woman before him, who seemed so in control of her surroundings, flailing about and wreaking havoc. "Perhaps you've chosen the wrong profession? You're quite good at serving. It might be a better path for you."

Her eyes narrowed. "Excuse me?"

"If you have a choice, why choose to do something you aren't good at?" he asked, and that didn't seem to improve her mood.

"Who said I wasn't good at it?"

Sweat began to form on Thabiso's temples. "No. Just. I mean . . . why are you telling me this?"

"I don't know," Ledi said, tone short, then shook her head. "I guess the point was that people mess up sometimes? I'm an amazing lab assistant now. So amazing that my postdoc wants me to do all his work for him." Her brow creased in consternation for a moment, then she met his gaze. "It's not your fault that we're understaffed and you don't have a chance to get trained in an easier situation. You'll get the hang of it eventually."

He had not been expecting this. He'd been a thorn in her side the entire night and she had given him cupcakes and a gonorrhea anecdote and support. She was looking at him, Thabiso, at his very worst, and telling him that she believed in him.

"Thank you," he said, his voice low and rough. The cupcake must have been dry.

She smiled and patted him on the arm. "Look, just hang back for now. Maybe you can help with something that doesn't require touching the food or interacting with customers, like . . . changing the burner under the chocolate fondue? It was pretty low last time I checked. Ask Chef Yves to give you a new burner and a lighter. Can you do that?"

It was somewhat comforting for someone to ask if he could do something in such a tone. She was doubtful, but throwing her support behind him anyway. At home, no one was allowed to doubt whether a prince was capable of something—not even the prince himself. Her lack of surety made him all the more eager to please her.

"Of course I can do that," he said.

"Good," she said. "I'll go do a round and make sure the guests are okay."

She held her fist up to him expectantly.

"Black power?" he guessed. He had just watched a documentary about the Civil Rights movement but wasn't aware that Americans used it as a form of salutation. He had kept abreast of the latest social justice movement in the states, and supposed it was related to that. He lifted his fist high into the air.

She laughed that tinkling laugh again, but this time it didn't anger him. It made him want to know what he'd done to cause it so he could create the sound again and again.

"Um, that's not what I was going for, but yes, that too. Chef is in his office."

Thabiso marched off toward the chef's office, invigorated by Ledi's belief in him.

This is ridiculous. You've climbed Kilimanjaro. You've told the Prime Minister of Belgium to get stuffed. You will not be defeated by a chocolate fondue!

When he arrived at the chef's office, it was empty. He waited, but as the minutes ticked by, he grew more agitated, knowing Naledi must be thinking he'd not been up to the task.

I can figure this out.

Of course he hadn't been quite sure what Naledi had meant by "burner," but he marched up to the dessert table with purpose. He possessed deductive reasoning skills, didn't he?

He noticed a decorative candle holder on the buffet table. Instead of a wax candle inside, there was a wick with a small plastic reservoir filled with kerosene. He'd seen those used for all manner of things back home.

It didn't match the small metal can under the fondue, but it should work just as well. Thabiso placed it under the fondue dish and smiled. He *would* get the hang of things. He wouldn't be a disappointment, to Naledi or his people.

He turned to search her out in the crowd, to see what else he could accomplish that would ease her burden. It was after three steps that he felt the burst of heat at his back.

"Oh, looks like they're going with flambé," one of the guests said. "Maybe there will be Bananas Foster!"

Thabiso turned to discover flames dancing around the metal fondue pot, racing across the tablecloth and devouring the napkins and decorations strewn across its surface. Dread and a crushing sense of failure froze him for a moment, but then he grabbed the closest thing to hand—a suit jacket hung over the back of a chair—and began batting at the fire.

Ah, Goddess, what a catastrophe. The flames were undeterred by his attempts to smother them. They climbed up the jacket and nipped at his hands but he was focused on stopping it before—

"Out of the way, Jamal!"

Naledi charged past him with a fire extinguisher, fierce as Mujaji the rain goddess. It was over in a few seconds. She blasted the flames, and him in the process, the party attendees clapped, and everything went back to normal, minus the chemical-covered dessert table.

Thabiso was still on his ass coughing up flame retardant when Naledi held the melted gas reservoir in front of his face.

"This . . . isn't a burner." Her eyes were wide and her chest heaved with quick breaths. She had looked at him with disappointment before, but now she looked at him like he was a fool. Like she had been wrong to believe he could ever handle a seemingly simple task.

Shame raced through Thabiso's blood, quickly followed by indignation. "Well, how was I supposed to know what a burner is? Aren't you supposed to be training me?"

"I have been training you. I've also been cleaning up your messes. And Dan's messes. And the guests' messes. I shouldn't have to worry about you starting a fire while I'm busy with that." Her words came through gritted teeth, as if he were the one at fault.

"You really shouldn't talk about cleaning up after others as if it's something to be proud of." His indignation flared, higher perhaps than the flames that had nearly singed his beard. "Only a dog seeks reward for performing lowly tasks for others. Fetch! Pour! Serve! You're no better than a—than a Saint Bernard!"

He leaned forward into the charged space between them, ready to continue their battle, but Naledi's expression had gone completely blank, even those expressive eyes.

Regret washed through Thabiso as his anger sapped away yet another unfamiliar emotion. Maybe there was something in the water in the US causing these fluctuations. Fluoride? He'd read about that, too.

He had started this subterfuge in the name of getting to know his betrothed, but he'd made a mess of it, like the buffoon in a fairy tale before the prince comes sweeping in. Except he *was* the prince.

"Did you burn yourself?" she asked quietly.

"Only a little. I'm fine."

"That's great," she said. "Because now I won't feel bad about firing you. Get out."

She turned and walked away, and then stopped. Hope flared. Maybe he could fix this . . .

"The tux shirt costs twenty dollars. Make sure you leave it on the counter because I'm not covering anything else for you tonight."

Thabiso stood there, hands throbbing, ego badly bruised. His ruse had failed in every way. He'd wanted to learn more about Naledi, and he'd wanted to learn one thing specifically: that his life had been better off without her. That her leaving hadn't mattered. But as he watched her walk away, he didn't feel relief, or like his curiosity had been sated.

He'd need a new strategy.

Chapter 7

*I*f you will not take my advice as your assistant, then please take it as a woman. This is a bad idea. Very bad."

Likotsi shifted and the overstuffed couch she was perched on squeaked in protest beneath her tailored pants.

"Why is this couch wrapped in plastic?" she asked, nose wrinkling as she poked at the uncomfortable clear covering. "There is absolutely no reason to preserve this floral print monstrosity. And this wallpaper!"

Fading evening rays of sunlight from the window in the small kitchen highlighted the overstuffed couch and its outdated print, the mix of plastic flowers and real plants that occupied shelves and corners. The place was nothing like the penthouse suite in the hotel they'd reserved for the trip. That room commanded a view overlooking the city. This apartment looked out onto cracked sidewalks and a combination beauty salon and barber shop across the street.

"The place has a vintage look I thought would appeal to you," Thabiso said from the bedroom down the hall. "I'm honestly surprised you haven't already staged a photo shoot for InstaPhoto."

Likotsi carefully crossed her leg over her knee, so as not to wrinkle her pants. "I was waiting for you to play photographer, Your Highness. My arms are long, but a selfie would not capture the majesty of this unorthodox rental you've chosen."

Thabiso smiled as he hung his clothing in the closet Naledi's neighbor, Mrs. Garcia, had cleared out for him. Likotsi had insisted she unpack for him, but Thabiso was trying the method acting approach: a common man would hang up his own clothing, no?

Mrs. Garcia had been reluctant to accept the all-expense paid trip to visit her family in Puerto Rico, and to rent him her place while she was gone, but once Thabiso learned her hometown had been severely damaged in recent storms, he'd offered a substantial donation to a local rebuilding fund. Thesolo already had people on the ground helping with the rebuilding efforts, so a bit more money for a good cause wouldn't hurt. She'd accepted, her people would benefit, and he'd gotten what he wanted. All good, right?

He did feel a pang of conscience. There was something at least a little untoward about bribing the old woman who lived across the hall from the woman you were trying to get to know better . . .

". . . stalking," Likotsi said. The couch squeaked in agreement. "Like, just a hairbreadth away from it really. This behavior is unbecoming, and to a woman of Naledi's cultural background, you could be seen as a threat."

"I am no threat," Thabiso said. "I just need a way to continue observing her without her knowledge or revealing that I lied about my identity when we first met."

The only response was the *mmchew* of Likotsi sucking her teeth. He should have chided her for forgetting her place, but he was in Jamal mode, so he let it slide.

"I certainly wouldn't like it if a strange man pursued me in such a way," she said tersely.

"I'm not a strange man," he bit out as he hung up the linen shirt. He was Naledi's betrothed. But still . . . Likotsi's words had some truth to them. He wouldn't like a strange man pursuing Likotsi, who didn't desire the attentions of *any* man.

Wait . . .

He strode into the living room. "Do you think perhaps Naledi has the same predilections as you?"

"Predilections?" She tilted her head to regard him like he was a jumping spider she was tracking before she stomped on it. "How should I know if she enjoys her popcorn with salt instead of sugar?"

Thabiso's face scrunched into an expression of contrition. "My apologies. I meant, in your research, was there any evidence that she might be attracted to women? Well, exclusively women?"

He'd felt sparks of heat from Ledi several times during his ill-fated attempt at serving. That is, before he'd put off sparks of his own and nearly set her workplace on fire. But perhaps he'd read too much into her reaction to him?

Likotsi burst into laughter, her hands slapping her knees as she doubled over from it. "Your Highness. While I admit that you are a fine specimen of a man, being a lesbian is not the only possible reason a woman wouldn't respond to your attentions."

That bit stung. Mostly because it was the truth—for a normal man. For all of his life, people liking him or desiring him had been a predetermined thing, inextricably tied to his royal status. He'd thought himself so clever when he'd decided to go along with

Naledi's misunderstanding and pretend to be Jamal, but maybe being a prince was the only thing about him that would interest a woman.

"I am determined to get to know her, Likotsi. That is my right."

He just needed a second chance; he couldn't let things end as they had. Just thinking of his petulant behavior brought heat to his face.

Another *mmchew*. "Seriously, sire. I'm starting to wonder if I shouldn't have loaned you that book everyone was passing around the palace. I know you have never had to work for female attention, so let me be clear. In reality, women don't like when strangers show up at their jobs and track their every move under the auspices of 'getting to know them.' Please keep in mind that just because you have the money to do things doesn't mean they should be done."

"Enough." Thabiso waved her and her common sense away. He had a plan. Or the beginnings of one. Or the seed of the beginning of a plan, which would have to suffice for now. "I thought you said you were going to go grocery shopping? I might like to visit one of these American markets."

Likotsi pulled out her tablet, eyes glued to the screen as she spoke. "Actually, there is a delivery service I thought would be perfect for you. It's quite intriguing. They send you recipes along with the correct proportion of gourmet ingredients so there is no food waste. Apparently, even a simpleton can use it."

"Really?" Thabiso thought about the last meeting he'd attended before leaving Thesolo. He thought of Naledi holding her cupcake.

I hate seeing food go to waste.

"I wonder if the agricultural minister would be interested in such a program. I've heard that the lower-income citizens who receive assistance from the kingdom sometimes eat little more than mealie pap—a program like this could be converted to something that gives them more choice. Production and delivery would create jobs, and we could contract the local farmers to provide ingredients. Oh, and perhaps the Minister of Culture would like to get involved, providing recipes that have started to fade from memory. Mark that down in my agenda for the next ministerial session."

Likotsi glanced at him with pride.

"This is an excellent idea," she said as she tapped away. "I'm sure the ministers will be happy to see you more involved than you have been of late. I added it to the notes for next week's meeting."

Next week. His UN summit and meetings with PharmaMundial, Omega Corp, and various dignitaries wouldn't take longer than a few days; he hadn't scheduled in additional time for getting to know his betrothed. After the incredible display of ego he'd put on after she'd saved him from a fiery demise, he had only a week with Naledi. A week to . . . What?

Make her fall in love with you.

No. That had never been the plan. He was curious, that was all; he'd spent most of his life feeling the loss of a person he'd never truly known. He wanted to know her.

And after that?

"Highness?" Likotsi pulled him away from his thoughts. "I am here as your assistant first and foremost, but I am insubordinate enough to consider myself your friend as well. I cannot make you stop this madness, but I can ask you to be careful, yes?"

Thabiso paused for a moment. He'd been told to be careful all his life, but he sensed Likotsi wasn't talking about tarnishing the image of the Kingdom of Thesolo. She was talking about him, Thabiso with no royal title attached.

He cleared his throat. "I will be, Kotsi. Now feel free to take your leave. You may have this evening for yourself."

"Thanks, sire." She put away the tablet and pulled out her phone. "One of the women I swiped right on, located zero point three miles away, has requested that I meet her for a drink. Perhaps you shan't be the only one with an American conquest?"

She executed a little shoulder shimmy.

"Naledi is not a conquest," he said gruffly.

"'Every woman is a conquest,' Your Highness. That's a direct quote, from you, during our visit to the Miss West Africa pageant six months back," Likotsi said cheerily before grabbing her houndstooth suit jacket and slipping into her brown-and-white spats. "I told you to be careful—pretending this is anything other than an itch to be scratched could be dangerous. For you and for her."

"You make me out to be some kind of heartless beast."

"I manage your correspondence, sire, so I get to be the heartless beast when it comes to the women you date." She gave him a smile that was actually an indictment.

"But—"

"I'll be sleeping at the hotel, possibly not alone, so don't wait up and don't get into too much trouble," she said with a wink, then glanced mistrustfully at the couch. "And be careful not to get a heat rash from that thing."

With that she was gone, ready to conquer the NYC dating scene after shivving him with the truth about himself in just a few sentences. He was known as the Playboy PanAfrique in certain tabloids for a reason. He was rich, he was handsome, and he had been known to go through women like a zebra through the fresh grass of the veldt.

He walked over to the couch and sat down slowly so as not to pop the cushion like a balloon. Somewhere down the hall, he could hear the slap of tennis shoes as children raced up the steps.

He looked around the small, clean apartment that would be his home for the next few days. Mrs. Garcia told him she'd lived there for thirty years. Thirty! She'd raised children there. In a place that was barely the size of one of his walk-in closets back home. The walls were crowded with frames of various shapes and colors; some of the faces were familiar to him, as the older counterparts had shown up and shook his hand before climbing into the limo. They'd all radiated a thankfulness that Thabiso wasn't sure he'd ever felt. No, that wasn't true. He'd felt it just yesterday, when Naledi had touched his arm and told him he would get the hang of things. It had been a lie, of course, but one made in kindness, to assuage his fears.

Keys jingled in the hallway and Thabiso rose from the couch, slowly, to avoid any untoward sounds from the couch. He crept to the door and looked through the peephole.

Before him was Naledi. At least he was fairly sure that the cloud of thick curly hair and the spectacular bottom that poked out from beneath a heavy backpack belonged to her. She fumbled with her keys, and then dropped them. He could tell by the way she bent to retrieve them that she wasn't clumsy or drunk; she was exhausted.

The urge to go to her welled up in him, but he found he couldn't move. Likotsi's chastisement rang in his ears.

Stalker.

What had he been thinking? Moving in across the hall from Naledi? Peering at her behind without her knowledge? Just a few days before he'd had to reprimand a palace guard for sniffing after one of the maids. Was he any better?

She looked up suddenly, apprehensively, and Thabiso jumped away from the peephole. Sweat broke out on his brow and his stomach tightened. Had she seen him? What was he going to say if she had? That was one of the many parts of this plan he hadn't thought through. He had recently completed an exhaustive ten-year outlook for Thesolo's projected growth, but he couldn't think of a single thing to say to Naledi that could ensure their next few hours.

He heard footsteps and a male voice. This one had an accent like he'd heard in films. The approaching man was what had caught her attention, not Thabiso's peephole creeping.

"D'you order Yellow Spatula Dinner on Demand?"

"No." There was a thread of apprehension in her voice, as if she wanted the man to leave her alone.

"It says here there's a delivery for seven p.m. for apartment 7 M."

Silence, followed by the shuffling of paper. "No, that's an *N*. Mrs. Garcia's apartment."

The tightening in Thabiso's stomach transformed into a sick pulse of fear as a heavy knock sounded on the door. Thabiso took a step away from it as another knock fell.

"Look, I can't hang around. It's dinnertime and I got a ton of deliveries to make."

He heard Naledi sigh. "I'll get it to her. She's always home at this time. *La Mujere Morena* is on right now and she never misses her stories . . . Here, hand it over."

Footsteps echoed in the hall, and then there was another knock at the door. This one was quiet. Tentative.

"Mrs. Garcia?" Another knock, a little more insistent this time. "Mrs. Garcia, are you there?"

The concern in her voice was unmistakable. He could hide there like a coward and let her think her neighbor had suffered a heart attack, or he could open the door and face her. That was the point of the whole ridiculous plan, wasn't it?

He took a deep breath and exhaled.

"One moment!" he called out. He'd meant the words to be a warning—*not Mrs. Garcia!*—but when he opened the door fear rippled across her face. She shuffled away from him until her backpack bumped into her own apartment door.

Thabiso remembered that this was supposed to be a surprise to him, too. He gasped.

"Naledi? What are you doing here?"

"What am I? What are you? Where is Mrs. Garcia?" He didn't miss the way she readjusted the fingers of her hand holding her keys into a fist, with one pointy key sticking out from between the knuckles.

Stalker.

"She went to Puerto Rico to visit family," he said. "I'm renting her place while she's away. About yesterday—"

Naledi didn't relax the grip on her key. "She didn't mention any trip. And she hates having strangers in her apartment."

"It came up quite suddenly, and apparently my renting helped her afford her hotel accommodations," he said, shoving his hands in his pockets. That was true, somewhat, but he still felt like a creep.

She betrayed you, the priestesses, and your people. A lie or two won't harm her compared to what she's done.

"I'm sorry if I freaked you out. I didn't mean to," he said. That part was completely true.

"Freaked me out? Last night you flew off the handle like you have anger control issues when *you* were at fault, left me with fire damage to clean up, ruined my mood for the entire day, and you called me a dog. I'm more than freaked out—I'm pissed. I can't even escape asshole co-workers at home now."

Thabiso had spent the entire day recriminating himself over the fire and his behavior, but he hadn't given much thought to cleaning up either situation.

"My behavior yesterday was unacceptable," he said. "I'm not used to failure, and I took my frustration at myself out on you."

"Well, what's done is done." She shook her head, then pinned him a sharp look. "Though I'm not sure Mrs. Garcia would have let you stay if she knew about your pyromaniac tendencies."

"My flirtation with pyromania was a one-night event," he said calmly.

"Well, aren't I the luckiest Saint Bernard in the world to have witnessed it?"

Apparently he'd struck a nerve with that insult. He cursed his big mouth and wondered how one handled such things. His relationships with women never generally reached the point where there was arguing and making up. He tired of them, bade them adieu, and then Likotsi handled anything that came up after that. He wasn't quite sure how to apologize to her. He supposed it couldn't be much different than dealing with a head of state who felt slighted.

Thabiso caught her gaze and held it. This was the moment on which the rest of his week rested.

And perhaps more.

"I called you a Saint Bernard as if it was something bad, but they're a breed known for their intelligence, loyalty, and keeping their wits about them in touchy situations. I should be so lucky to have anyone think me so useful."

Naledi stared at him, those large eyes wide with indignation, but something else, too. Something startled but pleased. He imagined she'd look that way when the man she loved pulled her close against him with no warning.

Expectation. That's what it was, and she wasn't the only one feeling it. A path was forming between them, brick by brick, spanning the width of the hallway and the length of the time that had separated them. Something drew him to her, a force that made his body go taut and his breathing slow down. Her lips parted and the tug between them grew stronger.

She cut her gaze away from him, and when it met his again, there was a distance there, like the bridge connecting them had fallen away—or she had demolished it with a controlled explosion. There was no coldness; she was warm as ever when her mouth pulled into a smile. But that distance left him feeling miles away instead of across the hall.

"Was that supposed to be an apology?" she asked. "Because if it was, I'm assuming you've never spoken to a human woman in your life."

Thabiso let out a brief laugh of relief. She hadn't told him to fuck off. There was a chance he hadn't blown this entirely. He stepped forward tentatively, leaning forward at the waist to reach for the box she clutched in her arms so that he didn't crowd her in front of her door.

"That wasn't my apology." He plucked the box from her hands. "But this could be. Or the start of one at least."

"What is it?" she asked suspiciously.

"Dinner," he replied, and then scanned the receipt taped to the box. "Specifically, lemon sage chicken thighs with a cucumber quinoa side."

She stood still for a long time. "I'm trying to calculate the probability of this encounter we're having right now but I don't even know where to begin," she finally said, shaking her head. "This is a really weird coincidence, don't you think?"

"I don't believe in coincidence," he said. He hated that something so true was wrapped in a lie, but loved the way her lips parted at the words.

"I was completely out of line yesterday," he rushed on. "You should have let me burn to a crisp, but you didn't. I'd like to thank you for that, and nothing more."

Her gaze skittered away from him.

"If you can put up with me for the amount of time it takes to cook and eat this, of course," he added.

The sound of her stomach growling echoed in the hallway's strange acoustics.

She sighed, but released her grip on her key and pulled out her phone.

"I'm telling my friend I'm having dinner with some asshole named Jamal who is definitely an arsonist and may or may not be a serial killer. So if you try to make lemon sage Ledi instead, the police will be here before you have time to book it to LaGuardia."

The shift from hope to fruition was a tangible thing

that Thabiso felt in the pounding of his heart and the surge of joy that forced the corners of his lips into a smile. That she called him by another man's name wasn't ideal, but the fact that she was talking to him at all was some kind of miracle.

He bit back the diplomatic immunity joke on the tip of his tongue and turned back toward the small flat that suddenly seemed to contain a world of opportunity.

"I'm not a serial killer," he said. "And I'm no chef either."

When he turned back to look at her, her gaze lifted from his butt. She had been caught in the act. For a moment their gazes held, and there was that same flash of heat that had simmered beneath her rambling talk of kale when they'd first met.

"Don't expect any help from me in the kitchen. I can't cook," she said suddenly. "And don't expect anything else either. I'm extremely frugal and tired of eating ramen, which is the only reason I'm accepting this invitation."

Thabiso was definitely not used to this type of talk from a woman. He very often had to ask them to stop helping him, and those who shared a meal with him were generally expecting more themselves. But he liked her laying out what she wanted from him. Food, and nothing more. It was a start.

"I'll take care of this," he said, mustering his confidence as they entered the apartment. There was a recipe that must be simple enough to follow and no candle wicks were going to be involved. Still, his gaze scanned the room and settled on the small fire extinguisher in the corner of the kitchen with relief. Confidence was good, but he was learning that knowing one's limitations could be useful as well.

Chapter 8

Ledi glanced at her phone just as Portia's reply came through:

> Whooooa. You're having dinner with a strange dude? *checks horoscopes to see what planet is wilding out right now*

Ledi rolled her eyes. It wasn't that weird, was it?

> This is totally weird, but I'm intrigued. Fill me in tomorrow (check in when you can though).

Okay, it *was* totally weird. But Jamal didn't really feel like a strange dude; the sense of familiarity had hit her as soon as he'd walked into the kitchen at the Institute. And though she was used to dealing with assholes, she'd spent the day angry and uneasy over what happened because the way their night had ended had felt wrong. She certainly hadn't felt the same about Dan.

Worse, when Jamal had opened Mrs. Garcia's door, some part of her had been glad to see him. It must have been her soft, stupid nucleus; the reason she needed a social cell membrane for protection to begin with.

Now she was closing the door behind herself and getting ready to share a meal with him.

You'd probably share more than some quinoa if he asked nicely.

Her gaze slid over the flex of Jamal's muscular back beneath his shirt as he placed the box onto Mrs. Garcia's dining table. She imagined feeling those muscles bunch beneath her palms as he pressed into her, and then clutched her hands into fists at the explicit image that flashed in her mind. Her body warmed as she watched his lithe movements and understood that though she had only agreed to dinner, she was hungry for Jamal, too.

No. He's an asshole. Focus on the free food.

"So how did you rent this apartment of all places in New York?" she asked as she examined Mrs. Garcia's family photos lining the walls. She looked away, hating that her first reaction to the photos was envy.

"A friend made the introduction and the situation worked in both my and Mrs. Garcia's best interests," Jamal said as he scanned through the printout that he'd found inside the box. As he pulled each ingredient out, he cross-referenced it with the list, then brought it into the small kitchen. It wasn't the most efficient method of transport, but she got to watch him walk so she couldn't complain. He moved with a grace she wasn't used to; many of the guys in her neighborhood had swagger, but Jamal walked as if he expected everything to fall away before him, and like he was justified in thinking it.

He had the bearings of a rich boy—she knew that well enough from years of dealing with Portia and clients at the various catering gigs she took on in addition to serving at the Institute—but he'd seemed unsure of himself as he stood before her in the hallway. Chagrined. She'd told him what an ass he'd been, and he hadn't even tried to turn it around and explain to her how she had *made* him behave like an ass. And now he was trying to make it up to her.

She wondered if this was some new species of fuckboy, an evolved version that was more effective at luring women into its trap before showing its true nature. If that was the case, it was working.

She was still wary, but some part of her was already lowering the drawbridge and inviting him in. He'd make quite the efficient virus if he weren't approximately a gazillion times too large.

As she watched him try to figure out how to light the gas stove without letting her know he had no idea what he was doing, the figurative drawbridge shuddered to a stop and reversed course.

"Seriously?" She trudged over to the stove and nudged him out of the way. "Have you never used a gas stove before?"

"I've seen one used," he said stubbornly.

"Let me rephrase that—have you ever used *any* kind of stove before?"

"The ones back home are electric. Honestly, it can't be that difficult," he said, holding the match to the wrong burner again.

Ledi rolled her eyes. Of course a hot man offering to make her dinner would turn into more drudge work for her.

"I'll do it."

"You said you couldn't cook," his deep voice rumbled next to her as she grabbed the box of matches, struck one, and held it near the burner. The correct burner.

"I meant 'I can't cook for you.' Once someone knows you can do something for them, they'll want you to do it all the time." She turned the knob on the stove and pulled her hand back just as the gas ignited with a *whoosh* of blue and orange. She'd learned to cook early; not because she'd been a mistreated Cinderella, but because it had made her useful to her foster parents. People didn't get rid of things they found useful. In theory, that is.

"You know, that is true," he said gravely, pausing to strike a contemplative pose as she used her fingertips to push him out of her way. He didn't resist, simply stepped back. "My parents constantly say that I have to lead by example, but once I do one thing and it succeeds, people expect me to do more and more."

"Such is the tragedy of being marginally talented," she said. "I'm great at doing grant applications it seems, so my lab's postdoc has decided I should do all of his."

"You mentioned this man yesterday. He makes you do his work for him?"

"It's fine. It's how things are. It just seems that he thinks I'm his personal assistant instead of a fellow researcher."

"Why don't you say no?" His tone was serious, as if he was presenting her with an option she'd never considered.

"Because men make life harder for women who say no, especially women who look like me," she said. "STEM is already hard to navigate—being marked as someone who doesn't work well in teams or contribute enough could tank my career."

He didn't respond and Ledi sighed. This was why she was single. She needed a bearded hottie who wouldn't be flummoxed by the simplest conversation about what she experienced every day. Clarence had told her to stop complaining and work harder when she'd brought up Brian; he'd thought his own success meant that anyone who failed just wasn't trying hard enough.

"Ah. This is like the research indicating that a woman who speaks once or twice in a professional or academic setting is seen as monopolizing the conversation. Tell a co-worker no once or twice and that is all he remembers of you, I suppose."

Ledi almost dropped the chicken thigh she'd been seasoning. When she looked at him, he was leaning back against the window molding. His fingers stroked his beard, and for a moment he looked like The Thinker, but dipped in a smooth dark chocolate shell and, judging from the folds at the crotch of his pants, packing a bit more heat.

"Yes," she said carefully. This was a new thing for her, and she didn't want to make any sudden movements. But she would push him harder; there was no need to give him the benefit of the doubt. "And there's also the gaslighting."

"Gaslighting?" He looked quizzically at the light switch in the kitchen.

"It's when you point out something that upsets you, or you try to set boundaries, and the other person tries to make you feel like you're overreacting or it's all in your head. Like when I tell Brian it's not fair that he's offloading his work on me, and then he acts like I'm the one being difficult."

"I thought that was called being an asshole," Jamal growled. "This Brian is an asshole."

Ledi laughed; somehow she could laugh about it now that Jamal sat looking so angry on her behalf.

"And yesterday I was just another man making

things harder for you," he said. "*I* was the asshole. I don't like that."

"It wasn't great for me either, my guy," Ledi said. She'd pushed and instead of revealing himself for the fuckboy he was, he'd surprised her. "Just don't blame other people for your mistakes and stop embellishing your résumé and you'll be all right."

His low laugh seemed to caress her even though he was across the room and even though she was feeling a surge of residual anger at him as she recalled his behavior at the Institute.

"How apt," was all he said in reply. "Do you want me to take care of this co-worker? So that he doesn't bother you again?"

Ledi's head whipped around. Had he really just casually dropped that into the conversation? "I thought you said you weren't a killer."

"I said I wasn't a serial killer. This would be a one-off thing." The corner of his mouth stretched up into a grin, and she relaxed.

"But seriously, he has made you afraid to refuse him because you fear for your career. I have associates who could make him understand that he should also fear for his."

Was she supposed to feel slightly giddy that a near stranger was leveling threats at her co-worker? Surely there was something wrong with her.

"Ummm, I'm gonna have to go with no thank you, though I appreciate the offer."

"Hmph. Well, I'm glad that you're not afraid to say no to me," he said. "Maybe next time he tries to tell you what to do, you should summon the Naledi who fired me in no uncertain terms."

"Maybe I will," she said. She took the recipe from his hands and scanned it. *Rinse chicken thighs. Sear.*

Melt butter. It was like following experimental procedure, but with more delicious and edible results.

She glanced over to find Jamal staring at her.

"Where did you learn to cook?" he asked suddenly. "From your parents?"

She couldn't tell if he was being purposely nosy or just making idle conversation.

"I don't have parents," she said bluntly.

"I invited a divine being over for dinner? Brilliant. We need some wine to go with this, if you want to work your magic on the tap water." He smiled a little, but it was the weird, tight smile people deployed when something you said had worried them. She realized too late that he wouldn't be around long; she could've just lied and said yes and been done with the conversation. Now she'd have to talk about *that.*

"Well, I did. Then I didn't. I was too young to cook when they were around. I don't even remember what my favorite food was as a kid."

Or much of anything about my childhood.

"Your parents left when you were very young?" Jamal's accent made the words seem heavier somehow, like something from a Shakespearean tragedy instead of her everyday life.

She put on water for the quinoa. Salted it so she wouldn't forget when the excitement of the boil distracted her.

"They died."

She'd underestimated how tired she was. That was the only thing that could explain why she'd just blurted out her sad orphan story. She hated talking about it, and couldn't even remember the last time she had.

"Oh." He sucked in a breath. "I'm sorry."

His voice had gone deep and strained, as if their

death meant something to him. Most people were brusque and changed the subject, allowing her to follow their lead. It didn't bother her. Her emotions were at pH 7.0 when it came to her parents—she'd made sure of it. But the sincerity of Jamal's apology nudged something inside of her, changing the balance that she had maintained so well.

"Car accident. I barely remember it. Or them," she said, shrugging away his kindness as she stirred the food.

"That is quite unfortunate." When she looked at him, hoping her glare would remedy his nosiness, he was staring down at the ground, lost in thought. "And I assume you had no relatives to take you in."

A pigeon sat on the rail of the fire escape outside the window behind him, tilting its head and staring as it schemed how to get at their meal.

"Nope. I got put into the system. I was a layaway foster kid. A few families put a deposit on me, but none of them ever made the final payment, so to speak. They were nice, with a couple of exceptions. Just never clicked enough with any of them to do the whole 'forever family' thing."

She refrained from telling him about her defective Velcro theory.

"Do you need help?" he asked suddenly. "I noticed yesterday that you have issues with delegating. Rather, you delegate the easier tasks and take on the harder ones for yourself."

"Well, maybe you also noticed yesterday that sometimes it's easier for me to do things myself because I'm better at them."

He let out a short, sharp laugh. "Well, yes, but doing everything yourself isn't really sustainable, is it? Please. Delegate."

She stopped stirring the quinoa. "Come chop this cucumber. Dice it so it's in cubes. Don't cut your fingers."

He stood next to her and fumbled with the knife a bit before getting into a chopping rhythm. "What's layaway?"

She stopped with her fork over a thigh that needed to be flipped.

"Are you some kind of trust fund baby who got his allowance cut off?" She'd asked the question because she was curious, but the contempt in her voice sizzled like the meat in the pan. He was probably the kind of guy who paid cash up front and thought Sallie Mae was a country singer.

There was a pause in his chopping. "Something like that."

He wasn't going to elaborate. Well good. She didn't feel like elaborating anymore either. Ledi flipped the pieces of chicken and pulled out a small cast-iron pan to make the sauce. "Chop the sage next," was all she said. "And then juice the lemons."

Jamal's bicep brushed against hers as they worked quietly. The fresh, green smell of sage mixed with the scent of the meaty carmelization of the chicken. Someone drove by with the latest everpresent pop anthem playing at full blast, but they prepared their meal in silence.

The pigeon cooed outside the window and stepped closer to the glass, and Ledi thought of a study she'd read that described how well the birds remembered human faces. They were more observant than people gave them credit for. She wondered what she and Jamal looked like to it. Paired-off humans who chose to cook dinner together each night, and to share other parts of their lives, too?

It's just a free meal. And the pigeon isn't thinking about jack except how to get in on the quinoa action.

"My parents expect a lot from me," Jamal said. Apparently, he was one of those people who found chopping meditative. "They pin their every hope for the future onto me, so they also want to decide everything for me, down to how I do my job and who I marry. But at least I have parents, so I shouldn't complain."

Ledi dropped the sage leaves into the citrus butter, then removed the pan from the heat. "We can stop talking about parents and the lack thereof now," she said as she poured the sauce over the chicken.

She didn't look at him as he moved around behind her. She focused on taking up a small bit of quinoa, blowing on it, testing its give between her teeth.

When she finally turned around, he stood next to the table, hands in his pockets. On each of Mrs. Garcia's bleach-stained plastic place mats sat a perfect dinner setting. The silverware wasn't as fancy, but he'd apparently retained some of what she'd taught him at the Institute. He'd even folded some paper towels in the elaborate way she'd shown him. She shouldn't have cared, but it was the look in his eye that got her. She'd been in his position, standing beside a set table hoping that somehow that small gesture made her foster parents happy, showed them how useful she could be . . .

Ledi gave a grunt of approval and turned back to the food. She knew he'd expected a different reaction from the way she caught his shoulders slump from the corner of her eye. He couldn't know that the coarse sound had been the result of whatever strange reaction was happening in her chest, and happening because of him. Fluttering and fizzing and fluffiness: all kinds of *f* words.

Feelings. Good ones, that couldn't be solely attributed to the high of getting a free meal.

She moved away from the stove as he stepped back into the kitchen. The cooking area was bigger than her measly Pullman, but suddenly much too small for the two of them.

When she looked up at him, his gaze was on her face in general, and specifically homed in on her mouth. And then his eyes lifted to hers and the fluttering and fizzing spread from her chest to a portion of her anatomy that she was fairly certain wasn't part of the respiratory and circulatory systems. She'd have to double-check her anatomy books, because the pulse between her legs felt as strong as a heartbeat and as natural as breathing.

Men had looked at Ledi with lust in their eyes before. The way Jamal looked at her was something entirely new to her. No, that wasn't true. She'd seen it before. It was the look on Charming's face when Sleeping Beauty's eyes fluttered open. The expression of awe that Eric sported when he woke to find Ariel cradling him on the beach. It was the look that she thought only existed in Disney cartoons because it seemed so highly improbable that anyone would ever look at her that way.

And yet, there he was, gaze sparking with mischief and want, corners of his mouth turned up in a hopeful smile. She considered giving him whatever a smile like that would cost her, but she knew all too well how things would turn out.

Defective Velcro. Phospholipid bilayer, activate.

"I have to go," she said suddenly. Washing her

hands and then grabbing her backpack and slipping the heavy load onto her back were autonomic functions.

"Ledi."

She was heading for the door and kept walking, ignoring him. "I'm really tired, and I have to get up early to run some tests at the lab—"

"Ledi." This time his voice was commanding, a tone that wouldn't be ignored, and she turned to face him before she realized it. "Here."

The open cabinet behind him revealed a treasure trove of Tupperware, and the one in his hand held a portion of the meal they'd made together.

"Thank you for preparing dinner for me," he said as he handed her the warm plastic rectangle.

"No, that's okay," she said, taking a step back.

His gaze narrowed.

"What wouldn't be okay is you leaving here without some portion of the meal you made," he said, and pushed the dish into her hands. He opened the door wide enough that she could pass through it without having to touch him. "I had fun. Thank you for spending time with me."

He wasn't looking at her with Disney eyes anymore, but the smile he gave bathed her in warmth, like the first ray of sunshine to slip over her after hours spent in the lab.

What the hell are you doing, for real this time?!

She rushed out the door, tossing her thanks over her shoulder as she fumbled her key into the lock and let herself into her apartment. He didn't linger like a weirdo—his door was closed before she got hers open. She doubted he was watching through the peephole either, although she did just that when she closed her door behind her.

Naledi ignored the delicious smell coming from the Tupperware.

Home. Alive(ish), she texted Portia.

She fed the Grams, took a shower, and then oiled her scalp with the fragrant mixture she'd made after watching several YouTube videos, even though her stomach growled. She pulled her hair up into a bun atop her head and tied on the silk sleep scarf with "I <3 SCIENCE" printed all over it that Portia had gifted her.

When she finally picked up the food, it was barely lukewarm. But as she took the first delicious bite, she wondered if Jamal was doing the same just a few feet away.

She regretted denying herself the sight of him biting into the tender chicken, of the grease and sauce making his already-perfect lips shine enticingly.

She silently cursed Mrs. Garcia and whatever fluke of statistics had brought Jamal much too close to the nucleus of her small world. It didn't matter in the end—she was going to be so busy with work at the Institute and studying that she doubted she'd see him again. And that was exactly how she wanted it.

Chapter 9

Ledi had already groggily pulled on her black trousers and was halfway through rebuttoning her tuxedo shirt when the phone rang. She was annoyed for a moment—people who called instead of texting were a plague on humanity—but then felt a brief flash of fear. Portia had never responded to her text the previous night. Maybe she'd had too much to drink again. Maybe . . .

But when she grabbed her phone, the name YVES lit up the screen.

"Hello?"

Yves's angry voice hissed through her phone.

"Don't come in today. We're closed for a few days at least," he growled.

"What happened?" Ledi asked.

"Several people got sick after lunch yesterday and they're saying they can trace it back to this kitchen! MY KITCHEN."

"Oh no." Ledi's hand went to her stomach as she imagined all the possible bacterial agents she might have been exposed to while working. She didn't have time for food poisoning. But she'd likely already be sick if she'd eaten anything contaminated.

"See, I told them not to order that prepackaged salad shit and to keep buying from the farmer's market, but they complained about costs. Now we're paying for it!" Ledi held the phone away from her ear. "You should see the emails flying back and forth on the Institute's listserv! Diarrhea this, and projectile vomit that. Everyone is acting like I wiped my ass with the Bibb lettuce before serving them. *Jävla fan!* The only way I could keep this kitchen cleaner is if I took a blowtorch to it!"

That didn't seem outside the realm of possibility to Ledi. He might take a blowtorch to the Institute itself if they kept allowing people to besmirch his kitchen.

"I'm sorry, Yves. I know cleanliness is a priority for you." That earned her a hum of approval. "So I shouldn't come in at all?"

"No, I'm sorry, but your shifts today and tomorrow are canceled. I'll give you a call when things settle down but I know you're leaving for your internship soon. We'll play it by ear, yes?"

She felt a new surge of panic as he said his goodbyes and hung up, this time thinking about her bank account. She reminded herself that she was fine— she scrimped and saved so that she wouldn't have to freak out in case of emergency. Or at least not freak out A LOT.

As frustrating as it was, not having to work was one of the nicer things to happen to Ledi in a long time.

Besides the hot dude across the hall, that is.

She thought about Jamal, and the meal they'd cooked the night before. She'd been annoyed at having to take over the preparation, but working side by side had actually been kind of cool. She was used to impersonal dates. Movie theaters and coffee shops and possibly a few hours in the guy's bed—if that long. She never brought men to her place, let alone cooked with them. She'd certainly never shared so much about her past.

She'd told Jamal about her parents. It didn't seem like much in the current terrain of social media over-share, but it was way more than she'd ever told a stranger who didn't work at Child Services. And it hadn't felt like talking to a stranger, which made it all the more uncomfortable for her.

Her phone vibrated in her hand and she fumbled it, watching with horror and then relief as it landed on the less-hard-than-the-floor surface of her bed.

> Hey! I'm on my walk of shameless. Your date with guy next door went well?

Ledi smiled.

> It was fine. I ended up bringing my dinner back to my place, so not much of a date.

> **Wait. What? Was he a weirdo?**

> He was cool.

> **Cool enough that you left before sitting down to eat with him?**

> Yeah.

> **Did you guys talk?**

> Yes.

> **. . . and you liked talking to him?**

Yup.

👀 🌊

You see what? Ledi began unbuttoning her tuxedo shirt, passed her phone from hand to hand as she tugged it off by the sleeves. She wondered what Jamal was doing across the hall, and then reminded herself she didn't care.

> You've sucked it up through some of the shittiest, most boring dates known to humankind. But you left before eating with a cool guy last night. 👀 🌊.

Ledi rolled her eyes and tapped out her response.

> I worked at the lab all day and then the Institute. I was tired.

Suuure.

In other news, I have off from work today.

Wait. What? Which work?

Both. Oh my god, I can go back to bed. 😊

She eyed her textbooks and notes.

> Yes! Don't even think about studying. Go get some sleep.

Ledi felt a little giddy at the possibility of a block of time with nothing to do but recharge.

Maybe we can get lunch at that Brazilian restaurant you mentioned when it opened? My treat! And my former coworker at the Museum of New York City posted that they have an exhibition about historical epidemics. Friend date?

Ledi knew this was, in part, Portia's way of making up for her late-night wake-up call, but also because despite her flaws, Portia was a caring friend and wanted to give her a reprieve from her daily grind. Ledi wanted to see her—to actually have a conversation that was coherent and would be remembered by both of them—but it was always uncomfortable when Portia made offers like this. The Brazilian restaurant was Michelin starred—lunch there would cost way too much. But Ledi thought maybe that was the point. She wasn't the only one who confused being useful with being indispensable.

How about we get some pizza? That's more in my budget.

Hey, you can take free food from some weird guy but not your best friend? I got you. I'll pick you up at your place.

Ledi sighed and brushed away her annoyance. She had a nap calling her name.

LEDI HAD CHANGED into less formal attire by the time Portia arrived: straight-legged jeans, bright pink slip-on sneakers, and a black scoop neck sweatshirt that hung off of her shoulders. She had nice shoulders, and she suddenly had the urge to show them off.

"Look at you!" Portia gave Ledi a pleased once-over paired with an encouraging nod. "You look so pretty! Is that mascara? And lipstick?"

"It's lip *stain*," Ledi said. "I actually found it on Regina's website. GirlsWithGlasses has a great 'makeup for all shades and budgets' section. The site has really blown up. You must be proud."

"Yeah, Regina always succeeds when she puts her mind to something," Portia replied, her gaze becoming distant as it always did when Ledi brought up her twin sister. Ledi knew twinhood could be a fraught thing, but when your sister ran one of the most popular geek sites, it was bound to come up from time to time.

"Do you want to do the museum or get drinks instead?" Portia asked suddenly.

"The museum. It's like noon," Ledi said. "Your liver sent me a text asking for the day off, too."

Portia was silent for a long moment, apparently not appreciating the not-quite joke, and the fun day that Ledi had imagined began to slip through her fingers. She didn't feel like arguing. She wanted to enjoy her brief window of freedom.

Portia seemed to shake off whatever was bugging her and smiled. "You're right. And I'm kind of excited about this exhibit. I can introduce you to the curator afterward if you want, and you can talk about science shit. Oh! Maybe they'd want to have you come in and do a talk!"

Ledi's tension disappeared as Portia launched into some grand plan for Ledi's future as a world renowned public scientist. She was always trying to push Ledi toward better things, even when she seemed to have no idea what she wanted from her own life.

Ledi grabbed her favorite purse, which was shaped

like an amoeba, and declined to tell Portia which website she'd spotted it on as they headed out into the hall and she locked up behind them.

Ledi had always been extra perceptive of her surroundings, or for as long as she could remember at least. It was a necessary skill when you moved from one stranger's house to another and had to adjust to new guardians and siblings on a somewhat-regular basis, no matter how caring they were. Maybe that was why she was already staring toward 7 N when the door swung open.

Jamal stood still for a moment, looking as good as ever in a V-neck tee patterned with swirls of black and gold, a dashiki of sorts, and those perfectly fitted jeans of his, in dark blue this time.

"Howdy, neighbor," he said with a grin, as if that was a completely normal thing people said to one another.

"Well, hello," Portia replied, her amusement clear. "Did you just move here from Mayberry?"

"They play reruns of that show where I'm from, too." he said, flashing his smile. "We're no New York City, but not quite as provincial as that."

"And where are you from, exactly?" Portia asked, but Jamal had already transferred his gaze to Ledi. She remembered how he'd looked at her the night before, but could find little trace of it now. Only a reserved friendliness. He bent forward at the waist a little.

Is he . . . bowing?

"How was your dinner?" he asked. "Mine was delicious. There was only one thing that could have made it better."

Ah. *There* was the look. Heat rose to the surface of Ledi's cheeks and neck.

"Paprika?" Ledi guessed. "I thought it could have used some paprika."

He shook his head and his gaze quickly traced the curve of her shoulder before returning to her face.

"Not paprika."

Two simple words that sent up blooms of sensation in her breasts and belly.

"My dinner was good," Ledi said, suddenly regretting not staying the previous night, which was a sign she'd made the right decision. "Probably not as good as the packet of ramen I would have eaten if you hadn't been here."

He laughed. His eyes squeezed shut as he did, and it was a relief. She had boundaries—everyone needed those—but when Jamal looked at her, she could feel just how tightly closed in on herself she was, and how tiring it was to always be that way. His gaze made her feel like opening.

She took a deep breath to center herself and something floral sweet and grassy green hit her scent receptors and kept going. It made a beeline for her brain and rustled around in her memory, nudging at shadowy outlines that she couldn't quite make out. There was a flash of yellow against brown skin— and was that a smile?—but more than that there were feelings.

Again with the feelings?

Happiness. Belonging. The knowledge that she was loved.

Jamal closed his door and stepped fully into the hallway and she realized the scent was coming from him.

What the hell?

Ledi backed away from him a bit, not because the scent was cloying, but because she had no idea why it evoked the burning at her eyes or made her want to be held.

"Ohhhhhhhhhh. You're the one who made Ledi dinner? The possible serial killer?" Portia's gaze flicked speculatively between the two of them, the glance pulling Ledi from the memories and emotions that hovered just on the periphery of her perception. Portia was zeroing in on Jamal, and that was a problem.

Oh god. No.

Portia had offered to help kill her ex the other night, and although it had been hyperbolic, her friend could be a bit overprotective when it came to men. Men and Ledi, that was. She showed no such discernment for herself.

Ledi began to drag Portia away. "The Institute is closed because of an emergency, so I'm going to actually do something fun before studying this evening."

"Closed? Is it . . . Was it because of the fire?" he asked, walking alongside them as they headed for the stairwell. His expression was so contrite that Ledi couldn't help but feel a little sorry for him. A little.

"No. The restaurant survived your arson attempt, only to be felled by nature's greatest asshole—the bacterium."

He looked confused.

"Food poisoning."

His confusion changed to worry and she remembered that he'd recently eaten there, too. She'd let him figure out that he was fine on his own as a final repayment for his behavior that night.

"Wait, what fire? What are you talking about?" Portia asked, turning back to look up at Ledi. That was when Ledi realized that she was walking next to Jamal instead of her friend. She hopped down a step so that she was next to Portia.

"Nothing," Ledi said. At the same time, Jamal announced, "I set fire to the fondue station."

Now it was Ledi's turn to look up and back.

"I'll never forget the sight of you racing to save the day," he continued. The white of his teeth broke up the uniform blackness of his beard as he smiled. "You were like—"

He began to move in an exaggerated slow motion, mimicking the pivotal scene in just about every summer blockbuster. He pointed an imaginary fire extinguisher in Ledi's direction. "The foooooonnndduuuuuuueeeeee!" he yelled in a voice that he also slowed and deepened as he pretended to spray an imaginary extinguisher that threatened to slip from his control. "Not on my watch!"

When he finally stopped and met her gaze, his arms still raised as if they held the extinguisher, they both burst into laughter. Ledi didn't know what was happening, but her stomach hurt from the heaving and she had to stop and hold on to the banister with one hand and her chest with the other.

"That's not what happened!" she managed to gasp.

"I'm the one who nearly set himself on fire, Naledi. It is quite literally burned into my memory, and also my left forearm," he said. "Trust me on this."

And then they were laughing again, and Ledi realized she felt the same way she had outside her door when she'd caught a whiff of his cologne. Happy. Like she belonged.

"I don't get it," Portia said. Her thin brows furrowed and Ledi saw the slight hunch of her shoulders. Unlike Ledi, who was perfectly happy on the sidelines, being out of the loop was something that made Portia uneasy.

"Eh, you had to be there," she said as they touched

down on the landing. She slipped her arm through her friend's and headed for the exit.

Standing in the vestibule was someone dressed in a suit that made Jamal look like a beggar. Tan slacks with a crease so sharp Ledi would find her jeans fashionably slit if she walked too close. A dark brown suit jacket that tapered at the waist—oh.

The besuited woman was texting with a dreamy little smile on her face.

"Who is that?" Portia whispered. "That outfit is everything!"

"I don't think she lives here," Ledi whispered back. "But let's jump her for those spats. I think I can fit into them if I cut off a few toes."

When they pushed through the door the woman glanced up from her phone, taking hold of the door as they passed through, like their very own dapper doorwoman. Her gaze locked on Ledi, and for a moment Ledi was sure that she knew her from somewhere; the woman looked at her as if they were old acquaintances. She said nothing, but gave a nod of acknowledgment that made Ledi feel almost regal.

I really should wear this lipstick more often.

Then she was looking past Ledi and Portia, and her expression grew more reserved. "High—Hi . . . man," she said to Jamal. She had an accent similar to his, but with the "something else" more pronounced. It was closer to the lyrical English of the women who braided Ledi's hair every now and then. "I regret that I have distressing news about, uh, stuff. Things. You know."

The smile she had sported while engrossed in her phone screen was gone.

"Stuff and things. Quite." Jamal turned to Ledi and Portia and gave another of his little bows. "Well, ladies. I hope you enjoy the museum," he said, then turned to talk to the fabulously dressed woman. His demeanor was suddenly serious. He seemed taller, more rigid, more in control.

Ledi liked this side of him, too.

"Bye!" Portia was a bit too enthusiastic with her farewell.

Ledi glanced back as she walked out of the building. She wasn't jealous—she didn't know him well enough for that. But still, curiosity bloomed. This woman was well acquainted with him, whereas Ledi knew nothing about him at all beyond the fact that he smelled good and didn't want to disappoint his family. There seemed to be something more going on beyond the story Jamal was feeding her, though. It wasn't that she wanted an excuse to see him again, or anything, but she had to make sure he wasn't doing anything that Mrs. Garcia wouldn't approve of in her apartment.

If she had to meet up with him again, she was just being a good neighbor. That was it.

Chapter 10

*I*t appears that you've crossed the fiery gulf that lay between you and your betrothed?"

Likotsi's voice echoed in the vestibule. She pulled out her trusty tablet from a perfectly aged leather satchel, swiped in her passcode, and began scrolling, but her eyes lifted from the screen to him every few seconds to let him know that she was awaiting a response.

"Things are amicable between us," he said, thinking of their dinner yesterday. Thabiso had rarely cooked for himself—when he had, on a whim, he'd had the backing of the entire palace kitchen staff. With Naledi it had been fun. Intimate. He wished he had been able to impress her with his skills, but he had shown his deficiency yet again, and she hadn't heaped invective on him.

After she'd left, he'd sat alone at the dining table and wished for a knock at the door that never came. And that he could bypass the messy part of his plan, the telling-her-who-he-really-was part, so that they could move to the stage where his lips moved against hers and his hands traced the shape of her body.

He'd tried not to let his mind stray too far in that direction, but even the food inspired lustful thoughts. Although gourmet cuisine made up much of his diet when he was abroad, the simple chicken thighs were the most delicious thing he'd tasted in recent memory. As he'd savored the citrusy sage sauce, he'd wondered whether Naledi's essence itself weren't mixed in, giving it some extra, addictive quality that had him licking his fingers. Thoughts of her "essence" had led to a night sleeping on his back, painfully hard but unable to pleasure himself in Mrs. Garcia's frilly pink bedroom without feeling like even more of a pervert.

He'd looked up the term *gaslighting* instead, and then *layaway* and *foster child*, and a deep sense of sadness had spread through him as he thought of Ledi alone in her apartment, with not even memories of her family to keep her company. He'd rarely ever been alone—if his busy but attentive parents hadn't been with him, then a nanny, or advisor, or tutor, or coach, and eventually Likotsi, had been around. His lack of privacy had always been a bother to him, but now— without romanticizing his past—he could see that it had been a privilege. One he hadn't asked for, but benefited from nevertheless.

He'd thought of the smiling little girl in the picture from their betrothal, then imagined her in an enormous country like America—and a huge and frightening city like New York—all alone, shuffled between people who knew nothing of her homeland.

In Thesolo, when a child was orphaned, they were placed with relatives, or with a family who could not conceive, or in one of the communal orphanages that tried very hard to reproduce the feeling of a family and usually succeeded. He'd looked at the high brick buildings outside the window, and the dirty concrete sidewalks. Manhattan did not seem like an easy place to be an orphan.

"Sire? What's wrong?" Likotsi asked, breaking his reverie.

"Last night, I learned a little about Naledi's life after she came to the States."

"You know the location of the traitors Libiko and Kembe? I had no luck finding them during my search, and she had no information listed on the genealogy site." Likotsi's eyes narrowed the way any good Thesoloian's would when Ledi's parents were discussed. It had never bothered Thabiso before, but he hadn't known Naledi then, or what had happened to her parents.

"They are walking with the ancestors," Thabiso said. "They died when she was very young, perhaps not long after they arrived here. She was placed into the care of the state, raised by strangers."

Likotsi gasped, her eyes wide and suddenly glossy with emotion. The reverence of the ancestors was ingrained into every Thesoloian, whether they were a beggar or a king. The remembrance of those who came before you and the passing on of familial knowledge was something sacred. To not even know one's parents or one's roots . . .

Thabiso understood Likotsi's sudden upset—it was horrifying to think of someone being denied that birthright.

"Highness, does she know who she is?" she asked in a low voice. "Where she's from?"

Thabiso looked over at her, feeling the weight of Ledi's loss as if it were his own. It was, in a way. "I don't think so."

The vestibule was suddenly stifling. Likotsi swung

the door open, as if she sensed it too, and let in some fresh air. Fresh by New York standards.

"If her parents died soon after they arrived . . ." Likotsi looked anguished. "This changes everything. This means they never returned because they did not have the opportunity. This means they never communicated because they could not. This means . . ."

Likotsi's expressive face contorted in confusion.

Thabiso nodded. "She says she does not remember her family at all. I assumed her parents had changed her name to Smith to avoid detection, but it could have been done by the state if they did not know who she was. It is a very common name here."

"I will look into it, sire."

Likotsi had a determined look in her eye, and that usually boded well.

"Just—perhaps you should tell her who you are now?"

"How was the penthouse?" Thabiso asked, changing the subject. "And I believe that you never wear the same suit twice in a row, but what have we here?"

He tugged at her lapel, which bore a red stain of some sort. Lipstick?

"There is a term native to this region. I learned it last night. 'nunya.'"

"Nunya?"

"'Nunya business' is the full colloquialism." Likotsi got a faraway look in her eye and smiled as she said it, as if there was some joke in the words that Thabiso couldn't decipher.

"I understand. I think. I will stay out of your affairs, but I'm glad to see you smiling like a schoolgirl."

Likotsi was quite the bachelorette back in Thesolo, though she, too, had lost her taste for dating of late. Many disappointed mothers hoping to have the prince's right hand, and eventually the King's right hand, as a daughter-in-law had been sorely disappointed.

"Bah," she said, brushing past him to step outside. "There are matters of more import than my love life."

He was going to point out that love was a rather strong word to use so quickly, but then he saw how grave her expression had become.

"What is it?" he asked as he stepped outside behind her. A group of teenagers bopped past the front of the building, their posturing reminding Thabiso of the students who attended the high school that bore his name. Youthful braggadocio was the same worldwide it seemed.

She sighed and shook her head. "There has been a report from Lek Hemane. The wife of one of the elders has fallen ill."

His stomach lurched. "Who?"

"Annie," Likotsi whispered. Annie Jarami was a legend in Thesoloian politics, and her husband, Makalele, was just as respected. They were keepers of knowledge, those who had lived through generations of change in the kingdom and who told tales at times of festivity. They'd both been old for as long as Thabiso could remember, but Annie was hardy, like the twisty trees that sprout on the windiest mountain and bear the brunt of the gale, leaning but never falling.

Annie was also Ledi's grandmother.

"Ingoka makes no mistakes, Highness. For Annie to become gravely ill now? You must tell Naledi who you are, and who she is, soon," Likotsi said. "In case the worst comes to pass."

Thabiso gave a quick nod. The burden of the secret he was keeping seemed to grow heavier by the hour, but there were other issues at hand. "Will Annie's sickness impact the tribal representation at the land stewardship meeting?"

"Yes. Makalele refuses to leave Annie's side, so Finance Minister Alehk is going to represent them. He is . . . cut from a different cloth than his parents, as you well know."

That was Likotsi's delicate way of saying the man was greedy, stubborn, and didn't care about the well-being of his tribe, only about lining his pockets. He was the primary push for the Omega Corp deal, which was reason enough for Thabiso to distrust the company. Alehk had convinced the majority of the other ministers though, forcing Thabiso's hand. He had always wondered why the goddess had punished Annie and Makalele with not one dishonorable child, but two; though now everything he thought he knew about Libiko might be wrong.

"This is disappointing, but hopefully Annie will recover before the council meeting. What ails her?"

"That's just it, sire. No one is sure—"

"Thesolo has the best doctors on seven continents, unless there's a crack team of penguins we've yet to discover in Antarctica," Thabiso said, letting his frustration get the best of him. "What do you mean no one is sure?"

Likotsi nodded. "You have not spoken falsely, sire. The doctors are working hard to find the cause of the problem and to ensure that she recovers quickly."

Unease slithered around Thabiso's ankles like a cobra, and he was worried that the venomous strike would come sooner rather than later.

"The timing of this is unfortunate, but she's elderly so it's not entirely unexpected." Elderly, but not frail. The way Likotsi's brow creased convinced him that she thought the same. "Keep me updated of her status, and have the doctors send us their initial findings."

His thoughts went to Naledi. He'd looked up epidemiology; this was in her wheelhouse, something that would interest her. But discussing it would require him to provide specifics such as location, and she hadn't responded well to Likotsi's emails. If he mentioned Thesolo at the wrong moment, in the wrong way, he would also have to drop the news of her past on her like a hippo from a tall building—it would crush her in the messiest way possible, and whatever it was that was growing between them as well.

His resistance to telling her had grown instead of diminished. He liked the way Naledi looked at Jamal; he liked being able to talk and joke freely. Once she knew who he truly was, all of that would change.

"What else is on the docket for today?" he asked. Best to focus on his actual reason for being in New York: improving the welfare of his country.

"After your lunch with the representatives from PharmaMundial this afternoon, there's a General Assembly at the UN that requires your presence. Cocktails at the South African consulate afterward—"

Thabiso grimaced. "Does that diplomat still work there? The woman who wouldn't stop calling after our liaison?"

"You mean the woman who you made think she might have a shot at princess-hood? No, she requested to be relocated. I believe she is at the consulate in Iceland now."

Thabiso wasn't fond of the censure in Likotsi's words.

"I didn't make her *think* anything. I told her that our arrangement was temporary, while I was here hammering out the details of our environmental treaty."

"And then you turned on your charm," Likotsi said, keeping her gaze fixed on the cars passing by. "Just like you're doing with Naledi."

"Charm? Aren't you the same Likotsi who tuts at my supposed rudeness every chance she gets?"

Likotsi made a sound of impatience. "You're rude and demanding, but that has nothing to do with charm. I don't know what happened last night to make your betrothed smile at you like that today, but I'm quite certain it wasn't a confession of your true identity. Or hers."

Thabiso's anger flared. "Hectoring me about my interactions with women doesn't fall under the auspices of your assistantship. What happened last night was . . ." Wonderful? Frightening? "Nunya business."

Likotsi snorted, but her smile was sincere when she looked at him.

"Your honor, and your sanity, are both under my purview. If you hurt this woman the way you've hurt others, you will not brush it off and be the same Prince Thabiso. What started as a search for a shirking betrothed has turned into something entirely different." Likotsi shook her head. "She doesn't even know who she is, sire. Is it fair to her to continue on this path? Remember what they say. Sometimes it's best to bind the finger before it is cut."

The suggestion made sense; if he ended things now, Ledi would escape unscathed. She would continue living her life, unburdened by the news of who she truly was. He immediately rejected the idea, though. Likotsi might think he was engaging in a strange form of nostalgia, but being around Ledi made him happy. Happiness hadn't been something he thought was within his reach. Infatuation or not, he wasn't ready to give up the possibility of . . . Of what he couldn't rightly say.

He refused to discuss the matter further. "Is the limo coming to take me to the meeting?"

"Given your ongoing deception, I did not think that would be wise. You can live as the humble Jamal would, just in case Naledi sees you in transit."

She glanced at her phone just as a beat-up sedan pulled up.

"Are you from SuperLifts?" she asked the driver.

The man behind the wheel wore a Yankees cap and a hoodie instead of the chauffer uniform Thabiso was used to. He nodded.

"Yeah. Gonna be around thirty bucks with the surge right now, I think."

"Twenty." Likotsi was haggling like an auntie at the marketplace with the person who would be keeping him safe during his ride. Unbelievable.

"You booked the ride in the app. You know I don't control the price," the man said.

Likotsi gave a harried sigh. "I thought it wouldn't hurt to try. It seems I'm a bit old-fashioned." She turned to Thabiso while pulling the back door open. "Get in."

"You'd send me off in a stranger's car?" Thabiso asked horrified.

"It's a taxi, sire."

"Taxis are yellow. This car has no bumper, a ripped seat, and a strange fluid smeared on the windows."

"You getting in or what?" the driver asked. He was looking at his phone, probably searching for the next fare.

Likotsi pulled the door open a bit wider. "Have a pleasant day, *Jamal*. I'll text to update you of any changes to your schedule and I'll meet you at the consulate at five."

Thabiso grimaced and slipped into the car. Likotsi waved happily from the curb as it pulled away.

"She's lucky she's the best assistant in Thesolo," he muttered as he inhaled the scent of fake pine and leather.

And because she was, he knew her advice about Naledi should be heeded. But when he'd watched Naledi walk off arm in arm with her friend, his only concern had been how many hours would pass before he saw her again. He rarely disagreed with Likotsi when she presented him with the facts, but just this once, he hoped she was mistaken.

Chapter 11

Ledi couldn't remember the last time she'd had such a relaxing day. The cheese bread and mountain of meat at the Brazilian restaurant had left her and Portia in a stupor, so they'd people watched in Central Park before checking out the museum exhibit. Portia had filled Ledi in on her latest hookups and her newest obsession—she was taking a course on social engineering. Portia generally stuck to arts-related fields, but she changed interests more often than some people changed shoes—she could afford to deep dive into whatever captured her interest. It was occasionally frustrating, but it was one of the things Ledi appreciated most about her friend. She always had something new and fascinating to discuss, and she was always genuinely excited about whatever Ledi wanted to discuss with her.

She'd forgotten how good it felt to just sit in the sun and talk without worriedly counting off how many drinks Portia was having. She'd missed that.

After getting their second wind, they'd gone to the museum—one of the many places around the city Portia had interned. Ledi had gotten to talk about the history of epidemics in Manhattan with the exhibit's curator, and Portia had casually introduced the idea of a future event and Ledi and the curator had exchanged information so they could discuss it more formally.

Afterward, Ledi had met up with Trishna for a study date. Hours of force-feeding each other the information they needed not only to pass but to ace their exams had left Ledi feeling surer of herself. She was confident about the following week's exams, but Dr. Kreillig was still MIA, and even a great day couldn't negate that.

Everyone else had received instructions about travel expenses and where to meet and what to bring for their practicums. Ledi hadn't. After hearing Trishna gush about her plans for a summer spent at a rural public health office in Maine, Ledi had finally accepted she needed to take action. Drafting an email to Dean Bell, her advisor's superior, with Trishna's help had sapped the last of her energy.

She knew it had to be done, but the moment she'd hit Send had brought a horrible flashback—sitting in the child welfare office scared and confused, talking to the older boy who'd sat down next to her. She couldn't remember his face or what his voice sounded like, but she remembered his words.

"If you tell on an adult, even if they do something really bad, they always make you pay for it."

Then his caseworker had called him into her office, brows drawn, her mouth a thin slash of red. The boy had walked toward the office slowly, like every frightening creature a child's imagination could muster waited behind the smoked glass, and then the door had shut behind him.

Ledi had taken that advice to heart, and old habits were hard to break.

She'd thought of Jamal when her finger had hovered over the Send button on her screen, trying to find an excuse not to involve her dean.

"Doing everything yourself isn't really sustainable, is it?"

Of course Jamal had been talking about chopping vegetables and not her career, but it wasn't as if she was great at delegating in any sphere of her life. She'd taken a deep breath and hit Send. What was done was done. She wasn't a child, she wasn't in the wrong, and she wouldn't feel guilty about asking for help.

She was almost at her apartment building's door when she noticed the man standing out front. She repositioned her key for best eyeball jab-ability, just in case, but when he turned at the sound of her footsteps she recognized the delivery guy from the night before. He held another Yellow Spatula box.

"A little late for dinner, huh?" She loosened her grip on her keys, but only a little.

"Traffic was a bitch tonight. Someone rear-ended my van, then jumped out of their car and booked it. The police showed up, and getting information to them took forever. Now I've got angry customers blowing up my phone and no one will buzz me in."

"Is this going to 7 N?" she asked. He nodded, the hope of a man who doesn't want to walk up seven flights of stairs flashing in his eyes.

"I'll take it," she said. "It'd be the neighborly thing to do."

"Thanks, miss." He handed over the box. "You're a lifesaver."

She was a little excited at the possibility of seeing Jamal, but by the time she reached his door, she was rethinking things. Plus, although she'd looked cute that morning, after a day spent shuttling from subways to museums to park benches to coffee shops, she felt like a wrinkled, smudged facsimile of the woman who'd left her apartment with a jaunty step.

She'd have to do this smoothly. She looked down the hall—no other neighbors were around to see her acting like a weirdo.

She placed the box in front of Jamal's door, turned and unlocked her door, then crept back to his and pressed the doorbell. A sound that Ledi imagined was similar to a gnome crying out in pain echoed in the hall, and she whirled and ran toward her door. It was cowardly, but her sense of self-preservation was strong—just not quite fast enough.

"Naledi?"

She stopped in her tracks and turned guiltily at the sound of Jamal's voice. "Hey! I ran into the delivery guy again. You know how this city is . . . millions of people, but once you meet a person it's as if you swap some kind of chemical attractant that draws you together. Like you. And me. Not that I'm saying you're attracted to me."

Oh come ON. Ledi remembered the research she'd read for class that'd concluded that fatigue had more serious side effects than alcohol consumption.

Jamal grinned and picked up the box.

"Have you already eaten dinner?" He didn't acknowledge her gaffe, and she was grateful for it. "Perhaps you dined out with a friend. Or had a date?"

"I was out studying with a classmate, and I haven't eaten." She'd splurged on a fancy latte while out with Trishna, but had still been full from her huge lunch with Portia.

Jamal sighed and relaxed a little. In relief? No, that would be bizarre.

"Well, *bon appetit*," she said, turning back to her front door. Her shower was calling her name; perhaps she would explore the high-intensity setting on the handheld showerhead instead of rambling to her hot neighbor.

"You're not curious about what the meal is for tonight?" he asked. He held the box toward her enticingly, as if what was inside could possibly be more appetizing than the man holding it.

"I don't feel like cooking," she said reflexively, and Jamal frowned.

Smooth.

"Sorry. It's just—I'm tired."

For some reason her voice wobbled on the word *tired*, making her feel even sillier. Sure she had studied, but she hadn't even worked either of her jobs! She should have been able to take on the world. Instead, she just wanted to curl up on the couch and veg out. This was what happened when you slowed down; it was one of the reasons she rarely did.

"You are tired. And you were last night. I shouldn't have let you take over for me—it was thoughtless. I'll prepare the meal on my own, as long as you're willing to take a risk and eat it."

She inhaled deeply. He didn't understand just how much of a risk she'd already taken just by talking to him. Just by not running away as soon as she realized his effect on her. She had exams and a possibly fucked-up practicum to worry about. There was no time for a handsome, bearded foreign man who wanted to cook for her.

Wait, when you put it like that . . .

His back went straight and he suddenly didn't meet her eye. "I don't have much cooking experience, as you know, but I watched some instructional videos between appointments today. I think I have the basics down, but I need a test subject."

"I know what happens to test subjects," she said softly. Now she was the one avoiding eye contact. She told herself he hadn't watched the videos because of her, then she remembered how expectantly he'd looked at her after setting the table. Right before she'd left him to sit at that table alone.

"There was only one thing that could have made it better."

"I have wine, too," Jamal added, sensing her indecision. "It was a gift from a meeting I had today. A door prize, if you will."

"What kind?" The offer of dinner alone was already tempting, but she wasn't going to give up precious sleep over some two-buck chuck.

"Malbec. 1997."

Ledi wasn't a wine snob, but she knew from years of waitressing that it was a good vintage.

"Fine," she said. "You've convinced me. I have to check in with the Grams first, though."

"Grams?" He startled and fumbled the box. "How—I thought you didn't know your family?"

"Well, I guess you could say they're my family, in a way. Want to meet them?"

She nodded her head toward her apartment, then stepped in and turned on the light. His eyes widened.

"That's a very small space for more than one person," he said diplomatically. Then he heard the squeaking and his eyes darted toward the window.

"Vermin. I'll take care of this."

He pushed past her, and she quickly replicated his motion, pushing him behind her as she moved toward the mouse cage.

"Not vermin. Well, not unknown vermin. These are my Grams, Gram Negative and Positive. One is evil, but they look exactly the same, so I'm never sure which one." The two mice ran joyously around the cage as she approached and dropped some food pellets in.

When she turned, Jamal was regarding her with wide eyes.

"You . . . allow them to reside in your home? And provide them sustenance?"

She laughed at the horror lacing his tone.

"This is my penance. I've killed a lot of rodents in my day, you know."

His face scrunched in horror.

"For science! It's part of the lab work," she explained. "The part no one likes to talk about. I didn't *want* mice. But these guys escaped from their cages and no one could tell which experiment they'd been a part of. Sacrificing a rodent for an experiment is one thing, but I couldn't just let them die, or worse, find a glue trap."

"You're remarkable, you know that?" he asked. The tone of his voice sounded like he was talking to someone working for an NGO, not a woman with questionable taste in pets.

She looked up at him, the heat in her cheeks moving faster than the speed of light so that she was already blushing before he came into her line of sight.

"They're just mice. I mean, likely genetically engineered mutant mice, so I guess they're more remarkable than I am."

He shook his head. "Come to dinner. But wash your hands first. The Grams are cute, in a way, but I'd rather you not contract the bubonic plague. Or share it with me."

"You're thinking of rats, not mice, and that's actually a smear campaign against them. I'll wash my hands because I touched a subway pole on my way home. You really don't want to know what kind of disgusting bacteria use the subway as a means of transportation."

Jamal shuddered.

"Yes. I've heard the subways are covered in filth and that beggars accost you at every turn."

Ledi laughed. "It's not quite that bad, Jamal. Only people who've never taken the train say things like that."

He focused his attention on the box in his hands and Ledi was dumbstruck.

No. There was no way . . .

"Have you never taken the subway before?"

He shook his head back and forth stiffly, as if he were unsure whether to express embarrassment or pride over the fact. Ledi had figured he was a rich kid slumming it, but even the richest people she knew had taken the train at some point in their lives. What was Jamal's deal?

"How is that possible?" she asked, not caring if the question was invasive. He'd dug into her most painful memories—he could stand a query about his transportation methods.

"It's not that strange," he said after a long pause. "Have you personally tried every means of travel? I've traveled by blimp, have you?"

"Well, no," she said. Who the hell had been on a blimp but not a train?

"Hot air balloon?" he asked.

"No."

"Helicopter?"

"What? No."

"Plane?" He asked that the same way she would have said city bus.

"No. I've never flown anywhere before," she said. She met his gaze in challenge. "But a flight is way more expensive than a train fare. Well, slightly more expensive with all of these MTA fare hikes, but not the same thing at all. And all of this just raises more questions instead of answering mine."

"Aren't you hungry?" he asked.

"There aren't any trains where you're from?" she pressed. She could sense that he was holding something back. "And where exactly is that since you dodged the question earlier?"

"My country has an aboveground light rail system in the main city, not a subway. I'm from Africa," he said. Ledi's stomach jerked as she remembered the strange emails she'd been receiving. The emails that had mysteriously stopped when Jamal arrived.

"Africa isn't a country," she said as dread tingled in her fingertips. It didn't seem possible, but could the scammers have found her somehow? Was this some long con? Worm their way into her life, and then rob her of what little she had? That would be crazy, but she enjoyed putting on true crime podcasts as background noise while she worked. Stranger things had happened.

"I'm from the south of Africa," he said.

The vibrating of her phone distracted her, and she pulled it out hoping it was an email from Dr. Kreillig.

Today was so much fun! If you hang with Jamal again, make sure you do some vetting. He might not be a serial killer, but the fuckboy pandemic is too real.

She wondered if Portia's bestie sense had been tingling.

Interrogating him now. 🙃

Yasss. Interrogate him like you're peer reviewing dat ass.

Naledi laughed, then glimpsed the notification for a new email. She felt a surge of hope, but when she navigated to her inbox and saw the subject line, she groaned.

The People of Thesolo Welcome You: Our History

It seemed Likotsi the Scammer hadn't given up and moved on to greener bank accounts. Frustrating, but her suspicions about Jamal eased. Africa was a huge continent; it was like someone assuming she knew their cousin in Toronto just because she lived in North America.

"So you're from South Africa? That's interesting," she said as she put her phone away.

"Yes. Very interesting region," he said. "Let's see what's for dinner, shall we?"

"Sure. We'll cook at your place again." She guided him to the door of 7 N. In addition to not cooking, she also wasn't going to do dishes, she decided. She was really starting to enjoy this delegation stuff. Her night was going to be awesome. "What's for dinner?"

She saw his relief in the loosening of his shoulders and the way his smile made a tentative return.

"Gourmet grilled cheese sandwiches," he said. "I doubt even I could mess that up."

Chapter 12

$\mathcal{I}$t was the wail of a fire truck screaming past, the harsh siren reverberating off of brick and asphalt, that jostled Ledi from sleep. It was a sound that she should have been used to after a life in NYC, but it still made her heart beat fast sometimes when it caught her unawares. Her brain searched for a foothold in time and space.

Where was she?

Mommy? Daddy?

There was no response, just as there had been none all those years ago.

Mommy? Daddy?

No, she hadn't called them that, it had been something else, foreign words on the tip of her tongue and a scent that smelled like home surrounding her . . .

She awoke fully and moved to get up, to escape the panic that a sudden scrap of memory had elicited, when the sound of squelching plastic alerted her to the fact that she wasn't in her bed. That and the weight of a large, muscular man slumped against her.

Her dream faded away, details forgotten, as she realized she was still in Mrs. Garcia's apartment. The room was lit by the muted flatscreen television, where a woman was excitedly chopping vegetables with some weird contraption that was available for three easy payments of nine ninety-nine. Ledi risked a glance to her left. The flickering blue light revealed Jamal to be fast asleep, his head resting on her shoulder.

He's gorgeous.

His skin was smooth and unblemished, his brows thick and well-shaped, his lashes dark shadows jumping against his cheeks in the light from the TV. His beard was immaculate as always, despite the gooey grilled cheese he'd prepared for them, all on his own. The pride in his eyes when he'd presented the only slightly burned mozzarella, tomato, and basil sandwiches had been cute, but it had nothing on sleeping Jamal.

She hadn't ever been one for watching a man sleep. It was creepy, and sleep was a necessary function to ensure optimal bodily health, like using the bathroom. But looking down at him she had an inkling of why people deigned to share their bed with the same person night after night. It was nice—intimate. Ledi wasn't sure she'd ever fallen asleep so easily next to a man, and it wasn't just because she was tired.

Jesus Christ, you need to stop eavesdropping on Mrs. Garcia's telenovelas.

Ledi moved to get up again; she was fairly certain staring creepily at your neighbor as he slept placed her squarely in the weirdo zone. Playtime was over. She had a lot to do the next day, and getting a few more hours of shut-eye wouldn't be the worst thing that could happen.

I can think of the best thing.

She was suddenly all too aware of the feel of Jamal's arm resting against hers, of *all* the places where he pressed into her. She knew the weight of him now, could imagine how it would feel anchoring her into a mattress as he—

His arm went around her waist as his lashes fluttered, then his eyes opened. He just looked at her for a long moment, then a sleepy smile tugged at his full lips.

"It's not often a man can say that reality is better than the dream he was having. And my dream was *very* good."

His hold tightened and Ledi swallowed against the dryness in her throat and wished she had taken it easy with the garlic powder on her sandwich.

"Sorry I fell asleep," she said. "You could have woken me up."

"You needed rest," he said. He sat up, but didn't shift away from her. "And in case you haven't noticed, I like having you here."

He was looking down into her eyes, heat and intent in his gaze, and his body and its delicious weight were so, so close. If she swung her legs to the left she could easily slide into his lap. She could press her mouth to his and see if his lips were as soft as they looked, and if his kisses would live up to the way he was looking at her.

She could think of lots of things she might explore with Jamal, but she wasn't sure she could bring herself to take that first step. She stared at him, hoping he would understand that though she didn't move, she was trying her hand at unspoken delegation.

His hand slowly slid up her denim-clad shin, fingers curving down over her calf. When his palm reached her knees he tugged at first one and then the other, guiding her legs over his thighs. His other hand slid behind her back, cradling her. Maybe she was still dreaming. What the hell had been in that grilled cheese?

"I . . . I . . ." Ledi felt as if her entire body was under a magnifying glass in the midday sun. She was pretty damn sure that her clothes might turn to ashes and fall off at any moment, and from the way Jamal was looking at her, he wouldn't be opposed to that.

"I'm going to kiss you," he said. She could see the reflection of the television screen in his eyes as his mouth moved toward hers. LIMITED TIME OFFER was emblazoned there, in reverse, then AS SEEN ON TV, which made sense because no way was hooking up with sexy neighbors something that happened in Ledi's world.

"Okay," she whispered.

His lips pressed into hers, proving her theory that all it took was a millisecond for a world-changing discovery to take place. Hooking up with sexy neighbors *was* something that was possible on this plane of reality, and it was fantastic.

His lips were incredibly smooth and lush as they brushed over hers, just the lightest touches of skin against sensitive skin that shouldn't have sent a rush of sensation through her body, but did. His beard was rough against the sensitive skin of her chin and cheeks, a counterpoint to his gentle kiss. Her mind blanked at the intense reaction to just that slight pressure, and then her reflexes kicked in, reminding her that being kissed was one thing and kissing another. She returned the pressure of his mouth, tongue darting out the slightest bit to allow herself just a taste of him. A taste was all she could afford with a man who affected her like this.

Fuck.

She pressed into him harder, trying to regulate

the sensation, control it in some way, but his fingers stroked her back and she moaned, her self-control slipping away when he groaned and gripped her thigh more tightly.

His tongue lapped over her bottom lip, and she parted for him, welcoming him in. He moved slowly, but there was nothing tentative about his technique—the stroke of his tongue was warm and strong. Probing. Insistent. He kissed her with a deliberateness that had her moaning into his mouth not just from the sensation but from the possibilities they opened up for her.

Oh, the things that tongue could probably do.

Jamal's hand moved over her thighs and rested at the curve of her hip, grasping a handful of her sweatshirt as he finally kissed her full-on without reservation. A sharp, delicious pressure thrummed between her legs and she slid farther onto his lap, returning his kiss as well as she could.

There was no trace of the bumbling Jamal who hadn't even known which knife to use to cut a loaf of bread at the Institute. His hands and mouth and body moved with assurance, with finesse. Apparently there was at least one thing he was really, *really* good at.

She pressed her body against his, reveling in the solid feel of him.

"Ledi," he breathed into her mouth, and holy shit, no one had ever said her name like that. Like she was oxygen and he was desperate for it. "I want to touch you. Badly. Can I touch you?"

That was when she realized she was likely in over her head. Because she was already lost in a haze of sensation, ready to risk it all, and Jamal had barely put his hands on her.

Double fuck.

"Definitely. Yes. Go for it."

She'd barely gotten the words out when the hand that had been bunched in her sweatshirt tugged harder. The fabric that had rested provocatively on the swells of her shoulders all day slid down her arms. He pulled until the fabric was taut over her aching breasts, the friction of it both restricting and teasing until finally the soft cups of her bra were revealed. The new position of the shirt forced her arms to her sides with just enough pressure to hold them there, and for some reason Ledi's response was a clench of the pussy and an unprecedented gush of moisture that she hoped wouldn't seep through her jeans.

Jamal ran his fingertips down the nape of her neck, over her exposed shoulders. He traced his finger over her jawline, her collarbone, and she moaned and arched her back, greedy for the touch that left sparks of sensation in its wake.

"Do you like that?"

When his hand stopped moving, she looked up at him and realized he was asking a question, not just making idle dirty talk to fill the silence. His gaze was hot and intense, and she almost closed her eyes against the feeling it caused in her chest.

"Yes. I like it," she said quickly, because she wanted his hands moving again, wanted the distraction of a sensation that wasn't this pressure beneath her rib cage that she hoped was heartburn.

"Brilliant," Jamal said. His thumbs brushed over her hard nipples through the soft fabric of her bra. She expected him to lunge, to get right to it like so many of the men she'd been with, but he moved so slowly that after a moment Ledi wanted to scream with frustrated pleasure. His gaze was locked on hers as he brushed and squeezed and twisted, like he was calibrating her to the right frequency, one that left her gasping and trembling for him. Waves of pleasure rolled through her as he alternated soft brushes with hard pinches.

He wasn't driving her crazy because of lack of technique; that *was* the technique.

"Oh god."

She squirmed in his lap, scooting herself right up against the erection that tented his pants. If he was searching for the right frequency, she'd found his antenna; the length of it pressed up against her through his jeans, twitching and hardening in response to her soft cries as he teased her to the point of insanity with his hands. Her arms were still against her sides, but she could move her ass and she did, gliding it over the length of him.

Jamal hissed and rocked up against her, but both of his hands were busy with her breasts. His fingertips traced the cheap material edging her bra reverently, making her feel as if she was decked out in lace and silk instead. He hooked an index finger in each cup, pulling them down and exposing her.

"So lovely," he said, hefting the weight of each breast in his hands. Then he bent down. He lapped at one breast, and then the other, the strokes of his tongue alternating between punishment and adoration. He licked and sucked, and when she thought she couldn't stand any more, he brushed the rough hairs of his beard over her sensitive nipples.

"Oh fuck." Her voice was strained, caught between a scream and a whisper as sensation threatened to overwhelm her. Ledi pressed her chest up toward his torturous beard, then away, then back up, as if her body couldn't decide what was worse: the excess of pleasure or the lack of it.

His hands slid up behind her back, holding her in place now as he teased her with tongue and lips and beard. His hard length pressed against the seam of her jeans, as he worked his hips.

"Oh fuck!" Pleasure threaded through her, spreading over her body and pulling tight until she was caught in the web of her desire for him. She wanted to touch him, but her arms were pinned against her sides. Her ass ground against his groin though, and if she stretched her fingers she could stroke the confined length of him through his jeans.

"Mmm." The sound rumbled out of him and his head dropped back as he ground up against her hand. She was just getting a hold of him through his jeans, but then he shifted his hips so that he was just out of reach of her hands.

"I'm taking care of you tonight, remember?" he asked.

Ledi's throat went tight at the words, words she rarely heard from anyone.

I'm taking care of you.

Tonight. She couldn't forget that crucial part. *Limited time offer.*

"Then do it," she said. Her body ached with need and she didn't want him to say anything else. She wanted to feel.

One of his hands left her breast to unbutton her jeans, to roughly slide the stretchy denim down until it was around her ankles. His hand traced the path up her shin and took a detour at the knee toward her inner thigh. Ledi gasped at the gentle friction of his advancing fingertips, at the way they traced her slit through her underwear. He rubbed his palm over her mound through the thin fabric and Ledi's whole body tensed at the sudden, direct pressure.

His other arm was behind her and she felt the flex of his biceps supporting her as she arched wildly in response to the intense pressure of the heel of his palm.

Her hands splayed against his hard chest, curling into the fabric of his shirt as sensation shuddered through her.

He slid his thick fingers through the side of the underwear, tracing her clit down to her slick opening. "Goddess, you're so wet."

"It's a somewhat common physical reaction to arousal," she muttered around a gasp, and he laughed.

"I guess I won't get too cocky about it, then," he said, leaning in to kiss her. She moaned into his mouth.

"No," she said. "Not about that at least."

He teased her like that for much too long, murmuring as he slipped his fingertips firmly over the hood of her clit until she had no idea what he was saying, could only focus on the pleasure his hand was giving her. Finally, finally, he worked one thick finger inside of her, and then another. He slicked his fingers in and out, slowly, then quickly, alternating speeds.

He worked some kind of magic from the inside, caressing her in a way that had her riding his hand unabashedly. The damp fabric of her underwear was one friction and the drive of his fingers another; they combined to completely undo her. Her breath came in gasps, and she wanted to beg him for release but she was unable to make more than desperate, high-pitched noises as he drove her toward climax.

It wasn't just the way he touched her. His gaze was on her the entire time. He looked at her like she was a goddess. A queen. *His* queen.

"Oh yes. Jamal," she cried out, and his brow creased. His thumb pressed into her clit then, joining forces with the two digits that were already sending desire arcing across her body. He lowered his head to her breast again and sucked just roughly enough to make her cry out and clench around his fingers. He was working her like he had something to prove, and as her body bent, bent, and finally broke as release surged through her—her sobs of pleasure heralded his success.

Ledi'd had good sex before, but the rush of heat up her spine and the toes curling and the wave after wave of goodness, even as he withdrew his fingers? That certainly hadn't happened before. Certainly not all at once.

Her gaze met his as the last tremors of her orgasm shook her from head to toe, and the fierceness in his gaze shocked her. He smiled, but there was worry in his eyes, and something else.

She sat up and shimmied her sweatshirt back up her arms, then pulled her bra up and pulled the front of her shirt back up over them.

"Um. Maybe I should wipe down Mrs. Garcia's couch," she said, voice still shaky.

Jamal closed his eyes and chuckled.

"Let me handle that," he said. "You should go get some sleep."

She jumped up as if scalded, buttoning her pants as she searched for her keys. "Oh. Yeah. I was going to leave anyway—"

Jamal raised a finger—one that hadn't just given her an orgasm that still had her thighs shaking—and held it against her lips. "I'm not kicking you out. Well, I am, but only because if you don't leave I'm going to be tempted to fuck you senseless."

He exhaled sharply and ran a hand over his short locks, as if that temptation was a bad thing. He'd just fingerbanged her senseless, so Ledi couldn't understand how his penis could possibly add anything else to the equation unless he was one of those "penetration equals commitment" kind of guys.

Commitment?

"Yeah, that sounds terrible. Horrible, even. Definitely need my senses, so . . ." She made the sign of the cross using her index fingers and pointed it toward his crotch.

He stalked toward her, grabbed her by the chin, and kissed her. This kiss was better, and maybe worse because of the betterness, than the one they'd shared on the couch. That had been explainable: he'd gotten the middle-of-the-night hornies, and she'd been right there. But this? The way he kissed her slowly and reverently, but also like he was about to fuck her against the door? This meant that their ruination of Mrs. Garcia's couch hadn't been a sleep-induced aberration for him.

"Do you work tomorrow?" he asked when he pulled his mouth away. His commanding air was back.

"I have to go into the lab in the morning and check on some experiments," she said, willing her chest to stop heaving like she'd run a marathon. "And study."

"Are you free in the afternoon?"

Ledi looked away, then back at him. "For a couple of hours. Maybe."

He nodded. "I would like . . ."

Afternoon delight? Please say afternoon delight.

". . . an escort. On the subway. I hear it can be very dangerous, you see."

Ledi's excitement faltered.

"Where do you have to go?" she asked. Of course he'd only asked because he needed something from her. What else was new?

"Nowhere. But now I feel foolish for never having braved the subways and I want my first time to be with you. So we can go anywhere you want. Maybe someplace that makes you happy." He grinned at her, and that cut right through her disappointment. "I know you're very busy, Ledi. If you can fit me in, I'd be honored to be one of the many things that take up your time."

Ledi didn't know what to say to that. Why couldn't he call her a Saint Bernard again so she could flip him off and go back to life as she knew it?

"We'll see," she said carefully, and then slipped through the door.

This was not okay. She wasn't supposed to be feeling butterflies in her stomach and doing a happy shimmy as she crossed the hall. She let herself in to her studio, the vibration and flash of light across the room a reminder that she'd left her phone at her place. When she saw the solid block of message notifications from Portia, she wished she hadn't.

> Hey, I have to ask you something. URGENT.
> Call me!

The texts started off normal, growing more annoyed as the night wore on—probably commensurate with Portia's alcohol consumption. Ledi scrolled down, reading the increasingly hostile messages with numb acceptance, until she reached the last one.

> Wow. The 🍆 is that good? Thanks for making it clear what your priorities are. Nevermind.

Ledi knew Portia was drunk, knew she didn't mean what she'd written, but the unfairness of the accusation cut through her like a hot knife, melting away the residual giddiness of her orgasm and of Jamal's clear interest in her.

After all the sleepless nights keeping an eye on her, making sure she didn't drunkenly stumble into either the East River or the Hudson . . .

Ledi fought against the sudden urge to cry. She had never done anything for Portia with the expectation that Portia would owe her. She did things because Portia was her friend, and usually a good one. It was when she drank that this negative side sometimes emerged, but drinking had become too common a pastime for Portia. Her friend's bad habit had become Ledi's albatross, and she was tired of carrying that particular weight along with her own.

Ledi started to type in a response, out of habit, to ask where Portia was and if she was all right, but then she held down the power button on her phone and swiped it off instead.

She thought of Jamal's face when he'd asked her to take him somewhere that would make *her* happy. When was the last time someone had really cared about that? Not to assuage their own guilt, but sincerely?

She pushed away the tension that came with breaking years of habit and headed to shower. Sleep came first; she would deal with everything else in the morning.

Chapter 13

Thabiso shifted in the ridiculous and uncomfortable chair in the fancy restaurant where his lunch meeting was being held. The chair was composed of various parts of animals you'd see on safari in Kenya—the legs were those of a zebra's, the back a lion's hide stretched across two large horns that curved up and back—an unironic display of how, when it came to Africa, foreigners had no qualms about taking the pieces they wanted and rearranging them as they saw fit.

The two representatives of Omega Corp who sat across the table from him were just such men. They stared at him with smiles on their faces that were as contrived as the "nouveau Africaine" meal they'd just shared. Thabiso had tried to maintain his composure, but the backing track to their conversation had been that first conversation he'd had with Ledi. Not the kale plating confusion, but about power and what one did with it. As he listened to the men hash out the details of the deal to begin excavating in Thesolo, he'd been acutely aware that though he hadn't asked for it, he had the power to change the world—or to change his kingdom. Was this how he wanted to use it?

Thabiso took a sip of his bitter coffee and placed it down in the asymmetrical saucer with what he supposed was someone's idea of a kente cloth pattern.

"So, what do you think?" one of the men said. Tad? Todd? Thabiso could never remember these silly American names.

"I think I need time to mull this over," he said diplomatically. He really wanted to tell them to strap themselves to the twenty tons of condescending bullshit they'd just tried to sell him and jump into the nearest body of water, but he gave a short nod that he supposed looked thoughtful and gracious. He'd promised Alehk that this deal would go through, but there was a smugness about the men that raised the hairs on his neck. He needed more time. "There are a great many factors that influence a decision such as this. But I will relay this message to the king, queen, and High Council at my earliest convenience and contact you as soon as we've reached a final decision."

What he'd really do at his earliest convenience was get back to apartment 7 N so he wouldn't miss Naledi. If she even showed up. He'd told her to stop by if she could. She very well might stand him up, given the way she'd fled while still flushed from the afterglow. He'd seen poachers caught in the glare of a military lantern shove off with less haste. He held out hope she would come, but that hadn't made the last few hours of inane business combat any less torturous. It also didn't mean he would give in to the demands of these men, just to be done with it.

The two executives glanced at each other, their grins slipping.

"We were really hoping to settle this today," Tad/Todd said. "When we spoke with Minister Jarami, he indicated that things would be settled while you were here. That it was, in fact, the purpose of your trip."

"I see," Thabiso said. "There must be some confusion, as Minister Jarami does not have the final say in this matter."

He wasn't happy to hear that there had been discussions which he hadn't been kept abreast of.

"We're positive that this deal is something that would benefit Thesolo greatly, especially given the economic decline in the region," the other exec said, steepling his fingers and holding Thabiso's gaze.

Thabiso ran his fingertips over his beard, glad that the facial hair hid the sudden tightness of his jaw.

"What economic decline?" he asked. "I'm not sure I follow."

"Well, the data speaks for itself," one of the execs said calmly. "Outdated practices and dwindling natural resources present a pretty bleak forecast for Thesolo's future."

Thabiso remembered the gaslighting Naledi had told him about and was fairly certain that was what was happening. He had no idea what bleak forecast the man was speaking of, but he still felt pricked by dread, by the possibility that if he didn't go along with their plan he'd be hurting his people in the long run. Unfortunately for the men, one benefit of being the sole heir to the crown was a fairly large ego; Thabiso had the Moshoeshoe stubbornness to boot.

He laughed as if the man had told a mildly amusing but offensive joke.

"Thesolo's economy is the strongest it's ever been, having experienced explosive growth in the import, export, tourism, and renewable energy fields to name just a few," he said. "We are not some stripling nation ready to jump on the first piece of meat waved in our direction. Chinese, Korean, and Brazilian companies have also submitted proposals for coltan extraction, and a few local outfits as well. We're currently assessing all of those, as well as the long-term environmental impact such an undertaking would have on the country."

The men didn't look at each other this time, but their expressions both hardened. "Omega Corp is the number one producer of smartphone technology in the world. We have coltan mining operations in six African nations, and several in South America. Considering partnering with anyone else would be absurd—and dangerous."

He wondered what Minister Jarami had promised these men—what he'd told them he could deliver—that they thought escalating from gaslighting to full-on threats was a sound plan.

Thabiso's anger flared. "I'm well aware of Omega Corp's worldwide interests—as well as the civil wars, unexplained maladies, and governmental strife that seem to follow your operations like flies on shit." So much for diplomacy. But if they wanted to discuss data, Thabiso had done some research outside of the dockets that Alehk Jarami had given him, and thank goodness for that.

"I cannot know what Minister Jarami has discussed with you, but *my* interest is and will always be the well-being of my people." He checked his wrist although he wore no watch, and then stood. "I must be going. Thank you for the lunch, and I'll be in contact."

Thabiso shook their hands, and then strode out of the restaurant. A nice, but basic, compact car waited out front, its driver halfheartedly holding up a sign with "Jamal" scrawled on it. Likotsi was still having her fun, it seemed.

He nodded at the man, who opened the door for him. Thabiso exhaled around the pressure in his chest. He wasn't sure if he'd committed his first major political misstep. He was the sole heir, in truth, but just as that meant that his people didn't have another option, neither did Thabiso. If he did something not to their liking, he would bear the full brunt of it for so long as he reigned.

His suit suddenly seemed too tight, and he fidgeted with his cuff links. He didn't believe himself to be wrong, but he knew he'd have to defend his behavior. *If the deal was sound, why the rush? Why the anger? Shouldn't vetting it and examining all possible outcomes, good and bad, be a priority instead of a hindrance?*

"Work got ya down?" the driver asked as he pulled into midtown traffic.

Thabiso wasn't used to his drivers speaking to him. The palace chauffeurs certainly wouldn't dare be so unprofessional, but things were different in America. When in New York . . .

"Yes," he answered. "The world is full of opportunistic parasites, looking for their next resource to suck dry. Dealing with people such as this becomes tiresome."

"Don't I know it," the man said, meeting Thabiso's gaze in the rearview mirror before focusing on the road. "You know how much a taxi license costs? One hundred grand! Nobody who has a hundred grand lying around wants to be a driver. So poor guys get together and pay our little part, share the license with others, but every day there's some new law, some new bullshit to deal with. Someone always wanting *something* from you. That's why so many people are switching to working for these app companies. It's a kick in the ass to everyone who shelled out money for a medallion, though."

Thabiso had never considered that a job driving a car would be so fraught, or costly. One hundred thousand was a significant amount, even to him—he couldn't imagine how many drivers it took to scrape up that much. And they didn't get to go home to a palace afterward.

"I did not know that," he said. "I'm sorry that your job is vexing."

The driver scoffed. "Eh, everything is vexing. Climate change, government trying to kill us, education standards dwindling. Sometimes I wonder why my parents came to this country, the way things are now. But you know? Every night when I get home from work, my Divya is waiting for me. We cook together, and I tell her about the people I've met during my shift and she tells me about the people she met during hers. And those moments make everything worth it."

"She's also a driver?" Thabiso asked.

"A nurse," the man said, the pride in his voice unmistakable. "She studied very hard for a very long time. Those loans will take forever to pay off, but she's never been happier. So I'm happy, too."

They pulled up to a red light, and when the driver looked over his shoulder at Thabiso, the glower that had been in his eyes was gone, the creases smoothed from his forehead. His eyebrows rose as if he'd had a revelation.

"Actually, I need to change what I said. Everybody wants *something* from you, but sometimes there's a person you *want* to give to. Sometimes what you give them makes you better for having given it. And it makes having to give to everyone else not so bad."

The driver turned back to the road just as the light switched to green. Thabiso sat back against his seat as if a gust from the summits of Thesolo's mountains had swept down and bowled him back. Giving of himself had always been a job requirement—his education, his travels, his public persona—had all been calibrated in the way that would best benefit his people. In return, he got to be a prince. That was nothing to scoff at, but of late it had felt like bits of him were being pecked away. Bits that he could never get back.

Was there anyone he *wanted* to give to? The answer echoed in his head before the question was complete.

Naledi. She had come home to him, like this man did to his Divya, for the last two nights. And the night before, she had come *on* him. His fingers twitched at the memory of how tight she'd been around them, and how the scent of her had filled the apartment after she'd gone.

But it was more than that; just a few conversations with Naledi had made him want to give more to his people as well. He wanted to do more than go along with the minister's plans. He had always cared a lot, but now he didn't feel hemmed in by that caring, so afraid to make the wrong move that he made none at all.

"You got anyone like that?" the driver asked.

"I'm working on it," Thabiso said. He wished he could say yes, but all he could think about was the way Ledi's eyes had squeezed shut and her mouth had stretched wide in ecstasy as he'd touched her. He'd wanted to take her as she writhed on his hand, to lift her up and guide her onto his cock. But then she'd cried out "Jamal," and he'd realized he was behaving like a craven thief at the market. She gave herself to him willingly, took pleasure from his touch, but she didn't even know his true name. He couldn't touch her again while this comedy of errors played out.

He thought of the Omega Corp executives smiling greedily across the table from him, already imagining how they'd slice and dice his country to increase their profit margin. Were his fantasies about Ledi any less selfish?

He pulled out his phone and sent a string of messages to Likotsi, letting her know what had happened at the meeting and that he would be back at the apartment soon.

"Good luck," the driver said when he pulled up in front of Thabiso's building. Naledi's building.

Thabiso nodded and left before the man could count out the tip he'd given him. He took the steps two at a time and changed from the suit into something more casual as soon as he entered the apartment. And then he waited.

"SIRE? THIS IS planet Earth calling Prince Thabiso." Likotsi snapped her fingers in front of his face. Thabiso noticed that she sported a pinkie ring now, filigreed gold with a clear green stone.

"New bling?" he asked, grabbing at her finger. She tugged her hand away.

"It was a gift from a friend," she said. She tried to be stern, but a smile hovered at the edges of her mouth. "An incredibly beautiful friend. So beautiful it should be a crime to look upon her. And intelligent, and witty, and . . ." She sighed, and Thabiso imagined he knew exactly how she felt.

"So these dating apps work, it seems?" Thabiso asked.

"Yes. Especially when the majority of the people in your dating radius aren't cousins or cousins twice

removed," she groused. "But enough about me—
did you really storm out of the meeting with Omega
Corp just to skulk around the apartment this afternoon?"

Maybe Thabiso should have regretted his behavior
toward Tad/Todd and Todd/Tad, but the thought of
having spent a moment longer with men who wanted
to gut his country for the sake of a microchip made
his fists clench.

"Bah. There was nothing further to discuss with
them."

"Minister Jarami certainly feels otherwise. He
called immediately after the meeting to voice his dis-
pleasure about how it was handled. An emergency
meeting of the finance ministers has been planned
for tomorrow."

"Pardon?" Thabiso couldn't have possibly heard correctly.

"Minister Jarami feels this was a grave blow to the
people of Thesolo and has called an emergency meeting." Likotsi's voice was calm, but anger blazed in her
eyes.

"This is unprecedented," Thabiso said. His stomach tightened as if preparing for a blow. "And shows
a lack of respect that cannot be tolerated."

"What will you do to Alehk Jarami to put him in
his place? Right now you court his niece, a niece he
does not know is still alive, while he spreads malicious
rumors about you to your people."

Thabiso got up and began to pace.

"Do you know what my meeting with Omega Corp
was about?"

"I do not know the details, sire."

"They want to dig. They want to excavate. Every
plan they proposed involves uprooting some portion

of our people from their native land and doing damage, likely irreparable damage, to our environment."

Likotsi looked at the ground, a frown tugging at her mouth. "Minister Jarami has promised them this? How can he plan such an affront to the goddess?"

Ingoka aside, Thesolo was a small kingdom. Disturbing even a portion of it for such an endeavor would have ecological ramifications. The worship of the ancestors was sacred, but so was preservation for those to come—Thabiso wanted to be worthy of any worship given to him by an accident of birth.

"The man is persuasive. He makes it seem as if this is our only choice," Thabiso said. "But it isn't. We have fought off colonizers and invaders for generations. I am not yet king, but I will not have my legacy be 'the man who let Thesolo be ravaged.'"

"And to think I thought you'd rushed from the meeting because you had a date with Naledi," Likotsi said. "I hadn't realized the gravity of this matter."

"It is indeed more serious than even I imagined. And I have nothing definitive planned with Naledi at this point in time," Thabiso said. That wasn't entirely false, or rather it was more true than several other things going on in his life.

"Will you tell her today?" Likotsi asked, seeing right through him.

"It's not quite that simple," Thabiso began, then stopped at the chilling look his assistant gave him.

She sucked her teeth. "Telling her is simple. Her reaction, which is what you fear, is what will not be simple. But how long can this farce go on? Actually, I can tell you—exactly four more days."

The same thought had been circling in his mind all morning. He had to tell her as soon as possible, or he risked losing her trust for good.

"How is Annie doing?" he asked. It wasn't smooth as subject changes went, but it was something he needed to know.

"Another two people from her tribe have fallen ill," Likotsi said quietly. "They do not know why. Yes, our medical specialists have been working themselves to the bone trying to figure it out."

Thabiso stood and began pacing. Between this and Alehk's scheming he had a definite sense of unease. "Should we go back?"

Likotsi shook her head. "As you said—you are not yet king. Your parents have the problem in hand, though you should let them know about your meeting with Omega Corp yourself. The only thing you can do apart from that is make sure that your decisions here reflect well on Thesolo, and that they are being made with our people's—and Annie and Makalele's granddaughter's—best interests in mind."

She didn't have to add *And not your cock's*—the lift of her brow was enough.

"I will."

Just then, the hideous buzzer squawked and Thabiso's heart thumped harder in response. He turned and jogged to the door and opened it before it could sound again.

Ledi stood there, eyes wide and a nervous smile gracing her lips. The unease that had seized him after hearing the news from home receded just a bit. There was something comforting about her presence, in the way she always seemed to know what to do if presented with a problem. It made him think maybe he could do the same if put to the test.

"Hi," she said.

The word was barely a whisper, and the rasp of it unlocked the desire to draw her into his arms and kiss her. It was as if she'd made him her Manchurian Candidate when she'd moaned and shuddered in his lap only hours before, and now she was calling him to action. But there could be no more shuddering, or anything else, until he told her the truth.

"Hey," he replied, gripping the door frame instead of her hips.

Her hair was down, a billow of curls that framed her face. She wore a purple T-shirt with a cartoon image of a brown-skinned woman in a lab coat holding a test tube on it. Tight black jeans accentuated her curves, and he supposed she was wearing shoes of some sort but his gaze had retraced its path back up and over the formfitting jeans and T-shirt. Desire stirred low in his belly, but when he met her gaze there was that distance again.

Thabiso's Adam's apple suddenly felt too large for his throat. What was this nonsense? He wasn't a boy being asked to go to the flower festival for the first time.

"Are you still up for a train adventure?" she asked. "I've been studying and doing Western blots since five a.m. and I could use a break."

"Yes. I'll be just a moment."

He walked back inside, grabbed his keys and wallet, and rubbed a dab of scented oil on his neck. It had been blessed by the royal priestesses of Thesolo and was supposed to bring luck. He'd need it if he was truly going to reveal his perfidy.

"Make sure you tell her," Likotsi whispered harshly. "And remember that your schedule is packed before the gala tomorrow evening. No running off like a boy shirking school."

"Okayyy." He held up his hands. "Later, drill sergeant."

When he stepped out into the hall, Ledi turned to him, then wrinkled her nose. "What is that smell?"

Thabiso froze, embarrassment stopping him in his tracks. Perhaps he'd applied too much of the oil? He lifted a hand to his beard, sniffing surreptitiously. He thought it smelled fine . . .

"You were wearing it yesterday, too," she said. "It seems so familiar, but I can't pin down where I've smelled it."

She moved closer to him and went up on her tiptoes, her nose close enough to his neck that it tickled him, and inhaled. Thabiso clenched his hands behind his back, although he craved to pull her warmth closer, or perhaps to rub the oil over her body so her skin was slick and pliant under his fingers.

"It's eng oil," he said, taking a step back from her as he reined in his racing imagination. "Made from a plant native to my country. It's very common there."

Common enough that her parents would have worn it. He and Ledi were surely doused in it during their betrothal ceremony.

Now! Tell her now!

Thabiso struggled to find the right words and kicked himself for wasting his time before her arrival fantasizing about her body when he should have been planning how to break the bond that had been solidifying between them—and how to mend it afterward.

If you can mend it.

"Strange." She shook her head. "Maybe one of the street vendors around here sells it?"

"Perhaps, although it's quite rare in the States." He glanced at her and dipped his toe into the waters of truth. "Or perhaps it's a scent from your childhood? Maybe your parents—"

"Let's go," she said. "We only have a few hours before I have to study again." Then she was marching down the hall, leaving him and his question behind. Her reaction to a simple inquiry about her parents didn't bode well for his confession and all that would come with it.

For the first time since he'd assumed his false identity, Thabiso wished he actually was Jamal: an American boy who had fallen for his coworker. If he were, there would be no lies to dispel and no truth hanging over his head like the sword of Damocles.

Chapter 14

"Why is it so hot down here? What is that strange smell? Are those cats frolicking on the tracks? Dear goddess, they're rats!"

Ledi rolled her eyes, though it was hard not to be amused. Jamal had been acting like a lamb taking its first steps from the moment they left the apartment.

When they'd stopped at the bodega on the corner and she'd ordered them sandwiches, his nostrils had flared in alarm. He'd stared in horror at the line of people calling out their daily lottery numbers near the cash register, and had recoiled from the display case of deli meats as she ordered their food.

"What is your deal? These are the best sandwiches in the city," she'd said under her breath.

"Best?" Jamal's nose had wrinkled in disgust. "Who knows how long that meat has been idling under glass? And the meat slicer looks like it hasn't been cleaned since Bush was in the White House."

Julio, the co-owner of the store and the man making their sandwiches, had looked up with an angry glint in his eyes. "We've got a four point five Yelp rating, homie. You want some fancy shit, go to Gentrification Café or whatever, down the street."

"Ignore him," Ledi had said to Julio, pushing Jamal farther into an aisle. "We're going to buy more stuff. Definitely don't spit in our sandwiches or anything, okay?"

Julio had nodded while glaring after Jamal, who was wiping a film of dust off of a box of Grape-Nuts and holding his finger out to Ledi for inspection.

Now they stood on the subway platform with a bag full of sandwiches, beverages, and random items she'd pulled off the shelves just to appease Julio, waiting for the Uptown A train. Jamal was still looking at her after his barrage of questions, so Ledi held up three fingers.

"To answer your questions, it's hot because the subway has its own weather system that varies by station. It can be a beautiful day outside, then you step onto a train platform and it's like you're standing in the devil's asscrack." She folded one finger down. "That smell is prooooobably stagnant water. Or the decomposing body of one of the mole people who live in the tunnels." She folded her middle finger down, leaving her index finger, which she pointed in the direction of two rats who were circling each other, about to engage in pawsticuffs over a half-eaten slice of pizza. "Definitely rats. This is their kingdom and we're just passing through. Don't ever think you have priority on these platforms, because they don't back down and, despite the bubonic plague smear campaign, a rat bite will mess you up good."

"You're kidding, right?" he asked. The rats on the track in front of them started squealing and rearing up. Ledi shuddered and dragged him down the length of the platform. The Grams in their cage was one thing. Wild sewer rats were entirely another.

"Honestly, this station looks like it could collapse at

any moment. I've read reports of America's crumbling infrastructure but I'd assumed it was exaggeration." He looked around at the stained ceilings and cracked, flaking paint.

"This city is held together by hope and insomnia," she said. "Who needs infrastructure?"

"Americans," he muttered, shaking his head.

Ledi shrugged. "But seriously though, I hope you have traveler's insurance because there've been some derailments lately."

Jamal's head whipped toward her. "Wait, what?"

A gust of warm air carried the familiar subterranean scent that preceded the rumble and screech of the train as it pulled into the station, then a rectangular steel car emblazoned with a circle of blue and white appeared. Jamal made a perplexed grunt.

"It looks like the trains in movies, but . . . the movies I watched as a child. I imagined they'd be more modern by now," he said as it pulled to a stop in front of them.

One crowded car passed, but the one pulling up before them was empty, which set off Ledi's subway sense. She grabbed him again and jogged to the next car down, which held a good number of people but wasn't sardine-can packed.

"Why did we run?" he asked. "More rats?"

"Maybe. Never get on the empty train car when the ones on either side are full," she explained. "That means that something not okay is going on in there. The doors between train cars are locked sometimes, and you don't want to be trapped in a car with rats, random human excretions, or something worse."

"Why do I feel like I'm navigating some kind of dystopian nightmare instead of one of the most famous cities in the world?" Jamal asked with an incredulous laugh. He was smiling that big smile of his again, like they were on an adventure, and Ledi's stomach fluttered in a way she couldn't blame on the rickety train. His fingers curved around the train pole, and heat stroked through her as she remembered the press of them into her body. She looked away. They were just two friends out for a day at the park. It didn't matter that he had seen her *O* face, had touched the embarrassing underwear she'd been forced to wear because a neighbor had been hogging the building's shared laundry room.

She glanced at him and realized he was studying her face.

"One fun thing you learn when you study Public Health, especially infectious diseases, is that most societies are one step away from dystopia, really," she said, trying to sound deep and like she hadn't been thinking about their trip to fingerbangville.

"You really know how to put a man at ease," he said. "Next you'll tell me the mole people who live in the subway tunnels are real."

Ledi widened her eyes in mock horror, looked around the car, and then leaned closer to him. "Someone told you the mole people *weren't* real? Oh you poor little lamb. You don't stand a chance."

He leaned closer, too. "I'd say my chances are pretty good. I'm quite lucky, you see, at least in my choice of shepherdess."

The stale air of the train car caught in Ledi's throat. It wasn't Jamal's words. It was the way he looked at her when he said "choice." Every interaction with another human was a choice, really, but the way the word rolled off of his tongue seemed intimate. She'd never really known the feeling of being chosen—it had been denied to her each time a foster parent sat her down with a guilty expression on his or her face. But Jamal said it like choosing her was something anyone would do.

You're reading too much into this. It's not like he chose to be your neighbor. That was a fluke. Don't get excited— you know what happens when you do.

Suddenly an adolescent voice boomed through the train car. "Showtime! Showtime, ladies and gentlemen!"

Jamal jumped, startled by the obnoxious shouts of a group of teen boys on the other side of the car.

"What's happening?" Jamal asked, stepping protectively in front of her. Ledi laughed, although she appreciated his chivalry.

"Oh perfect, you'll get the full New York City experience," she said, tugging his arm so he was flush against the doors with her. "Stand back, and watch out for flying limbs."

One of the teens tapped on his cell phone and held up a small wireless speaker above his head. A second later, the train was filled with the thumping bass of the latest top 40 hip-hop song. Ledi hadn't been listening to much music lately, but she'd heard strains of it from the windows of passing cars in her neighborhood and at the bodega as she waited for coffee, and bopped her head along to the familiar beat. One of the teens took off his fitted hat and began a popping and locking routine, tossing the cap up and around, spinning and catching it.

"Hat dancing?" he asked, leaning close to her ear. "Is this what the youth are doing these days?"

"Just keep watching," she explained, curving a smile in his direction. She had grown up seeing these train performances—different boys, different dances, but always the same amazing athleticism. She'd long ago grown tired of them, but getting to be with Jamal as he watched for the first time made it all new for her. She kept her gaze locked on him, waiting for it . . .

"Go! Go! Go!" the boys shouted as they began clapping. Jamal looked on skeptically, brows furrowed one moment, and then shooting up toward his hairline the next. She heard the telltale thump and looked back at the teen who had just flipped forward and landed on his feet in time to watch him Milly Rock for a few seconds, then segue seamlessly into a tight front somersault, followed by two backflips down the center of the moving train car. The dab he hit after that combination was well earned.

"Holy shit," Jamal said. "Is this normal? Boys flipping about on moving subway cars? I can barely stand without holding the pole and this child just reenacted an Olympic gold medal gymnastics routine."

"It's pretty normal," Ledi said. "It's amusing until the first time you accidentally get kicked in the face."

"Brilliant," was all he said, his attention locked on the dancers. He laughed and clapped along as each of the three boys cycled through their particular routines, doing a little two-step along to the beat and occasionally pressing his shoulder into Ledi's as if urging her to join him. She couldn't quite bring herself to let go enough to dance, though the rhythm of the music pulled at her. She clapped along, instead.

The song wound down, and Jamal cheered, drawing a few looks from some of the jaded New Yorkers sharing the car with them. He was particularly impressed with the last boy, a break-dancer.

"Anyone willing to fling himself on this floor after the information you've given me about bacteria should be considered an artiste of the highest caliber—obviously prepared to suffer for his art."

"I'd never thought of it that way, but I guess you're right," Ledi said.

One of the boys walked by with an open backpack, holding it out for donations. People who had been rapt a moment before suddenly had their faces resolutely stuck behind e-readers and books, ignoring him. Ledi could see the bag was empty, but she rarely carried cash on her. She searched her purse, hoping she had a couple of bucks.

"I've got it. You paid for lunch after all." He rifled through his wallet and casually tossed in a few bills as the kid went by.

"Thanks, mister," the kid said with a nod and kept walking. Then he stopped and turned back, confusion on his face. He looked into the bag, then at Jamal, and then back into the bag. "Um . . ."

Jamal waved a hand. "Thanks for a great show."

"*Thanks*, mister!" The boy turned and ran toward his friends on the other end of the car as the train pulled into the station.

"Yooooo!"

They ran out through the open doors, congregating behind a pole that blocked them from view.

"What was that about?" Ledi turned and peered through the window as the train pulled away. The boys were peering into the backpack and shouting, the sound amplified by the acoustics of the train station. She leaned back against the door and crossed her arms over her chest to look up at him.

"You know how children are," he said, shrugging it off. "By the way, the sign instructs you not to do that." He pointed to the peeling, scratched-up DO NOT LEAN ON DOOR sticker over her head.

"Okay. Now that I have you trapped on a train, I have to ask. How have you never taken the subway, or gone to a bodega? Never seen train dancers before? I know rich people—like, pretty rich—and they're not quite as . . . disconnected as this." She tried to cushion the bluntness of the questions in a teasing tone, but if she was going to give him some of her valuable time, she deserved to know who she was dealing with.

The laughter left his eyes; it was strange to see him tuck away his emotions so quickly. It reminded her that she didn't know him at all, despite the fact that she'd talked to him—and let him touch her—as if she did.

"I'm just used to traveling in a rather different style, and moving in different circles, when I'm here."

The train began to slow down again as it pulled into the next station, the loud screech of its brakes against the rails drowning out the sound in the train car and drowning out the rest of his response.

She moved aside to let a man off of the train, and then resumed her position in front of the door.

"So, that 'different style' you're accustomed to? I'm guessing it doesn't mean you're usually at an alpaca farm upstate?"

He chuckled. "No."

"So you haven't been traveling around the city via dromedary instead of train. I guess I would have seen video of that online." She resumed her position against the door.

"I had chauffeurs." He took a deep breath and when he looked at her again a familiar fear sprang up in her. He was wearing the expression. The one that looked the same regardless of skin tone or age or gender. It was the expression her various foster parents had sported when they called her into the kitchen or living room, avoiding eye contact as they explained she would be leaving.

Guilt.

"I was hesitant to tell you about my wealth and my background because I wanted you to see me for me," he said. "I'm used to people judging me for everything I own and represent, and not me as a person."

His brows drew together, and Ledi ached to reach out a hand and smooth away his worries, but she was still waiting for the other shoe to drop.

He opened his mouth and then closed it. "It's just . . ."

He sucked in a deep breath.

Here it comes. Ledi steeled herself for the impact. Why had she stepped out onto this thin branch of possibility, knowing that when it came to her dating life, any experimentation always yielded the same results? She should have stayed home to study. Reading case studies about a flesh-eating virus would be a step up from her imminent rejection.

"I'm just going to say it." Jamal's mouth twisted beneath the bristles of his beard. "I like you."

Ledi wasn't expecting that. Three words, imbued with confusion and fear and hope, all woven together like strands of DNA. She stared at him, waiting for the *but*, and got his consternated gaze instead.

"I'm rubbish at this." He shook his head. "I've never had to divulge my feelings, or really had any to divulge for that matter. I've spent most of my life focused on preparing for the job that awaits me. Relationships were just an extracurricular."

Ledi was a bit surprised at that—it didn't sound very different from her own life.

Jamal's fingers were trailing up her arm now, leaving gooseflesh in their wake even though the train car was a bit warm and stuffy. She leaned back into the door, farther away from him, as if trying to escape his gravitational pull. He wasn't trying to resist hers though, not with those featherlight touches that made her want more. His gaze on her was so intense, like he was truly trying to see her and willing her to return the favor.

Ledi had never felt more exposed. She wanted to run screaming, but that feeling of recognition that had briefly grabbed her when she'd first met him returned even stronger than before.

Jamal smiled, though his gaze didn't soften. "This, at least, is the truth. I like you, Naledi. I like who I am when I'm with you, the man you make me want to be. I want to get to know you, and I want you to know me—the real me."

His mouth set into a firm line, the way it had been at the Institute the night she'd trained him. Like he was waiting for her to reprimand him. Ledi didn't know what to say, and his fingertips moving on her arm were as distracting as his words had been. She didn't know how to respond; her defenses should have kicked in, but this type of attack was unknown and crept around them.

His gaze suddenly became serious. "And that's why you should know . . ."

It was silly, but she suddenly felt weightless—and that's when she realized she was falling.

"Dyckman Street!" the train conductor called out. The doors had opened behind her with no warning, or no warning she'd been capable of hearing in her state, and she was about to assplant on the platform.

But then Jamal's hands were on her shoulders, and he was stumbling forward into her ungainly descent and pulling her upright and close against him. The chime sounded the close of the doors, and they snapped shut with both of them safely upright.

He didn't let her go, though, and she was getting a refresher on just how warm and solid his body felt pressed against hers.

"That's why you're not supposed to lean against the door!" the conductor called out from her small window as the train pulled out of the station.

Jamal laughed and looked down at her. "Told you so. Score one for team lamb."

The muscular length of him was pressed against her, holding her close, but his expression wasn't seductive. He looked at her like a man who really liked her, and she was sure she was looking at him the same way. Because she did like him. Even though it was illogical. Even though she was defective Velcro, and Jamal would figure that out soon enough. In that moment, pressed up against him on a dirty subway platform, Ledi took a deep breath and decided maybe being out on a limb wasn't the worst position in the world.

"I'm probably breaking some kind of shepherdess ethics law right now, but . . ."

She leaned up and kissed him. His soft lips molded to hers and his hands went to her hips and gripped hard. His tongue slipped into her mouth, searching, and he groaned when her tongue slicked against his.

For a blissful moment, her mind was blank—no worries about busted friendships or missing advisors or skipped shifts—just the scent and taste and feel of Jamal. Jamal who liked her.

Studying was overrated.

Chapter 15

Thabiso focused on the feeling of lightness that had buffeted his steps since Ledi had kissed him long and hard in the dirty, leaky, rat-infested bowels of New York City. His adrenaline had died down, but he still felt like lifting Ledi up and spinning her as the strings section of the National Orchestra of Thesolo played behind them. But that would have been over-the-top, even for a prince, and the only backing music they had was the reggaeton bumping from the cell phone of one of the men playing dominoes at the rickety table nearby.

Thabiso repressed the urge to act out cheesy romantic clichés—all save one. He lifted the hand he held in his own, the one that was softer than he'd imagined given how hard Ledi worked, and kissed the back of it.

She smiled, and then pushed her hair behind her ear with her other hand. She was obviously nervous; she'd turned into a neighborhood tour guide as soon as they left the station, giving him a detailed overview of the neighborhood and avoiding meeting his gaze.

They'd done a round of the park, Fort Tryon, an oasis of unexpected green that was still filled with all of the noise and liveliness of the city. She'd shown him the outside of the Cloisters, a French monastery transported to the city stone by stone because America had to import its antiquity. Ledi had filled him in on the history of the neighborhood, its role in the American Revolution, the vibrant Latino enclave that had sprung up in the area and the gentrification that threatened it. He noticed that she was quite talkative when she spoke of something other than herself. He doubted that was a coincidence.

They were nearing the top of a steep incline, but that didn't stop her skillful avoidance technique.

"And in the summer, sometimes they show films here, and—"

"Naledi."

She looked up at him, eyes wide. For perhaps the first time since he'd met her, her gaze was unguarded, and he could see the turmoil there. The turmoil caused by their kiss. He didn't want to know what her face would look like when he revealed the truth, but he would soon find out.

"Let's sit," he said, gesturing toward a bench that faced out toward the Hudson. Spring sunlight dappled the muddy green waves of the river, making them as beautiful as the waterfalls that careened over Thesolo's mountains, wild and heedless. Or perhaps it was Naledi exerting that effect on his perception. "I asked you to do something that you wanted to do today, and I highly doubt that giving me a detailed recounting of the local history is your way of relaxing. You're always doing for others. Let me do something for you."

He hadn't meant to say that, but as she'd rambled on and on, he'd realized she was building a wall of words between him and her. Between their kiss belowground and their time in the park. He couldn't abide that.

What will she do when she discovers your lie?

Ledi blinked a few times and pulled her hand away slowly.

"Well, then," she said. She walked over to the bench, turned and sat down, as regal as the queen she was destined to become. "If that's the case, entertain me."

A shiver rushed through him that had nothing to do with the breeze from the river. More with the way her thighs pressed together when she crossed her legs, or the gaze she fixed him with. She wasn't just letting her guard down, which he knew was rather a big thing for her—she was inviting him.

"Shall I dance?" he asked.

"Did you pick up some moves from the train performers?" She raised a brow.

"I have moves of my own, thank you very much." He hopped to the side, bent his knees, and worked his hips in the traditional dance all Thesoloian boys had to master for the coming-of-age ceremony performed during each spring festival.

Ledi erupted in laughter, which wasn't the actual effect the dance of manhood was supposed to have, but she couldn't know. If she'd grown up in Thesolo, she likely would have performed her dance of womanhood alongside him at the ceremony, given that she was his betrothed. She hadn't been there, though, and a stubborn Thabiso had danced alone. The fact that he'd imagined a brown-skinned girl with happy eyes across from him as he'd performed the ceremony was his secret.

He finished the dance to amused applause from Naledi.

"Don't act like that didn't steam your headwrap," he said as he dropped onto the bench beside her, throwing his arm along the back of it in spite of the splinters. Another peal of laughter rang out from her lips, the sound breaking from her like the evening call of the birds surrounding his palace back home.

"Steam my headwrap? What does that even mean?" She looked up at him, wiping tears of mirth from her cheeks.

Thabiso leaned in a bit closer. "It means, to reach a state of arousal such that the heat produced by the body steams the traditionally starched headwrap until it is . . . limp."

Ledi blinked a few times. "Okay, I need to know more about where you're from, where this is an actual thing people say to each other."

His delight turned to panic, and then to inspiration. Maybe there was a way he could reveal the truth to her that would negate the lies he'd told. It often worked out in the fairy tales—Beauty had still loved the Beast once he revealed he was truly a prince, hadn't she? Thabiso had a flash of a story in his mind; the Beast in pain and dying alone because Beauty had left him for some reason or another. Not the outcome he was hoping for.

"Okay, okay," he said, mental wheels spinning in merciless desert sand, until finally, they caught traction. "You've given me a tour of your local park, and now I'll give you one of mine. Just . . . work with me." He glanced at her to be sure she was giving him her full attention. "We're in a garden full of lush greenery and beautiful flowers imported from all over the world. That majestic bird over there. You see it?"

"Um, the pigeon?" she asked skeptically. Her brow raised as the bird puffed itself up and began chasing a female bird through a puddle.

"Pigeon? That's a peacock! They roam the grounds of the park near my home, although they are not a local breed. That over there?" He pointed to a pug walking by, bowlegged and snorting. "That is one of the pigs that live behind the kitchen eating scraps and providing compost material. We don't eat them, not because they're unclean, but because they're much too smart."

"I'm sure the cows feel some kind of way about that," she said wryly.

"The cows live a very good life, as do the goats, even if they can't appreciate it as well as a pig can. Some animals are more equal than others, you know."

Her mouth curved up into a smile and something in his chest moved out of alignment. He loved seeing her smile. He loved being the cause of it. That smile would fade soon; he hoped that she would be able to forgive him.

"Is there a playground?" Ledi asked as they watched a father walk by with a group of kids on scooters, rushing toward the swings and slides.

"My parents had a play area set up for me, yes." He was sure she was imagining a small plastic swing set, not the gymnastics arena and amusement park-grade water slide his parents had built for him.

"This was my local park for a while," Ledi said. "When I was thirteen. I lived with this family, the Davises, and I'd come here on the weekend and ride my bike around. Sometimes I'd see kids from the school I'd transferred to and hang with them. Over there by the monkey bars is where I had my first kiss."

"Romantic," Thabiso said.

"Disgusting," she replied with a small grin. "He had braces and we'd just eaten take-out Chinese. That's all I'll say about that."

Thabiso wasn't jealous exactly, but he wondered what would have happened if her family hadn't taken her from Thesolo. There were no true constraints on the betrothed of a prince that said she must date only him, but might her first awkward kiss have been with him?

"I didn't even like the guy really," Ledi said. "My foster dad got wind of what happened, though, and said he didn't want a fast girl under his roof because they were too much trouble. So all that kiss got me was some prechewed chunks of sesame chicken and a new foster family." She looked up at him. "It's funny, I'm so sure that none of this stuff bothers me, and then you bat your lashes at me and I take a left turn into emo-ville."

She looked embarrassed, and maybe a little angry. She had every right to be angry. Kicking a young girl out for natural exploration was cruel.

"I'm honored that you trust me to be your copilot into emo-ville, as you call it," he said. And suddenly the thistled path to the truth that he'd been fighting through fell away before him. He knew how to tell her. He knew how to make things right.

"I can tell you my own embarrassing story," he said.

"Have you been involved in other ego-driven acts of arson?" she asked with raised brows.

"Figuratively, yes," he said, leaning close to her. "I've only ever tried to burn a building down to get a woman's attention once, though." She laughed again. He took her hand, brushed his fingertip over her palm. "When I was a boy, I was certain I had a soul mate, even though many people told me otherwise. For a short period, I required those around me to pretend that she was real. A place was set for her at snack time. I asked that gifts be purchased for her. I was often found talking to an empty chair as if she were beside me. Eventually, my parents became worried and tried to wean me off of this imaginary soul mate, so I tried to run away and find her. I was seven, so this didn't go over too well."

Ledi smiled. "OMG, this is so sweet. I can imagine exactly what you would have looked like as a kid."

Her brow furrowed as she stared at him, and he wondered if she was conjuring an image of him or pulling one from the recesses of her memory.

"What happened to your soul mate?" she asked.

"I stopped believing for a while there," he said. "Became too busy with grown-up things and stopped thinking of her."

"Hey, sometimes you do what you have to," she said. "I stopped thinking of my parents because it hurt too badly, and then one day I tried to remember them and I couldn't."

She stared out toward the river.

Thabiso saw the opportunity before him like a neatly wrapped present. He made his move. "Would you want to know about them, if it was possible?"

An expression of distaste passed over her face. "Why? They're dead and I've gotten along just fine on my own. Knowing who they were wouldn't change any of that."

"But—"

"My friend got me one of those DNA tests and I still haven't looked at the results. I'm Naledi Smith. I eat biostats for breakfast and produce the cleanest gel images on the East Coast. I don't need a past."

Damn it.

The thorny path to the truth sprang up before him again. He had asked her if she wanted to know and she didn't. If he told her who he was, in a way he'd be going against her wishes. What was he supposed to do now?

I know you just explicitly stated you don't want to know about your past, buuuuut I'm going to tell you anyway because I also need to explain how I'm a lying prick.

Thabiso was scrambling to think of a way to tell her without alienating her even more when he felt a vibration against the bench. Ledi pulled her hands away from his and dived for her phone.

"Sorry, I'm expecting a call from my dean," she explained as she tapped at her phone and raised it to her ear. Thabiso could see the worry in her eyes. "Hello? Yes, Dr. Bell, this is Naledi. I hope my email wasn't too—oh. Oh."

She stood from the bench and began pacing. "That doesn't make sense, I—how could they? *Why* would they?" She paused, nodding slowly as if the person on the other line could see her. "Yes. I understand. I can be there in half an hour. Thank you."

When she turned to him, her expression was blank but her eyes were glossy and her lower lip trembled for just a moment before she pressed her teeth against it to stop the movement.

"Naledi?"

Thabiso jumped to his feet, to stand beside her, but she backed away from him.

"I . . . Wow. I hadn't been able to get in contact with my advisor about my field study for this summer. It was supposed to be at the Disease Task Force, this group that monitors infectious disease outbreaks."

That sounded interesting and terrifying, though Thabiso had interned at The Hague, which also sounded vaguely menacing, and had been bored out of his mind.

"I'm assuming something is amiss?"

"My advisor is the director. He hadn't been following up with me, and I just found out that the funding for the Task Force has been cut. The reason he's been MIA is he's been trying to save as much information as he can, protect vulnerable communities in the midst of possible epidemics, and whatever else you do when a major governmental agency is shut down without warning."

Thabiso was concerned on several levels. For Naledi, as a friend, and for what cutting infectious disease outbreak detection could portend, as a leader.

"I'm sorry. Do you know why?"

It was simply bad governance, and he couldn't understand what would drive such a decision. Then he remembered Tad/Todd. He remembered Naledi's uncle, Alehk. Money. Somewhere along the line money was involved, he was sure.

"Because the government has been hacking at science funding indiscriminately. Forget my practicum. They're cutting funding for research that will stop people from dying." Her expression was blank, as if she couldn't fathom it. "I just need . . ."

Thabiso prepared himself to comfort her. He was opening his arms when she stepped away from him.

"I need to go."

Thabiso shoved his hands into his pockets. "Sure. I mean, do you want me to . . . ?"

He looked at her, brows raised in question.

Can I help?

She shook her head.

"I just have to get to school. For this meeting." She touched his arm, and then took off down the hill, phone in her hand. She had been opening for him on the bench. Even after he'd painted himself into a corner. But now she'd slammed shut again.

She was in trouble and wouldn't turn to him. Worse, he still hadn't revealed himself to her.

He looked around the park and sighed as he tried to figure out his way back to the train. He'd gotten himself into a fine mess, indeed.

Chapter 16

I'm sorry.

$\mathcal{L}$edi ignored the text from Portia that popped up on her phone screen as she sat in her living room, sipping a well-deserved wine cooler. The Harbor Fog was the best Julio the bodegaman had to offer, and even if it was sickly sweet, it was better than thinking of her horrible news.

It was also better than thinking of the silent apartment across the hall, and how she'd had to fight the urge to go knock on the door and ask Jamal to make her feel better when she returned from her emergency appointment at the dean's office, despite the fact that she'd run off on their date. She knew he could make her feel better—that he would—and that made it even more imperative that she sit tight in her apartment, just as she always had when shit hit the fan.

Since when had she needed outside help with anything? Even Portia had no idea when Ledi's life got really rough, most times, because what was the use of burdening others with her bad news? She'd always kept her deepest feelings more safely hidden than porn on an unlocked laptop—folder after figurative subfolder of false file names to mask her true feelings from those who might click through. But Jamal had gained access to the folder labeled NothingToSeeHere after just a few days. She'd opened herself to him and, frightening as it was, she wanted more. Oh god, she wanted more. She wanted to curl into his lap again, to let him touch her and kiss her and make her forget that her life was in the midst of derailment.

Heat throbbed between her legs and she pressed her thighs together as if that could ward off thoughts of the man who'd barged into her life. The one who would likely be just a few yards away from her at some point soon. The skeptical, superstitious part of her wondered if his presence wasn't connected to her bad luck.

You let your defenses down. When you do that, the bad can get in with the good.

There was nothing scientific about that line of thinking. There was no way that a few days with Jamal had led to her current situation, but it *felt* like it. Just like getting excited about the practicum hadn't caused the government to shut down the Task Force, even though it felt like it. Feelings couldn't be quantified like data in R, but that didn't make their effects any less real.

She sighed and took a sip of the sweet wine.

It didn't matter in the end. Jamal was temporary. Mrs. Garcia would be back soon, and all Ledi would have left of him would be memories of how he'd given her the best and most inappropriate orgasm of her life. She'd regretted having to leave him in the park, but now she was wondering if that wasn't for the better. He was a complication she just didn't need at the moment.

That didn't stop her heart from racing every time she heard a sound in the hallway.

Her phone buzzed again, and she finally gave in and picked it up to read Portia's message.

> Look, I was worried and drunk, and I acted like a jerk. I went too far.

A picture of a growling Doberman came through, followed by a pic of a sad Doberman puppy. Portia knew Ledi couldn't resist random dog pics. She sighed and texted back before she could think better of it.

> I forgive you. Mostly because my life is falling apart and I need you to do friend-type things like tell me everything will be all right.

> **Whoa. Naledi Smith is admitting she needs help.**

> *looks out window*
> *sees pig flying*
> *shoots pig with bow and arrow and brings Naledi bacon*

> What happened? Did you find out something about Jamal?

Let me just call you. Ledi tapped on the phone widget in the messenger app.

Portia picked up on the first ring, groveling like the pro that she was. Then she listened sympathetically as Ledi explained how her field study had imploded.

"Damn. Well, I was going to invite you out tomorrow night anyway, but you definitely have to come now."

Ledi sighed. "Going on a bender won't help this." She took a sip of her wine. A moderate amount of booze would, but moderation wasn't a concept that Portia was always on familiar terms with.

"I wasn't going to suggest one." Portia sighed. "My parents want me to go to some fund-raiser tomorrow night and I have an extra ticket—I guess they were hoping I'd magically find a guy who didn't give me hives after one date to drag along with me."

Ledi was going to point out that Portia didn't do dating so much as hooking up, but it seemed superfluous.

"Their friend who works for the Department of Public Health, Dr. Okri, will be there. She's way into mentorship and all that socially upright stuff, so I can make an introduction and see if she can get you an internship or whatever it is you need."

Hope fluttered gently in Ledi's chest. Could it be that simple? Really? She didn't want to use her friend's connections to get ahead, but she'd tried playing it straight and that hadn't gotten her anywhere. She'd avoided all the extracurricular meetings, eschewing the networking that would've provided her with more options, so now she'd have to get over herself and get out into the world.

"I'd really appreciate that, Portia. Thank you."

"Don't thank me. I'm your friend and I care about you." Portia's voice had gone serious, and Ledi couldn't help but wonder what that was about. "Ledi, look. I saw something kind of weird on social media yesterday . . ."

Ledi put her wine down on the chipped particleboard surface of her coffee table and sat up straight on her futon. She'd been so busy talking about her own problems that, for maybe the first time ever, she hadn't inquired about Portia's well-being.

"Everything okay?" she asked. Portia was somewhat popular on social media and had cultivated a small following with her artsy pictures, trivia spanning a wide range of subjects, and interest in everything and everyone. It wasn't a problem, but sometimes she drew the ire of weirdos.

"Yes. It's just something about the fund-raiser." Portia went silent then.

"Um. Okay. And what would that be?"

There was a long pause, one that was nine months along, at least, as far as tension went.

"Oh it's just . . . the dress code is formal." Portia said, following it up with a short, clipped laugh. "Make sure you look stunning. I can lend you a dress if you want. Or pick something out for you if you want to hit up Nordstrom."

"I have a dress," Ledi said. "But thank you."

"Great. I'll pick you up at eight tomorrow."

When Portia disconnected, Ledi was tempted to call back and ask what was really going on, but she had to worry about herself first, even if just for that night. She opened the web browser on her phone and continued searching for open epidemiology field studies, as she'd been doing for most of the afternoon; having a backup for your backup was just common sense.

After an hour of searching, she'd compiled a list of four positions that were still unfilled and three people she could cold email. She wasn't convinced that any of the leads would work out, but she'd at least reminded herself that she was capable of rolling with the punches and handling problems as they arose.

She stuck her phone on the charger and flopped back on her futon. She heard the footsteps in the hallway, but her stomach had stopped flipping after several false alarms—it was a busy night in her building. From the smell of weed drifting under the door, the hipster down the hall seemed to be having a party.

This time, though, she heard the keys jingle, and the door to Mrs. Garcia's apartment open and close. Disappointment diffused through her as she lay splayed on the bed.

Sure, she'd ditched Jamal on a hilltop in upper Manhattan; she'd still expected that he'd check in. She grabbed her pillow from across the bed and pressed it against her face, embarrassed for herself. A few days and one great fingerbang didn't mean anything on the NYC dating scene. Connections in this city were fly-by-night, at best, and in this case more than others, but she'd allowed herself to have expectations, like a fool.

That was when the knock came.

Maybe it's a lost party guest.

The knock came again, more insistent.

"Who's there?" she called out, wanting to save herself the inevitable disappointment when she opened the door full of silly hope and found some random dude dropping Visine in his eyes instead.

"Special delivery for a graduate student having a no good, very bad day," a rich, accented voice answered. The hope she felt was still silly, but it pulled her up off her futon and toward the door almost as fast as when the UPS guy was waiting outside the building with a package for her.

She pulled the door open and, just like that, her protective membrane was pierced, her defenses were down, and the draining events of the day were wiped away by Jamal's bright smile. Her heart beat faster and elation sped through her. She'd once worked in a lab that researched addiction, and had watched as rats provided with cocaine-laced glucose would mope about until a researcher approached with their refill; then they'd be zooming all over the cage, eager for their next hit. Ledi thought perhaps she understood their reaction a little better now.

"Hi." Why did she want to touch him so much? Why was she smiling so hard that her cheeks hurt, despite her definitively shitty day?

"Hello," he said. He held up a bag, and she didn't have to open it to know what was inside. She could smell the lunch meat, oil, and vinegar of her favorite sandwich as soon as the bag moved. "We didn't get to eat, and maybe you were too busy to grab food since you had meetings, I assume? I just happened to pass the bodega—" He stopped talking, and his smile faded as he shook his head. When his gaze met hers again, it was intense, insistent. "Enough of these false pretenses. I don't care about these carcinogenic sandwiches, however delicious they might be. I'm here because I wanted to see you. I know you're used to doing everything yourself, but I wanted to make sure you were okay after receiving that news. Are you okay?"

Everything Ledi thought she'd known about her needs and wants slid away, leaving her open, exposed, and shocked by his gruff demand. She'd had support, she'd had friendship, but she'd never had a man standing before her looking so frustrated on her behalf that he might track down whoever had shut down the Disease Task Force and throttle them himself.

Ledi thought she might cry, but that was unacceptable, so she did the next best thing: she grabbed Jamal by the front of his shirt and, for the second time that day, she kissed the hell out of him. This time, she didn't intend on stopping.

Chapter 17

This was going all wrong, even if it felt all too right.

Thabiso had spent his evening distracted at a last-minute gathering at the Thesoloian embassy that Likotsi had arranged after he'd been left behind in the park. Thoughts of Ledi's shattered hopes and the way she'd run before she let him see her break had taken too much of his attention. He'd saluted the Kenyan ambassador in French instead of Swahili, had offered the Moroccan envoy a bacon-wrapped scallop, and then turned and done the same to an Israeli minister.

"You're a mess, friend," Johan had noted, handing Thabiso a glass of wine. The tabloid Prince of Liechtienbourg, Johan was known in equal measure for his shocking red hair, his weekly brushes with infamy, and for being the stepson of a king—"all the fame, none of the responsibility" he'd teased Thabiso during their boarding school days.

"It's a woman, isn't it? *Schietze de mierde.*" Even the Liechtienbourger mashup of French and German hadn't lifted Thabiso's spirits.

"Any advice?" Thabiso had asked. Johan wasn't exactly a font of wisdom on creating lasting relationships, but perhaps having a new woman every week had given him some special insight.

"Don't get attached," Johan had replied drily, before taking a sip of his own wine.

"Sounds like something she would say," Thabiso had said.

"My kind of woman. Is she here?"

Thabiso had given Johan a playful shove before changing the subject to the upcoming climate talks in Paris.

He'd eventually recovered his wits enough to smooth everything over and send the guests of the Thesoloian embassy home happy; trade deals were unofficially set into motion, mutually beneficial political discourse had occurred without fisticuffs. He was the only one solemn and sullen after what had somehow turned out to be a success.

His return date loomed nearer, and the length of time left for him to tell Naledi the truth and beg her forgiveness was a ticking time bomb that grew ever larger in his mind. Likotsi's suddenly expert opinions on relationships hadn't helped either. She'd been smiling and sneaking text messages all night, and Thabiso was jealous. Jealous of his own assistant's happiness.

So he'd stopped at the bodega on the way from the UN and bought two of the sandwiches Ledi loved, as well as some beer that seemed much too fancy for the cracked glass door it resided behind. He had a plan: he'd check in on her, make sure her school situation was in hand, and reveal every single lie he'd told, starting with his name.

But then she kissed him.

Her soft lips pressed against his and her tongue grazed over his mouth, which had sealed shut in prudish surprise. When he opened for her, she released such a moan of relief—of want—that it spiraled through him, sliding over his skin and down his spine like a living, hungry thing. With her tongue slicking over his as it did—with her soft cry reverberating through him as it did—Thabiso's cock responded without further prodding. It wanted in on some of the action, his intentions be damned.

Thabiso backed her into the apartment and kicked the door shut behind them, his mouth not budging from hers, mostly because she had grabbed his face with both hands to keep him close. Her palms roughed over his beard as her hands slid behind his neck and her fingers interlaced, pulling him down, down toward the futon. He dropped the bag along the way, not even listening to hear whether the bottles clinked or shattered. His attention was fully directed on the heat of her mouth, of how her shirt was riding up beneath his hands, exposing the bare skin of her waist to his touch. His blood thrummed and his heart was doing some bizarre dance that knew no choreography but the joy of Naledi.

She was on the futon beneath him, her tongue tracing his mouth as her hands slid up under his shirt. Thabiso had never really given much thought to the palms of a woman's hands, but Ledi's were warm and capable and scorched over his bare skin. He'd compared her to the goddess of rain, but he'd been wrong. She was pure fire.

"Oh fuck, Naledi. Hold on. Hold on, hold on." His forehead rested against hers and he gripped both of her wrists in one hand. She gazed at him, eyes wide and reflecting lust back at him.

"Oh, sorry. I kind of tackled you."

Her brows drew and she moved to roll away from him, but he leaned and caught her lips with his. He kissed her slowly, sipping at her like a butterfly savoring the sweetest nectar. She arched up beneath him, pressing the V where the seams of her jeans met right up against the hard length of him, undulating her hips as she kissed him back with abandon.

"I need to tell you," he said between kisses. "Who I am."

"I know who you are," she said. She pushed away from him and pulled off the screenprinted T-shirt she was wearing, revealing a soft, worn-looking gray bra cupping her silky brown breasts. "You're the guy who learned to cook for me. The guy who's made me laugh harder than I have maybe ever. Who made me come so hard I thought I'd peed myself."

That shouldn't have made him harder, but it did. Oh, praise the goddess for American oversharing, it did. He ran a fingertip over the frayed faux lace that edged her bra. She shuddered at the merest accidental brush against her skin, and he chuckled.

"I love that you speak so freely," he said. Her hand came to cover his, and when he looked up at her, she was shaking her head.

"I usually don't, to be honest. I feel like my entire life has been me trying to keep everything together, but right now I want to fall apart. And I want you to be the guy that makes me." She was gazing at him hard, and he could see the want in her eyes and the loneliness that he'd caught glimpses of. One of the things he'd grown to adore about her was how in control she was, but now she'd bared herself to him.

"You're leaving soon," she said, and those were the words that broke him.

"We still have to talk," he said, but he was on his knees on the futon now, pulling her toward him. He unhooked her bra with one deft flick of his thumb, and then eased her bra down her arms. He'd been draped in the smoothest silks, the softest wools, as a matter of course, but her skin was the finest texture to ever grace his sense of touch.

"Okay. I know you're some kind of runaway trust fund baby. But you have me here saying corny things that will kill me from mortification in the morning." She shook her head and squeezed her eyes shut. "Ugh. Make sure my last night is a good one, okay?"

Thabiso ran his hands up her torso and cupped the weight of her breasts in his hands. "I can do that."

And he did.

He pushed her breasts together and licked and sucked at her nipples, wasting no time with soft caresses. He licked at her with his tongue rigid and flat, circled and teased her peaks with its tip, then caught a nipple between his teeth and pulled, ever so slightly.

"Ooookay," she said, her voice going breathy. "You might kill me before my embarrassment does. That works, too."

Her hands went to his jeans, tugged at the button fly until she had enough room to work her hand inside and grip him. Thabiso paused midnibble as the heat of her hand registered, and then the clumsy stroke as she tried to work over the length of him in such a restricted space.

He leaned back and pulled his shirt over his head, stood and shucked his jeans, moving with efficient motions that meant his mouth and his hands wouldn't be away from her for long. On the bed, she was pulling off her pajama pants, revealing underwear that were a different color and material from her bra but hugged her curves and accented her hips so perfectly he wondered at the appeal of matching sets.

"You're gorgeous." He dropped back down into the bed, pinning the hot, soft length of her beneath him. She giggled, but looked away.

"Naledi, you have no idea . . ." He didn't think it respectful to compare her to other women, or other women to her. She was beautiful, just as other women he'd been with had been beautiful, but they hadn't made him *feel* like this. "You are lovely, yes, but you make me feel . . . you make me feel like I can be anything."

And it was true. Everyone else had been taught to treat him like a future king, but Ledi released him from that confinement, showed him that he was more than the Moshoeshoe lineage he'd been born into.

She smiled and her arms went around him, banding him in something that felt like much more than lust. "And you make me feel like I'm already something."

He kissed her then, and all the words left them. Her hands rubbed over his back, sending tiny, electric thrills coursing through him. He worked his hand between them, to the juncture between her thighs where she was wet and hot. His fingers teased along her slit, and then rubbed hard, and when he could see she preferred his touch rough he kept at it, kissing her all the while.

"Oh god, yes." She writhed under him, her soft body going stiff as the climax claimed her, bit by bit. First her toes pointing, then her legs pressing into him, and then she arched up and broke with a cry that almost dragged him along with her. She was suddenly pliant beneath him, breathing heavily.

"Do you have condoms?" he asked.

"I'm a public health student," she replied with a sharp look. She pulled off the top of a small footstool beside her bed and fished lazily around, until she came up with a catch—a silvery sleeve of condoms.

He took it, carefully tore open a packet and sheathed himself before resettling himself between her legs and slowly pushing his way in. Her muscles clenched at him, immediately, and the squeeze of her against his cock was excruciating.

"Ledi," he whispered, and then prayed she didn't respond with a name that wasn't his. He paused, reality creeping in at the edges of his pleasure.

"I'm fine," she whispered, misunderstanding. "Better than fine."

She pulled his mouth to hers and thrust her hips toward him, taking him into her completely. Thabiso couldn't say what happened then. He went up onto his elbows so he could look at her as he thrust like a madman, performing acrobatics with his hips that most certainly could only have been the result of possession. He was fit, he knew that, and he put every ounce of his musculature to work with the single goal of giving her pleasure. And when her eyes went wide with shocked arousal, when her head pressed back into the futon and her hands grasped his hips and the sheets and anything that could provide purchase, he slid his hand between them again and pressed at her clit.

She let out a short, sharp cry as the orgasm crashed into her, but he'd already felt it coming from deep within. Her inner walls squeezed him tightly, again and again, and he let go a hoarse cry of his own as his senses shorted out from pleasure.

He collapsed on top of her and she swatted weakly

at him, so he used his last ounce of strength to roll onto his side and take her with him. He inhaled, taking in the scent of her hair oils, her sweat, her soap.

"Are you sniffing me?" she asked, snuggling closer to him. Her kinky curls pressed into his arm, and her breath tickled his chest hairs.

"Maybe." He grabbed some tissues from the box next to the bed and disposed of the condom. He heard scuttling across the room and turned to find two sets of beady eyes focused on him.

"Your mice were watching us," he said as he pulled her back into his embrace. "Voyeuristic vermin. That's a first."

"I knew those two were freaky." She giggled, truly carefree for perhaps the first time since he'd known her. His heart constricted painfully as he looked at her. Being watched by rodents wasn't the only first for him that night. He didn't want to investigate whatever it was he was feeling for her—not when everything he hadn't said came crashing back down, sucking all of the amazing after-sex feeling from him and leaving him with the realization that she still thought he was Jamal. Just Jamal.

She still didn't know about him, or her parents, or her homeland, and she shouldn't have known what he felt like pushing inside of her before any one of those things.

His body went cold, his hold on her slackened.

"Ledi. Look, we really need to talk." He pinched his nose as he sorted just exactly how he was going to explain himself, especially while sitting naked as a mangy hyena.

She stopped laughing and leaned back, away from

him. Just like that, the openness was gone. "Hey, don't go getting weird now. It was just sex."

She hopped out of the bed and headed for the bathroom.

He sat up, and stared after her, her words dashing away even his own self-loathing. "Pardon? Just sex? That was not just sex."

"It definitely was. Exhibit A, I'm going to pee now so I don't get a urinary tract infection. Something you do after just having sex." She shrugged and went into the bathroom; she didn't slam the door.

"Ledi, there is a misunderstanding underway right now." Thabiso paused, and then dropped his head in his hands. "There are actually several misunderstandings going on. How about we clear up this fairly simple one. That wasn't 'just sex' for me. I like you a lot and nothing has changed."

The toilet flushed. Water ran, and he heard her humming the happy birthday song, and then the water stopped.

He pulled on his boxers and jeans and shirt and finally she stepped out, now wearing a pink bathrobe that would have been cute if her gaze hadn't been so wary.

"Okay. It was pretty good just sex," she said with a shrug that he supposed was meant to indicate she was indifferent. But she sat down beside him anyway, folding her legs beneath her and exposing a smooth brown stretch of thigh. He traced his knuckle down her knee and over the sensitive skin, then stopped and took her hand.

"Look—"

Just then, there was a pounding at the door. Ledi squeezed her eyes shut in frustration, hopping out of bed as a second barrage of knocks sounded in the quiet.

"Portia, I'm sorry but this really isn't a good time," she said as she swung the door open. "Oh."

She looked back over her shoulder at him. "It's for you."

Dread gathered in his stomach, but he rose and faced Likotsi's stern glare anyway.

"*Jamal.*"

The single word was rife with accusation and disgust.

"Erm. Hello." He didn't know how to explain her presence to Naledi. "This is my friend."

"Pleasure to meet you again," Likotsi said with a sweet smile for Naledi, but her dour expression returned when she faced him. "There is a problem. I've received news from your family and, before you ask, no, it cannot wait. I'm sorry to interrupt your fun, but this is extremely important."

"Well," Ledi said, obviously uncomfortable, "we can talk tomorrow about the trust fund stuff. Wait, you're not like, a rich serial killer or an investment banker or anything, right?"

Thabiso huffed. "I already told you I'm not a serial killer."

"So you're a banker?" she asked with mock horror. Thabiso couldn't help but laugh. She could pull that out of him, even though he was neck deep in shit.

"I have to study all day," Ledi said, and her gaze darted toward the door across the hall. She sighed and he knew what she was thinking. Mrs. Garcia would be back soon—Likotsi had received the online check-in info for her flight in an email. Thabiso didn't want to think of going back to his real life.

"Do you have plans tomorrow night?" he asked.

"*You* have plans tomorrow night," Likotsi interjected.

"I do," Ledi said, gaze darting between them. "Maybe I can make time for you afterward."

Thabiso knew her well enough to understand many men probably hadn't received that grace from her. He was tempted to have Likotsi tell Ledi the truth right then so it could be done—wasn't that part of her duties as a royal assistant?—but he owed Ledi more than that.

Likotsi cleared her throat. Thabiso squeezed Ledi's hand, and then stepped out the door and crossed the hall with his enraged assistant.

As soon they got into the apartment, she whirled on him. "You silly, self-important, rhinoceros-skulled man! What are you thinking? How could you toy with her like this?"

He noticed the tears standing in Likotsi's eyes then, but she quickly dashed them away. "Oh never mind. Some people enjoy playing games with others' emotions, it seems. I'm tired of being your conscience. You'll have to develop your own."

Thabiso was unsure of how to proceed. Earlier in the evening, she'd been walking on cloud nine as she headed off for a date with her mystery woman. "Do you want to talk? Did something happen with the woman you're seeing? Is that why you fetched me?"

Likotsi sucked her teeth. "I would never be so unprofessional as to burst into a room and demand you listen to my problems. That's your job."

Thabiso couldn't argue with that.

She sighed. "I'm not seeing her anymore, so there's nothing to talk about." Her eyes glistened but she kept her face expressionless. "You, on the other hand, have a problem."

"I was trying to solve that problem by telling Naledi the truth when you interrupted us," Thabiso gritted out. Why was everyone making this so bloody difficult?

"No, actually there's a new problem," Likotsi said as she pulled her handy tablet out and tapped and dragged. "An email from your parents, Your Highness."

She handed the tablet over.

Subject: Your Fiancée Has Been Selected.

Thabiso glanced up at Likotsi, whose expression was perfectly blank.

"What am I supposed to do now?" he asked, scraping a hand through his beard. He still smelled of Ledi.

Likotsi shrugged. "I've offered you romantic advice several times over this trip, to no avail. Figure it out yourself. Sire."

With that, she clicked the heels of her spats and wandered into the bathroom, one of the few places in the apartment where she wouldn't have to look at him.

Thabiso dropped down onto the couch. Perhaps he could be Thesolo's first bachelor king? At this rate, his love life was more complicated than keeping a small nation thriving.

Chapter 18

Ledi spent the following day at the lab and then studying with Trishna, despite the temptation to cancel, leave her door open, and spread herself out suggestively on her bed. But even Jamal and his amazing body couldn't make her forgo her studies. She'd worked too hard and had too much still stacked against her to let her infatuation get that deep.

Still, her attention span wasn't up to her usual high standards. Her brain was more interested in replaying brief snippets of the most amazing sex of her life than reading case studies. When she could push thoughts of Jamal away, and thoughts about having so many thoughts about Jamal, her nervousness about her introduction to Dr. Okri that evening was already lined up and ready to tag in for Team Distracto.

When Trishna had finally demanded to know why she was acting so strange, Ledi had hedged, but then she remembered Jamal telling her to delegate. That she didn't have to do everything herself. She'd explained her dilemma, and Trishna had gone into action, emailing her network of friends for help in finding a new practicum for Ledi in case Dr. Okri didn't work out.

Ledi wondered at the strange burning behind her eyes as she watched her classmate's fingers fly over her laptop keyboard. First Portia, and now Trishna, who she'd shielded herself from all of these months.

It's almost as if people will help you out if you let them in, a not so subtly sarcastic part of her mind chimed in. *It's almost like it's okay to need that sometimes.*

After parting from Trishna with a hug, Ledi returned home, fed the Grams, and hurriedly got dressed for the fundraiser. She chose a purple knee-length sheath dress that hugged and enhanced her curves, paired with a black shawl and her fanciest heels. She moisturized her hair and fluffed it so it framed her face and dabbed on simple but elegant makeup. As she prepared herself, she couldn't stop hoping that Jamal would knock on the door with a Yellow Spatula box and a smile. Maybe nothing else. Even if she'd have to turn down an offer of dinner, there was always the possibility of dessert when she returned.

But that brief fantasy was doused by the reality that even if she saw him later in the night, by next week he'd be another notch on her bedpost. That was all he could be, especially given the fact that he was apparently some rich kid and she was decidedly not. Her stomach flipped, but she focused on blotting her lipstick instead.

Her phone buzzed, letting her know that Portia was outside. She grabbed her purse and rushed out, hopping over a small box that had been left outside her door. She turned her key in the lock and picked up the package as she hurried out of the apartment; her street was narrow and she hated the honking and cursing that ensued when a car double-parked.

Still, she couldn't wait until she got downstairs to

know what was inside. She unwrapped it and pulled off the top as she ran down the stairs—she'd waitressed in heels and was fairly sure she could run at least a 5k in them while balancing trays. Opening a box was nothing.

A small slip of rich, heavy paper rested inside; for a moment she had the ridiculous fear that it would say "Greetings from Thesolo," but the smooth, beautiful cursive apparently belonged to Jamal.

> *Ledi,*
>
> *I apologize for the way last night ended—worrisome news from home awaited me, and more arrived this morning. I've spent the day attempting to put out fires (figurative ones—I learned my lesson, oh Ledi, goddess of fire extinguishers). I don't have much time left in New York, and it's imperative that I see you tonight. There is something we must discuss, and it is of the utmost importance, but besides that, I want to see you. I should be focused on my work, but I've spent every free moment thinking of you. You've become rather important to me, it seems. Here is something to bring you luck.*
>
> *Your neighbor, Jamal (for now)*

When she moved the paper aside, she saw a small glass vial encased in ornate metalwork nestled into the cotton lining the box. A silver chain was connected to the vial, meaning it could also be worn. She lifted it by the delicate metallic links and flipped back the small cork at the top. A strange warmth spiraled in her chest as the scent of the eng oil hit her, one that wasn't caused by the squeeze of her push-up bra. Why did he have this effect on her? How could a guy she'd only known for a few days and met under the strangest circumstances leave her feeling breathless?

She dabbed a drop of oil onto her wrist, then secured the cork and slid the necklace around her neck. She hurried to the giant SUV waiting at the curb and was reaching for the door handle when a giant of a man stepped around the car and pulled it open for her.

Well.

"What's up with the fancy car and driver?" she asked Portia as she slid onto the buttery leather seat. Her friend looked at her, uncomprehending, and she realized that this was part of the life Portia protected as much as Ledi did her own privacy. Ledi had gone to fancy clubs and fancy restaurants with Portia, had joined her and her artsy acquaintances for a winter weekend at her parents' ski chalet and a Fourth of July cookout at the Sag Harbor summer bungalow. Those had seemed like rare, wondrous treats for Ledi, but for Portia, multiple homes and drivers who could take on a defensive line were normal.

"You smell good. And you look amazing," Portia said, ignoring the awkward question with a refinement borne of years of charm school. "That color just pops, and you're glowing! And that necklace is exquisite."

Ledi ran a finger over the metal vines encasing the glass vial. "Well, I'm guessing Dr. Okri won't be that interested in my looks, but every little bit counts."

"You bet your ass it does," Portia said, eyes narrowing. She opened a small cooler compartment and pulled out a can.

"Soda?" Ledi asked. Her public health side was already tsk-tsking at the high sugar levels in the drink, but Portia laughed and shook her head.

"Champagne. In a can! I think my dad is an investor in the company or something."

"No thanks." Ledi shook her head. "I can't be slurring my words while begging for a practicum."

Portia chattered away as the car moved through the Friday night traffic. She'd signed up for yet another art internship, after deciding she didn't like her current gallery. She was taking a metalworking class, in addition to the social engineering course, and was thinking about getting into social media management. She presented these new possibilities with the unvarnished optimism that she always had for new endeavors at the beginning; Ledi hoped one of the projects would hold the key to making her friend happy.

"What kind of fund-raiser is this?" Ledi asked abruptly, realizing she had no idea what she was walking into.

Portia pulled out a compact and reapplied her lipstick. "It's an annual charity event for a pan-African organization. I usually just go for the Jollof rice, but they actually do really important work. Vaccinations, microloans, PTSD counseling in countries recovering from strife, etc. And everyone always looks stunning. I've made some great connections with artists and educators here, too."

"That actually sounds really interesting. Thanks again for inviting me."

Portia eyed her speculatively, and then put the compact away. "I think interesting may be an understatement for tonight, but we'll see."

Ledi turned and looked out of the window, glancing up at the tall buildings that lined Park Avenue. She inhaled deeply. If luck was on her side, what happened at the benefit would change her life.

Chapter 19

Ledi had thought herself dressed up, but as soon as she stepped into the lobby of the Waldorf Astoria she felt like a dull black-and-white microgel next to beautiful color-stained cells. Beneath the high ceilings and Corinthian columns, throngs of women in elaborate headwraps and wax print dresses in patterns that put peacocks to shame chatted in a variety of languages. Men wearing equally elegant and bright African print suits stood by their sides or wandered into the lounge area. One woman floated toward the elevator bank in a skirt that billowed out behind her like a blazing orange phoenix's tail.

"Oh my goodness," Ledi said. "It's like Africa's Next Top Model up in here."

Ledi was still dazzled as they rode the elevator up to the ballroom on the hotel's top floor. Music with a heavy drumbeat tugged at her hips before she even got through the door, and serving staff in aprons of kente cloth bustled by with plates of delicious smelling hors d'oeuvres. Ledi grabbed a small meat pie, and then another, partly because she was hungry and partly because she knew that parties where no one ate the appetizers were hell on a server's wrists.

It was also a cardinal sin to let free food pass her by. They moved against a wall as Portia searched out her parents.

"My dad should be somewhere around here—"

"Mom and Dad are playing musical chairs right now. We have to move because someone fucked up the RSVP and there's no way I'm fitting between those tables." The voice was low, its cadence a bit slow and overenunciated. Ledi looked down into a face that was so similar to Portia's that she startled.

Regina, Portia's twin sister.

They weren't identical, but it was close. Her hair was much shorter, her curl pattern tighter, but it was the same dark auburn. Her eyes were the same shade of maple, and her mouth wore the same smile, except where Portia's was sad, Regina's was sharp. She sat in a sleek, high-tech wheelchair. The wheels were encased in fire-engine red rims and looked like something out of a comic book. Ledi was certain that was on purpose. The bright dresses weren't the only things that would draw people's eye at the gala.

Portia sometimes referred to a time "when my sister was sick" when she was drunk, but she was pretty tight-lipped about her sister otherwise, despite Regina's rising internet stardom. Ledi had thought it sibling rivalry, but now she wasn't sure.

"Hey, sis. Good to see you." Regina looked up at her sister with an inscrutable expression.

"Reggie! I didn't know you'd be here," Portia said, bending down to give her sister a peck on the cheek.

"You would know if you ever answered my texts," Regina said. Another sharp smile.

"Sorry. Just. You know how it is."

Regina did not seem to know how it is. She raised a brow.

Instead of elaborating, Portia gestured toward Ledi. "This is my friend Ledi."

"Oh, this is the Ledi you're always hanging out with?" Regina sounded . . . Jealous?

A little rush of nerves went through Ledi, despite the obvious sisterly tension she was smack dab in the middle of. She tried to be cool, but that lasted about five seconds. "It's so nice to meet you and also OMG I love your site so much! I read it every day! Thank you so much."

So much for playing it cool.

Regina reached a hand up toward Ledi, and even though her hand shook en route, her grip was strong. "You're welcome? Is that the right response? I don't know what to say when people are excited about the site. This is why I hang out online instead." She squinted up at Ledi. "Wait, you look familiar. Do you comment as HeLaHoop?"

Ledi's face warmed and Regina looked embarrassed.

"Oh shit, I shouldn't ask that. Just, you have a cool avatar photo wearing lab gear and you always have such smart things to say on the science posts, so I remember your picture. I was thinking about asking if you, well HeLaHoop, wanted to do a column on lady scientists. We pay our columnists, in case you were wondering."

"Oh! That sounds like it could be fun," Ledi said, both shocked and flattered. "And I could always use extra cash."

"Oracle, take note. Email Ledi about lady scientists."

An LED screen on the arm of the wheelchair blinked red, then green. A robotic voice styled after HAL from *2001: A Space Odyssey* piped out of the armrest. "Note taken, Reggie."

"Did your chair just talk?" Ledi asked. "That is amazing!"

"Your phone talks, too, I'm sure," Regina said drily, but grinned at her. Ledi felt a hard tug on her arm. Portia.

"Dr. Okri is over there. I should go introduce you." Portia smiled, but it didn't reach her eyes, and Regina frowned and looked down.

"It was great meeting you," Ledi said before Portia could respond. "I'll see you at the table."

"Yeah," Portia said. "We'll be back."

Regina's expression lightened. "Okay. I'll just . . . wait for Mom and Dad I guess."

Then Ledi was being dragged toward an imposing woman who held court in front of a small group of admirers. She wore a royal blue gown printed with bright yellow images of birds in flight, paired with a matching headwrap. Her face had that smooth brown agelessness that meant she could be anywhere from thirty to seventy, and her eyes were bright with kindness.

"Why hello, Miss Portia," she boomed in an accent that could only be described as "rich New Yorker." Once you'd made a certain amount of cash, you could make up any accent you wanted and no one would call you on it. "And is this lovely lady the friend you told me about? Where are you from, dear?"

The last question was directed at Ledi.

"I bet she's from Eritrea," a woman in the group said. "She's the spitting image of my auntie."

"No," another man interrupted, his accent thick. "Look at those cheekbones. She has to be from Sudan. I'd know my people anywhere."

The defensiveness that arose whenever people

spoke of their past or their ancestors activated her defenses. "I'm from Manhattan," she said firmly.

"Hmph," said the Eritrean woman. "I guess your people just sprang from the soil here, then?"

"Ah, don't start now, Judy," Dr. Okri said, then clasped Ledi by the arm. "This young woman is training to be an epidemiologist, an asset to the community no matter where she is from. We have to go talk boring science stuff now, but please enjoy the food and the music. I'm very excited about tonight's program."

Dr. Okri led her to a corner away from the band. "So what's this about a practicum falling through?"

"Well, I was supposed to be working at the Disease Task Force."

"Which no longer exists thanks to people who've never cracked a science book in their lives," Dr. Okri said. "I wish I could say this was the last such closure we'd hear of." She sighed. "Well, you're welcome to come intern with me. It's not very exciting, but maybe we'll get another bird flu epidemic since no one is currently tracking such things to prevent it."

"Thank you so much! That would be great. The internship, not the epidemic." Ledi's body slackened with relief. Her career wasn't ruined. Things hadn't worked out as planned, but Portia had come through for her and now she could finally relax and focus on her exams. She wondered if she'd get to share the good news with Jamal—maybe he'd help her celebrate?

"Or perhaps we'll have to figure out a mystery disease, like they're dealing with in Thesolo?"

Ledi's head snapped up. "What?"

The woman was in full science-gossip mode, completely unaware of the shock she'd given Ledi with the mention of Thesolo. "It's not Ebola, or malaria.

The water sources are clean, and there's no discernible contagion pattern. It's been on everyone's tongue tonight, especially given our guest of honor, Prince Thabiso."

Led wasn't sure if the room tilted or if it was her.

Prince Thabiso. The man who had been the subject of her emails for weeks was now in New York City, at the same event as her?

Impossible. And yet Dr. Okri had no reason to lie, unless she was in on it, too? A ridiculous thought, but if Prince Thabiso was really there, couldn't anything be going on?

"Are you okay, Naledi?" Dr. Okri was staring into her eyes and Ledi knew she was checking to see if her pupils were dilated.

"I'm fine," she said. "I think that maybe all the stress of the field study lifting so suddenly made me a bit dizzy."

Dr. Okri nodded. "I understand. Grad school is stressful enough without setbacks like this. Go find Portia, eat some of the wonderful food, and relax. Everything is going to be okay now."

Ledi took a deep breath. Dr. Okri was right. Her academic career was moving back on track. She had at least one more night of incredible sex with Jamal to look forward to. The Prince Thabiso business was nothing to be worried about; in fact, she'd make it a point to find him later that night and let him know what scammers were doing in his name. It would be strange talking to a prince, but she was sure he was no different than any other guy.

Chapter 20

"Pardon me, Highness, but there is a man from Botswana who is rather insistent that you meet his daughter," Likotsi said in a low voice. "I told him you were occupied but I'm not certain he won't creep under the table during dinner and pop up from beside your seat."

Thabiso closed his eyes against the annoyance. The music provided by the live band was delightful, the food exquisite, but it was so much drone in his ear and ash on his tongue because Naledi wasn't there with him.

He still had to reveal his true self to her, although that wasn't entirely right. He'd never felt more like himself than in the time he'd spent with Naledi. The adulation and coy glances from women, the hearty handshakes and admiration from the men, the way everyone treated him like royalty—it grated on him. He wished he were back at the building uptown, on an uncomfortable futon or in a tiny kitchen or on a plastic-wrapped couch, as long as Ledi was there with him.

"You can tell him I'm not available to meet eligible young women right now," he said, pressing back against the wall of the alcove he was tucked into. He'd have to socialize at some point, but no one had recognized him just yet. "My parents finding me a bride has taken care of that annoyance at the very least."

"Yes, sire."

As Likotsi strode away, Thabiso noticed a young woman hovering nearby. He almost dismissed her, but then he saw the tray in her hand. She was a server, like he'd been for those fateful few hours when he worked with Naledi.

"Um, would you like more sparkling water, Prince, sir?"

"Yes," he said, holding out his empty glass, then added, "Thank you."

Her hand shook as she poured his water, and a bit splashed onto his shoe. "Oh, I'm sorry! I usually never spill."

"Don't worry," he said. "I know this job is difficult. It's not as if you set me on fire or anything. Then we would have a problem." He smiled, hoping that set her at ease, and was pleased when she returned it.

"Thank you, sir. And congratulations."

"I'm at this fund-raiser on behalf of my people, not myself, but thank you."

"Oh, congrats for that, too!" she said, and walked away grinning. Thabiso was slightly confused, but people often said strange thing when they realized they were talking to royalty.

A flash of purple fabric hugging a familiar hip in his peripheral vision caught his attention, but when Thabiso turned to investigate, all he saw was the wide, wax print skirt of a ball gown in the space where the purple apparition had been.

Perhaps he was still so enraptured with Naledi that

he'd begun conjuring her up? It wouldn't be the first time; he'd done the same when he was a child, after all. It would certainly be disquieting if that were the case, but that didn't stop his sudden sense of unease. He needed to see her. Needed to tell her. He'd created a ridiculous set of preconditions in his head, when in reality there was no good moment other than *as soon as possible, you cowering hyena.*

Likotsi returned, chewing something and brushing crumbs off of her lapels. "These stuffed plantains are addictive," she said. "Do you want one before you're announced?"

"No," he said, his voice rough from nerves that had nothing to do with speaking in front of a group of people. "What is the earliest time I can leave here?"

"Customarily, the guest of honor stays for at least two-thirds of an event," Likotsi said, disapproval icing over her words. "Don't tell me that you're considering leaving to see her. Do you really think she's sitting around waiting for you? She said she had plans. She could be out with another man—one who isn't lying to her."

The thought of it made Thabiso's fists clench. A crown of icy panic settled on his head at the thought of some other man, perhaps the one who'd comfort her when she found out Jamal was really Thabiso.

"She didn't mention any other man," he said defensively.

"And you didn't mention living in a palace," Likotsi said with a Cheshire cat grin. "Funny, the things people omit during love's first bloom."

Love? Could that be the ridiculous happiness that settled over him at the mere thought of Naledi, that made him sick with anger at the suggestion of her being with someone else?

Impossible.

Or inevitable, if the priestesses had been correct in their assessment.

The music quieted and the roar of the crowd grew louder for a moment before the shushing began. The MC took to the mike and began joking with the attendees.

"You're right," Thabiso said. "I have an obligation here and I can't go running off because I didn't tell her when I should have. But tonight—"

"I believe you once told me that your love life was not my purview," Likotsi said. "Shall we keep it that way until *after* you've told her? I'm not feeling very charitable this evening."

"Do you want to talk, Kotsi?" Thabiso was worried by the dullness in his assistant's eyes. When he looked closer now, he noticed the wrinkles that marred her shirt, and that the edges of her short hair were slightly overgrown. She'd had time to get a shape-up before the event, and she hadn't. In the world of Likotsi, this was catastrophic.

"If Naledi throws you out on your buttocks, as she has every right to, then perhaps we can commiserate about our failed American conquests one day," she said. "But not yet. I'm still a bit tender, you see."

Thabiso placed a hand on her shoulder. "You're a good woman. I don't know what happened, but I know she's a fool to have hurt you."

"I seem to be surrounded by fools, lately," she said, but her smile was affectionate. "For your sake, I hope Naledi is as fond of them as I am."

The MC's voice boomed out. "Dinner will be served shortly, but before that, allow me to introduce tonight's guest of honor. Voted Africa's most powerful man, and formerly known as one of the

world's most eligible bachelors, His Royal Highness,
Bringer of Light and Love, Prince Thabiso Moshoeshoe of Thesolo!"

Thabiso wanted to roll his eyes at the honorific, but
the man was just reading from a card. Besides, the
title had served as a great icebreaker with women
in the past. The not-so-distant past, in fact, but the
thought of it seemed gauche to him at the moment.
Anything but returning to Ledi and telling her the
truth, and then getting to his people, seemed unimportant.

"And it seems that we'll also be the first to congrat-
ulate the prince on his impending marriage! Congratulations!"

What? Word spread fast. He couldn't very well deny
it—that would cause a scandal. Thabiso gritted his
teeth. Yet another thing he'd have to pretend for the
moment.

He strode toward the stage and had taken his first
step up onto it when there was that purple flash just
out of view again, this time accompanied by a com-
motion. He turned, and his gaze met familiar brown
eyes that were wide with disbelief. His stomach gave
a sick jolt and tumble, as if he'd just gone over the side
of Thesolo's highest waterfall in a barrel.

Ledi. With her friend Portia from the other day
seated beside her. Ledi was standing, fists clenched
at her sides and fury scrawled into her features. She
knew he was a prince now. She thought he was an
engaged-to-be-married one. He prepared himself for
her to scream and shout and make a scene, but she
turned from him and glared at her friend.

"You knew," she said quietly, but the words carried.

"No! Yes. I suspected." Portia's shoulder hunched
guiltily.

"You suspected and you brought me here to humiliate me?" Ledi asked.

"What are you talking about?" Portia's voice rose in a panic. "He's the one who lied! He should be the one humiliated."

"Tell that to everyone watching," Ledi growled, then walked around her friend and through the now-buzzing crowd. Thabiso felt as if his feet were glued to the ground, as if he were in a silent film watching the leading lady make her escape, but then the noise of the crowd filled his ears and his legs began to move, carrying him through the slim paths between tables toward the door Ledi had just marched through.

He was about to break into a full-out run when a wheelchair pushed back and blocked his path. The short-haired woman seated in it gave him a smug look as she pushed a button on her chair.

"Oracle, text Kelly. Kelly pick up a friend named Ledi in front of the Waldorf, right now, and take her wherever she wants to go," she said, then released the button and smiled at Thabiso. "You'll have to go around. I hope she's long gone when you get down there."

Thabiso didn't know who the woman was or why she was blocking his route to the one thing that was important to him, but he scrambled around the table. The spaces between the seats was tight, and he pushed his way past shocked guests who were starting to stand in their seats and demand to know what was happening.

He reached the elevator bank just as the door was closing and shoved his hand into the slim opening, hoping the sensors weren't faulty but deciding it was a risk worth taking. The doors stopped and reversed their course, opening to reveal Ledi, pressed against the back of the elevator car. Her expression was one of terror—was she afraid of him?—and she was shaking her head.

"Let me explain," he said.

"What are you going to explain first? The crazy emails? How you showed up at my job? How you ended up in the apartment across the hall from me? How you lied to me about everything? Everything!"

She shut her eyes and her nostrils flared; she was fighting against pain, and he was the cause of it. Thabiso wanted to pull her into his arms, but that would assuage his hurt, not hers.

"Listen, Naledi—"

"Don't," she said, the croak in her voice a shock to him. "Please. Just . . . don't. Nothing you say can make this right."

Tears began slipping down her cheeks, and Thabiso knew then that it was over. He could admit that he didn't know everything about her after so short a period, but he knew he valued her pride and resilience. He had hurt her, and worse, he'd witnessed those tears break free against her will. That may just have been worse than causing them. He released the elevator door, flinching at the *ding* that announced the door was closing. Naledi's eyes opened just before the doors slid together, the pain in them driving home just how ridiculous and selfish he had been.

He leaned his forehead against the cool metal framing the elevator doors.

"Sire?"

"I'll be back inside in a moment, Kotsi," he said. It didn't matter where he was, really. He felt an odd numbness, but he was a prince. Feelings would wait. "I know I have obligations to uphold."

"I was going to suggest we leave, actually," she said. "Heartbreak and scandal are sufficient reason for the guest of honor to leave an event, customarily. But perhaps we should wait a moment."

She was giving Naledi time to make her escape; however nice she was being to him, she'd warned him that he'd hurt the woman from the beginning, and Likotsi was always right.

"Okay," he said. "Do you think the bodega sells Macallan?"

"No, but this is New York," she said. "You can get anything you want."

"Almost anything," Thabiso corrected. Likotsi nodded grimly.

He could hear people milling about and voices coming toward the elevator bank. "Let's take the stairs, shall we?"

Forty-seven flights of stairs later, Thabiso had almost convinced himself things were better this way.

Chapter 21

"Lediiiiii!"

Ledi knew her bad luck streak would continue as soon as she saw Brian's head poke out of his office the next afternoon. She'd wanted to build a pillow fort and hide away from the world, but grad school didn't allow for recovery from life's minor tragedies. Or comedies. Perhaps she was experiencing a bit of both. So she'd operated on autopilot that morning, feeding the Grams, and then sneaking out of her apartment and pretending her heart didn't hurt when she saw the door to 7 N. She had barely slept thinking that he might show up across the hall at any time, then reminded herself that his little game of slumming it with the commoners had been found out so he'd probably relocated to classier digs. Maybe with his new fiancée.

Deep breaths. You don't care. He's just another case study for Fuckboy Monthly.

The necklace he'd given her shifted under her shirt. If she was stronger, she would have thrown it at him as the elevator doors closed, a dramatic form of closure. But she couldn't. The scent brought her comfort, and it was the most perfect gift she'd ever gotten, even if it had come from a scumbag.

She'd left her phone at home; she'd removed the battery with shaking fingers on the ride down in the elevator to avoid Portia's impending barrage of messages. Jamal—Thabiso—had hurt her, and badly. But deception by a guy was unexceptional; from your best friend, it was unbearable.

"Good morning, Brian," she said politely, refusing to show emotion in front of him and also really not up for his shit.

"My favorite lab assistant! I've told you you're my favorite, right?" She wondered if he really thought the constipated grimace he was sporting passed as a smile. She supposed he thought if he asked nicely, it wouldn't matter that he somehow only had eyes for her when it came to foisting his work on her. "I know you're supposed to do the Wright-Giemsa staining today, but Kevin was on sac duty this morning and he's out sick."

"Again?" Ledi had been exhausted for a long time, but she was veering dangerously close to burnout. Going into the lab after the shitshow of the previous night was supposed to be a reprieve. Do some cytospins, stain some cells—try not to think about the handsome jackass who had gotten past her defenses, not once but twice.

Jamal's reveal had also unearthed a pressing question, one she had been hiding behind her anger and disappointment all night: if the prince was real, what was she supposed to make of all the "spam" emails she'd been receiving from Thesolo?

"Naledi?" Brian's brows lifted, crenellating his forehead like the tiny brains he wanted her to retrieve and slice up. "You can do the mouse sacrifice, right?" He held her lab coat and safety goggles out as if they were the sacred garments needed to perform such a ritual. "If you could do a transcardial perfusion on the C57BL/6-backcrossed group? That'd be super."

He dumped the coat and goggles onto the table beside her, as if she'd already said yes. She'd barely processed her own life and now she was supposed to serve as rodent executioner? Fucking Brian. Fucking Thabiso. Fucking *everything*.

"No."

Brian kept walking, so she said it again a little louder.

"No, Brian."

He turned around, annoyance plastered over his face. "What do you mean, no?"

Ledi inhaled deeply. "I mean, I have my own stuff to do this morning and I can't do the saccing. You asked me if I could, and the answer is no."

Brian's face went red. "What is it with you? Part of being a team member is helping out when you're needed."

"And part of being a supervisor is making sure that you delegate tasks equally," Ledi replied. She was shocked at how calm her voice sounded even though her face felt like it was flaming and her breathing was thin. "Whenever you have some grunt work you come searching for me, even though I'm one of the most experienced people in the lab. You call me out for being late, but give Kevin a pass for magically getting sick every time he's up for sac duty. I said 'no.'"

They stood glaring at each other. Ledi was already formulating rebuttals, was already prepared for whatever he would say to make her the offending party in the situation. She was done putting up with people's shit.

Apparently, oh-sure-I'll-do-that Ledi had been incinerated by the flames of her frustration and I-wish-a-motherfucker-would Ledi had risen from the ashes.

Try me, she thought as their standoff continued, but then the door to the lab opened. Ledi turned to see a woman enter, long dark hair brushing against her fuchsia blouse.

"Dr. Taketami?" Ledi hadn't seen her PI in three weeks. "I didn't know you were back yet."

"I got back from the immunology conference last night. Still jet-lagged," she said with a smile. "I'm calling in a favor today, though. I have someone who's interested in learning more about our laboratory, and I'd like you to show him around."

"Ledi was about to perform the saccing actually," Brian said, a smug smile on his face.

"I was actually about to do my own work. I'm pretty tired of doing yours, too."

Dr. Taketami looked back and forth between them. "Brian, go wait for me in my office."

He made a sound of objection, but Dr. Taketami was already focused on Ledi again. "I know you have work to do, but you've been specifically requested."

"That's a thing? Why would someone request me?"

Ledi was trying to process everything that had happened. She'd said no to Brian. And then again in front of their PI. And everything was fine. Relief coursed through her, but it was quickly replaced by apprehension. Nothing good had happened in the last few days without exacting a hefty toll. Why should that pattern suddenly deviate?

The door to the lab opened and all thoughts were blotted out by anger.

This motherfucker.

"What are you doing here?" she demanded as Thabiso strode into the lab with that damned long-legged regality of his. He wore dress pants and a finely woven shirt with some kind of hexagonal pattern in red, black, and yellow that almost distracted from the smooth dark brown skin of his forearms.

Naledi whirled toward Dr. Taketami. "No way. Sorry, you'll have to find someone else to show him around."

"Ms. Smith!" A firm grip landed on her bicep, even though Dr. Taketami was smiling with all of her teeth. "This man is a donor. A Very. Generous. Donor."

"So you're pawning me off to some strange man for money?" Ledi asked in a low voice. "There's a term for that you know."

Dr. Taketami leaned in close and whispered, "Is this guy a stalker or something? If so, I'll get security. If not, the deans would really appreciate you fulfilling this request. The governmental cuts have hit the program hard. They're unprecedented and without donations, we're in some real trouble."

Ledi glared at Thabiso. His chin was raised haughtily in the air, but his gaze was nervous?

Dr. Taketami continued. "And, if you take a minute to talk to him, he may have the solution to your practicum problem."

"I've already found a replacement field study since the university left me in the lurch," Ledi shot back, but then remembered the theatrics of the night before. Was Dr. Okri still interested in working with her after the scene she'd been a part of? People had undoubtedly started gossiping before she even left the room. Was that internship still even on the table?

She glared at Thabiso and Dr. Taketami stepped in front of her.

"I don't know what you found, but the probability of it being as useful to your career as this is doubtful. And I'm not just saying that to get you to do what I want. This could be huge, for both you and the program."

Ledi narrowed her gaze and crossed her arms over her chest. She hated that her career was being used as an enticement, but she was curious now and Dr. Taketami knew it. The woman looked back and forth between the Ledi and Thabiso. "Shall I leave you to it, then?"

"Sure," Ledi said. "If you have Brian do my data processing, as well as the saccing."

Dr. Taketami grinned. "He'll do it and he'll like it. Stop by my office when the tour is over." With that she hustled off.

Ledi dropped her gaze to Thabiso's shoes, then remembered that *she'd* done nothing wrong and met his gaze. A tremor ran through her when she did, and she desperately wished it was only disgust. She hated that she remembered how his hands felt brushing against her most sensitive skin, how lush his mouth felt against hers. She hated how he was looking at her, with that damned Disney-fied, wide-eyed innocence. Like he hadn't somehow wiggled his way into her life and exploded it from the inside. She'd thought he might be a virus from the moment she'd seen him, and she'd been right—she just hadn't realized how fast-acting he'd be.

"So this is the equipment for the vermin murder you mentioned the other day?" He asked the question as if he was entitled to reminisce after what he'd done. An angry flush spread over her skin.

"What are you doing here? You think throwing your money around will make things all better,

Prince?" she asked. She'd said she'd do the tour, not that she'd kiss his ass.

He laughed, a deep rich sound that insinuated itself under her clothing and pressed up against her skin. Ledi steeled herself against the sensation.

"Even I know there are some things money can't buy," he said, and now that she looked at him she could see the regret in his eyes. "But you have to know that I was going to tell you—"

"No. You paid for an informational session, not for the chance to worm your way back into my life."

Thabiso leaned back as if evading a blow. "I understand that I've ruined everything, but do you not think you deserve an explanation?"

Ledi rolled her eyes.

"Explanations are for people who care, and I'm not in that cohort. I don't need you," she said. "I don't need anyone."

The words had always been the truth before, but they felt like a lie now, one that tripped clumsily to the ground and drew everyone's pitying stares.

"I wish I could say the same," he said, shoving his hands into his pockets.

"This is the lab," Ledi said in a flat tone, spreading her hands out like a lethargic museum guide. She refused to listen to any more of his lies, especially when it was so tempting to believe them. "Science stuff happens. Kind of like magic, but with more paperwork."

"I don't want a tour, Naledi," Thabiso said quietly.

"Here are the high-powered microscopes," she said with a wave of her arm. "When you look into them you can see the tiniest details of a life-form. Nothing hides from that Zeiss lens. It's really too bad there isn't one for screening men like you."

She hadn't meant to say that, but seeing him in front of her and not hating his guts as much as she should have was upsetting.

"Naledi." His fingertips brushed her arm and she stepped away from the sensation that webbed over her skin. She refused to look up at him, but she could smell the familiar scent of him. The scent of happiness. Her throat went rough. If he made her cry in the lab, she would at the very least pretend to infect him with anthrax.

"I'm not engaged," he said. "If nothing else, you must know that. That was a misunderstanding—there is no one else."

Ledi didn't acknowledge the relief that perfused her, rushing through her veins, making visible just how foolish she was. There was no reason to give him the benefit of the doubt except for the fact that he was there in front of her instead of swimming in a pool of money or whatever it was princes did in their spare time. It didn't change anything though.

"I believe you mean there's no one at all," she corrected.

He inhaled sharply.

"I've always believed that once something is done, there is no going back," he said. "That people should pay for mistakes. That's mostly because I was also taught that it wasn't possible for me to make them."

She glanced up at him, wanting to smack the sheepish grin off of his face.

"I'm selfish. Entitled. You witnessed that firsthand the day you met me," he said. "But I'm a prince, Ledi. Before this week, I'd never had to think of anything beyond myself and my people. I saw getting what I wanted, when I wanted, as a fair bargain for a life of servitude."

"Servitude? I have Google you know. I finally looked you up and it seems like a pretty sweet life to me. Servants. A palace. Beloved by your people. Forgive me if I don't shed a tear for you."

Thabiso frowned. "You may sneer at my riches, but that's the life you would have had if your parents hadn't fled. You would likely already be my wife, living in that palace, being waited on by those servants, and beloved by your people. Our people."

Ledi took a deep breath, one that bordered much too close to a gasp. When she was a child, in those strange homes, she'd told herself the silliest stories as she lay awake at night. Stories with castles and royalty, and where foster homes only showed up in nightmares. She'd long ago buried all of those foolish dreams, but now they were being dragged back to the surface.

"Why are you doing this? If what you say is true, my parents are the only thing that tied me to Thesolo. They're dead. Any ridiculous pact they made when I was a child has nothing to do with me."

The words were cold, but she needed cold to fight the hot tears rising in her. He knew everything about her, and she knew nothing. This was about more than his betrayal now; living in the dark had allowed her to go through life in her self-contained way. Now he was offering to bring her into the light, and that would change everything. Fear gripped her tight with this one simple truth: if she knew who her parents were, she would know what she'd lost, what she'd been denied.

She wasn't sure she could take that.

Jamal—Thabiso—nodded. "I shouldn't ask anything of you, but a good prince is also a businessman. I have an offer that is mutually beneficial."

Ledi wanted to turn and walk off, but she couldn't even if she tried. If those emails were true . . .

"Spit it out," she said.

"My country is in the midst of a medical crisis," he said. "My people are falling ill with a sickness that seemingly has no source and our best doctors have been unable to resolve it. This has caused several problems, including people turning to witchcraft and superstition for explanations."

He sighed and scrubbed his hand through his beard.

"There is a small but important sect of religious leaders who believe that this sickness has befallen my people because the goddess is unhappy with me."

Ledi tilted her head, as if that would help her to understand better. "For being a lying jerk?" she asked.

His gaze flicked to hers, then away. "For remaining unmarried."

"Are you fucking—"

"Hear me out, Naledi." He held out his hand to stay her, but his fingers curled away from her skin and into his own palm at the last second. Ledi wished she didn't feel a pang of regret at the near miss with his fingertips. "This is my proposal. Come to Thesolo. I will give you unfettered access to my team of epidemiologists and doctors as they track this situation. Novel, is what the scientists are calling it. Novelties are quite important in your field, if I'm not mistaken."

Dammit, he was right. Working at the NYC Health Department would give her something to write about, but it would be a bottom of the barrel thesis unless something remarkable happened. She was fairly certain no other grad students in her contingent, and perhaps the whole of the US, would have access to a small-scale outbreak in a homogenous African kingdom. She hated that people were suffering, but if she went, she'd get to help stop that and to make a name for herself all in one shot. And . . .

"You can also learn about your history. Your people. The country you never knew."

"I told you that I don't care about that," Ledi said, even though her heart squeezed at his words.

"You can meet your family," he said quietly, as if he were ashamed to pull that card.

"I . . . I have family?" She felt a brief, unexpected burst of joy, followed by a chaser of rage. "I have family and you waited to tell me?"

The words came out louder than she had controlled for. Thabiso flinched and Ledi pressed her lips together, mentally slicing away at the anger and hope and betrayal that were coagulating around her. She couldn't be overwhelmed. She refused.

"I asked you directly and you said you didn't want to know," he said. "Was I supposed to force the information on you against your will?"

"Yes!" A fierce whisper, then she remembered how adamant she'd been at Fort Tryon Park. "No. Well, just tell me now."

"You have an uncle and a cousin. Your grandparents, your mother's parents, are among those who have fallen ill. We're trying to save them."

Ledi stared at him; she was shit at telling if he was lying, but she couldn't believe he'd sink so low as to lie about that.

"What do I have to do? And what's in this for you?"

Thabiso sighed, but this time he didn't look away.

"You don't have to do anything more than you've ever done, really," he said. "You just have to be my betrothed."

Ledi held one hand to her forehead and another up in front of Thabiso. "Wait. *Wait*. You came here to apologize for lying about your identity, and now you're asking me to lie about mine? You're ridiculous."

"I'm not asking you to lie," he said. "You are my betrothed, by royal and religious decree. I'm not asking you to pretend that you love me—"

"Good. I'm a scientist, not an actress, Bones."

"Bones?"

She stared at him, and he dropped the query.

"Never mind. Right." Thabiso shoved his hands deeper into his pockets. "Rumors are already spreading after the event last night, but we can spin this. We can go with the story that you were unaware of who I was, who you were, and you can return a prodigal daughter. That should placate people who were angry about your parents fleeing. Then, once the outbreak is handled and things go back to normal, you can say that you miss the US and go back home."

Ledi was trying so hard not to care, but his last words shanked her right in a vulnerable spot. Some stupid romantic part of her had hoped he might beg her to stay, even if that was the last thing she wanted. Didn't she deserve that lie, too? Then she remembered that no one ever wanted her around for long.

Defective Velcro.

She almost told him no.

This is for work. This could make your career.

"Fine. I'll pretend to be your betrothed," she said holding out her hand. She squeezed his hand hard, and then dropped it. "And then I'll leave."

Chapter 22

*L*edi had packed and repacked her suitcase several times over the course of the last week, between bench exams, finding a mouse sitter for the Grams, and getting last-minute vaccinations, a passport, and special visas that were expedited at the behest of the Thesoloian Consulate.

All that, and dodging Portia.

> I should have just confronted him myself and asked once I was suspicious. I didn't think it would hurt you this much if I was right.

Ledi had to admit that she'd spent years convincing Portia, and herself, that nothing a man did could hurt her. But Portia should have known how much *she* could hurt Ledi.

> I shouldn't make excuses. What I did was wrong, and I'm so sorry.

Ledi put the phone away, her sadness weighing down on her. She missed her friend, despite Portia's ridiculous, thoughtless behavior, but she needed time to think before speaking to her. She needed to figure out how to break the bad patterns of their friendship and create better ones, and whether Portia would be able to do the same.

This was why her phospholipid bilayer was so important. Once someone got through, it was all over. They could hurt deeply and she'd still care about them. Caring was the worst, despite its evolutionary necessity.

She refocused on her packing, deciding between a more reserved skirt set and bright pink skinny jeans. She stuffed both into the suitcase and zipped it resolutely. There was no perfect outfit for meeting your countrypeople for the first time. Or for making a prince eat his heart out.

Don't be ridiculous.

She'd barely see Thabiso—she hated that name. Each time she had to mentally correct from Jamal to Thabiso it was a reminder of how she'd been played for a fool. What's in a name? Acute embarrassment, apparently.

She had plenty of things to keep her occupied while she was there; she'd downloaded all available info about the possible epidemic and dozens of case studies onto her phone to read during the long flight. She'd also compiled the emails about Thesolo, the most recent ones that had suddenly started explaining the country's history and culture. She now realized those emails had been Likotsi—Thabiso's mystery friend, actually his assistant, who she'd met in the hallway of her building—prepping her for Thabiso's confession that never came to fruition.

She'd read through all of those already, soaking up the facts and photos like a sponge left away from the water until it was hard and dry. It was too much to absorb at once, and she'd read them again and again, telling herself it was the same thing she'd do with any assignment she received in class. The only unread email's subject was right to the point: **Libiko and Kembe Ajoua, Your Parents.** Ledi hadn't been able to lie to herself about that one, so she hadn't opened it. Not yet.

Her phone rang, the sound jolting her out of her reverie.

"Ms. Naledi Ajoua, betrothed to His Royal Highness Prince, Bringer of Light and Love, Thabiso Moshoeshoe of Thesolo?" The man on the other line could have been an auctioneer with his smooth, fast delivery.

It jolted her, hearing her real surname instead of the one on all of her legal documents. Smith had given her anonymity, ensured she was always at the back of the class and at the bottom of lists. Ajoua was a front of the class, top of alphabetically ordered lists kind of name. It was a name that didn't allow for shrinking. She wondered what her life would have been like if the social workers hadn't found her parents' fake identification papers, but that led down the perilous path of wondering what her life would have been like if her parents had lived and why they'd had fake IDs to begin with.

"This is she," Ledi said, automatically slipping into formality even though she was considering hanging up and throwing her phone into the trash compactor, for real this time.

"I'm your driver, hired by the Thesoloian Consulate to bring you to the airport. Do you need me to come up and get your bags?"

Well, that was certainly way better service than she was used to. Likotsi had said she needn't worry about a thing in regards to her trip to Thesolo, and the woman had meant it.

"No, I'm good," she said. "I'll be down in five."

"I'd be more than happy to assist," the driver pressed.

"I need a moment," Ledi said, looking around her tidy apartment. She touched the space on the windowsill where the Grams' cage usually sat and took a deep breath.

"I understand. Take your time."

"Thanks." She locked the phone and slipped it into her pocket.

She steeled herself against the enormity of what awaited her as she rolled her suitcase out of the apartment and locked the door behind her. She had lived her entire life—what she could remember of it—rootless, being passed around like brussels sprouts at dinner before they became trendy. Now she was about to take a trip to the motherland, her actual motherland, and she had no idea of what she should be feeling.

The door to apartment 7 N opened and Mrs. Garcia, tanned and radiant, peeked her head out.

"Hey, *linda*! I've barely seen you since I got back and now you're leaving?"

Ledi tried not to look like someone who'd done unmentionable things on her neighbor's sofa. "Hi! How was your trip?"

"It was amazing! I got to go to the beach—a real beach—see my family, and catch up with friends I hadn't spoken to since I left when I was a teenager." Mrs. Garcia grinned. "That rich guy who sent me on the vacation so he could stay here? I think he was an angel. Really. It's crazy how one person can show up and *boom*! Suddenly your life is completely different."

Ledi decided against telling Mrs. Garcia that Thabiso was a lying fraud who used his wealth to get what he wanted.

What had he wanted, exactly?

It didn't matter. Mrs. Garcia was happy, and she wasn't necessarily wrong. Ledi's life had certainly taken a turn in the last two weeks. Whether it was for the better or the worse was still up for debate.

"DiDi! *Ven aqui, mi amor!*" A gruff male voice called out from the recesses of the apartment. That's when Ledi realized that only Mrs. Garcia's head and shoulder—bare shoulder—were visible through the cracked door.

"I have to go," she said with a sly smile. Ledi distinctly heard the sound of footsteps approaching, and then Mrs. Garcia's face went pink. "An old friend I reconnected with in PR is visiting. You know how it is. Um. Ah! Have a good trip!"

The door slammed closed and low laughter—male and female—sounded from behind it, followed by the squeal of plastic. Ledi wished Mrs. Garcia better luck in love than she'd had.

She took the seven flights of stairs slower than she ever had, and was so lost in her trepidation as she stepped out of the building that it took her a moment to notice the small crowd. Several people were holding up their cell phones.

"You think someone famous is in there?" a teenager zooming in on his iPhone asked.

"Yo, what if it's Beyoncé?" his friend asked.

The crowd was staring excitedly at the long, sleek limo double-parked in front of the building. Ledi got pulled into the excitement; if Beyoncé had randomly dropped by the neighborhood, she might have to tell her driver to wait.

The car door opened and a balding man in a black suit got out and scanned the crowd.

He smiled in recognition when his gaze landed on her. "Ms. Ajoua?"

He began walking toward her, and the crowd parted, their camera phones turning toward her as the driver took her suitcase from her. "Follow me, please."

Ledi stood still for a moment. "I'm not Beyoncé," she said, confused.

"Damn right you're not," an older woman in the crowd said.

"No need to be rude, madam," the driver said with a disapproving look, then took Ledi's arm and escorted her toward the limo. He opened the door and inclined slightly, waiting for her to enter.

"I think there's been some kind of mistake," Ledi said.

"Are you Naledi Ajoua, betrothed of His Ro—"

"Yes, that's me," she said, cutting him off. People were recording and she didn't need word of her fake engagement getting around the neighborhood, or the internet. She'd kept a low profile for years, and this limo business would be hard enough to explain when she got back. Because she'd be back eventually, alone as ever, and didn't need her neighbors thinking she'd lost a prince when the truth was she'd never had him.

"Then there is no mistake. Get in, and I'll have you to the airport in no time at all."

Ledi climbed into the limo and sat awkwardly in the middle of the backseat. She felt ridiculous in the enormous interior of the car, which was decked out in sleek wood and smelled of leather and something she couldn't quite place.

Money, she thought. *A scent you're not too familiar with.*

"Are you comfortable?" The driver's voice filled the car, emanating from hidden surround sound speakers, as they pulled into traffic. "There are beverages in the refrigerator and a crudité platter and some appetizers. If you'd prefer something warm, there are some microwaveable items."

"There's a microwave?" she asked.

"Of course," the driver replied, as if she'd questioned his honor. "There's also a Keurig if you need coffee or tea."

"Thank you," Ledi said. Traffic was moving pretty smoothly, but she worried they would hit a snarl along the way. "What is the exact time of my flight, by the way? Likotsi only told me when to be ready for the car service to pick me up."

There was a pause. "Pardon?"

"What time is my flight?" Ledi repeated. She looked around to see if there was some kind of intercom button so he could hear her better. When she pressed a small button on the interior wall beside her head, a panel slid away revealing a touch screen dotted with various icons. One with a martini glass likely represented the bar. One with wavy lines seemed to represent the AC. She wasn't sure what the icon with the flames represented, but figured it was best not to touch that lest she end up a victim of her curiosity.

"I imagine it's in about an hour and a half," he said, much too vague for Ledi's liking.

"Are you sure?" she asked. She tapped an icon with a bottle of water on it and another panel slid open, revealing an empty cubbyhole. A second later a petite bottle of mineral water dropped down.

What the hell?

"I read that you're supposed to get to the airport two hours ahead of time. I don't want to miss the flight and have to rebook."

A chuckle came through the speakers. "The flight won't leave without you, so please relax and enjoy the ride. If there's any particular music you'd like to listen to, you can sync your phone to the car's audio system."

Ledi pulled out her phone and selected the latest episode of her favorite science podcast. The familiar voices of the hosts bantering about gut microbiota soothed her for the rest of the ride.

They hit a bit of traffic and Ledi fought panic that she'd show up at the airport just in time to see her plane take off. She'd never been through security before, but Portia always said it was a nightmare if you didn't have TSA PreCheck.

Portia.

Ledi wished she could have asked her friend what to expect on the flight, what to wear to meet a royal family. Portia knew the ins and outs of this high society kind of stuff, but Ledi would have to figure it out on her own.

She felt a twinge of guilt; she was flying to see Thabiso but ignoring her best friend? She stopped herself from going down that self-recriminating path. The bottom line was she was still mad as hell and her trust was bruised and battered. Whatever she was doing with Thabiso was a sham and would be over soon enough. Her next steps with Portia . . . She needed time, and she would take it. If their friendship couldn't survive that, it wasn't much of one.

The limo pulled up to the airport, and Ledi gave in to the impulse she'd been fighting the entire ride. She glanced around the limo, then quickly tapped the flames icon on the digital menu. For a moment there was silence and she was sure she'd activated the self-destruct sequence, but then a panel at the opposite end of the car slid up and a fireplace roared to life.

Who needs a fireplace in a car?

Ledi's door opened and she quickly tapped the icon so that the fireplace went out. A dark-skinned woman in a pink suit poked her head in.

"Ms. Ajoua?"

"Yes." Ledi appreciated that the woman had kept it simple and left out Thabiso's titles.

"I'm Natalie, your airport liaison. Come with me, please."

The driver wished her a good flight and handed off her suitcase to Natalie, who was walking so quickly that Ledi had to jog to keep up.

"I have your passport," Natalie said as they walked by a snaking line of people. "You're much lovelier in person."

"Thanks. I think. Is that the line for security?" Ledi asked. She was definitely going to miss her flight.

"For commoners," Natalie replied briskly. "You get an expedited check in."

"Like preapproval?"

The woman laughed. "Also for commoners. Do you think the Queen of England waits in the TSA preapproved line?"

Ledi had never had to consider such things. She couldn't imagine the queen hanging out in an airport, but she supposed she had to get around somehow.

Natalie stopped in front of a door that read Authorized Personnel Only and swiped a key.

"Right this way."

Behind the door was a long hallway that led them to an area with an entirely different atmosphere from the echoing chaos they had just passed through. Classical music piped out through low speakers and the light was warm instead of fluorescent. Beyond the metal detector, there were framed photos on the wall and velvety wallpaper and plush couches instead of plastic seats. She was underdressed in her jeans and sneakers, which was overdressed for flights where people could often be found wearing their pajama pants.

"Wait right here," the woman said, and approached the TSA officer seated at a wooden desk. She showed him Ledi's passport and placed her bag through a scanner, then walked through a metal detector. "Come on, Ms. Ajoua."

Ledi followed her, and a moment later they were walking through a clean comfortable-looking seating area. Expensive looking chairs rested on bright area rugs, interspersed with wooden tables outfitted with chargers, magazines, lotions, and other necessities.

"I didn't know this kind of place existed," Ledi said, gawking at the opulence around her. She'd heard so many terrible stories about what a shitshow LaGuardia was. If only people knew that while they waited for three-day-old pizza from Sbarro's, there was a four-star restaurant with comfy leather chairs and gourmet meals.

"Very few people do," the woman said. "Celebrities sometimes try to get in here, but to no avail. This is Gate R, the Royal boarding area. Come, come."

Ledi was falling behind Natalie's high-speed pace again.

"Is everyone else boarded?" Ledi asked, noticing how empty the area was.

Natalie glanced back at her, not missing a step. "There is no one else. You're it."

They stepped up to the huge glass windows that looked out onto the tarmac. Sitting outside was the kind of jet Ledi had only seen in articles decrying the carbon footprints of the rich and famous. A yellow flower was painted onto the fin of the plane.

Ledi's stomach flipped and she stopped, letting Natalie continue on without her.

It was crazy enough to be going to Thesolo. But the limo. The secret gate. The sleek plane waiting to ferry her around the world. She was a woman who lived in a tiny apartment with two mice, who ate a steady diet of ramen and swaddled her phone in layers of protection because breaking it would be unthinkable.

Is this real life?

Up ahead, Natalie was at the door to the tarmac handing off Ledi's bag to a member of the flight crew.

"Princess! Time to go!"

Ledi looked around to see who she was talking to, then remembered what she was heading toward. She walked to Natalie on shaky legs.

"I'm not a princess," she said.

Natalie shrugged. "You're close enough. If you weren't, you wouldn't be listed as 'fiancée of Prince Thabiso' and you wouldn't be at Gate R."

Ledi placed a hand over her stomach, willing herself not to puke. Not to run away before she got to Thesolo and was faced with the fact that no one there wanted her either. "I can't do this. I *can* vomit, though, and I might do that instead."

Natalie sighed. When she spoke, some of the stiff formality was gone from her voice. "Look, I'm not a therapist or anything, but I'm going to advise you to chill. You're about to get on a plane and have a delicious meal, get you some wine, sleep in a comfortable bed—"

"There's a bed?"

"There's a bed, and I guarantee it's more comfortable than anything you've slept on in your life," Natalie said with a bit of envy. "You're gonna do all that, and then wake up in a place where you can either tell people you're not a princess or do what I would do given the opportunity."

"And what's that?" Ledi asked.

"Live a little." Natalie smiled. "Do it for those of us who are stuck at LaGuardia every day, watching the planes fly out and never getting on them. Gate R is fancy, but it's still in Queens."

Ledi nodded. This was the opportunity of a lifetime, and she wasn't going to let nerves—or an annoying prince—blow it for her.

"Thank you, Natalie."

"Just doing my job! Enjoy your flight."

With that she was off.

The crewman with Ledi's luggage beckoned her out onto the tarmac. She stepped outside, where the roar of the engine filled her ears, blocking out the sound of her rapidly beating heart.

"Thesolo, here I come."

Chapter 23

Thabiso stood on the tarmac at Kwetsi International Airport with the highland winds at his front and the royal retinue at his back—he wasn't sure which was colder.

His gaze tracked the plane as it emerged from behind Thesolo's world-famous mountain range and began its descent. He took a fortifying breath and glanced at his parents: the king tall and slim; the queen matching her husband in height, stature, and frown of disapproval. Thabiso's plan to cede to the demands of his people while doctors and scientists tracked the disease that stalked them hadn't gone quite as planned.

"Really, Thabiso," his mother said, glaring at him from the corner of her eye, "you should have told us about this search for the defector. We would have told you it was unnecessary. Between this and making that scene at the gala—so every auntie from here to Khartoum was wagging their tongues about it—what are we supposed to tell Shanti's parents?"

Shanti, the woman who was living proof that his parents had not been joking when they'd said that if he didn't find a bride they'd find one for him, was back at the palace, doing whatever it was a woman did when her life's purpose was to become a queen. He'd met with her briefly to inform her that they would not be marrying, but his parents and hers had put other ideas into her head. She was nice enough, but nice wasn't what he wanted. Right now, she was just another worry to add to a plate that was already piled high with them.

"Tell them that you're sorry but you'll have to return her," he said bluntly. "If you weren't going about snapping up fiancées for me like they were half-ripe fruit at the market, we wouldn't be in this situation."

"Son." It was just one word from his father, but Thabiso heard all that lay beneath it. *Boy, don't think just because you're grown you can talk to your mother in that tone.*

It was the verbal equivalent of a tug at the ear.

"I apologize, Mother. I'm just nervous right now."

"Why should you be nervous? Just because this girl's deceitful parents abandoned their duties is no reason to think she'll desert you and make a fool of you before your people. Is there?" The queen's smile was a bit too knowing for Thabiso's taste.

"You should be happy she's returned to fulfill the will of the goddess, Mother," Thabiso said quietly.

"Her parents should have never left. It was an unforgivable betrayal, and one they can't be held to account for because—" Thabiso glanced at her when the words cut off, but her face was carefully neutral. An outsider would have thought her completely calm, but Thabiso knew it was a front; she was the one who had taught him to do the same, after all.

Public displays of emotion are for commoners, Thabiso.

"We shall see whether this child of the traitors Libi and Kembe is worthy," she said grimly.

The man behind her cleared his throat loudly.

"I'm sure my niece is quite up to the standards of *your* family, Your Highness." Alehk Jarami had been a boil on Thabiso's ass since his return, more interested in the failed Omega Corp deal than the fact that his niece had been found, so Thabiso was glad that he seemed to have finally begun to take her return seriously. Naledi needed people on her side, and though he wished her uncle wasn't a self-interested buffoon, Alehk was one of the few family members she had.

"We shall see," was all his mother replied, not bothering to hide her doubt.

Thabiso had never thought his mother exceptionally rude, but then again his outlook on life had shifted drastically over the last week.

The drone of the jet's engine drowned out any further awkward conversation, and all of Thabiso's attention focused on the plane as it taxied down the tarmac. The noise from the crowd grew as people shouted over the engine noise—it was the largest crowd Thabiso had seen in ages, spread out over the snow-dusted grass on either side of the tarmac. He'd known there'd be some interest, but the welcoming party had quickly turned into unprecedented crowds. They'd had to call in additional security to ensure everyone's safety. Vendors had set up stands selling caps and T-shirts emblazoned with #RoyalReunion, which was apparently the official social media hashtag. They also sold surgical masks for those worried about the mystery disease. Press from all over the continent had arrived to capture the moment when Africa's Most Eligible Bachelor introduced his betrothed.

No pressure.

When the plane finally drew to a stop and the engines powered down, several tribal representatives, each clad in the intricately woven cloaks of their people, formed a procession behind the ground crew. A red carpet was unfurled at the foot of the Jetway and strewn with flower petals, scenting the air with hope. The citizens of the council lined up along the carpet, some smiling uncertainly, others wearing dubious expressions. Ledi's family's betrayal had been a source of national discontent, but now the populace was being told to welcome her back unconditionally. For a moment, Thabiso wished he could play the role of Jamal amongst his own people, to move among them as a normal citizen so that he could know their thoughts and feelings. But Jamal was retired, and the people's doubtful expressions would have to suffice.

Only the children—whether the goatherds barely taller than their wards or the young choir members nervously awaiting their moment in the sun—were unequivocally happy about the arrival of their soon-to-be princess.

The children and Thabiso.

He'd tried to resign himself to the fact that he had ruined things. When it came to love, people were often given second chances. Unfortunately, he'd already used up his second chance and was sure that third ones were rather rare.

But even though she detested him—even though he deserved her detestation—she had still come. He'd been alerted as soon as she'd boarded the plane. He would get to see her rediscover the country she had forgotten, and he just might be able to help with the career that was so important to her. It was a paltry consolation prize compared to having her as his own, but it still made him happy to know that perhaps her life could be different—better—now. That she wouldn't be alone anymore, even if she wasn't with him.

The low-level murmuring of the crowd grew louder as the door of the plane opened and she stepped out. Her T-shirt, completely inappropriate for the low temperatures of winter in the mountains, was rumpled from the long flight and she blinked like an owl in the bright afternoon sun. She wore no makeup, and the thick hair that he knew was soft to the touch was pulled into a messy ponytail atop her head and wrapped in a scarf. She moved to smooth a palm over her hair, and then a look of shock crossed her face. She ran back into the plane only to emerge a moment later, scarf gone, hair down around her shoulders. She smiled nervously and brought a hand to her stomach.

"This is who you choose over Shanti?" his mother asked through her tight smile.

"Indeed."

He realized in that moment that he was exactly the selfish bastard that Naledi thought he was. That he would be happy for her altruistically, platonically? Yet another lie in a long string of them. She stood at the door to the plane, green under her brown skin and dressed like she was going to the bodega, and he wanted her so badly that he had to close his fists against it.

He wanted to feel those hips that swayed as she walked down the plane's steps beneath his hands. He wanted to taste the lips that pulled into a smile as a boy approached and handed her a bouquet of flowers. He wanted Naledi Ajoua, even though he had no right to her—despite their betrothal, only she could bequeath him with that honor. The warmth in his chest transformed into a throb, one that synced with each step Ledi took toward him.

"Sire. You are making her walk into a strange land, toward a strange people, alone." The tip of Likotsi's pointy Italian loafer dug into the back of his ankle, propelling him into action.

Thabiso moved toward Ledi, and although the first step was one of uncertainty, the next brought him closer to her, and there was assuredly nothing he wanted more than that. He knew that she knew he was approaching, although she kept her attention on a little girl who had grabbed her by the hand and gazed up adoringly.

"Welcome home, my dear Naledi," he said as he approached, his voice almost drowned out by the children's chorus that had begun to sing their national anthem. She finally turned to him.

"Oh hi, *dear*," she said with a wry smile. "Nice crown."

He touched the ring of platinum encircling his head. He'd forgotten it was there, even though it was supposed to serve as a constant reminder, like a wedding band.

He shrugged. "Oh this old thing? This is my casual crown. The formal one is eight inches tall."

She wrinkled her nose.

"We Moshoeshoes are not known for our subtlety," he said.

"The princess is boo-the-ful," the little girl holding Ledi's hand said, ducking her head shyly.

"That she is."

The girl darted back into the crowd when Thabiso addressed her, hiding behind her mother's long patterned skirt.

"*She* is also underdressed," Ledi said through chattering teeth. "Isn't it supposed to be hot in Africa?"

He could see her shivering; she was still dressed for spring in the Northern Hemisphere, not winter in the Southern. He removed his thick wool cloak and wrapped it around her. A gasp went through the crowd. Sharing one's cloak was an act of intimacy; it was like sharing your second skin. As he pulled the collar closed, he noticed the thin, serpentine metal glinting against her collarbone.

The necklace.

What did it mean that she still wore his gift? Hope, stronger than the logic that told him nothing could bring Ledi back to him, spread in his chest like one of the great winged creatures said to serve Ingoka's will.

He inhaled deeply as he tucked the collar of the cloak and fixed it in place with a button. "It is hot on some parts of the continent. Your current location is fifteen hundred feet above sea level, nestled in the mountains, and it is winter. It's ski season here."

"Of course," Ledi muttered.

Thabiso wondered how Naledi, lover of data, had been remiss in reading up on the local climate. He was sure Likotsi would have informed her in one of her emails, but then he remembered how Naledi ignored that which caused her emotional discomfort.

"Are you ready to meet your people?"

"I guess." She was looking down at her sneakers.

He held his hand out, and when she took it warily, he tugged her toward him, gently folding her arm under his so that she was pressed against him along one side.

"What—"

"Mother, Father, esteemed citizens of Thesolo, and our guests. I present to you my future wife, and your future queen: Naledi Ajoua." Polite clapping broke out from the crowds that had gathered to witness this historic event. He felt Ledi stiffen beside him. "Although she is one of us, it has been many years since her feet touched this sacred soil. The people of Thesolo are world renowned for their kindness and hospitality, and I have no doubt you will help show her just how wonderful her homeland—our homeland—truly is."

That bit was met with thunderous applause. It never hurt to compliment people when you were asking them to do you a favor. He was trying to recruit two hundred thousand wingmen—he needed all the help he could get.

"Um. There are a lot of people. Looking at me. And holding up their cell phones and taking pictures."

Thabiso glanced down and noticed that Ledi was breathing shallowly and her eyes were wide with panic.

"Thousands. Like cells on a hemocytometer. If there are eight people per square foot, and you multiply that by . . ."

Thabiso hadn't even thought of how she'd react to the crowd. Although she'd made a crack about putting him under a microscope, the truth of the matter was that he always had been. He expected to be stared at and photographed as soon as he left the privacy of the palace grounds.

He didn't know what to say to calm her.

Instead, he lifted his hand to her face and brushed his knuckles along her jawline. Her gaze darted to his, but her breathing didn't slow. In fact, she was breathing more quickly now, and her eyes had gone a little unfocused—how she'd looked before he'd thrust into her back in her tiny apartment. Before she'd clenched and cried out at only the smallest fraction of the pleasure he'd wanted to give her.

Desire stirred, but the biggest photo opportunity in

a generation wasn't the ideal place to display the royal member.

"People are looking at you, yes, but you need fear nothing from their judgment."

Her skin warmed beneath his hand.

"Is this what your life is like here?" The sounds of thousands of digital shutters clicking made her glance away from him. She squeezed her eyes shut.

"It's usually not quite this intense, but I am royalty. Celebrity is part of the package." He shrugged. "I guess it's the princely equivalent of the ritual animal murder you participate in."

"Sacrifice," she corrected. Thabiso felt her smile against his knuckles, and it washed over him like the rush of a great waterfall.

"Whatever you wish to call it. Like your sacrifice, it's not fun, but it's necessary for achieving my goals."

If he moved his hand just a bit, he could trace the outline of her mouth with his fingertips . . .

"You can stop touching me now," she said, turning her head and breaking contact with him. "I thought we weren't going to pretend."

He hated to lose the feel of her soft skin, but he pulled his hand away. "I'm not pretending."

He turned to find his parents watching with the bland, regal expression that had frightened him as a child because it was so different from the loving, expressive parents he knew.

"Come. It is time to meet my parents."

He could feel Ledi's intake of breath and the straightening of her spine. Likotsi had wondered whether she'd be up to the task; Thabiso's only question was if it was worthy of her.

They stopped in front of his parents, who had gone into full "frosty royal" mode. They looked down at her as if she were a gaudy souvenir he'd picked up at the airport gift shop.

"Mother. Father. Allow me to reintroduce my bride-to-be, Naledi Ajoua."

Naledi shifted nervously then gave a little wave. "Queen Ramatla, King Lerumo. It's a pleasure to meet you."

The queen ran her eyes over Ledi in frank assessment and sniffed.

"I hope in the future she chooses more appropriate attire for public appearances. This sartorial choice is quite unbecoming of a supposed future queen."

Thabiso had known his parents would be upset, but he'd thought his finally being committed to marriage would smooth over any rough edges. That would be too damn simple of course.

"The view from the plane was beautiful," Ledi said. "I was looking down at the mountains and waterfalls and wondering why my parents would leave such a place." She returned the assessing look his mother had just given her. "Thank you for clearing that up for me."

The queen inhaled sharply and the king's thick eyebrows rose.

Naledi looked up at Thabiso. "Your family is *delightful*, but I'd prefer to meet mine now if that's all right."

"I am here, my niece." Alehk stepped forward, and before Thabiso could make an appropriate introduction, Ledi was pulled from his side and engulfed in a hug. "My god, you are so grown-up! The last time I saw you, you were up to my knee!"

Ledi stared at him. "I'm sorry, I don't remember. I—"

"Do not apologize." Alehk wiped at his eyes. "I am your uncle Alehk. I represent the Jaramis, as your grandparents, our village elders, are at hospital. This is your cousin, Nyakalla."

A thin, slightly hunched over young woman wearing a dark blue cloak and black headwrap stepped from beside Alehk and embraced Naledi, too. Nyakalla's frailty was shocking after not seeing her for some time. She'd always been sickly; she'd been born with health issues and her mother had died from complications in the delivery room, despite Thesolo's low maternal mortality rate. Nyakalla's survival had been alternately considered a miracle and a pity by whispering aunties. She didn't leave Lek Hemane, their hometown, often, and had been raised in part by Annie and Makalele. He wondered if her somber appearance was spurred by their sickness.

Thabiso detested Alehk, but the expression on Ledi's face washed all of that away, just for a moment. She pulled back from her cousin's embrace and looked at her. "We have the same nose. And smile," she added when Nyakalla twitched her nose and laughed.

"I am happy to see you again after all of these years, my cousin. Our grandmother always believed you would return." Her eyes filled with tears that she blinked away. "You can call me Nya, as you did when we were children, if you'd like."

Naledi blinked several times, then cleared her throat. "And you can call me Ledi."

They looked at each other, assessing each other with wide smiles.

Nya looked away, as if she were embarrassed. "I would love to learn about New York. I've dreamed of going there, but I've never left Thesolo."

"There are rats in New York. Huge ones," Thabiso interjected.

Nya and Ledi looked even more alike as they rolled their eyes in unison.

"Maybe you can tell me about Thesolo, and I can tell you about New York?" Ledi said. "He's right about the rats, but there are giant vermin here, too, I'm sure."

She didn't glance at him, but the barb still hit its mark.

"We should return to the palace to prepare for the engagement celebration," the king said. His voice boomed, but there was a glint of amusement in his eyes.

"Naledi will ride with us," Alehk said, stepping between her and Thabiso.

"No, she'll ride in the royal carriage," Thabiso said.

"It's cool," Naledi said, giving Thabiso's arm a pat. "I'd like to talk to my—my family more. I'll see you later."

With that she turned and walked away from him.

Likotsi stepped up and pulled at the collar of her shirt, eyes trained on Alehk, who had thrown his arm around Naledi. "Is this advisable, Highness?"

"Perhaps not, but it's what she wants. I am at her mercy."

"The Jaramis are known for their stubbornness, sire," Likotsi reminded him. "Mercy is not in her DNA."

Thabiso hoped that Ledi had taken after her father's side of the family.

Chapter 24

This wasn't exactly how Ledi had imagined her evening would play out. Clad in a too short robe and perched on a stool—a fancy, upholstered one, but a stool nonetheless. The fabric covering the seat was itchy against the backs of her thighs. Or maybe that was her nerves. Whatever it was, Ledi couldn't sit still.

"I would rather not be known as the woman who maimed the future queen," Nya warned with a faint smile before attempting to line Ledi's eyes with kohl for the tenth time. Ledi sucked in a breath and stilled herself as Nya finished.

Nothing was as she'd expected. She thought she'd immediately be taken to her room, be able to gather her wits alone, and then meet with the local epidemiologists. But although she was thinking of the trip as field study, everyone else saw this as her homecoming and the reinstatement of her betrothal to Thabiso. Both had to be celebrated before she could get down to work, apparently.

She regretted not consulting Portia about her wardrobe; most of what she'd brought with her was laughably inappropriate, and she was cringing thinking of the photos taken at the airport. Her uncle had ordered her a dress, which was en route; he was apparently an important person in the Thesoloian kingdom because people seemed happy to do his bidding at the snap of a finger. Ledi had often fantasized about breaking the thumbs of restaurant patrons who snapped at her, but she'd decided to cut her uncle some slack. He'd been nice enough, though she'd nodded off in the car as he discussed Jarami pride and how Ledi could change the future of Thesolo. That was after interrogating her about her parents, which, while understandable, wasn't exactly fun for someone who couldn't remember them at all. He was . . . Focused. But he treated her with a somewhat cloying affection that she'd heard other people complain about when relatives visited.

I have a family. She tried not to get too excited about it. Alehk hadn't spoken much about her grandparents in the midst of his discussion of duty to one's country, probably because they weren't doing so well. Nya's somber expression spoke volumes, though.

"Can I have some more of that tea your dad gave me?" Ledi asked. "It was good." She'd tried to stay hydrated on the plane, and the stewardess had urged her to drink water and use the scented oils and facial masks, but she was more parched than when she'd landed.

"You should taste the water fresh from our mountain springs. They say they were blessed by Ingoka and that the water is imbued with the essence of Thesolo itself." Nya headed over to a glazed clay pitcher and poured Ledi a drink into a matching cup.

Ledi had read enough to know that Ingoka was the main deity worshipped in Thesolo and that she, and the priestesses who worshipped her, were an important part of Thesoloian culture.

She took a sip of the water, and though it wasn't quite as tasty as good old New York City tap water, it was a close second.

There was a knock at the door of the dressing room, and two women dressed in the purple shirts and black slacks that identified palace staff rushed in. One woman held a garment bag high over her head, the other had a small utility case in each hand, and the expressions on both of their faces were so serious as to be comical. They were like some tactical fashion team from the reality shows Ledi put on while studying sometimes.

"You did your makeup already?" the taller, curvier woman asked, crestfallen.

"Was I not supposed to?" Judging from the way they loomed over her, that answer was no.

"Jolie is an experienced makeup artist, in demand by all the Nollywood starlets," the woman holding the dress explained.

"I can remove the makeup," Nya said quickly, reaching for a box of tissues, but Ledi stopped her. There was something about how quickly she acquiesced that Ledi didn't like.

"No. It's my face and I love what you did, so it stays," Ledi said, feeling oddly protective. "And I have my own lipstick, too. I'm sorry, Jolie."

"Fine," the dress woman said, muscling Nya out of the way. "First, we'll do something with your hair, and then we'll get you into this dress."

Jolie set down her makeup case and moved behind Ledi, tugging at the tight curls that framed her face.

"I thought my hair was already done," Ledi said. Both women had their hair straightened, and she wasn't going to submit to a hot comb for Thabiso or anyone. The two women looked at each other.

"Come now, girl. You are betrothed to His Royal Highness Prince—"

"Yes, I know who he is," Ledi interrupted.

"Do you know that he's topped the Continent's Hottest Man list three years running? Not to mention making lists around the globe?" Jolie asked as she began gathering Ledi's hair into a ponytail, smoothing the thick curls back with her hand before reaching for a soft brush. She caught Ledi's gaze in the mirror and pointed the brush at her. "The line of hopeful brides could stretch from here to the Maghreb."

Ledi tried not to show how sick that thought made her. "And your point is?"

She knew what the point was: Thabiso had a huge pool of possible brides to choose from. Ledi knew what her chances were in that kind of situation. She'd learned it over and over again every time she'd stuffed her belongings into a black garbage bag and left her temporary home with a social worker at her side.

No one chooses you.

"All we mean to say is that certain families here have set their hats for him. Each time he turned down what could have been prosperous alliances, they believed their chances increased. If you go out there looking like anything other than the woman destined to be princess, there's a line of people waiting to tear you apart," Jolie said, curling her hands into claws and slashing in Ledi's general direction. "You may have been born here, but right now you're a greedy American coming to take what's ours."

The dress woman cleared her throat and Jolie looked chastened.

"Or so people might say."

Ledi's palms were sweating and nervous nausea made her clutch her stomach. The problem with compartmentalization was that she had separated all the emotional aspects of the trip—fear, anger, apprehension, anxiety—into various boxes. One by one those boxes were being knocked over, and the resulting mess wouldn't be pretty.

"Anyone who might say that would be a fool," Nya said, coming to stand beside Ledi. "Thabiso is a man, not a prize, and if he and Ledi have been lucky enough to find love, everyone should celebrate that." She spoke in a voice that brooked no discussion. "And any Thesoloian with a problem might want to take it up with the priestesses."

There was silence after that, except for the rustling of the dress as the other woman prepared it and the sound of Ledi's hair being twisted and pinned.

"All done," Jolie said after what seemed like an eternity. Ledi turned to look into the mirror and did a double take. Her hair had been pulled into a high, round bun, a simple sleek look that had been made regal by dozens of crystal-tipped rose gold pins. Her bun had become an elegant, jewel-studded crown. She pulled her shoulders back and raised a hand to touch it.

"Thank you. It looks beautiful."

Jolie made a sound that was both "you're welcome" and "duh," as if it had never been in doubt that she'd make her look amazing.

"Now for the dress," the other woman said. "Alehk really went all out with this one."

Ledi turned and saw the woman holding out what seemed to be a pile of black and red silk. She stepped into the opening and sucked in her breath as it was zipped from behind, watching the dress take shape as the zipper made its way up. When the woman stepped away, Ledi stared at herself in disbelief.

The black bodice was formfitting, with a sweetheart neckline and frilly off-the-shoulder straps. The skirt billowed out around her, frothy black and red layers of silk and taffeta that gave the effect of a blooming, fantastical rose. The lavish dress paired with the elegant crown updo and Nya's top-notch makeup job had transformed her into someone else entirely. Perhaps the woman she would have been if her parents had never taken her to New York.

"The prince will not be able to tear his gaze from you tonight," Nya said. "And your red lip stain will match perfectly."

Ledi let Jolie apply the lip liner and stain, not wanting to step on any more toes, then checked herself out in the mirror.

"Wow," she said, allowing herself a moment of vanity.

"Wow," Jolie repeated with a little laugh. Ledi thought she was mocking her, but when she glanced at her, Jolie seemed to be genuinely entertained. "Is that what Americans say? Yes. 'Wow,' indeed. Cool."

In the mirror, Ledi noticed Nya looking at the tube of lip stain wistfully. Nya's dress was simple instead of sumptuous, loose fitting instead of accentuating her slim curves. Her hair was wrapped in a black headwrap, but that was simply done, too, not like the structural marvels Ledi had seen at the gala. She wore no makeup. She was lovely, but there was an air of neglect about her that was concerning. Ledi wondered why Alehk had lavished her with this gift while his own daughter was in Cinderelly-clean-the-kitchen mode.

"Do you want to try some?" she asked.

"That is too bold for me. Red is not for dark-skinned girls anyway," Nya said.

"Says who?" Ledi tilted her head and regarded her cousin. "I'm the same color as you."

"But." Nya eyed the lip stain covetously. "You're a New Yorker. I'm just a village teacher."

Ah. That explained the "shut up and sit down" tone she'd used on Jolie.

"I'm a waitress and a glorified number cruncher," Ledi countered. "You're not exactly speaking to a paragon of glamor."

Ledi hadn't known the woman for more than a few hours, but already she could see the resemblances that went deeper than the surface. The way Nya folded in on herself and tried to be inconspicuous, for example.

"Tell anyone who asks that the bossy American made you do it," Ledi said, unscrewing the wand from the tube and handing it over. She watched as Nya carefully applied the bright color, and saw the way her eyes lit up when she looked at herself in the mirror.

"Jolie, since you didn't get to do my makeup, can you do hers instead?"

A few minutes later, Nya had been contoured, concealed, rouged, and eyelashed. Her headwrap had also been redone in a style they'd called gele, a fancier, more structured shape. She had already been lovely, but now she looked like a star.

"This calls for a selfie," Ledi said, and struck a ridiculous pose beside Nya in the mirror. She snapped a series of photos and chose the best one: when both of them had burst out laughing, red lips stretched wide.

She was in the process of texting it to Portia before she remembered that she wasn't talking to her. It seemed like a sin to waste such a good selfie though, so she went to her InstaPhoto account to upload it. So what if she only had three followers and one of them was Portia? She had no one else to share the current weirdness of her life with.

When she opened the account she noticed what must have been an error: thousands of notifications. She definitely had more than three followers now, and she'd been tagged in at least a hundred photos. Her stepping off of the plane. Thabiso looking down into her eyes like he actually cared.

"Yasssss (Literal) Queen! Relationship goals: someone who looks at me like PT looks at his fiancé! 💙! #RoyalReunion" the caption read.

"Ugh, so jealous!" read the first response.

"Her? Really?" read the third.

She left the app without uploading her photo and put the phone away. She hadn't entirely thought this thing through. She reminded herself that it didn't matter what strangers on the internet said, anyway. This whole relationship was a scam, and Thabiso was just another person who didn't particularly care if she stuck around.

"And then you can go home."

Still . . . That "Her? Really?" pricked at Ledi's pride. She pulled out the phone and uploaded the photo of her and Nya, captioning it with a sly smile emoji.

Yes, her, you jerk. Really.

"Come, ladies, enough dillydallying. Time for us to make our entrance!" Alehk knocked at the door with an annoyed vigor, as if it was his fifth time coming around when it was really his first.

"Sorry," Nya said, and Ledi could tell that she was used to apologizing for the man. It was then Ledi realized that her cousin hadn't spoken of a significant other or children or home of her own. Not for the first time that day, she wondered if she would have turned out more like Nya if she'd never left Thesolo, or if Nya would have been more like her.

They stepped out into the hall and were whisked into a whirl of color that made the African charity gala look like small potatoes. Alehk kept up a steady stream of conversation that Ledi pretended to follow, although she didn't catch a word of it. There was too much to see.

The royal guard lined the long hallway leading to the ballroom, each clad in a crisp blue uniform with a sabre hanging from one hip and a horn from the other. The hall was full of people making their way into the room, but her eyes immediately focused on one.

Thabiso stood at the end of the line of sentries, gazing at her. He wore what appeared to be a traditional black suit, the top a longer robe-type garment with a high collar, instead of a formal tux like Alehk was wearing.

"Clinging to the old ways, as usual," Alehk muttered before clapping her on the shoulder. "Hopefully, you can change that."

"Hmm," she replied.

Thesolo was consistently listed as one of the most progressive countries in the world, with more technological and environmental advancements being put in place as Thabiso took on a larger role in government. She'd never seen him use a cell phone, but she wouldn't exactly call him backward thinking. And if that outfit signified the old ways, then the old ways were quite all right by her.

The suit was finely tailored, enhancing his broad shoulders, accentuating the width of his chest and the taper of his waist. The hems of his sleeves were piped in scarlet, matching her dress.

Alehk released her arm and gave Thabiso a grimace. Nya gave her a thumbs-up before being pulled along with her father. Then she was gone, and there was just Ledi and the weight of Thabiso's gaze.

Her skin felt suddenly taut and sensitive, betraying her resolve to be unmoved when it came to Thabiso. She knew the technical reason behind her arousal; what she didn't understand was how she could still feel that way after he'd lied to her. After he'd pretended to be Jamal, making her laugh, making her lov—

Hey now. What was that?

Just the possibility of the unfinished thought made her want to turn and run back to the airport, but her traitorous feet kept carrying her forward until she stood close enough that she had to look up at him. She steeled herself, reminded herself that this was not the man she'd grown close to over the last week.

"Prince Thabiso," she said, his name another barrier she could throw up between them.

"My beautiful betrothed," he responded. He said the last word so warmly that anyone watching would think he was a man looking forward to marriage. Then again, she'd never thought Jamal might be a prince in disguise before the night he'd stepped onstage. Her chest tightened at the memory.

"Are you sure you're not too tired to attend this event?" he asked. His hand went to her shoulder in concern, and she closed her eyes against the pleasure of his touch on her bare skin.

She was exhausted. She had no idea what time it was in NYC, but she was jet-lagged, and meeting her family and an entire nation of people had compounded that. She hadn't factored in that Thabiso's presence would be this hard; she'd only known him a few days—he should have been out of her system. Men had done hurtful things to her before, and Ledi had always been able to move on quickly. With Thabiso, she'd actually *been* hurt, which made things a bit more difficult.

"I'm fine," she said.

He nodded, then took her arm gently. "A Thesoloian celebration can last for days, but I'll have you out of here in a couple of hours, just in case you stop feeling *fine*."

"I think I can handle a dinner," she replied curtly, then they stepped into the dining room and she regretted her attitude. The dining room was huge, with cantilevered ceilings and rich tapestries hanging from the walls. The long dining table on a raised area, clearly for the guests of honor, was on the other side of the room. To get to it, they had to walk a gauntlet of people who were apparently all there to meet Naledi.

"Here we go," he whispered, brushing a caress over the back of her hand, and then they were off. After the first ten people, Ledi barely remembered shaking anyone's hand or kissing anyone's cheek. She couldn't recall a single name, and she didn't know what she was laughing at when people joked—she simply followed Thabiso's lead.

"My my, you look just like your mother!" an older man said, after nearly cutting off circulation in her hand. All of the older people she'd met had said something similar, although there was no consensus on which of her parents she resembled more. She smiled and nodded, but all she could think of each time someone mentioned it was that they'd known her parents better than she had.

"Yes, Ledi is surpassingly beautiful," Thabiso said, clapping the man on the back heartily enough that he dropped Ledi's hand. He ran interference for her constantly, stepping in every time she was at a loss for words or overwhelmed. "They're about to serve the salads. We should get to our seats."

He tucked her arm in his again, and though Ledi had resented the gesture before, she was fairly certain he was holding her up. She wasn't sure how much time had passed since they'd descended onto the main floor, but it could have been days given how many hands she'd shaken and how tired she was. She didn't want to lean into him, but she was a practical woman and he was the nearest source of support. She leaned.

"You're doing very well," he said in the same tone a teacher would use when giving out participation trophies.

She laughed and even that small action left her feeling a bit unsteady. She stumbled and Thabiso stopped and looked down at her. "Ledi. You do not seem *fine*."

"I'm not," she admitted. "Can we sit down?"

He led her to her seat, near the head of the table, and the other guests began to follow suit.

The king and queen were already seated, and she greeted them with as much energy as she could muster. Her head was spinning and she wanted nothing more than to sleep.

"There we go," Thabiso said as he helped her into her seat. He was so gentle with her that she had to close her eyes against it. Perhaps a bit *too* gentle.

"Don't tell me she's pregnant!" The queen's indignant whisper jolted Ledi's eyes open.

"Mother," Thabiso warned.

"Is that what this is all about? Honestly—"

"I'm not pregnant," Ledi said. She was too tired and out of sorts to feign politeness. "I know how to use a condom correctly, but I also have an IUD in case of accidents and just had my period. Need anything else cleared up? Want me to pee on a stick for you?"

"Naledi," Thabiso choked.

The king picked up his glass of wine and took a hearty drink. The queen regarded her with a strange look that Ledi ignored.

She wondered if that's what everyone thought. That she had entrapped him with a baby, or some other soap opera nonsense. The thought distressed her, then she remembered that they were actually pulling off something even more audacious and she smiled. She wasn't pleased to be his pretend betrothed, but having that secret felt like a special fuck you to his parents, who were doing their best to make her feel unwelcome.

"You're smiling," Nya said as she sat down beside her. "I hope you're enjoying yourself."

"I'm feeling a bit ill, but I think it's just the jet lag," Ledi said.

Nya's smile faltered. She reached into her purse and handed Ledi a small bottle. "Can't have you feeling out of sorts. It's a local cure-all. It should help with any queasiness and fatigue. Take one with some water."

Ledi scanned the ingredients before opening the bottle, shaking out one of the giant capsules and swallowing. When she tried to hand it back, Nya shook her head. "I have more at home. I'm sure you'll need it, since the next few days are going to be very busy for you. Take one in the morning and one before bed."

"Thanks," she said.

Ledi began to feel better shortly after, but as dinner progressed she started to wonder if maybe Nya had slipped her a hallucinogen.

Is this really my life?

She was fairly well versed in international cuisine, but the variety of rich stews, tender meats, and desserts that ran the gamut from sweet to sour was like some kind of fairy-tale feast. Ledi considered herself an awesome server, but she had nothing on the palace waitstaff. At times it felt as if food was appearing by magic in front of her and her dirty plates were disappearing into the ether. She half expected one of the candelabras to start singing and offer her a treat by the time the last dish was taken away.

Nya helped her navigate through Thesoloian society from one side, pointing out important people and providing gossip about others. The king and queen sat across the table, occasionally asking questions of Ledi that were either purposefully insulting or only sounded that way because of cultural miscommunication. Ledi was fairly certain it was the former, though; she only spoke English, but was fluent in shade.

"So an epidemiologist?" the queen asked between delicate bites of her meal. "Not a doctor? It's best when one knows one's limitations."

"Doctors diagnose diseases, Mother. Epidemiologists save the world from them," Thabiso said from her other side, where he'd remained mostly silent throughout the meal. Instead of making jokes, he'd responded to his parents' questions with clipped responses. Each time he tried to talk to her, he'd been interrupted by a minister or an advisor or a priestess, all demanding his time and pressuring him about one thing or another. She started to feel vicariously stressed on his behalf, and she was only half listening.

Ledi thought of his silly jokes in Mrs. Garcia's apartment, and of how he'd made her dinner and been so proud of that small accomplishment. Jamal was truly a different person from the stiff, overburdened Thabiso, who seemed to be on the job even in the midst of his own celebration. A small part of her, just a few molecules really, thought maybe it was understandable that he'd wanted to be someone else, even if just for a short while.

"So you have no memory of your parents at all?" the king jumped in, continuing the tag team pattern he and his wife had established. "That's quite . . . convenient."

Ledi choked on the bite of cake she'd been swallowing, and both Thabiso and Nya pounded at her back. She'd allowed the king and queen their polite rudeness, but she'd had about enough. Heat rushed to her face as she stood and glared down at them. "There are many ways to describe growing up an orphan, but *convenient* isn't one of them."

"Enough," Thabiso said in a tone Ledi hadn't heard from him before. It was deep and rough and shot straight through Ledi's eardrums and down between her legs. She liked his commanding tone, it seemed. A lot.

"Yes, tell her to have a seat," the queen said.

"Actually, it's you who should have a seat, Mother."

The queen tilted her head at him, genuinely confused. "I'm already sitting."

The king leaned toward her. "Oh, that's something the youth are saying these days. It means—"

"It means you're going to stop blatantly disrespecting your future daughter-in-law," Thabiso said. "Immediately."

There was a taut silence, and then the king picked up his fork and dug into his dessert. "This cake is delicious, isn't it?"

Ledi slowly sank down into her seat. "Yes. Delicious. My compliments to the chef."

"Our culinary school turns out some of the best chefs in the world." The king made congenial small talk about cakes, pies, and pastries for the next few minutes. The queen sipped her coffee in silence. Her gaze slipped to Naledi every once in a while, but her expression was unreadable.

The rest of the dinner passed amicably enough. There was dancing and performances by groups from various tribes, and Ledi got a short-lived second wind, although she steered clear of the dance floor. She was enraptured by the bright colors and the music that almost tempted her past her reservedness, but that didn't stop her from falling asleep in her seat. Even the strong, bitter coffee couldn't keep her from nodding off.

She awoke in Thabiso's arms as he carried her to her room. For a moment she just blinked up at him. His face was handsome as ever, but his eyes were tired, and a frown rested on the lips she'd grown so used to seeing stretched in a smile. The desire to wipe away that frown rose in her so strongly that she shifted in his hold, trying to escape the feeling.

"Hello, Sleeping Beauty," he said, and her heart lifted to see his grin again.

Stupid heart. It hadn't done anything but pump blood at a steady pace before Thabiso had come into her life, but it had been engaging in all kinds of bizarre behaviors since he'd stepped into the kitchen at the Institute.

"You've read too many fairy tales," she said grumpily as he deposited her in front of her suite. "I hate to break it to you, but there's no such thing as a happy ending."

"One can never read too many fairy tales," he replied. He moved closer, the bulk of him reminding her of how good it had felt to be pressed beneath his weight as he pushed into her. Her body was suddenly warm, and the heaviness of the material wasn't the only reason she wanted out of her dress.

Thabiso lifted his hand and skimmed his knuckles down the length of her neck, and if there was anything fairy tale about the feeling it produced, it was from the naughty retellings she'd found on the internet. Lust. Slickness between her legs and a tremble in her knees, just from that one touch.

"And I know you've experienced a happy ending. At least two." His hand stopped feathering down her neck. "I've felt you shake in my arms, cry out with my name on your tongue. Your next happy ending is waiting for you whenever you desire it, Naledi."

And then his hand slipped away, and he turned and made his way back down the long hallway. Ledi realized that she was on her tiptoes, every sensitive part of her body angled up toward the space Thabiso had just vacated.

She lowered herself onto her heels and exhaled. She'd thought that Jamal and Thabiso were entirely different men, but unfortunately for her, they had one thing in common: her defenses were useless against them.

Chapter 25

Ledi stared out the window of her room, which was three times the size of her apartment, sipping a cup of the tea Alehk had gifted her and wishing it had more caffeine. She'd already had two cups but felt more muddled instead of less. Jet lag was no joke.

She'd awoken in the middle of the night and, unable to sleep, finally opened Likotsi's email about her parents. It had been embarrassing, the way people had spoken to her about them at the celebration and she'd nodded along because she knew nothing at all.

There were the basics: the towns they'd been born in. Libiko, Libi, had one brother while Kembe was an only child. They'd met in high school and married as soon as they graduated. At the University of Thesolo, Libi had studied laboratory technology and Kembe mathematics. That was where Naledi sat up in bed, gripping her phone hard.

She had to have known. She thought she'd erased every trace of her parents, but perhaps her desire to be a scientist hadn't been driven by a *National Geographic* cover at all, but by the memory of her mother, who had been one as well.

She'd closed her eyes against the hot pressure of

tears until it abated, then scrolled down to an attachment: a short video clip. Thirty seconds of tiny versions of her and Thabiso on a bed of pillows in the middle of a gazebo-like structure, chubby-cheeked toddlers playing with the flower petals surrounding them. A woman dressed in a yellow and green robe was speaking blessings over them as their parents stood and watched. Just before the clip ended, her mother leaned over and whispered something to Queen Ramatla, who laughed and clasped her mother's hand. Her heart had ached at the way they looked at each other; it had made her miss Portia with a fierceness she hadn't imagined.

Ledi had put her phone away then and pulled out the book she'd picked up about Twentieth Century African epidemics, mostly because it was lighter reading than her parents' biography.

Now she watched as morning sunlight spread over the winter garden below her room; she'd been told it was called the lesser garden. She couldn't imagine what the greater garden looked like. Hardy cold-resistant shrubs and trees lined snow-dusted pathways, and small animals darted here and there. A burst of color caught her eye. For a moment she thought the jet lag and fatigue were really getting to her, but that was, in fact, a peacock walking proudly down one of the paths. Thabiso hadn't been lying when he described his childhood park, though he'd omitted some vital information, such as the fact that the park was part of the palace grounds. He'd been describing the place that might have been her home already if she had stayed.

She was too overwhelmed to parse that. And way too confused by her reaction to Thabiso after the celebration; she'd been exhausted when she stumbled into her ridiculously large suite, but also so annoyed and so horny that she hadn't been able to sleep until she slid her hands between her legs and massaged away the ache that Thabiso had started in her. And just as she had that first night he arrived in apartment 7 N, as she'd eaten the dinner they'd made together, she wondered if he was doing the same. Could the way her body had arched and trembled at the thought of him stroking himself be blamed on jet lag, too?

Probably.

She moved away from the window, put down her lukewarm tea, and sat down on her bed just as a knock sounded at the door.

"Come in!" She stood, twisted her hands together nervously, then tightened the drawstring of her robe.

The door swung open and a rack of clothes wheeled itself in—or so it seemed at first. Another magical aspect of the palace? Then Naledi spotted the feet underneath and realized there was a woman on the other side.

"*Mmoro! O fela jang?*" the woman called out from behind the rack stuffed with clothing.

"Oh, um." Ledi scrambled to the desk to grab the index card with basic Thesoloian phrases she'd copied down. "*Lanthe fela, anwo fela jang?*"

A hoot of laughter rang out, and then a short, middle-aged woman stepped out from behind the rack clad in her purple shirt and black pants.

"Oh, they were not joking when they said you'd been Americanized!" she tsked, but she was still smiling. "Your accent is very cute, but I can speak in English, okay? We all speak English here, too, so there is no problem for you."

The woman gave her a thumbs-up and Ledi returned it, both annoyed and appreciative. It was frustrating to know that Thesoloo had been her native language, and now she stumbled over the words with the clumsiness of a stranger. She *was* a stranger—her parents had made her one.

Why did we leave? The question lingered around every palatial corner now, and just as in her lab research, there was no guarantee she'd ever find the answer.

"Here is your wardrobe. The prince picked all of this out for you, personally. He said, of course, that you should let me know what you'd like made specifically."

Ledi would have no idea where to even begin with ordering specially made clothing. Most of her wardrobe had been plucked off of a sales rack. Besides, Thabiso seemed to have ordered enough to last a lifetime.

"I've known that boy since he was in short robes and he never cared this much for fashion!" The woman gave her a sly look.

"But Thabiso is always well dressed," Ledi said.

The woman laughed. "That is all Likotsi. He simply wears what she suggests, and she is never wrong. Well, there was that one time with the genie pants."

The woman screwed up her face and Ledi laughed.

"Last week was the first time he came to me with specific interest. Make of that what you will. Okay, here are some warm wool pants, and you will need this sweater." It was a little strange disrobing in front of the woman, but the woman urged her on. Ledi pulled on the thick, legging-like black pants and the soft black cashmere turtleneck she'd been handed. In the mirror, she could see that they had been perfectly tailored, hugging her curves and falling just right at her wrists and waist.

"Ah. I thought sizing you by photograph would be hard, but I've still got it. Now try this." She handed her a cloak similar to the one Thabiso had wrapped around her the day before, and what many people had been wearing at the airport.

"This is a blanket of Thesolo. They are a very important part of our culture," the woman explained as she showed Naledi how to wrap and fold the blanket so it fit snugly. "We use them for many purposes. You can get similar ones from the tourist shops, but some people prefer having a distinctive pattern, made just for them. The prince chose this for you. The design was difficult, but my weavers did their best."

Ledi stared down at the pink coffee-bean-like shapes floating in a field of purple and suddenly realized what the pattern had been based on. She gasped, and then burst into laughter as she stroked her fingers over the thick material.

"If you don't like it, I can make another." The woman looked down at the ground. "I am sorry if I've displeased you, my lady."

Ledi clasped the woman's arm. "No! I love it! It's just . . ." How did she explain that the design was based on the shape of a gonorrhea bacillus? That Thabiso had remembered the humiliating story she'd told him the first day she'd met him? "It's a private joke between the prince and I. This blanket is beautiful."

The hurt look dropped away from the woman's face, replaced by a bright smile.

"Very good. I hope everything else is to your liking, my lady. There are a variety of shoes and warm socks for you so you don't get frostbite on your toes."

She bowed to Ledi and left the room. Just as the door was closing, a familiar face peeped in.

"May we enter, my lady?" Likotsi asked politely.

"Yes, you may." The formal words seemed bizarre, but it was hard to speak normally when everyone was talking like they'd escaped from a period film.

Likotsi entered, dapper as usual in a slim-fitting green suit, followed by Thabiso.

"*Mmoro,*" Ledi said, trying not to cringe at the sound of the beautiful language being destroyed by her pronunciation. How could two syllables be so difficult? Still, her attempt was greeted by bright smiles from both Thabiso and his assistant.

"And good morning to you," Likotsi said. She pulled out her tablet and started swiping. "We were thinking we could take a short tour on the way to see Annie and Makalele. Your grandparents. They are at the Royal Hospital, here on the palace grounds."

Ledi tugged at her cloak.

"I see. Thank you for telling me more about them, by the way. In the emails. Your writing is beautiful." She'd discovered the source of the persistent emails, and now that she knew the truth behind them she realized what a kindness Likotsi had done her, even if she had been complicit in Thabiso's lies. As she'd read through the emails in the aftermath of the truth, they'd changed from demands for response to informal histories of the people Ledi had never known, more intimate than the Wikipedia pages and tourism websites she'd found could provide. She'd learned of the highest point in Thesolo from a website, but it was Likotsi who had described what the annual solstice festival held at the summit of the mountain looked, tasted, and smelled like. She'd learned her parents' names, but it was Likotsi who had shared stories of how they met, their hopes and dreams.

"It was my pleasure," Likotsi said.

"Also, I apologize for the rude email response. Before." Ledi cleared her throat.

"Already forgotten, my lady. Please let me know if you need anything. I am Thabiso's assistant, but I am also yours until other arrangements can be made."

She'd be gone before she needed an assistant, but Ledi didn't say that.

"This is for you," Likotsi said. She handed Ledi the envelope she was holding.

Ledi expected it to be light, but it was slightly heavier than a stack of papers that thickness should be, and firmer. She opened the envelope and slipped out a sleek, thin tablet, the kind she had seen everyone over at GirlsWithGlasses freaking out about a couple of weeks ago. The one Brian had been scrolling the internet and shouting the specs for on the day it was announced as she'd filled out his grant papers. The one she hadn't even bothered to look at the price for because it was way out of her league.

"This is too expensive. I can't." She meant to hand it back, but strangely she was still clutching the cool glass and plastic, imagining all the ways it could be helpful to her in her research.

"You can and you will. I had important papers, such as your birth records, a selection of your parents' papers from university, and family photos uploaded. It's already been personalized."

"I guess I'll keep it then." She placed the tablet down on her pillow. She would peruse the photos later when she was alone. She walked over to the rack of clothing and chose a pair of socks and pink leather ankle boots, and sat on a chair.

"May I suggest these instead?" Likotsi held out a

pair of knee-high black boots with thick, rugged soles. Her expression intimated that it wasn't actually a suggestion.

Ledi took the boots.

"Now you see what I live with every day," Thabiso said with a smile. He'd been surprisingly quiet, but Ledi had never forgotten he was there. Keeping her gaze from drifting to him was difficult, even when she was giving her full attention to Likotsi.

Likotsi sucked her teeth. "Trying to act like you don't ask me which shoes to wear every morning isn't becoming, sire."

Thabiso feigned shock. "That's not true. I haven't asked your opinion in days. Maybe even a week. Ignore her, Naledi."

Ledi smiled, even though the interaction made her chest hurt. This was the man she had known in Manhattan: playful, open, eager to make her laugh. She didn't know how she was supposed to react, couldn't even suss out how she actually felt, really.

Why was it so natural to sit and chat with Thabiso and Likotsi? Why was she eager to see her cousin Nya, and hear how the rest of her night had gone? Was she supposed to care about Annie and Makelele, people she didn't know at all but who were responsible in part for her existence? Would it make her a terrible human if she met them and she didn't feel anything at all?

She glanced up to find Thabiso staring at her feet as she slid on her socks.

She wiggled her toes, showing the pink polish. "It matches my cape," she said. "Do you give all the girls venereal diseases?"

"Your Highness!" Likotsi narrowed her eyes at Thabiso, who was attempting to keep a straight face.

"Only the ones I really like," he said. "It fits you well."

She finished zipping up the boots and sighed, spitting out the question that she really needed to ask. "Annie and Makalele. Are they going to die?"

"We don't know," Thabiso said, his expression solemn. "Dr. Bata, the woman you'll be working with, is out collecting data. You can speak to her more about the symptoms and the potential outcomes when she returns."

Naledi nodded. "I think I need some coffee before we head there."

"Your coffee awaits. Along with your chariot." Likotsi swung the door open to reveal three Segways parked outside her door. One had a cup holder already stocked with a travel coffee mug with a beautiful watercolor floral design.

Ledi was sure this was some kind of practical joke. She grabbed the coffee and took a sip, noting how expensive it tasted, then eyed the Segway with trepidation. "Are you serious with this?"

"The palace grounds are quite large, my lady." Likotsi stepped onto her Segway and turned it on. "In older times, royalty was conveyed about on rickshaw-type means of transportation. We upgraded to these babies from golf carts a few years ago. Much more fun, if I do say so."

"I don't know how to use it," Ledi said, stepping on. She put her coffee cup in the cup holder and pressed the on button, as she'd seen Likotsi do. "How do I make it move?"

"It's simple." Thabiso's familiar bulk stepped behind her, and his arms reached around her. "Just lean, like this. It moves in the direction you push it toward." He moved so that his whole body was pressed against hers and even through the thick cape she could feel the outlines of his muscles, the flex of them.

"That sounds too easy," she said, hating the tremor she heard in her voice.

Thabiso's voice dropped, husky and low. "It is simple, Ledi. It will do what you tell it to do. You decide what path to follow. You are in control."

Fuck. She wondered if Likotsi had provided Thabiso with a docket on her, or if he innately knew the right thing to say to make her want to turn around and wrap her legs around him.

"Ahem. Forward, my lady. You are currently leaning *back*." Likotsi didn't bother to hide the amusement in her tone.

"Oh! Right." Ledi leaned forward and felt the wheels kick into action, moving her away from Thabiso's heat. "This isn't so bad."

She got the Segway moving at a steady pace through the hall, fast enough that her hair fluttered around her face and she felt a burst of excitement at the sensation of freedom. She was driving! Kind of! She glanced back triumphantly, just in time to see Thabiso's smile turn to a frown and Likotsi reach a hand out. Then there was the thump of her vehicle coming to an abrupt stop that flopped her back onto her ass. The sound of two sets of footsteps running toward her echoed in the vast hallway.

"My lady. You have to lean forward, and look forward, too." Likotsi wiped at the indentation in the giant wooden carving—the very well-endowed wooden carving—that Ledi had crashed into.

Thabiso took her by the hand and helped her up. "Perhaps we should walk?"

"So much for creating my own path," Ledi said.

His hand flexed around hers. "Choosing a path straight through a likeness of the god of lust was an interesting choice. I like where you go when you decide to take control."

"Can you not?" She pulled her hand away and retrieved her coffee. The cup was warm against her skin, too, but it didn't make her body tighten like Thabiso's touch had.

It took them about fifteen minutes to get to the hospital. On the way, Ledi lost track of the priceless artwork, random wild animals, friendly palace staff, and the running commentary Likotsi gave about all of them. Her head buzzed and she started to lose the thread of the conversation as more and more information was thrown at her. She'd been training to be an information processing machine for the last five years, so it felt strange not to be able to keep up with simple conversation.

It's the jet lag.

She took one of the pills Nya had given her, downed it with the last of her coffee, and handed off her empty cup to a passing staffer who stopped and asked if she'd finished.

"Isn't it weird having people wait on you all the time?" she asked Thabiso as she watched the woman walk away. "Do you really need people roaming around, seeing if you need something done at any given moment?"

"Weird is relative," Thabiso said with a shrug. "I think living in a shoe box with vermin is a bit strange, but I don't judge you for it. And in case you're wondering, palace staff receive high pay, excellent benefits, and can retire at the age of forty-five with a lifetime pension and a home in the place of their choosing. The positions are highly competitive."

"I'm sure there's something comparable to this in

the States?" Likotsi asked with a wide smile. "Since I'm one of the weird people you're referring to, I need to keep my options open. Tell me all about the wonderful work environments, salaries, and retirement funds in your country."

"Oh no, I didn't mean you! Or anyone, really. I'm just rambling," Ledi said as they passed through the doors to the hospital. Thabiso snickered like a schoolboy laughing at a chastised classmate. She glared at him.

"Of course," Likotsi said.

Nurses dressed in crisp lilac uniforms bustled about, making their rounds. One of them, a tall, sturdy woman with braided hair, came over to greet them.

"Your Highness. My lady." She executed a slight bow, then looked at Likotsi with a much less formal expression. "Kotsi."

"Hi, Sesi," Likotsi said. She straightened her bow tie. "Long time no see."

"I assume it's because some lucky woman has snatched you up," Sesi said, grabbing a chart.

"Not yet. I'm still enjoying the bachelorette life." Likotsi smiled mischievously, but even Ledi could see it didn't reach her eyes.

Sesi seemed pleased with that information, but her flirting stopped as soon as she flipped open the chart. Her expression went from playful to sober. "Annie, Makelele, and the others are the same. They are not doing worse, but they aren't doing better either. People from their village come to sit and talk with them every day and bring them healing brews, but there are no visitors at the moment." She looked at Ledi. "You are their granddaughter, no?"

Ledi nodded, and Sesi smiled gently. "They spoke of your mother often, when they were well. They are not awake, but perhaps your presence will help."

Ledi knew the woman was trying to be comforting, but instead, the low-level nervousness she'd been feeling kicked it up a notch. She tried to smile back, but if it looked as forced as it felt, she wasn't fooling anyone. Then a familiar warmth slid over her fingers. Thabiso gripped her hand lightly as they followed Sesi, leaving her room to pull away again if she wished.

She didn't.

He leaned down and said in a low voice, "Do not pressure yourself, Naledi. You know how I feel about fairy tales, but no one is expecting them to hop out of bed and start dancing as soon as you walk into the room. If that does happen, I'll have to fight our priestesses from taking you into their order."

"Being a priestess sounds kind of cool," Ledi said, happy to talk about something apart from her sick grandparents. Her stomach lurched as they passed through a door into the intensive care wing.

Thabiso gave her a faux-serious look. "Yes. I forget you have experience with ritual sacrifice. I'm not sure if you'd appreciate the celibacy, though."

"I've been considering it, actually, given my last few experiences with men," she said, tugging her hand from his at the reminder of what had passed between them. She wanted his comfort, but last time she'd opened herself up to it, it had come at the price of her trust.

He took it in stride. "In the old days, the king got to wed the priestess of his choosing."

Ledi ignored him. He was trying to distract her, but Sesi was handing out masks for them to place over their mouths and paper robes and gloves, then pushing open a door.

"Here we are," she said. "My lady? Would you like to go in alone?"

Ledi didn't want to go in at all. She wanted to turn and run down the brightly lit white hallway. She wanted to throw up. Maybe she would do both at the same time. The thought of going into the room alone sent a surge of panic through her.

She turned and looked behind her. "Can you come with me?"

Thabiso stepped forward, but Likotsi brushed a touch over his arm. "I believe she was speaking to me, sire."

"Oh. Of course." Ledi ignored the disappointment that passed over his face and the corresponding pang she felt that it wasn't him accompanying her. Not that she cared if she'd hurt him—she'd be leaving Thesolo soon enough, anyway. His feelings weren't her priority. Whether she had made a difference for her grandparents and the other people who were sick was what mattered in the end.

She walked into the room and Likotsi followed, closing the door with a click.

The two standard hospital beds were pushed together, covered with green and brown traditional blankets bearing a circular pattern that seemed to be the same until you looked closer and saw that they were variations of each other. A teapot sat on the side table, and two mugs that had to have been brought from their home, given their well-used appearance.

Ledi allowed herself to take in their faces. Both dark brown, like hers, and aged, but not crowded with wrinkles. The raised bumps and splotchy red of a rash covered their cheeks and necks, down to below the neckline of their hospital gowns, but it didn't hide the obvious resemblances to what Ledi saw in the mirror every day. She felt an odd disconnect, as if she was watching some other orphan meet their grandparents for the first time.

"Hi." What did you say to someone in a coma? "I'm Naledi. Your granddaughter. Umm . . . nice to meet you? Not 'nice' nice with the whole coma thing, I guess."

There was no response. She walked closer and rested her hand on the safety railing.

"I like your blankets. That's a cool pattern. Mine is designed with gonorrhea because Thabiso thinks he's funny."

Their heart monitors beeped in sync, but her grandparents didn't move. The whole situation was a bit awkward, but if she could talk to her mice without expecting a response, her grandparents certainly merited it.

"I'm a grad student. I study infectious diseases. The workload is awful and it's super expensive and I spend half my time wondering if I've made terrible life choices. But I love it. And I just found out that love of science runs in the family. Funny, huh?"

More silence.

She sighed and glanced at the middle of the beds, and that was when emotion hit her like a rogue wave. Someone had placed a pillow between her grandparents, half on one bed, half on the other. Their hands rested atop each other there, their fingers lightly entwined. Even in this deep sleep, they held on to each other.

She took a sharp breath and looked at the two frail people who had helped create her. Who she had forgotten, and might never have the opportunity to know again.

She cleared her throat. The dry air in the room must have been giving it that scratchy feeling. "I wish I could have met you before. You guys look like you would've been great grandparents. Like, you would have snuck me candy even when my parents said no, and given really good hugs. Maybe you're assholes though, since my parents did run off, but you *look* nice. Really nice."

Ledi stopped talking because suddenly she couldn't. She had filled in her parents' faces on her mental family tree, and now her grandparents were there. Her imagination had this information, and while she didn't consider herself particularly creative, there was one area in which it had always excelled before she'd forced it to stop: imagining what might have been.

Birthdays, shared meals, teen hormone-driven arguments followed by forgiveness . . . Ledi now had the base factors to imagine them all. The feeling of unfairness she hadn't ever allowed to take hold began to get its hooks into her. In that moment, what she wanted more than anything was everything she'd missed out on, good and bad.

How could my parents take this from me?

Her grandmother's face twitched a few times, and then her eyes fluttered open, focusing on Ledi's face. A beatific smile lit up her features.

"Libiko." Her voice was thick, her accent almost masking her single word, but the shock of her mother's newly learned name went through Ledi like lightning. Her grandmother sighed and said something in Thesoloian that Ledi didn't understand.

"What?"

Annie smiled and closed her eyes again.

"She said, 'I knew you would return to us, my heart,'" Likotsi translated, her voice rough.

The beep of the machines keeping the elders alive filled the silence that followed her words, until the sound of Ledi's sniffles joined in. What was going on? If she didn't know these people, then why was her hand at her chest to stop the pain? Why were rivulets of tears coursing their way toward her chin? Why did it hurt to see them like this when she didn't even know what they had been like before?

The tears began to wet through the edges of her face mask, and then a handkerchief was pressed into her palm and she felt Likotsi's hand on her shoulder. She wiped at her eyes and cleared her throat before speaking. Emotions were a distraction, and she'd come to Thesolo on a mission.

"You said that you'll assist me with anything I need, right?"

"Of course, my lady." Likotsi drew herself up straighter, and Ledi thought she might salute. Instead, she pulled out her tablet from what had to be a custom-made pocket in the interior lining of her suit jacket. Her latex-gloved fingers hovered above the screen, ready to do Ledi's bidding.

"I need to speak with their doctors immediately. I'd also like copies of all of Dr. Bata's latest findings, and full access to the hospital records and a briefing on past epidemics, illnesses, and abnormalities over the last fifty years—to start."

Likotsi nodded and looked up at her, and Ledi was surprised to see what looked like pride in the assistant's eyes. "I will make it so, my lady."

"Please. Call me Ledi," she said. She turned and briefly placed her own gloved hand over her grandparents. She didn't know what compelled her, but when she felt the cool skin of her grandfather's hand she closed her eyes and made a pact with them.

I'm going to help find out what's going on here.

Chapter 26

"Ledi?"

Thabiso pushed open the door to Ledi's suite when he got no response, expecting—or hoping—to find her still ensconced in the silk sheets and fluffy down-stuffed duvet. Instead, she was hunched over her desk, her back to him. The blanket he'd had made for her was draped over her shoulders and trailed onto the floor, and the papers spread over the desk were illuminated by an ornate desk lamp and the glow of her tablet screen.

For a moment, he thought she'd fallen asleep there, but then he noticed her right hand was scribbling furiously while her left hand traced a path down the printed page beside her. She shifted the page to another pile and her fingertips traced over the words on the next page.

"I brought you breakfast in bed, but it seems I'm too late," he said as he moved across the suite.

"Too early," she replied in a gravelly voice. Her hands stopped moving, and then reached up into the air as she performed a stretch that shifted the blanket completely off of her. She wore a robe made of thick, warm flannel, and the curves of her breasts and the bend of her back were silhouetted against the weak predawn light filtering into the large window in front of her. Seeing her displayed in such a way was a moving sight, but it didn't inspire lust in Thabiso; instead, he felt a pang of sadness. The palace gardens and Thesolo's mountain range served as a backdrop to her beauty, but, if everything went to plan, soon she'd never look upon them again, or he upon her. Was the desperate urge to go to her that struck Thabiso what Ledi had felt that night when she opened herself to him in her apartment?

No, not to him. To Jamal. Thabiso was simply the man who had crushed the fragile sprout of trust she'd been kind enough to offer. She would not have him. That didn't stop him from savoring the memory of her in his arms after she'd fallen asleep during the welcome dinner. He'd had a preposterous thought as he'd carried her.

This is what our wedding night could be like. What kind of nonsense was that? Sentimental and as unlikely as him crawling back to Omega Corp. He'd compromised any future negotiations between he and Ledi, and they were simply fulfilling a temporary contract now.

He put the tray down on the bed and realized the sheets were still smooth and crisp, and the single eng flower the housekeepers laid on the palace pillows to induce prosperous dreaming hadn't been moved away or flattened.

Now that he was closer, he could see that her eyes were bloodshot and ringed with dark circles.

"You haven't slept?"

"Sleep is for the weak," Ledi said, then yawned again. "And for people not trying to help figure out a possible epidemic."

He carried over the bowl of mealy pap and the cup of coffee and placed them on the desk. "We should reschedule today's event at the temple so you can rest. I didn't bring you here for you to work yourself sick."

Ledi scoffed and grabbed for her coffee. She popped some kind of vitamin supplement into her mouth and washed it down with a sip of coffee. "I'm a grad student. Sleep is a bonus, but far from necessary. Don't worry about me."

Thabiso wanted to argue that she had been running on fumes from the moment he'd met her, but she wasn't the type of woman to be tucked into bed and given a glass of warm milk. He hoped that after their meeting with the priestesses of Ingoka he could convince her to at least take a nap, but rest didn't seem to be her style.

"Please eat. I can bring something else if this isn't to your taste. And I'd love to know how your day was yesterday, if you don't mind sharing that. I know seeing your grandparents must have been difficult."

"Why don't you tell me about your day, while I eat and caffeinate," she said. Thabiso doubted she was really interested—she was a master at changing the conversation away from herself—but she picked up a spoon and tucked into the porridge and that was good enough for him.

"Well, after you and Likotsi left to begin your research, I was called into an emergency meeting with the finance ministers. Very unhappy finance ministers."

"What were they mad about?" She spun her office chair around and leaned back, still annoyed but at least actually engaging in conversation. "Did you blow your allowance sending Mrs. Garcia to Puerto Rico?"

She took another bite, and Thabiso's gaze followed

the path of the spoon into her mouth, the way her lips pressed against the smooth metal and her tongue slipped over her lips afterward.

He lifted his gaze back to her eyes.

"No, that was a humanitarian mission, although Mrs. Garcia did quite enjoy the mini bar at the Ritz," he said. That pulled a grin from her. "While I was in New York, I decided against finalizing a multimillion-dollar investment deal with a powerful company," he said.

"Is that all? I mean, what's several million dollars?" She chewed sarcastically, which Thabiso hadn't even known was possible until that moment.

"Thesolo is wealthy nation, but hundreds of millions is still a lot," he said. "I could buy many Italian special sandwiches with that."

"Then why'd you tank the deal?" she asked, ignoring his reference. Her gaze dropped to her food, lashes fluttering down and hiding her eyes from him.

"Because even though I was told that this deal would usher Thesolo into the future, it felt like I was ensuring the destruction of our kingdom if I said yes. I decided against letting a company come to Thesolo, dig up our resources, and destroy our land, but the ministers see it as impertinence and overstepping my bounds."

Thabiso thought of the raised voices and the accusations of incompetence that had been hurled at him. "It's like they look at the other nations being robbed of their resources and think 'Oh, *they're* just stupid. That's why they were fooled.' These men are intelligent, but they ignore economic history, colonization, and globalization. They can only think in the moment, when we need to be thinking a hundred years ahead, and beyond for that matter."

Naledi was looking at him now, staring at him like one of the large spiders that inhabited the dusty corners of the palace had just rappelled down from the ceiling onto him. He ran a hand over his head to the back of his neck. "What?"

She stirred her porridge and glanced away from him. "I'm sorry, it's just . . . you actually know stuff."

Thabiso huffed. "I'm a prince. Of course I know stuff."

"Well, when you see princes in the news, they're usually just gallivanting around, riding horses or playing strip poker. But you *know* things."

He groaned. "Johan really ruined it for all of us with that strip poker game. A good prince knows you always frisk for cameras and cell phones before getting nude."

Ledi rolled her eyes.

"I'm kidding. Mostly." He cleared his throat. "The horses and gallivanting are marketing, and they are part of the job in this day and age, no matter what kingdom you hail from. But while I've led a privileged life, and perhaps a sheltered one, I've been preparing to lead a kingdom since I could sit up in my crib. What I know, I know well."

"I see that," she said. "I'm glad. I thought you were just a fuckboy with a crown, but you actually seem to care for your people."

Thabiso squelched the reflexive indignation that flared in him. "I don't know what a fuckboy is, but my behavior toward you was less than honorable so I don't doubt you for thinking the worst of me."

"'Less than honorable?' *That's* marketing. I suppose pretending to be a commoner in order to get laid is just part of your 'job.'"

She said the words without emotion, but the implications hit Thabiso in the chest like a blow.

"You think I lied to you to get you into bed?"

She looked down. "You lied to me. You got me into bed. Am I missing something?"

"I can't fault you for thinking the worst of me, but you of all people should know correlation does not equal causation."

Ledi wouldn't look at him, but he hoped she was listening. He had ruined everything, but she couldn't think that he'd had sex with her as some fucked-up royal mind game.

"I meant to tell you as soon as I walked into the kitchen at the Institute. I had this whole speech planned out, demanding an explanation for why your family had run from Thesolo and never returned." He moved his chair a bit closer to her now, looked down into the face that until just weeks ago had been a blurred curiosity at the periphery of his imagination. He remembered the moment when it had all come into focus.

"You've been this presence in my life since I was a child, you see. You may not remember me, but I was never allowed to forget you. You became a myth I couldn't escape, a path that had been closed off to me. I wanted to find you and finally snuff out that silly hope I'd harbored for all those years. And then suddenly there you were, calling me Jamal and handing me kale, like that was completely normal. I had expected some rude, thoughtless woman, and instead you were . . . you."

Ledi dropped her spoon into her bowl with a ringing clatter. "So, what, lying to me was some kind of revenge for me leaving? I hate to break it to you, but you're late to the party. I've been paying for my parents' decision for years. Pass the word on to your folks, by the way, since they didn't get the memo."

"Lying to you was a mistake," Thabiso said, but then amended that. "No, that's not true. Maybe part of me did want to punish you. Remember, most of my life has been spent hearing how your family betrayed mine. I rationalized my deception by using your family's as a measuring stick. But mostly, when I saw you, I wanted to know you. And I've found it's very hard to do that once you utter the words, 'I'm a prince.'"

"You think this justifies what you did?" Ledi asked. Her face scrunched up into an expression of incredulous rage.

"No," he said. "But knowing that if I'd told you the truth from the beginning means I would never have worked with you, or cooked with you, or ridden the subway and walked hand in hand in the park with you? That makes it very hard to say I would have done otherwise."

Ledi opened her mouth, then closed it and looked away from him. He didn't like how defeated she looked in that moment.

"I don't get close to people," she finally said. "It's something I've been pretty firm about because of the whole defective Velcro thing."

Thabiso had to have misheard. "What? Velcro?"

"No one ever sticks." The words came out quiet. Small. Not like Ledi at all, or perhaps exactly like the Ledi that she hid behind all those walls of hers. But then she shook her head and the anger returned. "But for some reason, I felt like maybe you were—Jamal was—someone worth letting in. Someone who might stick. And it was all a lie. You expect me to forget that? No." She shook her head. "Get out of here."

She turned and took up her stylus again and stared straight out the window, waiting for him to leave.

Thabiso couldn't move; he was still reeling from her words. He hadn't known how deeply he had hurt her, but he also hadn't understood how deeply he cared that he had.

Someone who might stick.

She hadn't known of his wealth or his fame, or anything of their past, and she had wanted him regardless. Thabiso tried to reconcile that with his lie, and what had happened because of the lie, and what would have happened if he hadn't lied at all.

"I don't expect you to forget. But, Ledi, what would you have said if I'd shown up at your job and proclaimed that I was a prince from some African kingdom you'd never heard of and you were my betrothed? Honestly."

She kept her back to him. "Get. Out."

"Exactly," he said. He exhaled loudly and stroked his palm over his beard. "Look, we have this ceremony with the priestesses in an hour or so. You've made it perfectly clear that you don't want to be around me, and rightfully so, but we do have a charade to keep up, Bones."

"Bones?" Her head tilted.

"You said that before, at your lab—" Thabiso was cut off by the thing he least expected at that moment—Naledi's laughter. Just like that, her expression went from pinched to soft and open. She threw her head back as she laughed, and his cock jumped at the memory of her tight around him as she executed a similar motion. Goddess, she was beautiful, all the time, but even more so when she was too preoccupied to push him away.

"You've never seen *Star Trek*, have you?" she asked.

"That's with the guy with the black helmet and the funny voice, yeah?" He knew better, but he wouldn't pass up this opportunity to make her smile one more time.

"I'm pretty sure I told you to get out." The words were firm, but there was no malice in them; there was the slightest hint of amusement. Thabiso would take it.

"Someone will come for you to bring you to the temple soon," he said on his way out.

"Oh, I got an alert for that. Likotsi added it to my planner," she said, picking up her tablet. Thabiso was sure Kotsi would be pleased that someone finally appreciated her attempts at modern planning. Ledi swiped, squinting at the screen. "Purification ceremony. This isn't going to get too weird, is it?"

"I think it's just a blessing ceremony, shouldn't be anything too extreme."

She didn't look up again, and after a moment Thabiso understood it was because she had already kicked him out three times.

Maybe his affection for her was futile, but if he'd hurt her more than anyone else, perhaps it was because she had cared for him more than anyone else. The minute chance that he was right meant he couldn't give up. Not yet.

Chapter 27

*A*fter Thabiso's departure, Ledi found herself unable to focus on the facts and figures before her. He'd broken her concentration, another thing to add to the list of reasons to hate him that she was compiling: liar, concentration breaker, shoddy cook, excellent kisser, master of making her toes curl . . .

Wait.

She was losing track of her thoughts. Perhaps pulling an all-nighter hadn't been the smartest idea. That had to be why she was giddy instead of angry, why her fingers had been itching to pull up a video montage of a droll, intergalactic doctor for her and Thabiso to laugh over instead of shooing the annoying prince out of her door. She was glad she hadn't asked him to stay; that would have been dangerous. She knew what happened when she watched TV next to Thabiso—or rather, what happened when she fell asleep watching television with him, and she was a few blinks away from slumber, despite her protests to the contrary.

She stood and stretched, almost toppling over from the rush of blood to the head. Yep. The all-nighter had definitely been no good. She grabbed her tablet and then moved slowly to her bed, where she perched on the edge to wait out her swimming head. She'd really underestimated how hard the jet lag would hit her, but her lack of travel meant she'd had no idea what jet lag even was. She'd be kinder to her lab mates returning from overseas conferences when she got back.

Because you are going back.

She tapped the photo widget on the tablet and flipped through the images in the device. She didn't linger on any particular photo; she couldn't bring herself to do that, although she'd already looked through them several times. A chubby toddler, presumably her, running through a garden, grabbing at flowers. Her parents, sitting on a couch and looking at each other; her father's hand resting on her mother's belly. Funny, how she thought she'd imagined certain features when she'd tried to recall her parents, like the way her father's eyebrows arched like the villain in a movie. His eyes were large and kind, though. She hadn't remembered that.

They looked so happy in all the photos. That made sense, since people rarely took photos when they felt like shit, but still. She couldn't understand what had driven them to leave. To take her away from all that she knew. She had never been angry at her parents before during all those years bouncing around foster care, but now each memory of the past, each reminder of what she'd had and lost, stoked her resentment.

A wave of fatigue crashed into her, and she placed the tablet at her side and leaned back onto the soft bed. It was like falling into a dark well, where thoughts of her parents and Thabiso and Thesolo couldn't reach.

"My lady?" There was a knock at the door, and Ledi jumped up. She'd only meant to close her eyes for a minute, but now she was sleep-drugged and unsure of how much time had passed.

"Crap," she whispered as she sprang unsteadily to her feet. "Coming!"

The attendant from the day before entered, this time without her rack of clothing. She had only one item draped over her arm.

"Are you ready for the ceremony?" she asked.

"I haven't showered or dressed. I'm sorry, but I need a few more minutes." Great. She was going to piss off the priestesses. Hopefully their goddess wasn't a vengeful one.

"Dress? Shower?" The attendant's brows rose. "Were you not told about the specifics of the ceremony?"

Ledi's shoulders sagged. "No."

"All you need is this"—she shook out the silk robe draped over her arm—"and a pure heart."

"Um, okay, one out of two isn't bad," Ledi muttered as she stepped toward the robe. The attendant pulled it away. "Oh, maybe I wasn't clear. This is *all* you need." She glanced pointedly at Ledi's sweater and jeans, and then turned her head away, while holding the robe up.

Ledi sighed and began stripping down. The quicker she was naked and in the robe, the faster she could get to Thabiso—and throttle him.

"YOU SAID THIS wouldn't be weird," Ledi said in a low voice. "So far I've been scrubbed down and oiled up by some random women, had my feet kissed by some *other* random women, had my aura massaged, and then had a staring contest."

After her examination by the priestesses, a white linen band had been tied around her chest bandeau style and another length of linen wrapped around her waist like a skirt. She'd been led out onto a stage to stand beside Thabiso, who had the same linen wrapped around his waist. Bare chest and linen skirt was a damn good look for him.

They knelt with bowed heads before a group of people, including the king and queen, who stared up at them with solemn expressions.

"Seriously, that massage delved into places I don't think even I've explored," she whispered, and Thabiso tried and failed to swallow a snort of laughter.

A priestess turned and shushed her, and Ledi felt like she'd been caught talking in the library, except the draft that swept up beneath her skirt reminded her she usually had on underwear when checking out books.

"People pay good money for spa services in New York, don't they?" Thabiso said. She could hear the grin in his voice.

"If I find out this has all been some cult recruitment long con, I will end you," she muttered.

"I assure you, it's not a cult. And weird is relative, anyway," Thabiso reminded her. "We think eating the body and drinking the blood of one's deity is fairly strange, but don't judge others for it."

A high, strong voice rang out from among the priestesses. They were all clad in the same loose linen dresses, with matching headwraps, and Ledi could not tell whether the median age was older than her or younger because apparently oil rubs and aura massages did a body good.

"We, the priestesses of Ingoka, mother of all and sculptress of Fate, have spent these last twenty years in doubt." A chorus of "yes" rose up behind her from the women. "Two decades of recrimination, of wondering whether the goddess had abandoned us or we had been misled by the Deceiver. All because of this girl."

She turned and pointed toward Ledi.

Ledi forgot that she was annoyed at Thabiso, forgot that he was beside her. The power of the woman's voice enveloped her, paralyzed her, like she was a pathogen and they were the neutrophils charged with casting her out. The anguish in the woman's voice . . . She had caused that? She wasn't religious, but had they examined her soul and found it impure? Unworthy? The thought of it spurred panic in her. It was defective Velcro writ large, and they were about to tell everyone exactly what was wrong with her.

Ledi began to rise, but then Thabiso's hand was closing over hers. Why did he keep her there, where she was unwanted, again?

Always.

Her chest heaved and he squeezed her hand tightly. It was too much, his fingers strong and warm around hers, like he wanted her there beside him when she so clearly didn't belong. Everyone could see that except him.

The priestess continued her speech. "We failed our kingdom by selecting a future queen who deserted us. Sickness stalks among our people, and the future of Thesolo is in jeopardy. Surely, Ingoka is punishing us for our mistake, yes?"

Ledi closed her eyes against tears—and against the murmurs in the crowd. Why had she agreed to come? Why had she thought anything would be different?

"NO."

The voices of all the priestesses combined in one loud, resolute word, one that left Ledi's defenses nothing but tattered strands of DNA.

"We have examined this woman, and she has the same pure heart and bright mind as the girl we chose all those years ago. The spirit of our people is strong in her. She is fit to be a prince's bride, and a future queen."

"Naledi's returned to us," sang out one of the women, her voice a high keen that floated through the temple.

"Sign of Ingoka's grace," sang another.

"Naledi's returned to us," all of the priestesses sang as one, some voices soaring high, others rumbling low. "Returned to take her rightful place."

The priestess broke out into whoops of jubilation and circled her and Thabiso in a joyful dance. Flowers, yellow and purple and pink, rained down around them. Ledi's heart felt like it would burst as the women graced her with their joyous smiles. They were happy she was there. Ecstatic.

These women don't know you. This is an act.

It might have been a performance for the royal court, but Ledi couldn't fight the warmth that flowed through her, the sense of belonging. She couldn't fight the fact that she felt like a princess.

Thabiso squeezed her hand and pulled her to her feet. "Come. It's about time we did this."

"What?" Her voice was barely there because she was exerting all her energy stopping herself from weeping.

"This."

He hopped to the side, bent his knees, and worked his hips, just as he had in the park that day. A cheer went up from the crowd and Ledi laughed, delight flooding her senses as the realization hit.

"You didn't make that dance up?" she asked.

"This dance is thousands of years old," he said, switching to the other leg.

"It is also a question. Only you can answer him,"

one of the priestesses said, coming to stand beside Ledi. She leaned forward, opened her arms wide, and then pulled them in, her hips moving in tighter circles than Thabiso's. "Like this."

Dancing on a stage in front of a crowd was not something Ledi felt capable of. But Thabiso was looking at her so earnestly as he danced, and the priestesses were clapping and singing, and then there was that connection. The connection she'd felt the moment he'd walked into the Institute pulsed within her, riding the rhythm created by the claps and trills of the priestesses. She'd gone rigid at the idea of dancing, but willed herself to relax, to let her hips sway the way the priestess beside her demonstrated. Her hips didn't move as fluidly, and she kept messing up the push and pull motion with her arms, but the priestess stepped away, and then there was just Thabiso before her.

His gaze burned into her as he inched closer. With each step, he paused to move his hips, the dance dragging out into something spiritual and sensual at the same time. Ledi's body tingled and her heart felt filled to overflowing, and after a moment she realized she wasn't focusing on moving correctly, but on moving naturally.

She understood the dance now, her arms and hips and entire being calling out to Thabiso, opening up to receive him as he moved toward her, ever so slowly. She *felt it*. Finally, he was before her and they both stopped moving, eyes locked on one another and nothing but the wild beating of her heart—*their hearts?*—in her ears. Ledi couldn't breathe, couldn't think, and didn't know how to proceed, but Thabiso did. He dropped to his knees and bowed down before her, and the entire room went silent as he did. She could feel his breath on her toes, something so intimate that it sent a shiver up her body.

"The betrothal ceremony, started all those years ago, is now complete. Naledi has accepted Thabiso's suit. Let us all welcome her into our hearts."

Everyone bowed down, following Thabiso's lead, except the king and queen, who knelt. The queen regarded her steadily, her expression unreadable. Ledi looked out over the room, unsure of what was happening even as the attendees began to stand.

As the euphoria died down, the priestess's words sank in.

"Accepted what?" she asked.

"Thabiso's request for your hand. You are now officially engaged in the eyes of Ingoka."

Chapter 28

"Son?"

Thabiso turned at the sound of his mother's voice echoing in the palace hallway. He hadn't really spoken to her since Ledi's arrival, in part because he was busy dealing with rebellious finance ministers and a possible epidemic, and in part because he hadn't wanted to. He couldn't think of much to say to her, given her treatment of Ledi, that wouldn't result in banishment. That wasn't what he was afraid of, though. He'd never fought with his parents over something substantial. Disagreements about how to rule their country and his deportment were one thing, but the low insults they'd resorted to of late were something he didn't know how to equate with the people he loved most. He didn't know how to navigate this new rocky terrain in the geography of their relationship.

"Mother."

He waited as her heels clicked noisily down the hall, the sound bouncing off of the walls of a palace that had stood strong for generations. That would one day be his.

She slid her arm through his and they fell into

step, continuing toward the private wing. They had walked like this so many times before, but it felt forced now, stiff.

"That was quite a spectacle earlier," she said.

Spectacle? As he had danced with Ledi, he'd felt something move in him. He wasn't sure if it was Ingoka, but it had been suspiciously close to the center of his chest and had throbbed painfully as Ledi beckoned him closer. Calling it a spectacle cheapened it.

"I was quite pleased with how the purification ceremony turned out," he said, putting his diplomatic training to good use. "I'm glad the priestesses did not find her wanting. I wish everyone shared their belief in Ingoka's will."

His mother sighed, then stopped and looked up at him. "Thabiso, you are our only child. We have tried to instill in you the importance of your role in this kingdom, but perhaps we were remiss in extolling the importance of choosing the proper wife."

"Interesting. You weren't quite so particular before I left, throwing any breathing woman my way, and going so far as to bring in Shanti while I was away."

"Shanti knows how to be a queen because she was raised for it. She would be an excellent and attentive wife, would see to your needs and—"

Thabiso disengaged his arm from hers as frustration made her touch irksome. "I don't love her, Mother!" Thabiso had never raised his voice to his mother before. Shame and anger and sadness washed over him, and dealing with that was hard enough without taking into account what he had just confessed.

She stared at him for a long while, and then shook her head sadly. "Maybe I shouldn't have indulged you when you were a child who insisted she and her parents would return."

"Why? I was right. She's here now."

The queen's gaze sharpened. "Are you willing to gamble the future of our country on whatever game it is you're playing?"

"This is not a game." He exhaled through flared nostrils. "I'm sorry, but I refuse to discuss this further. You've raised me to be a man who does not give up on what he believes in. I can't begin to figure out why you're set against Naledi, but my choice is made."

"Is hers?" the queen pressed.

Thabiso had no response that wasn't a lie, and he was done with lying.

"I have things to attend to," he said.

She nodded. "Your father and I have pressured you, but you know we only want what is best for you, right? You must know that."

Thabiso couldn't stand the sight of the uncertainty in his mother's face. He leaned down and pulled her into a hug.

"I know you do, mother. But you're going to have to trust me here."

"I trust you. It's her I'm worried about." She pulled her head back to look him in the face, concern etched into her expression. "Thabiso, you have never truly experienced loss. Loving someone, letting them into your heart, and then losing them, or worse, being betrayed? It's something we must all face at some point, but if I can prevent you from being hurt unnecessarily, I will." She turned on her heels, clicking her way back in the direction she'd come from.

Thabiso looked after his mother. She had always been protective, and perhaps indulgent, but had never coddled him. His mother had always been particularly incensed by the betrayal of the Ajouas, but he'd thought that would fade once she knew that they had died, and perhaps would have returned. He had been wrong.

He made his way to Naledi's room, his mother's words echoing in his head. When he'd been kneeling down before Naledi during the ceremony, the first time he'd so abased himself before anyone, something had clicked for Thabiso. He couldn't let her go. He wouldn't. He wanted her, not out of some twisted nostalgia or because she wasn't a prize easily won, but because she was perfect for him and—perhaps just as important—perfect for his people. She pushed him to try harder, just through her own example. What could they do together as husband and wife— king and queen?

His mother was right, though. No matter what he wanted, she wasn't planning to stay, and he wasn't selfish enough to hope that the medical crisis lasted long enough to keep her in his kingdom. He imagined her getting back on the plane to leave and his frustration grew again. Could he really just let her leave? Could he let another moment pass in which she thought he didn't care if she did?

His mind was racing by the time he'd made his way down the damned interminably long hallway and reached her room.

"Naledi."

He knocked hard, and she opened the door with the general look of annoyance she seemed to reserve for him.

"I'm busy, so unless there's an emergency—"

"I think this counts as an emergency."

His hands went to her waist, fingertips sinking into her curves as he pulled her toward him. He dropped his head, angling for her lips, but stopped just before their mouths touched, resting his forehead against hers.

"Can I?" he asked. He wasn't going to kiss her into submission. He had already submitted to the force that drew him to her—he could only ask her to join him willingly.

"Um." Her breath was coming fast and she hadn't pulled away, but she looked ready to bolt. "This is novel. Guys don't usually ask after the first time."

Frustration tautened within him.

"I'm a fucking gentleman, Naledi. Gentlemen don't assume, they ask. So. Can I kiss you?"

"Wow. No pressure at all," she said, raising her eyebrows.

"Oh, there's a ton of pressure," he said, and realized how ridiculous the line sounded without the part he'd left unspoken. *In my pants.* He wasn't entirely a gentleman.

Ledi huffed a breath. "In your pants?" she asked.

The tension between them deflated, pierced by the sharp laughter that burst from them both. He let his head fall back, away from hers, but his hands still rested on her hips.

"Goddess. And to think I was once voted World's Smoothest Royal." He shook his head.

"Wait, people vote on these things?"

He dropped his hands from her waist, walked over to her bed, and flopped down on it.

"Well, luckily for me it's usually a group of strangers who've never heard my attempts at seduction."

"Obviously." The door clicked shut.

"No need to agree so heartily," he muttered.

"I needed that laugh," she said with a sigh, sitting on the edge of the bed. "Today has been really intense.

I've barely slept, I've been reading case studies all day, and that ceremony really fucked me up. Emotionally."

"You're not the only one," he said, folding her pillow beneath his head so he was propped up and looking at her.

"I grew up with no one, Thabiso. No one. And now?" Her voice cracked, and she cleared her throat. "I don't know how to take in what happened today, or what I'm feeling. It's just too much. Priestesses singing to me. Welcoming me. People bowing to me." Her eyes squeezed shut. "And you. There's you."

"What about me?" He leaned up away from the pillow, and her eyes fluttered open. Her gaze ran over his face and the pain and confusion he saw there lanced through him.

"This isn't real." She motioned to the air between them. "But it's starting to feel way too real and . . . I can't. I just can't."

"And what if it feels real to me, too?" he asked quietly. "What if it feels real because it is?"

His heart thumped heavy in his chest, because yes, that was it. It was real for him, always had been, and she might never feel the same way.

She shook her head. "The only reason you think we should be together is because you were told we should be, and now you need a wife. Let's say I agree that this is real. What then? One day you'll realize what everyone does eventually." She shook her head. "I can't."

Thabiso's frustration pushed him up to a sitting position.

"Has it ever occurred to you that I like you? You. Naledi. And that I would have liked you even if there was no betrothal ceremony?"

"No, it hasn't," she said stiffly.

He thought back to her comment from their previous conversation and was struck by something. "This is the Velcro thing, isn't it? The not sticking? Ledi, if you haven't noticed, let me tell you, I'm stuck. Intractably so."

"Enough, Thabiso." Her voice was barely a whisper.

"Why? Would us being together really be the most terrible thing to happen to you?"

"No, being left parentless in a foreign country was the worst thing to happen to me," she said. Her expression closed off again.

"Ledi." He pitched his voice gentle, trying to ease in between the bricks of the wall she was rapidly rebuilding.

She looked at him, expressionless. "It's funny that you resented me for abandoning you. You with your family and servants and people. Meanwhile, halfway across the globe, I was the one who was alone." She swiped at her eyes. "You should have told me. The minute you knew that I had no idea who I was, you should have told me. But you didn't. So no, I can't say yes when you come to my door all handsome and Disney-eyed, asking if you can kiss me."

There it was. Thabiso had been so fixated on forcing her to forget he'd lied about Jamal that he'd missed the forest for the trees. He'd done more than that; he'd lied to Ledi about herself. Likotsi had called him a coward and she had been right.

He exhaled, a deep weary sound. "What can I say? I'm sorry for being a fuckboy, Naledi."

Ledi shrugged, swiped surreptitiously at her eyes again. "Fuckboyism is a fairly common disease in men aged eighteen to thirty-five."

"What's the cure?" he asked.

"You'll have to ask your doctor about that. But I can tell you right now that it's not me."

With that, she got up and walked back to her desk.

Thabiso fought the urge to stalk over and command her to forgive him; she wasn't one of his subjects. He headed for the door.

"We have the trip to Lek Hemone, your hometown, tomorrow morning. Dress warmly because it's at a higher altitude."

"Thanks. Hopefully we'll find what we're looking for there because nothing in the research is giving any clues as to what's going on here. I need to figure this out."

So you can go.

"May the goddess make it so," he said, and then walked back into the hallway, closing the door behind him.

Thabiso stood for a moment. Although he'd been told otherwise his entire life, he was learning that there was something stronger than a Moshoeshoe prince's will.

Reality.

Chapter 29

*L*edi thought daily subway commutes had prepared her to handle any means of transportation,
but she'd been mistaken.

She readjusted herself on D'artagnan—the donkey
that was conveying her to Lek Hemane—as it ambled
up the winding mountain trail at a slow, steady pace,
and prayed that the animal didn't make any sudden
moves. It was super cute, and had looked at her like
she was its best friend after she gave it some apple
slices, but she couldn't quite get with transportation
that could also take a bite out of her.

When the Land Rover carrying her and Thabiso to
Lek Hemane had stopped at the base of a winding trail
where a few goat herdsmen awaited with their flock,
Ledi had thought it was a cultural break, not the next
leg of their journey. She'd tentatively fed some goats
and chatted with a shepherd. She'd even felt a spark
of adventure when she was hoisted onto D'artagnan,
that is, until Thabiso had climbed on behind her. An
hour riding a donkey up steep, mountainous terrain
surrounded by goats was jarring enough—goats were
way chattier than she'd realized—but having Thabiso
settled in behind her was even more disorienting.

Their conversation the previous evening had left her unsettled. She wanted so badly to believe what he'd said. But he had lied before. Could she really trust him?

"Doing okay?" he asked from behind her.

"I still don't see why we couldn't have taken a helicopter up here," she said, then shivered as a cold blast of wind swept across the exposed skin of her face.

"Because the mountain winds are too strong to ensure a safe landing," he said. "This is the safest route."

Safe? Thabiso's thighs pressed into her hips, his strong arms caged her as he held the reins, and his body heat inscribed warm memories of their night together into the skin of her back. There was nothing safe about that. She'd spent the entire ride ashamed at the way she wanted to push her ass back into him, to feel the length of him grow against her, like he wasn't a man who'd betrayed her.

She arched her back away from Thabiso and sucked in a breath of air so cold that she thought she might be able to feel each individual bronchiole as it froze. She focused on that instead of how her body protested being separated from his. "You could have found your own donkey," she said.

"I could have," he said, leaning forward just enough to close the space she'd created between them without pressing himself against her. "I think you would find the trip much colder without me here at your back. Sorry, but you're stuck with me."

Her breath caught at his words and she wished she had never let her silly Velcro hang-up slip. He couldn't be telling the truth. She had years and years of evidence to back her up—people might give her a try, but in the end, she was not the kind of person anyone kept around.

"I really hate having people behind me, actually," she bit out. "Especially people I can't trust." She needed to remind herself of why she couldn't just relax against him. Why she couldn't believe it when he said that maybe they could have something more.

She felt the expansion of his chest as he sighed. "Well, I watch the backs of people I care about, whether they trust me to or not. It's a princely requirement, though my wanting to protect you has nothing to do with my job. That's one thing we should be clear on."

"Oh, now you want to be clear?" she snapped. That wasn't entirely fair, though. He'd been trying to clarify things ever since she'd discovered the truth. And before that. She remembered that day in Fort Tryon Park, and that night, and how many times he'd tried to tell her before the gala.

His arms tightened against her sides a bit as he leaned closer to her ear.

"Yes. I want to be clear now. I should have been honest with you sooner, but I was frightened of losing you. I believe this is called irony." She felt a laugh rumble through his chest, but could tell it wasn't a happy one. "Even if you never forgive me, even if you leave Thesolo and don't look back, know that I will regret hurting you for the rest of my days. And, I'm sure you already know this from your research, but Thesoloians have quite a long life span."

She told herself that it was the cold wind that was making her eyes water. Why did it seem like the more determined she was to keep him at arm's length, the easier it was for his words to affect her? And his touch, too?

"Thabiso—"

"The town is just around the bend," one of the herdsmen called out.

They made a sharp turn and the rocky cliff face gave way to a sprawling town like something out of a nativity scene. Most of the snow-dusted houses appeared to be traditional Thesoloian huts like the ones she'd read about during her research—round structures with thatch roofs—but as they drew closer, Naledi realized they were made of concrete, not clay, and painted brown. The thatch was real, but it had to cover some other structure judging from the weight of the satellite dishes and solar panels that rested on each house. They looked like large, fancy yurts, and Ledi half expected to see a crew from the House & Home channel filming a segment.

In the distance, larger, less traditional houses loomed—Victorians, Georgians, and a couple of blocky condominiums.

Snow had been packed down and worn away on the cobblestones beneath D'artagnan's hooves, but the sidewalks were completely clear. They were also steaming.

"Is this mountain a volcano?" she asked. "Because with the luck I've been having, it might be better for everyone if I left."

Thabiso chuckled.

"There are heated coils in the sidewalks that melt the snow," he said. "The meltwater is collected in drains and used to heat homes, so people no longer have to use wood or coal. Energy efficient and good for the atmosphere, although not ideal when the livestock decide to stray from the street."

"That's impressive," Ledi said. "Is every town this advanced?"

"Not yet. Lek Hemane was the site of our pilot project because they receive the most snowfall, but we hope to expand the project soon. It had been put on hold when the Omega Corp deal was in play."

"Why?" she asked.

"Because there was no use investing in a town where the people would be uprooted and the infrastructure razed."

"Oh." A frisson of foreboding went down her spine. "I imagine that would have been a hard choice to make."

"Unfortunately, it came quite easily to some."

She remembered his talk of the finance ministers and how they were upset about the deal he hadn't agreed to. Making large-scale decisions like this must have been the equivalent of a group assignment with some major assholes, but where the fate of a country rested on it instead of a grade.

"You made the right choice," she said, and felt him stiffen behind her. "I give you a lot of shit, but you do seem to have the well-being of your people in mind. I can't say the same of most people in power."

"Nearly everyone is unhappy with me right now, so that's refreshing," he said. "Honestly? It feels like I'm doing everything wrong, and I've only been given a portion of the royal responsibility. I feel like I can't make any mistakes at all, but everything I do causes discontent."

There was vulnerability in his voice. Ledi knew that feeling well. She'd spent most of her life thinking if she did everything just right, things would work out. She'd be adopted, she'd get into a good school, she'd get the right practicum. In the end, nothing had worked out as planned, but everything had still worked out. She had her practicum, she had found her family, and she was on a noble steed with a handsome prince. Not too shabby.

"If I have to say one thing about you it's that you're persistent and you own up to your mistakes. And you care. That's a good start for a future king."

She closed her eyes and for a moment imagined what it would be like to be his future queen. To have such responsibility would be nerve-racking, but the trade-off would be getting to help people. Being royalty might have its upside, but thinking about it in relation to herself was asking for trouble.

"You won't ever be perfect—"

"Because of the fuckboyism?" he cut in.

"Because you're human," she said. "And humans make mistakes."

"So I've heard. So. I've. Heard." He maneuvered the donkey around an SUV.

She thought of Thabiso's expression that day in the park when he'd tried to tell her the truth; that night when he'd tried again. And again. She thought of Portia, who had made mistakes but who she missed so much it hurt. That was the thing with people getting past your defenses. They were bound to fuck up, maybe a little, maybe a lot. It was what they did afterward that counted. Ledi wondered if her Velcro was always defective, or if sometimes she was so scared of being hurt that she preemptively ripped herself away.

She turned her attention back to the town instead of digging deeper into that revelation. The sky was slate gray and overcast, and glowing streetlights illuminated cars and motorbikes and goats that rambled along the streets, a mix of ancient and modern.

"This is where my family is from."

Thabiso murmured a sound of confirmation behind her. Ledi strained, tried so hard to remember a life with her parents that she briefly felt dizzy, but came up with nothing. She didn't remember a damn thing about this place.

"Funny. I hate snow."

He didn't say anything, but it didn't feel like a careless silence. He seemed to be giving her space to breathe.

It was hard to take in, the differences from the life she'd known in New York and what she saw before her. As they passed a larger house, a group of children came bolting out of the gate, pelting each other with snowballs. Their happy laughter echoed off of the cobblestones, and a couple of women in parkas came out and joined in the snowball fight. Ledi caught sight of the sign in front and sucked in a breath.

LEK HEMANE ORPHANAGE

"It looks like any other home here," she said. "The group homes I was in always felt like what they were. A place for kids they didn't know what to do with. Not because the social workers didn't try, but they were underpaid, overworked, and fighting a system that should have been helping them along."

Thabiso dropped the rein with one hand and circled his arm around her so she was cradled against him. It felt good, too good, but she allowed herself the comfort. "Children who lose their parents in Thesolo are raised by the community. They live with the caretakers at the orphanage, but the orphanage is at the center of town because we believe everyone should interact with and take care of them. Nya works at the school that is attached."

She thought of the lonely halfway houses and overcrowded foster homes. Those children had run past like they were free and happy, and unafraid of anything. Had she ever felt that safe?

You do now, in Thabiso's arms.

She ignored the emotions that threatened to overtake her when he pulled her closer and sighed.

"Are we near the hospital?" she asked.

"It's straight ahead, just a few blocks down."

"Good." She grabbed the reins just a bit below where he held them and pulled, as she'd seen him do; he released his hold on her. The donkey stopped and she gave him a pat on the head. "I'll get off here and do some looking around before speaking with Dr. Bata."

She slid down to the ground, her body suddenly cool where Thabiso had kept her warm.

He nodded. "I will tell her you're on your way. Be careful, please."

With that he was off. How did he make riding a donkey look sexy? D'artagnan looked back at her, batting his long lashes as if to say *Girl, I know.*

Ledi took a deep breath. She needed to get her head right before they arrived at the hospital. No thoughts of what it would be like to be queen, or of orphans, of Thabiso up against her back and promising to watch out for her. She was coming into an investigation that was already underway, and though she had already been brought up to speed there was so much more work ahead of her. They were already at step five of the outbreak investigation, trying to orient the data they already had in terms of time, place, and people. She needed to prove herself useful to Dr. Bata; that was the real reason she was in Thesolo, after all.

Is it, though? Like her Velcro theory, her "I'm not here to make friends" theory was quickly unraveling.

Her social cell membrane had completely failed her, but maybe that wasn't always such a bad thing.

She passed a small restaurant; through the window she could see men squeezed into the small space and laughing as they told stories and ate delicious-looking meat. Her stomach growled, despite the rich breakfast she'd eaten. The one Thabiso had brought in to her, again, despite his gaggle of servants.

Ledi trudged forward to the hospital, but a familiar scent caught her attention as she walked by a small shop. She stepped inside, the rattle of beads above the door announcing her entry as she was enveloped in a mélange of smells, some floral, some musk.

An older woman with long, gray dreads and a round face turned toward her, and then her eyes widened. "My lady! Welcome back." She hurried from behind the counter and curtsied.

"Um . . ." Ledi curtsied back, or as close as she could get after spending the morning astride a donkey.

"Oh, I remember when you were a little potbellied thing, toddling around, and now look at you! The spitting image of your grandmother. We are all so happy you have returned," she said, her eyes filling with tears.

Ledi shifted uncomfortably under the woman's gaze. This was the first time she had been out on her own away from the palace and she hadn't thought about how people would react to her. She certainly hadn't expected this kind of reception.

The woman curtsied again, as if she also didn't know the protocol for interacting with a prodigal betrothed. "We prayed to the goddess that the prince would find a bride and end this terrible curse that has befallen our land, and our prayers were answered tenfold!"

"Thank you. I'm happy to be back, although this is all a bit overwhelming for me." Ledi lifted a sachet of leaves and sniffed it. "Why do you think the goddess would punish the country because Thabiso was unwed?"

Thabiso had mentioned there were rumors but she'd been on palace grounds since her arrival. No one would dare speak ill of him there.

The woman seemed surprised. "Well, you should talk to your uncle. He is a very educated man, but he is well versed in the traditional ways, too. Even before the illness started, he warned us of what would happen if the prince dawdled. Ingoka has given Alehk the gift of foresight, and he wishes to use it to aid the people of Lek Hemane, and of Thesolo."

The way the shopkeeper spoke of Alehk raised the hairs at the back of Ledi's neck. Maybe they had a little something going on, or maybe she just had a crush, but there was something beneath the woman's words that seemed off. Some people thought science was all about cold, hard facts, but that wasn't exactly true, especially when it came to fieldwork.

The facts come eventually, one of her professors had told their class. *But before that, there is instinct. It's not mumbo jumbo—we are animals, after all, and instinct is just a tool in our species' survival kit. Never forget that.*

"Are the townspeople unhappy?" Naledi asked. "Did they not feel my grandparents were leading them well?"

She thought of the frail couple hooked up to tubes and felt a flare of anger on their behalf.

"No, not at all, my lady!" The woman grimaced and looked about, as though they weren't the only ones in the tiny shop. "It's just . . . you have been away for a long while, living in the US with all of its opulence.

Annie and Makelele are content with slow change, but Alehk thinks we could do more to help all Thesoloians live richly, not just those in the palace."

Ledi was going to counter that her tiny studio wasn't opulent, but she swallowed that comeback because it was a lie, comparatively speaking. She was privileged, yes, but what she had seen of Lek Hemane didn't jibe with an underserved community. This woman had obviously never seen an overcrowded Bronx classroom or a housing project in Brooklyn in dire need of repair.

Ledi took another tack.

"Oh, is it Alehk who got the solar panels installed?" Ledi asked. "And the heated coils in the sidewalks?"

"That was your grandparents' doing," the woman admitted. "They have been working with Prince Thabiso on environmental initiatives."

"That seems very forward thinking to me," Ledi said.

"Indeed," the woman said, and then laughed nervously. Her smile was now of the "I said too much" variety. "We are all wishing for their quick return to health. Please take the tea as my gift."

She picked up the box of sachets Ledi had been sniffing and handed them over. "They are a combination of local herbs and it is said to bring clear thinking, luck, and . . . assistance in the bedroom."

The woman gave her a coquettish grin as she not so subtly guided her to the door, and Ledi couldn't help the heat that rose to her face. Thabiso didn't need any additional skills in the bedroom.

And why would you give the tea to him, *anyway?*

Ledi tucked the tea into her bag, gave her thanks, and headed for the hospital, mulling over the woman's strange behavior. She was only a visitor, but it seemed that Thesolo was a nation that took the well-being of its citizens seriously. She'd have to do more digging, but something wasn't adding up. The woman had spoken as if those in power didn't do enough—worse, as if Thabiso had actively brought harm to them. Ledi tried not to imagine the pressure of having thousands of people blame your bachelor lifestyle for a disease. No wonder Thabiso had risked asking her for help.

She had resented it, but thinking of him standing before the crowd with anyone else—pretending to love anyone else—made her want to kick something.

She stepped into the clean, bright waiting room of the hospital, only to find it packed with people, most of them anxious and looking about for help. Fathers clutched children to their chests, and people sat in visible clusters, shying away from their neighbors. A man stood at the front desk, his loud voice filled with frustration as he railed at the intake nurse. "How can you make us wait when we are sick with the Prince's plague? It is his fault, and he must fix this!"

Could all of the people before her possibly be sick? How could she help all of them? The urge to back out of the door was strong, but then she thought of her grandparents and girded herself. She wanted to help people, and now was her opportunity to do just that.

She made her way through the crowded waiting room and a nurse buzzed her through. "We've been waiting for you," the young woman said. "They're in the back."

Thabiso was talking to Dr. Bata, the epidemiologist, and Ledi ran over to them.

"Is what that man's yelling true? Are all of these people sick?" Nothing in the data she'd pored over the night before had indicated that such an explosive uptick in the number of cases was possible. In fact, the disease had seemed to be moving at a snail's pace, its spread following a yet-to-be identified and completely random pattern. If it hadn't stricken two of the most important people in the kingdom, it might have gone unnoticed for months.

Dr. Bata gave Ledi a tired smile and removed the round glasses perched on her nose to rub at the lenses with the hem of her shirt. "There have been no new cases reported, but apparently there was a town hall meeting last night. It seems that the symptoms of the disease were discussed in quite the convincing, and blatantly incorrect, fashion, and now half the town believes they have the Prince's plague. My apologies, Your Highness."

Thabiso smirked. "I quite like the ring of it actually. It isn't every ruler who will be known for bringing sickness upon his people. It's very biblical." His frown and the way he tilted his head to the side and stroked his beard belied the jokiness of his words. She had seen him make the gesture several times since she'd arrived. She remembered him doing the same that night in her apartment as he'd tried to talk to her—the night where she'd basically told him that nothing he said would change what she felt for him.

So he's not the only liar in the room, it seems.

Judging from the way she wanted to reassure him, to talk some sense into the people in the waiting room who had been misled by people they trusted into anger at him, perhaps nothing had changed at all. That was the thing about viruses—once they got through your defenses, sometimes they'd never go away, the remnants of them lingering in your bloodstream long after you thought you'd recovered. Sometimes they changed you down to the DNA.

"So this is basically like an old-school version of WebMD-itis?" she asked Dr. Bata, pulling her gaze away from Thabiso. "They were told vague symptoms and now they all believe they're sick?"

"Yes. Someone was irresponsible—reckless, in the event that any of the people here are actually sick and spread the illness to others. We'll have to evaluate every patient, just in case. The first day of your internship is going to be quite fun!"

"Great," Ledi said, and she wasn't entirely sarcastic about it.

"Likotsi told me she downloaded the appropriate apps on your tablet. Can you pull up the SansFrontiere app?"

Ledi did as she was told while Dr. Bata dug into a bag full of cords. She grabbed the end of a cord and plugged it into the jack on Ledi's tablet; the object on the other end wasn't a charger, it was a high-tech version of an otoscope. Without preamble, she stuck the device into Thabiso's ear and, a moment later, a reading popped up on Ledi's screen.

"Oh yesss!" Ledi exclaimed. "I didn't have the prereqs for the Modern Medicine class, but I'm fascinated by the use of technology in the field."

Dr. Bata grinned. "It's an app that's being developed for use in large-scale outbreaks, especially useful in places without much medical infrastructure and nomadic communities. That's not the case here, of course, but it's also just cool, yes?" The woman's eyes glinted with excitement. "There are three different attachments that take your readings and upload them, creating a digital file for each patient, an easily searchable database. It also cross-references other medical database apps to provide likely prognoses. You do have to input patient name, check off their symptoms, add notes, but at the end of the day we'll have lots of data to work with. Be sure to check for hives or rash developing along the neckline. That seems to be ground zero in the cases we've seen."

Ledi thrummed with excitement. Some of her cohorts had thought she'd be dealing with woebegone hospitals and difficult conditions when she'd mentioned her field study, but even Ledi hadn't realized she'd be working with equipment that wouldn't be common in the US for years—maybe never if the science regressivists got their way.

"Let's get to work," she said, feeling a surge of energy despite her lack of sleep.

She had a promise to keep, after all.

Chapter 30

*L*ater that evening, Ledi awoke under a warm quilt, wanting nothing more than to snuggle down and sleep for a hundred years. Was there an internship in sleep studies? She should have looked into that.

"Are you feeling better, my cousin?" Nya was at her side, and that was when she remembered that Alehk had showed up at the hospital just as she had wrapped up the morning's tiring work. Her uncle had invited her and Thabiso to lunch at his home. Ledi had asked to take a short nap and had been asleep before she hit the sheets.

"Still a bit groggy, but better," she said. "I guess my brain still hasn't caught up with the time zone. Did I miss lunch?"

Nya smiled indulgently. "Lunchtime has passed, cousin, and teatime. It is almost time for supper."

Ledi bolted up.

"What? How come no one woke me?" She scrambled for the boots she didn't remember taking off.

"Because Prince Thabiso said that you must sleep as long as necessary, and that you were not to be disturbed." Nya smiled and lowered her gaze. "He is very protective of you. And he cares enough to stay and be civil with my father, even after the castigation he received yesterday."

Ledi's brain was still halfway in the clouds, but she latched onto a fragment of the conversation she'd had with Thabiso that morning. "Alehk is a finance minister?"

"He is *the* finance minister, and he often doesn't see eye to eye with the royal family. Sometimes I think it's because . . ." Nya's cheeks showed just the slightest tinge of blush. "You see, after your parents left, he assumed that I would be chosen to be Thabiso's bride. Our mothers were the best of friends, and it was seen as a good omen when they all conceived during the same period."

Ledi processed that new information. "Wait, what? They were best friends?"

"Oh yes," Nya said. "One second."

She rushed across the room and came back with a framed photo. Three beautiful dark-skinned women—Ledi's mother, Queen Ramatla, and a woman she assumed to be Nya's mother. Three wide smiles, and three large bellies.

"They were devastated when my mother died, and when the priestesses chose you as Thabiso's betrothed, it made the bond between Libiko and Her Highness even stronger. When your family left without saying a word, the queen went into a state of shock. She wasn't the same after that." Nya shook her head. "This is all rumor, of course. But my father thought it went without saying that I would take your place as the prince's betrothed. After I fell ill, he became even more adamant, filling my head with all kinds of nonsense about the future, as though choosing a bride for a prince was as simple as transferring a property deed."

Ledi mentally sorted all of the information Nya had just provided her. There really was no replacement for boots on the ground investigation, because she'd yet to come across any of this in the emails Likotsi had sent her. Friendship, betrayal, and now a possible love triangle.

"Do you . . . do you love Thabiso?" Ledi asked carefully. Her chest went tight at just the possibility.

"Oh! No, of course not. I never wanted to marry Thabiso," Nya said with a shocked laugh. "Dealing with one spoiled, demanding man my entire life has quite cured me of any desire for another one. Although seeing how Thabiso treats you makes me believe that I misjudged him. Or perhaps the priestesses were right when they chose you as his betrothed, for you seem to be the one who brings out the best in him."

Ledi pulled on her boots. "He's okay, I guess."

"Mm-hmm," Nya said. "You know, when I watch television shows about New York, the women are always so cynical about love. I see this is one thing that is not false."

"That's the only thing those shows get right." Ledi laughed. "You can see for yourself when you come visit me. My apartment is the size of the bathroom in *Friends*."

Nya grew suddenly sober, and Ledi startled at just how frail her cousin was. "Yes, it would be quite lovely to leave Thesolo someday. Even if just for a little while."

"Hey, my niece, you are awake!" Alehk's voice carried into the room before he strode in with a steaming mug of tea, Thabiso trailing behind him. "Here, here, have something to warm you up before you leave."

"Night will fall soon," Thabiso explained as Alehk thrust the tea into her face. "If we want to make it back to the palace, we should go. Unless you want to stay."

"Oh, don't be silly," Nya said, rising to her feet and helping Ledi to hers. "Our accommodations are in no way fit for a prince and his future bride, family or not. Go, and I shall see you tomorrow."

Her cousin moved quickly, wrapping Ledi up in her blanket cloak and scarf and hat, slipping her gloves onto Ledi's hands, as her first set of foster parents had when she was a child. Alehk disappeared for a moment and returned with a large thermos. "For the cold road, then, where warmth is even more important."

Ledi tucked the thermos into her bag. "Thank you, Uncle."

She had always resisted being looked after and fretted over, always eager to show that she was an asset and not a burden, but she had to admit that it was surprisingly nice to have people who cared about your well-being, even if Alehk was kind of a jerk. Wasn't that how most people felt about their families?

She was soon atop D'artagnan, waving farewell to her family as Thabiso directed their not so valiant steed through the quiet streets of the town toward the trail that would lead them to the pickup point.

"Thanks for letting me sleep," she said eventually. "I feel a lot better. I've only worked in labs before, not in a clinical setting, so all of the interacting with patients wore me out. I'm glad none of them were actually sick, though."

"It's I who should be thanking you for working so hard today," he replied. "You know, I looked up epidemiology back in New York after I found out your field of study. And I didn't quite understand all the hard work that went into it. I remember once I asked you why you didn't remain a waitress, as you should perform the job you are best at. After seeing you today, I understand why."

Ledi grew a bit warmer under her layers of wool.

"I really want to understand what's happening here," she said. "I hate mysteries. I hate not knowing the 'why' behind things, and epidemiology is very much about answering that question."

"I'm sure there's good reason for that type of curiosity," Thabiso said.

"Can it, Freud." She felt his quiet laugh reverberate against her back.

They traveled in silence for a while, the sky darkening at a rapid rate as D'artagnan clomped his way down the trail. She shivered against the biting wind, which was no longer being filtered through the warming afternoon rays of the sun. "Do you think we'll make it back before the sun sets?"

"We could have, but it seems nature is having a bit of a laugh at our expense right now." He held out a hand in front of her and she watched a snowflake slowly drift down to his palm, only to be immediately whipped away by an icy gust of wind.

Annoyance ricocheted through her body. "Please don't tell me I'm gonna be the first Black person who went on a voyage to the motherland and froze to death," she gritted out through chattering teeth. "Social media would have a field day and I don't want to live on as a meme. Did you know it might snow?"

"This storm was not forecast," he said. "But the snow is coming down harder, so we should take shelter until we know how bad it will be."

Ledi looked around, then threw her hands up in the air, the only expression of her annoyance she was sure Thabiso would be able to see from behind. "Shelter? We're on the side of a mountain."

"I've heard that if you're going to be trapped in a snowstorm, it's useful to have a Saint Bernard with you," he said calmly.

"Thabiso—"

"I told you Naledi, what I know, I know well. Trust me."

And since she had no other choice in the matter, she did.

LESS THAN AN hour later, Ledi sat in front of the fire that Thabiso had made toward the back of a cave that wasn't exactly large but would have gone for two grand at least in New York. D'artagnan stood around the corner in the L-shaped entryway, tied near a weighted flap of fabric that dampened the strength of the wind.

"The goatherds need to take cover sometimes," Thabiso explained as he threw a tuft of fibrous dried grass into the fire. "This cave has been here for generations. I vexed many a nanny by running off to come here without their knowledge."

"Scaring your caretakers half to death by making them think they'd lost the prince? How cute," Ledi said. She was not pleased with their sudden camping excursion. Being stuck on a donkey had been adventure enough; sleeping in a rocky cave with no hot water or soft bed was cruel and unusual punishment. But there was something else stoking her impatience: another *f* word feeling that wouldn't let her be. Fear.

"There was no other place I could go in the kingdom to be alone," Thabiso said as he worked. "There was always someone trying to placate me, or reminding me of the responsibilities I would hold one day. Here, there was occasionally a lost goat or a herdsman on the outs with his partner."

Ledi took a deep breath. "I'm sorry for snapping at you. I don't like feeling like this."

"Like what?" Thabiso asked.

"Freaked out," she admitted. Their impromptu camping trip wasn't the only thing bothering her.

"Snow freaks you out?" he asked.

"My parents died in a car accident. Maybe you know that. I don't remember much, but I know there was a storm and the roads were icy, and then the car skidded. Was it a taxi? I think I was calling for them and getting no response. Even that might be a false memory, though. But this kind of storm *feels* bad."

She wrapped her arms around herself. She'd always told herself the nightmare was just a nightmare, but it was the closest thing to a memory she had.

"I'm sorry," he said. "I know you don't like to talk about what happened, but I was wondering if being back has brought any memories up to the surface?"

"No. I feel pretty silly, to be honest. How do you just forget a whole chunk of your life?"

"Sometimes it's easier to forget, I imagine." He stopped talking and Ledi did, too. She stretched her hands out toward the fire instead.

Thabiso went around the corner to give D'artagnan some feed from the supply of hay the goatherds had left in a corner of the cave. Wind rushed in, and then he called out. "We won't be able to go back tonight, and I don't want to risk anyone coming up to get us. It's really coming down out there. I sent a message to Likotsi; hopefully she got it."

Ledi ignored the little thrill that sneaked in behind her frustration, like those jerks who rushed through the subway turnstiles with strangers rather than pay. She ignored the fluidity of his walk as he returned, rubbing his hands together, and the way his body was put together so damn well beneath his sweater and jeans. None of that mattered. They'd sleep, get rescued at some point, and then she'd go back to her practicum and he'd go about his royal business. If she held out just a bit longer she'd be done with him for good. That was what she wanted. Totally.

"Does this place have reception?" she asked, pulling out the phone she'd been given.

"No. You'd have to go stand out in the snow," Thabiso said. "Me and my sparkling wit are your only form of entertainment for the foreseeable future."

He looked away quickly and she knew he'd had the same thought she'd had. There were many ways he could entertain her . . .

"I wish I had eaten lunch," she said, suddenly realizing that the prospect of an entire night without food lay ahead of her. Food talk was safer than thinking of the ways Thabiso could keep her preoccupied.

He grinned and dragged his travel pack closer to him, then dug inside and began pulling out aluminum foil–wrapped packets. He glanced up at her, his eyes bright. "You may detest me, but you can never say that I've let you go hungry."

He handed her one, and she tore it open and bit into a savory pastry stuffed with delicately spiced goat. "Oh my god. The goats walking around are cute and everything, but I can't feel an ounce of guilt about this."

She tried to eat with some decorum, finishing two pastries, and then making it through about half a serving of spicy rice before wisely cutting herself off. She had no idea how long they'd be in the cave.

"I'll save these for round two," Thabiso said, retrieving the unopened packages and placing them back inside his bag. "Nya is an excellent cook. Her mother, your aunt through marriage, passed away when she was born, so she's always had a lot of responsibility."

"She told me. And that our mothers were all best friends. How they were all pregnant at the same time." She kept any comments about the queen's behavior to her best friend's child to herself.

Ledi had spread her blanket out on one side of the fire, and Thabiso had done the same on the other. She rolled to her side and looked at him. "Is there a reason why you never replaced me when my family left? Like, with Nya, for example? She understands your people, and she knows what it's like to have unwanted responsibility."

Thabiso lay on his back with his hands beneath his head. He shrugged, and she could see his lips purse in thought despite the obstruction of his beard. "It is not wise to second-guess the priestesses," he said, then turned his head toward her. "Besides, I always hoped you'd come back. I believe in fairy tales, remember?"

He was looking at her with those Disney eyes again, this time with firelight dancing in their depths. The wind howled outside and the flames flickered as the cold air swept through the cave. Ledi remembered the story he'd told about his imaginary soul mate; she'd never forgotten it, but only now did she really connect the fact that he'd been talking about her. While she'd been alone in New York, Thabiso had held out hope. Saving her food, talking to her, keeping her company . . .

I stopped believing for a while there.

Did that mean he'd started believing again?

She'd grown up thinking that she wasn't wanted anywhere, but there had been a prince a world away who had been waiting for her and had apparently never stopped.

The emotion descended on her like the storm that had driven them into the cave. She held back the tears but she couldn't hide the way she shook thinking of the fact that he'd waited. He'd waited and wanted, and when she'd never returned, he had come looking for her. It was silly—she was romanticizing things—and yet . . .

"Are you cold?" he asked, his voice low.

Ledi stared into his fire-filled eyes and nodded. She was actually warm; her body had heated under his gaze. She should have said no, she was fine. She had always been fine. But she was tired of always being fine when fine meant alone, so this lie was okay.

She wasn't cold; she was hungry. Hungry for his touch and his soft smile that let her know she had never been alone. Or rather, that she had been, but he had been alone, too, because maybe Ingoka really *didn't* make mistakes, as the locals were fond of saying.

Thabiso eased himself up in one fluid motion and pulled his blanket after him. Ledi felt the puff of air displaced by the blanket as he flopped it onto the ground behind her. She felt his movements as he stretched out, and then scooted closer and closer.

"Is this okay?" he asked when there was a drafty couple of inches left between them.

"You can come closer," she said.

He did. Slowly.

His knees notched into the space created by hers as they bent. His shins pressed into the boots that covered her calves, and the muscles of his thighs rubbed over her glutes. Each new impression of his body against hers made it harder to breathe, harder to think of anything but how good he'd felt inside of her their one time together. Did it really only have to be once? Her body was presenting a serious rebuttal to that conclusion.

His muscled torso pressed against her back, and then his arms went around her to secure her.

"Warm now?" he asked. His voice was low, and just a bit cocky. He knew the answer.

She was. Everywhere. Her skin felt too tight and sensitive. Her nipples were pressing at the cups of her bra, just above where his arm rested. If he moved a bit he'd feel the hard peaks right through the fabric of her shirt. He could brush over them and drive her wild, like he had the last time he'd touched her. Ledi gasped at the thought, shifted the tiniest amount.

"I—I am."

That small, scared part of her mind tried to dredge up the feelings of humiliation to deter her, and that was when it hit her: she felt no shame about sleeping with him. She'd been pissed about his lie, hurt and angry and betrayed, but she also remembered the laughter they had shared and the way he'd made her feel. That part *had* been true. If that was true, and the fact that he had always wanted her was true, she wasn't sure what she was fighting against. She leaned back into him.

"Can you tell me about what you remember from when we were children?" she asked.

He pulled her closer. "I remember a bit of the betrothal ceremony. I remember thinking that you were very pretty, that you had happy eyes, and that you were a good friend so you would likely make a good wife. I don't know what I thought a wife was, though. Probably someone who played video games with me and shared her crayons."

Ledi laughed and he held her tighter.

"I was sad when you left, you know," he continued. "That was the first time I realized sometimes you could cry and scream and flail and it would do nothing to bring a person back."

"I learned that very soon after you, if it makes you feel any better," she said quietly. He just held her then, and it was exactly the thing she wanted in that moment. The synchronized rise and fall of their chests. Being held by a man who had presented her with two separate identities and seemed to care for her regardless of which he inhabited.

"This makes me feel better, actually," he said. "Having you here with me. I've always thought that the betrothal thing, especially of children, was outdated, but this feels right."

"You know it pains me to admit this, but it feels right to me, too." Ledi took a deep breath, then shifted in his hold and turned so that she faced him. In the firelight she could see the rounded sharpness of his cheekbones, the deep, dark brown of his perfect skin, and those eyes that stared at her as if she were both goddess and pilgrim.

"I don't know how to do this," she whispered.

"Do what?" he asked, whispering, too.

"Be with someone. I've only ever been alone, and that's worked pretty well for me."

"You had friends," he replied, not whispering anymore. "Portia was as protective of you as my Royal Guard."

Ledi shook her head and tears filled her eyes. "She hurt me, too."

Thabiso's hand moved to her face, and his fingertips brushed over her cheeks, traced the shell of her ear, and sent a shiver of want through her.

"That's the thing, Naledi. That the people who love you will hurt you the most is one of the great conundrums of the human condition. My philosophy tutor said so, and he had about five degrees on the subject, so I guess it holds some water."

She giggled despite the tears burning her eyes, then squeezed her eyes shut and finally said aloud the questions that had been trying to force their way out since she'd discovered Thabiso's identity and, as a result, her own. "How could my parents take me away from here and not leave me any connection to people who would have loved me? How could they have left me alone?"

She felt the press of his warm palm between her shoulder blades as he pulled her close and rubbed comforting circles down her back. His beard brushed against her face as she nestled into the comfort of the space between his neck and shoulder. It still smelled like happiness.

"I've been asking myself this, too. For years I'd thought it was greed, or pride, or insolence, but I cannot believe your parents would make such a rash decision without reason. I cannot believe that your mother would wound her best friend without reason. One thing is certain, though, Naledi."

She opened her eyes and looked up into his.

"You're not alone anymore." His lips pressed into hers then, warm and silky, and while his hands offered comfort, his kiss was pure desire.

Naledi closed her eyes and fell into the kiss. His familiar floral musk surrounded her, and she pressed fluttering kisses down his jaw to his neck to inhale it again. She retraced the path to his mouth and covered it with hers, relearning the taste and feel of a man she'd thought might be right for her, and was now turning out to be even better than she'd previously imagined.

"Goddess, I thought I'd never taste you again," Thabiso rasped against her lips. "I don't think I could live without this sweetness."

She pushed against his shoulder to press him back to the ground, and then straddled him.

"You'd live. Fuckboyitis isn't a terminal illness," she reminded him.

"But chronic lack of Naledi is," he said simply. "Leads to brittle bones."

She snorted, which wasn't very sexy, but she was glad that she wasn't the only one who turned into a complete cornball before sex. He leaned up on his elbows and nipped at her mouth before kissing her, hard. Her skin buzzed from the roughness of his beard, heightening the sensation.

She leaned back and pulled her sweater off. While the fabric was still over her head she felt his palms pass over her breasts and then a tug at the chain that hung around her neck.

"You still wear my gift," he said as she felt her bra pulled down and the caress of smooth, warm metal and glass over one of her nipples in contrast to the cool air of the cave. She shuddered and rocked against him, finally working her way out of the ridiculous cowl neck just as his mouth replaced the inorganic material against her skin.

His hands were at the buttons of her stretchy jeans as he sucked and nipped at the stiff peaks of her breasts.

Yes, there we go, she thought as his short, rough hair brushed her areola, making her jump from the shock before he soothed her with his tongue. She stood to shimmy out of her pants and underwear, so preoccupied with the heat in his gaze as he watched her that she almost threw her jeans into the fire.

She bent over to retrieve them and heard him groan. "Stop teasing me, Naledi." She threw them a safe distance from the flames and crawled back onto his lap. The bulge at his groin jumped invitingly as he thickened, pressing up against her as she moved to settle against his cock. He stopped her midkneel.

"Wrong seat," he said, then his strong hands were at the backs of her thighs, urging her up his torso and toward his face.

"Um—" That syllable was the only one she was able to emit before his hands clenched her ass and his beard nestled between her thighs.

"Holy shit," she gasped. His tongue pressed hard against her clit as he lapped and sucked and nibbled, pleasure dispersing through her body like a substance that would expand until it filled every part of its container.

Her knees pressed into the rocky ground that was barely softened by the blanket, but the nerve receptors there were dampened by the work being put in by Thabiso's tongue. Ledi ground into his face, crying out at the scrape of his beard against sensitive skin, at his fingers pressed hard into her thighs, but above all, at his tongue. That tongue alone made Thesolo one of the wonders of the modern world.

"Thabiso, fuck," she whimpered, and his name on her lips seemed to flip the switch on the tornado feature of his tongue. Thabiso swirled the hard warmth against her clit without mercy, and Ledi's arms flailed wildly in the air as she reached for something, anything, to keep her from being knocked over by the sensation. Finally, just as the orgasm curled her toes and bent her back, she grabbed his head and rode it out. At her abrupt cries, Thabiso slowed down, slackened his hold on her, and licked more softly. Her thighs trembled and she felt him smile against her, a shockingly intimate sensation.

She crawled down his body, and he sat up so that his face was level with hers when her ass came into contact with his still-clothed erection. He looped his arms around her and kissed her. "Are you okay, goddess of fire?"

She almost laughed at the ridiculous moniker, but then she stopped herself. She was feeling pretty powerful with all the good, postorgasmic bliss zinging through her.

"No," she said, then kissed him, tasting her own essence. "You're not inside of me."

Thabiso leaned over to reach into his bag and pulled out a sleeve of condoms. "I'm dating a public health student," he said by way of explanation, and she laughed, even though the word *dating* did send the tiniest amount of fear through her. Were people who everyone thought to be engaged allowed to date?

Then he kissed her and she closed her eyes and the only thought in her head was wondering how long it would take him to get the condom packet open.

She moved into a crouching position as he sheathed himself, and then sank down onto him when his hands moved to her hips. She was slick and pliable and there was no resistance, just a sweet friction and fullness as she took him in completely.

"Oh, sweet, sweet, Naledi," he groaned. His head dropped back and his nostrils flared and Ledi was emboldened by his reaction just to being held within her.

Her hands went to his shoulders as she slowly raised and lowered herself on his cock, moaning as he filled her again and again. Thabiso gritted his teeth and hissed, the sounds making her feel like the goddess he'd taken to calling her.

His arms moved behind him to brace himself as he began to pump up into her, meeting her downward stroke, and then Ledi was lost. She leaned forward and he met her halfway. Their foreheads were touching and their gazes were locked as they both worked their hips in a mad frenzy to see who could drive the other crazier. She reached between her legs and pressed her fingers there.

"Dammit, ah, Naledi." Thabiso jerked and his cock thickened inside of her, and then Ledi was gone, too, pulsing around him as their firelit shadows throbbed against the walls of the cave behind him.

Thabiso dropped back against the blanket and carefully withdrew from inside of her, and Naledi rolled off of him.

"Ouch! I forgot we weren't on a bed," she said, rubbing at her shoulder.

"My tailbone didn't have the luxury of forgetting, but it was well worth it." He kissed her, then got up to gather some napkins.

"Are you hungry again?" he asked.

"For food?" She watched the play of light against his body as he leaned over his bag.

She saw his cock jump again and he dropped the flap of the bag and began stalking toward her, a definitely non-Disney look in his eye.

"Food can wait," he said as he settled in beside her. "Warmth is the number one priority in surviving a storm."

Chapter 31

Thabiso kept glancing at Naledi from the corner of his eye as Likotsi railed at him for being gone overnight. Although Ledi had woken up cheerful, if somewhat sore and extremely bewildered to find D'artagnan curled up between her and Thabiso, he kept expecting her to rebuild her walls, to cut him off from the woman who had given herself so freely to him throughout the night and into the morning.

"Your Highness, do you know how worried your parents were?"

"You were right next to me as I spoke to the queen on the phone, Kotsi. You heard her disown me and threaten me with the dungeon, as did everyone else within six meters."

Beside him, Ledi opened her thermos of tea and poured the last of the amber liquid out, scenting the car with its sweet smell. He doubted she was thirsty—she seemed to be drinking to have something to do with her hands. Everyone had heard the queen rail at him, but they'd also heard her refer to Ledi as a ridiculous distraction that had gone on long enough. He understood his mother's upset, but Ledi's trust was such a fragile thing. It needed nourishment, not to be fed toxic doubts.

He reached across the car and took her hand, which trembled a bit against his palm. "I'm sorry," he said, raising a hand to silence Likotsi, who had opened her mouth to chastise him again. "My mother's behavior is bizarre, but I've made it clear that you are an important part of my life. You aren't a distraction and I'm so happy you're here."

Ledi smiled at him, and he noticed her pupils were wide, blocking out the beautiful brown he loved looking into.

"I'm happy I'm here, too. If I've learned one useful thing in life, it's that I can't make someone care for me. But I guess I can be better about letting in the people who do," she said, giving him a shy smile that warmed him like the sun rising over the mountains. Then she shivered hard, as if she'd stepped on a live wire, and his warmth drained away. "Guess I overcaffeinated."

Thabiso nodded, but gripped her hand tightly, feeling the steady tremor that hadn't been there before. He should have let her sleep more instead of making love to her until she was jelly-boned and couldn't keep her eyes open. Perhaps she'd taken ill from the snow? He was glad she'd be able to rest soon, and he'd have the doctor come to her chambers.

The car pulled into the palace compound, and his parents walked out toward them, a group of people at their rear as usual.

He glanced at Ledi. "Perhaps we should have stayed in the cave."

Ledi rolled her eyes. "If your mother is upset that you can't control the forces of nature, then I really do understand what you meant when you said your parents had high expectations."

He laughed, his anxiety dissipating.

"I would be upset if I thought something happened to you, too, though, so cut her some slack," Ledi added. Thabiso didn't comment on the fact that she'd admitted she cared about him unprompted.

"I think I can do that," he said, giving her hand a squeeze.

They stepped down from the vehicle, and he kept Ledi's hand firmly in his.

"Good morning, parents," he said brightly.

"Son," they said in unison.

"We've returned from our icy adventure, none the worse for the wear. I apologize if you were worried."

"Worried? Why would we be worried?" his father asked.

"Just because the sole heir to the Thesoloian crown took it upon himself to put himself in jeopardy to continue this farce of an engagement, nearly leaving his people without a future leader, doesn't mean we were worried," his mother said smoothly. "No, not worried, but quite done tolerating this."

"Your Highness, if anyone is to blame, it is me," Likotsi said, ever the mediator. "I should have checked the weather more carefully and not allowed them to travel alone."

"No, there is one person at fault here. This thoughtless woman who has distracted Thabiso and who threatens the prosperity of our kingdom."

"I'm sorry," Ledi said in a small voice that broke Thabiso's heart.

"Just like your mother," the queen said, an irrational rage in her voice. "You don't care who gets hurt by your selfish plans."

Ledi cringed, and Thabiso dropped her hand to place his arm around her shoulders. "Mother, Father,

I love and respect you both, but you are using an elephant's brute force when its intelligence would suffice. I don't know what farce you speak of, but I would advise you to forget you ever said such a thing."

His head throbbed with the anger building up inside of him. How was it that his parents had told him everything he wanted could be his, yet they would deny him this one thing? The most important thing?

His mother held out her hand and a beautiful young woman stepped out from the group behind her. She was slim, tall, regal. Her hair fell in wavy ringlets down her back and her features could have been sculpted from onyx by one of the masters. Shanti.

"We know that this was just an arrangement between you two to thumb your nose at us." The queen's voice was taut. "Did you think we wouldn't have our intelligence agency search her emails to ensure she wasn't spying for the meddlesome Americans, or worse? You two can end this now, and Thabiso will move forward with Shanti by his side."

Shanti curtsied beautifully. "Your Majesty, I have been trained in all the womanly arts, molded by my teachers and my parents to be the best possible bride to a king. If you allow me, I would be honored to show you what an excellent wife I can be."

Thabiso noticed that Naledi was abnormally quiet, and his anger flared. She was probably already rolling back the trust she'd placed in him, wondering why she had allowed him into her life again. He was bracing himself for her to pull away, but she sagged against him instead.

"She looks like a princess," Ledi murmured. "Your mother has a point."

"There's only one person I'd consider for my wife, and we're already betrothed," he said.

"Who?" Ledi asked angrily, her brows drawn in confusion. "Is there *another* woman?"

Something colder than the ice storm they'd evaded slid down his spine. "I'm talking about you. About us. Ledi, are you all right?"

"Oh! Right. I trust you, Jamal. You wouldn't hurt me. Except for when you tried to set me on fire."

She laughed, a slow and unnerving sound that was nothing like her usual laughter.

"What?" His mother started to approach, and she wasn't wearing the haughty mask she'd had on earlier. This was the face he'd always seen behind closed doors, drawn with concern when she placed her hand against his forehead or waved a thermometer in the air. "Thabiso, did she fall and hit her head? What happened out there?"

His mother stood before them, brows drawn as she studied Ledi's face. She raised a hand to touch her, then dropped it, intertwining the fingers of both hands with worry.

Thabiso adjusted Ledi in his arms. She was no longer leaning on him for moral support, as he'd thought, but because she couldn't have stood without his assistance.

"You're frightening me, Ledi. Tell me what's wrong."

"I'm fine. I just have to call Portia," she said cheerily. Then she bent over and was sick, right down the front of the queen's cloak.

"Son," his parents said in unison, this time in fear, but then Ledi began to sink to the ground. Thabiso didn't think. He scooped her up as she was falling and ran as fast as he could toward the hospital. She had been in the middle of all those people yesterday with no protection but rubber gloves and a silly little mask. And he'd brought her there.

He stopped himself from ramming through the slow automatic doors of the hospital, then barreled through the waiting room. He saw the nurse from the other day—what was her name, Ammina? Sesi? Unimportant!

"You! Help her, now!" he roared. She would listen to him because he was a prince and people did what he commanded, dammit.

She rushed forward and then stopped in her tracks. "Your Highness, please put her down right now and step away."

"What are you talking about? I told you to help her!"

Sesi picked up the phone and made an announcement over the loudspeakers. "Decontamination team, please report to the entrance. Immediately."

She put the phone down and advanced toward him as she pulled on gloves. "Sire, you cannot afford to get ill. Your people need you. Put her down." She pulled a gurney away from the wall and pushed it ahead of her.

It was only then that he saw the raised rash winding its way up Ledi's neck and over her jawline.

"No. No, Ledi." His world came crashing down around him in that split second. He'd invited Ledi to Thesolo to save his people, but he'd wanted her to save him too, if he was honest with himself. And now she was going to die because of his selfishness.

"Prince Thabiso, we can't help her until you put her down." A team of doctors had arrived without him noticing. They wore suits designed to protect them from disease, but it was too late to protect Ledi.

"I'm sorry," he said, his voice thick.

He placed Ledi on the gurney and they converged on her, wheeling her toward the ICU and out of his sight. He heard noise behind him, felt his mother and father's familiar presence at his side, and his father's hand cupping the back of his head as if he were a child again.

"She'll be all right. Ingoka did not bring her back to you just to take her away like this."

Thabiso wasn't so sure, but he prayed that his father was right.

Chapter 32

Ledi was looking up at her mother and father, who were hurriedly stuffing their belongings into bags. She couldn't understand what they were saying, except for two words: her name, and *Alehk*. The way her father's face contorted in fury when he said her uncle's name scared her. Then he picked her up and kissed her on the cheek, and they walked into the dark night . . .

Ledi awoke with a jump. For a moment she thought she was at Alehk's house again. Was that place real? Maybe she was at her studio on the cheap futon. Jamal was across the hall. Was *he* real? Had everything that passed been a dream? Sorrow clogged her throat at the thought, but then her eyes fluttered open and looked around her. The area was stark and white and she heard a steady beeping noise. Her alarm? She patted the bed beside her for her phone, and something stopped her arm from moving. She sat up, feeling woozy. And thirsty. So thirsty.

For a second she thought the woman at her bedside was Nya—had Nya been real or part of her dream?—but then she recognized the rust-brown curls and the smattering of freckles on the downturned face.

"Portia?"

Portia jumped up in her seat and rushed toward the bed. She wore hospital standard protective clothing for the ICU, including gloves, but she gripped Ledi's hand in hers and smiled through her tears.

"Only you would come all the way to Africa and catch some strange disease. I told you to stop using that antibacterial gel every time you got on the train. You lowered your immunity."

"What are you doing here?" Ledi asked, again wondering if she was dreaming. Had she really been mad at Portia? That feeling was gone. There was only happiness and a feeling like her chest would burst at the sight of her. "How did you even get here? Oh wait, I guess it's easy for rich people to just charter a plane."

Portia shook her head. "I'm a trust fund baby, but private jets aren't included in my particular tax bracket package. Thabiso flew me out after giving me a heart attack by telling me you were unconscious in the hospital. You've been knocked out for two days."

"What?" Ledi tried to throw her legs over the bed and her head started to spin. "I need to see him. No, I need to see Dr. Bata."

Portia stood and gently pushed her back down. "You need to rest. They didn't know when you were going to wake up. Or if you were going to." Portia exhaled a stuttering sigh. "I spent that whole trip terrified that you were going to die hating me. Ugh, that sounds selfish. It *is* selfish. But if you hate me, too . . ."

She shook her head. "I wanted to apologize. I was wrong and I should have admitted it from the beginning. You were so into Jamal, and I fucked up by not warning you of my suspicion before the gala. But part of me wanted it to be him, so you'd get mad and he'd go away. I guess I kind of maybe got scared that he was going to show you that you don't need me. And I wasn't exactly wrong because who needs a friend like me?"

Portia was miserable, and even if she had messed up, the pain on her face was too much to bear. Ledi had thought no one cared for her, but Portia cared possibly too much. Ledi realized a problem with her Velcro theory: Velcro was a temporary attachment. Portia, who always tried to help Ledi and would surely hide a body for her, if not do the actual killing, was a Krazy Glue kind of friend. They were stuck with one another by a bond that had been shaken but remained intact. Now they would have to decide how they used that bond.

"I need a friend like you," Ledi said, giving Portia a weak hug because it was all she could manage. "I don't hate you, but things can't be how they were before."

Portia shut her eyes but that didn't stop the tears from streaking down. She nodded.

Ledi sighed. "I'm going to work on not being a push-over. You have to work on not pushing." She paused. "And on not drinking so much. And on wanting as much for yourself as you want for other people."

Ledi had always been afraid to throw down an ultimatum. It wasn't what a health care professional would do, but as Ledi the human, she had to put herself first. She wasn't above leveraging hospital bed guilt, it seemed.

"Well, I had to reschedule my therapist appointment to come here," Portia said grouchily, wiping her tears away. "I'm working on things.

"Besides, I can't show up in the middle of the night

at a palace, drunkenly banging on the door. This is like having the ultimate doorman," Portia said. "I guess you can give up the ramen life now, huh?"

"Never," Ledi said, leaning back against her pillow. "But I'll consider upgrading to the classy brand."

The door to the room opened and Thabiso and Dr. Bata walked in, deep in conversation. She saw the exact moment he realized she was awake, the way relief and pain comingled on his face. He rushed to her bed and hugged her, probably breaking whatever protocol was in place, but making her feel a million times better.

"Goddess, I was so worried," he said on a shaky exhale. He looked haggard; she had never seen his beard and hair disheveled, dark circles under his eyes. He was a mess.

"Why were you worried? Shanti is waiting in the wings if anything should happen to me," she said. Just because he was a mess didn't mean she couldn't tease him. He released her to see if she was being serious and she just smiled.

"Ah, you really are better," he said happily. He was working the cartoon prince eyes hard-core, and if Ledi had just a bit more strength she would have grabbed him. "You know I had nothing to do with that. Besides, Shanti is long gone. As are my mother's favorite shoes."

"Good," Ledi said, not sorry in the slightest for either.

"Do I even want to know?" Portia asked diplomatically instead of hissing at Thabiso. She was improving already.

"Naledi, I'm sorry to interrupt, but I have to say that your recovery is fairly shocking," Dr. Bata said while scanning her chart. "None of the other patients are out of the woods, but here you are up and making conversation. And your rash is gone, as well."

Thabiso's brow furrowed. "So she wasn't sick with the Prince's plague?"

Ledi nudged him, and he shrugged. "What? That's what everyone is calling it."

"I'm glad to be better, but I have no idea why," Ledi said. "We don't even know how the illness spreads."

Dr. Bata put the chart down and stared at Ledi. "What did you do after you left the clinic? None of the people who were there have fallen ill, so it's unlikely you caught it from that group."

Ledi looked at Thabiso and her face warmed. "Um, I didn't do very much . . ."

"I wouldn't say that," Thabiso murmured.

"Oh my god, you two." Portia rolled her eyes and pulled out her phone and started typing.

Thabiso cleared his throat. "We went to her uncle's house, and she slept because she was exhausted. We got trapped by a snowstorm and spent the night in a cave. But, um, if this virus is transmissible, it doesn't seem to be through bodily fluids."

Thabiso looked awkwardly defiant but Dr. Bata simply grinned as she took notes.

"Well, what's different about you from the other patients?" Portia asked. "Are there any specific infection factors that you can think of?"

"Aren't you an artist?" Thabiso asked, face scrunched in confusion.

"I contain multitudes, Your Highness" Portia said in a sweet tone that wasn't sweet at all. "You should know a thing or two about that, *Jamal*."

She cringed and glanced at Ledi. "Sorry."

"None of the other patients are foreigners, are they?" Ledi asked, not bothering to mediate since

Portia wasn't wrong. Best friends who would shank your man for you were as valuable as any crown.

"No. As you know, the illness has been restricted to the mountainous region, until you," Dr. Bata said. "Though you are originally from that region and recently visited."

"So maybe we should be looking for some kind of genetic marker in the native population that might indicate sensitivity to a particular bacteria?" Ledi's mind was still muddled, but possibilities were coming fast and thick. "Or something in the local environment."

There was a knock at the door and Likotsi walked in carrying a tray laden with a ceramic teapot and several cups. "It's teatime. I figured since you were awake you might need to rehydrate."

"What kind of tea is it?" Portia asked. "She's more a coffee kind of girl."

Portia glanced at Ledi and gave a knowing nod and Ledi had to smile.

"It's our local bush tea, which is also said to help fight illness—"

The world around Ledi went very still as facts and data and suppositions congealed into hypothesis. "Wait. Wait, I think I might have something. When I got sick, it was right after chugging an entire thermos of strong bush tea."

"And after facing my mother," Thabiso added.

"Pfft." Ledi cut her eyes at him. "Your mother wouldn't last a day in New York without her retinue. She's not that scary. So, I drank a substance that my body is not accustomed to at a high volume, very quickly. I immediately threw up, passed out, and broke out in hives. Maybe . . ."

Ledi wished her brain wasn't still fuzzy with sleep.

The connection she was trying to make was *so close.* She began massaging her temples, hoping that would get the synapses popping even though it was entirely unscientific.

"Are you all right?" Thabiso leaned close, enveloping her in his signature scent. The same scent she had smelled in the tea she'd sniffed, and even more strongly in the tea she'd drunk from Alehk.

"May I taste that, please?" she asked Likotsi. It was light and delicate, nothing like the strong, earthy tea Alehk had given her and she'd been drinking from arrival. And it definitely didn't have the same floral scent.

"Dr. Bata, do you know anything about the effects of the eng plant on the human body when ingested in high doses?"

"Not particularly," the doctor said. "It's just part of our local culture. It has been used medicinally in the past, but most of those effects were considered to be psychosomatic."

Likotsi cut in. "I don't know much, but I do remember my grandmother always telling us to be careful that the balance of ingredients in the tea was right because just because something is natural doesn't mean it is safe. 'Less is more, and more can kill you' she'd always say."

Ledi nodded. "I'm guessing that my throwing up was caused by an overdose, of sorts. Most people here would have trace amounts built up in their bodies from everyday or occasional tea drinking, making the sickness more gradual. Because my body expelled the poison all over the queen's shoes, my eng overdose wore off comparatively quickly." Ledi looked at Thabiso as the idea in her head expanded and branched out into more sinister corners of her mind.

"Thabiso . . ."

"I'm guessing you don't suspect that this was just a bad batch of tea," he said gravely.

She shook her head. "Sesi said she was giving my grandparents a special blend provided by my uncle. And do you remember how Nya bundled me out of the house when he came in with the tea? That wasn't the first time."

Nya had given her vitamins, told her to take them every day. But Ledi had forgotten for the last couple of days, though she hadn't forgotten to drink her tea.

Thabiso's eyes widened. "You think your uncle is a fuckboy?"

She nodded. "And if what I think is correct, his case isn't curable."

He stood. "Likotsi. We must keep this quiet to prevent unrest, but please have Alehk Jarami brought in for immediate questioning."

Chapter 33

Two weeks later

$\mathcal{T}$he Thesoloian justice system was confusing, but it moved quickly.

Apparently, Lek Hemane sat on a valuable plot of land; it was the single most coltan-rich part of Thesolo. Alehk's talk of bringing Lek Hemane into the future had actually been a plan to destroy it by an insidious method—sickening several people and making it seem that the land was unfit to live on. The Prince's plague had been a detour in that plan, one that helped bolster his popularity amongst his fellow villagers before he planned to reveal the "true" source of their illness: the coltan that the selfish prince was refusing to dig up and get rid of.

Alehk's arrest, his poisoning of Ledi and others, all of it, should have made her even more doubtful about the human race. But her cousin Nya had come to the hospital and broken down into pitiful tears when she realized her attempt at stopping her father hadn't worked, and Ledi couldn't be angry at her.

"He is a man who creates grudges from nothing and holds on to them tightly," Nya said as they walked around the hospital greenhouse, safe from the cold. Ledi was better, and the other victims were recovering, but Nya had worried herself sick, literally. Her room was next to Annie and Makalele's, making visiting convenient for Ledi. "Your parents left years ago, and he still got so angry every time our grandparents spoke fondly of your mother. He felt that she'd gotten something he hadn't, and he never forgave her."

"What was that?" Ledi asked. "What could she have access to that he didn't?"

"You, my cousin," Nya said sadly. "And through you, power. We were born not far apart, but the Priestesses chose you instead of me to be the prince's betrothed. He had already lost my mother, and I suppose he felt deprived of something that was owed to him for that great loss. He loved her. He loves me too, in his own way."

Ledi rubbed her cousin's shoulder. "I'm sorry. It must be so painful for you, even though you're free of him now."

Nya smiled. "I don't think one can ever be free of their parents. I am sad, but then I remember that you have come into my life and I think this was a more than fair trade."

Her face warmed.

"I wish you didn't have to leave," Nya said sadly.

Ledi cleared her throat. In the weeks since her sickness, she'd been gathering data and trying to shore up the thesis she was writing about the experience, combining the fields of infectious disease, sociological epidemiology, and the degree in law she'd unofficially received after watching too many marathons of *Law & Order*.

Thabiso had been extremely busy, too. He'd been

charged with monitoring the investigation and searching out any other possible crimes committed by Alehk that could have endangered the people of Thesolo. He was also tracking Alehk's connections to companies that had been rejected flat out in their overtures to the Thesoloian government. Her uncle's email server had been loaded with shady deals and unauthorized interactions, meaning lots of work for Thabiso and little time for each other. He hadn't been kidding when he said being a prince wasn't all fun and games.

"I wouldn't mind staying a little longer," Ledi said. "New York can be much too hot in the summer."

Yes, that was what she was worried about.

"But you should come visit me."

"I like heat," Nya said as they walked back into the hospital's main building. "I want to try these bagels you keep talking about. And a slice of pizza."

"Oh my god. I'll take you to my favorite pizza place and you just might refuse to come back to Thesolo," Ledi said. "And there's this bagel store in Williamsburg. We'll do a food tour!"

Nya looked wistful. "Now that I am the daughter of a fraud and a criminal, perhaps leaving forever is not a bad choice."

Ledi threw an arm around her cousin. Spontaneous hugs were much easier when you were sure they wouldn't be rejected. She said what she wished someone had told her over the years. "If you need me, I'm here, okay? We're family, and not just because we're cousins. I mean, technically yes, but I like you for reasons outside of our shared DNA."

Nya nodded, swiping at her tears.

"And Portia likes you, too. She posted a photo of

you on her InstaPhoto, hashtagged '#frand' and I'm usually the only one who gets that treatment."

She left Nya near the entrance to the hospital and walked back to her suite alone. The staff, no longer strangers, waved at her and nodded encouragingly when she spoke her clipped Thesoloian greetings. A peacock with droopy feathers that she'd named Thurston kept pace with her for a moment before heading back to the garden. She was going to miss living in the palace, and not just because she didn't have to do dishes.

She was going to miss Thabiso.

But they hadn't spoken about the future, and she wasn't even sure what she wanted. Was she still betrothed to him? Did she want to be? After all, they'd never even gone out on a full date. She wasn't even sure if he was the kind of person who asked loud, annoying questions throughout a movie, although she'd heard there was a cinema in the palace somewhere. If she could confirm his boorish in-movie behavior before she left, she would feel a little better about saying good-bye. Or maybe he'd do naughty things to her in the dark theater. She'd be down with that as an alternative.

"Naledi?"

The voice from inside the library made her stiffen. The queen had been nicer to her since she'd gotten sick, but she was still unsure about the woman. Despite that, she followed the sound of her voice into the room. She found Queen Ramatla staring up at that picture of Ledi and Thabiso at their betrothal ceremony. Her eyes weren't on the toddlers in the picture, but on herself and Ledi's mom in the background.

"Have the royal taste testers been doing their job?" the queen asked.

"Yes," Ledi replied. "Though I think the threat has passed. I do appreciate it, Your Highness."

"I would like to offer a formal apology," the queen said suddenly, drawing herself up. "I was wrong to be so cold to you, but—" She closed her eyes for a moment and inhaled deeply, and when she opened them and looked at Ledi, there was a depth of emotion Ledi hadn't seen there before. "You resemble her so much. And she hurt me so badly. Every time I looked at you, or heard your voice, I felt that pain anew. I think . . . I *know* that I took my anger out on you. And that was unfair, and beneath both of us. I hope we can start over. Or rather, I would like to get to know you instead of trying to punish you for something you didn't do."

Ledi was still wary, but she glanced at the photo, at her mother and the queen laughing that special kind of friend laughter, and then back to the barely repressed pain on the queen's face.

"It's hard losing a friend," Ledi said quietly. "If it's your significant other, you're allowed to grieve. But people act like best friends are a dime a dozen, and if you lose one you can just replace them with another."

The queen nodded, her mouth pulling into a tight line. "I have never replaced Libi. After we lost Nya's mother, she was my sole support. I thought we were each other's support. And when I found out she'd left"—the queen shook her head—"I'd never felt such pain. When Thabiso told me that you had been found, for a moment I was so relieved. And then he told me the rest of the news . . ."

The queen looked away suddenly, but Ledi caught the tremble of her mouth and the way she sucked in a breath on a sob. Ledi had begun to mourn her parents anew, but she hadn't known her mother as the queen had known her. She tried to imagine what she would do if anything happened to Portia, and the hypothetical alone made her tear up.

She reached a hand out, tentatively, and placed it on the queen's shoulder.

"I'm so sorry. I wish you could have seen her again."

The queen nodded and cleared her throat. "Well. I will serve her memory better in my behavior toward you. And even if I did not get to meet her again . . . Ingoka makes no mistakes, Naledi Ajoua. I am glad you have returned, and Libi would be so proud of what you have become."

It was Ledi's turn to fight emotion then. Many people had said the same, but they hadn't known her mother as the queen had. And though the queen had apologized, she wasn't the type to lie to make someone feel better.

When she looked at the queen again, the emotion was gone from her eyes and her expression was smooth, regal. "Before you leave, we will have a memorial ceremony for them in the temple."

"Thank you." Ledi didn't know what else to say so she took a deep breath and headed back to her room. She was sure she wouldn't always see eye to eye with the queen, but she felt as if something had been mended between them. She hoped something had been mended within the queen as well.

When she got to her suite, the door was cracked. She pushed it open and found Thabiso stretched out on her bed, fast asleep. She quietly shut the door and approached him, smiling at the contrast between his ungainly sprawl and the sleek suit he wore.

She climbed onto the bed beside him and into the space created by his outthrown arm.

"Now I know what the baby bear felt like when it found Goldilocks in its bed," she said.

He smiled and his eyes slowly opened. "I thought you didn't like fairy tales."

"I don't. Goldilocks was a brazen home invasion artist." Ledi snuggled closer. "But I guess since you're the prince and all, I'll make an exception."

"I don't mind being an exception, as long as I get to wake up to this," Thabiso replied, hugging her close. "I did come here for a reason, though. Something was found in your uncle's papers. For a man with his fingers in so many nasty pies, he was something of a hoarder."

He sat up and Ledi mimicked his movement, staying on the bed while he walked over to the desk and brought over a ragged edged piece of paper enclosed in a plastic pouch. It was old, but not ancient, and the messy handwriting on it was scarily similar to her own.

"This was found between the pages of a book in his library," Thabiso said, settling beside her.

> *We will do as you say. I wish my own brother was not my enemy, but I cannot promise what you ask. I cannot risk my child's life for something so fleeting as money or power. I will pray for your soul, and for ours.*

Ledi wasn't exactly sure what the note meant.

"Was he going to kill me?" she asked.

"It appears he had some mad plan that your parents refused to take part in. Something that made them feel it was safer to flee with you than to stay. He refuses to tell us, but I thought you should know this."

Her uncle had driven her mother away. He'd hated his own sister so much that he'd allowed it to consume him. Or maybe he'd loved Nya and her mother so much that it was love that had consumed him in the end. It was frightening, what the emotion could do to you once it had you in its grip.

She took the little note and placed it on the bedside table, then stared down at her hands.

"Ledi?" Thabiso looked worried. "Is something wrong?"

"Yes," she said. She looked at him, examined that perfect face that made her want to hold him and protect him and, occasionally, kick him in the shin. "I think I might love you. Maybe."

"What?"

"I know. It's crazy, huh? I wouldn't mention it, but if I'm going to leave soon, I guess I should tell you." She waited for him to laugh, or to jump up and run away— after all, he didn't need her anymore. He was a hero to the masses at the moment, no bride necessary.

"Hmm. The thing is, I have some business to attend to in New York," he said, stroking his beard in the way he did when he was mulling something over. "I was thinking that since you were going to leave soon, I could go back with you. Crazy, as you were saying, huh?"

Ledi's heart started to beat faster, harder.

"What kind of business?"

"Well, there's always *something* to be done in New York when you're a prince." He pulled her into his lap and she wrapped her legs around him. "What was it you mentioned before? Riding horses and strip poker?"

"Horses? D'artagnan will be jealous."

"He gave me his blessing," Thabiso said. "That means I'm holding out on one more. Two."

Ledi was confused, then she laughed. "The Grams

are very protective of their space." She leaned into him. They were chest to chest and his heart was beating fast, too.

"I won't invade the Grams' space, but I really think they'll like the view from the brownstone Likotsi picked out for me, so I'll win them over eventually. It's no brick wall view, but Central Park is lovely in the autumn."

"It is," Ledi agreed, resting her forehead against his. His arms encircled her, with his hands cupped at the base of her spine, holding her close to him.

"Maybe, if they like me enough, they'd consider coming to Thesolo at some point in the future?" he asked.

Ledi closed her eyes. "Is there such a thing as being happily freaked out? Because that's what I'm feeling right now."

Thabiso laughed. "I'm pretty sure I prefer that to 'happily ever after.' Way less pressure."

"Oh, there's a ton of pressure, Bones," she said, mimicking his accent.

He sighed. "I'll never live that down, will I?"

"Let's find out," she said.

He kissed her then, more sweetly than he ever had. Ledi held him tight and wondered if their new home would have a washer and dryer. After all, she was kissing living proof that even her wildest dreams could come true.

**Keep reading for a sneak peek
at the next book in the
Reluctant Royals series**

A Duke by Default

Coming Summer 2018!

Chapter 1

*P*roject: New Portia was off to a fantastic start.

Old Portia was no stranger to hopping in cabs at the break of dawn, bleary-eyed and disheveled, but in the past she'd generally been hungover and making a hasty exit from her fuckboy of the night's bed.

New Portia was stone-cold sober, as she had been for months, halfway across the world from her usual New York City stomping grounds and entirely pissed.

She pulled her hair back out of her face, slipping the scrunchie she wore around her wrist over the mass of thick, kinky curls to secure them. She glanced out of the window, taking in the gated storefronts nestled in the incongruously beautiful old buildings of Edinburgh's Royal Mile. In the back of her mind, she noted the different architectural styles and probable time periods the buildings had been built in—her master's in art history and string of internships actually *hadn't* just been a way of putting off responsibility, despite what her family thought, or hadn't *just* been that—but she had more pressing problems than discerning between marble and gold leaf and Victorian or Georgian.

She checked her phone again—no new calls, no

new messages, and a shitload of social media notifications. The latter was the norm, the first two were a problem.

Next, she checked the website of her destination, the ugly fonts and terribly formatted photos giving her hives as she searched for and verified the phone number. The website was at the top of her "oh honey, no" to-do list for Bodotria Armory that she'd compiled since her application for apprenticeship had been chosen. She was a walking "oh honey, no" to-do list herself, but one step at a time.

She winced at the trite cliché—too many self-help books, or maybe her therapist, Dr. Lewis, was finally rubbing off on her.

Six months in Scotland? This apprenticeship sounds like exciting wonderful opportunity. You should be proud. Can you tell me a bit more about what you hope to get out of it? Moving to Scotland is exciting, but also a huge change. You've talked about the urge to run away before . . .

Change was exactly what Portia wanted, and even Dr. Lewis's annoying but necessary questions hadn't made her rethink her decision. Standing alone at Edinburgh station and realizing her boss wasn't showing up had her reconsidering, though.

Now she was in the back of her cab, ignoring her driver's slightly unnerving humming and hoping she hadn't made yet another terrible life decision.

She decided to call the place one more time. She'd called as her red-eye train from London, full of rowdy university kids returning from a night of partying, had pulled into the station. The scent of stale booze and cigarettes that had permeated the train car had both grossed her out and made her desperately nostalgic for wild nights on the town, though how one could be nostalgic for less than a year ago was a mystery. She'd called when she'd found herself the last person in the station halls, except for the dude who'd decided that the corner next to a vending machine would serve double duty as a urinal.

She'd frantically searched through the emails regarding her internship, all starred, tagged, and sorted into a special folder in her email browser—yet another aspect of Project: New Portia. The project had three main aspects really, as she'd discussed with her therapist: getting organized, being a better friend and family member, not using booze and men as an escape from reality. Instead, she was using an internship in Scotland as an escape from reality, which seemed much healthier.

A message from her twin sister, Reggie, slid into view on her phone screen.

Hey, hope you haven't been eaten by Nessie yet (unless you're into that type of thing). Some of the GirlsWithGlasses community members saw your InstaPhoto post about being in Scotland for the apprenticeship and asked if you would do updates on the site in the Travel section. I understand if you won't have the time, but would love it you could. People really dig the Wonder Twins aspect of us making content together. I dig it too, I guess. Later, loser. ✌️

Portia smiled and took a deep breath. She and Reggie were still in the process of rebuilding their relationship, mostly via chatting about Reggie's über-popular site, GirlsWithGlasses. It was Reggie who had forwarded Portia the link about the apprenticeship after one of her followers had sent it in for the weekly Cool Opportunities posting.

Of course! she replied. Another key aspect of Project: New Portia—stop avoiding things that were hard. Letting down Reggie was all too easy, but Portia wouldn't do that ever again if she could help it.

How did your sister's illness affect you, Portia?

"Oracle, call Bodotria Armory," Portia bit out. She left out the "again," not wanting to confuse the phone, which had already tried and failed to do her bidding at least ten times.

"What's that, lass?" her driver, who had introduced himself as Kevin, asked. The guy was young, white, with gelled brown hair more fitting for a night at the bar than driving people around in his old Renault.

"Just talking to my phone," she said brightly, her gaze automatically heading to the left of the car before readjusting and flicking to the right, where it landed on the back of his head. She'd been ignoring his attempts to meet her gaze in the rearview, and she did the same as the peculiar buzzing ring tone that had taunted her all morning sounded through her earpiece.

Hello, you've reached Tavish McKenzie, master in arms and proprietor of Bodotria Armory. Please leave a message.

The voice was Scottish. Like, really fucking Scottish—deep with a strong burr that had Portia frantically clicking on the "Yes, I would like to subscribe to your sexy accented newsletter" box. She hadn't found much info when she'd performed her obligatory internet dirt search on her new boss: a grainy picture on the website, where he was clad like a cosplayer at a fantasy con. A video of him in some type of armor that covered his face, displaying the proper technique for wielding a broadsword. She'd felt the tingles of interest then and had pulled the hand brake before they started barreling toward the Bad Ydeas Towne section of the renaissance fair.

Men were definitely not a part of Project: New Portia, most especially not her boss, who seemed to have forgotten her existence before she'd even arrived. She was done with fuckboys, and fuckbosses for that matter, no matter how sexy their accents were.

"Aye, ye Americans are a strange lot, aren't ye?" Kevin said with amusement, cutting into her thoughts. "Talking to your phones, kissing your pets, destabilizing countries around the globe."

Here we go. One of the benefits of being a rich American was traveling the globe, and one of the downsides was getting to be the sounding board against whatever fucked-up policies your country was pushing.

"You have voice command technology here," she said, then peered around his old car. "Though maybe not you in particular, I guess."

She had never kissed a pet or destabilized a country—except perhaps for that small incident when her bumbling attempt at "saving" her best friend from her now fiancé had almost cost her their friendship—and nearly deprived the kingdom of Thesolo of their future queen.

"I prefer a phone that doesn't do my bidding, or anyone else's, if you see what I'm saying," Kevin said earnestly. "I hope you cover that camera on the phone. You know the NSA can tap in and peer at you while you're doing, oh, just about anything."

Portia sighed deeply and opened her text app, tapped the conversation, International Friend Emporium.

Ledi: I saw the selfie you posted from the train station, with the guy peeing like five feet away. WTF? Where are you now.

> **Portia:** Yes, that was a sweet moment that reminded me of home. My boss never showed at the station and I'm in a taxi with a weird, conspiracy theory-touting Scottish driver.

> **Ledi:** Do you have the pepper spray I bought you?

> **Portia:** Yes, mom. What are you doing up?!

> **Ledi:** Same thing I do every night, Pinky: studying. Let me know when you get to the armory. If you don't, Thabiso will call the embassy there and have them send out SWAT. Is there SWAT in Scotland? SCWAT? You know what I mean.♥

Portia laughed. Her best friend Ledi was a princess, after eloping with the prince she'd been betrothed to at birth, but she still studied like a pauper and would use her pull to protect Portia if necessary. That knowledge eased the tension in her neck a bit. Someone had her back, even if only through an invisible link between their mutual phones.

"Did you get a hold of anyone?" Kevin asked. "At the armory?"

Portia's "mind your business" hackles rose, and she dug in her purse so that her pepper spray sat atop all the other crap. He looked harmless enough, but after months of her mother warning her how rough Edinburgh could be—*Have you seen* Trainspotting?!—better safe than sorry.

"Yes. I'm messaging with him now."

"Tav knows how to send a text?" Kevin caught her eye in the rearview mirror and Portia stiffened, though he was smiling. "I guess maybe he's finally getting it together now that he'll have you for an apprentice."

"Am I going to have to mace you?" she asked, too tired and frustrated to execute the niceties that had been ingrained in her through years of deportment lessons and dealing with her parents' rich family friends.

He barked out a laugh and smacked the wheel. "Aye! Definitely American!" Portia wasn't sure if the statement was meant to be an insult. "Don't fash yourself. I take lessons at the armory, and everyone's been on about this American apprentice arriving this week. Cheryl checked her InstaPhoto and said she was beautiful and glamorous, and seeing as how you're going to the armory and you're. . . ."

Portia didn't think psychopaths had the ability to blush as bright red as Kevin was up in the front seat, so she relaxed her hold on the pepper spray. Anyone who would call her glamorous after hours in transit deserved the benefit of the doubt.

"Well, I'm glad someone is looking forward to my arrival. Mr. McKenzie seems to have forgotten I'd be arriving this morning, and that he was supposed to be meeting me."

"Oh, yeah. Tav is . . ." Kevin paused, and in the rearview she could see his brow crease. "Tav is a right bawbag at times. But a bawbag who grows on you, I suppose."

Portia pulled up her browser and searched "bawbag scottish slang."

The term bawbag is a Scots word for "scrotum," which is also slang for an annoying or irritating person.

Considering how little contact she'd had with the man who would soon be teaching her the ins and outs of Scottish swordmaking, she couldn't quite disagree. They'd spoken briefly on the phone, once, and he'd kept the conversation to a minimum—at the end of the call she'd realized that he'd barely spoken at all. Her other correspondence had been with someone named Jamie, who seemed pretty cool.

"Yes, leaving me stranded at the station is a bawbag move," she said, and Kevin laughed.

"Aye, this is going to be grand," he said, then the car slowed and stopped just in front of what looked like a blue wooden telephone box. Portia was fairly certain she'd seen Regina wearing a T-shirt with one of those things on it, with the words *police box* around the top.

"Here we are, Bodotria Armory," Kevin said, hopping out.

Portia stepped out as Kevin busied himself pulling her bags from the trunk—boot—of the car. In the two pictures on the website, the building had looked charming, but in the early morning dark with mist rolling in from the sea and creeping over the cobblestone streets, it had a distinctly menacing air. It was Georgian neoclassical, if she was guessing correctly, three stories of perfect symmetry and imposing bulk. The gray sandstone was dark and grimy with age and moss grew in fissures between the stones. The windows were all dark, except for a circular Palladian window at the very top floor.

"There better not be any wives locked in the attic," Portia muttered.

"No, Tav is single, though not for lack of ladies trying, so no worries there," Kevin said as he handed off her rolling suitcase. "I'll wait for ye to get in, lass."

"Thanks," she said, then took a deep breath.

I could use a shot or two, for fortitude.

She'd forgotten how scary trying new things was

when you were sober. She shook her head and began moving for the door when a loud cry broke through the fog.

"Oh, stop it, you fucking tosser!" It was a woman, and she was mad or scared or both. "I said cut it out!"

Portia ran to the police box, but the door was locked.

"Oh, those were decommissioned ages ago," Kevin said calmly, as if there weren't a crime in progress.

All of the crime alerts from Bodotria her mother had flooded her inbox with popped into Portia's head and she didn't think. Her hand shot into her purse, her suitcase clattered to the cobblestone, and she ran off toward the sound.

"Och. Wait!" Kevin called out, but she was already turning around the side of the building and stepping through the fog into what seemed to be a courtyard. She heard the sounds of struggle, then saw movement in the fog. The courtyard was illuminated by a few dim lamps, and she could make out a small-ish woman with a crown of pink hair trying to fend off an attacker. He was large, broad shouldered, and looked like he could bench-press both Portia and the woman at the same time. The woman kicked out.

"Let go!" she growled, and the man laughed.

"Make me."

Portia was paralyzed by panic for a moment, but she had taken self-defense courses. She had played this out in her head, what to do if she saw someone being attacked.

She took a deep breath then ran up—holy *shit* this guy was huge—and elbowed the guy from behind, bouncing back a few feet from the force of the impact. Her hit didn't seem to faze him, but it got his attention. He turned to face her. His skin was tanned, surprising for all the talk of cloudy days and pasty

British men she'd heard about. His eyes were a beautiful shade of olive green beneath the fringe of salt-and-pepper hair that fell into his face. It was cropped shorter on the side, revealing that the hair at his temples had already completed the transition from salt and pepper to salt. His face was that of a man too young to be going gray, though rough-hewn, with gray-tinged stubble. Portia blinked, and then she saw a flash of metal and the man's attractiveness became the most trivial of matters.

He had a knife.

Portia focused on those gorgeous green eyes, lifted her hand, and sprayed like he was a cockroach in her living room.

"What the fuck!" the man dropped to his knees, hands pressed to his eyes. He muttered a string of words Portia didn't understand except that they were invective against her.

"She told you to let go," Portia said, feeling a strange light-headedness that was probably an adrenaline rush. She also felt a little rush of pride—she'd only been in Scotland for about an hour and had already stopped a crime in progress. She was already composing the text message to her parents, some variation of *See? I'm not a total fuck-up*, when she felt a burning that had nothing to do with victory.

"Ow, ow, OW!" Her can of pepper spray clattered to the ground and she brought her hands to her eyes, too.

"Did you stand downwind?" the man said, and for a moment she thought he was crying but then realized the strange sound was his low laughter. "Oh, you bloody tosser."

"Tav, are you okay?"

Through her tears Portia could make out the woman who'd just been attacked run to her attacker and begin to help him up. Her attacker named Tav.

Wait.

"Go get some milk, Cheryl," he said, pulling himself to his feet.

She heard Kevin then. "Did you just mace Tav? Oh, this is brilliant, man."

She heard the sound of a cell phone camera shutter, which in modern times was the equivalent to a death knell. She spread her hands to cover her face more fully, regretting that she'd pulled her hair back.

"Sprayed herself, too," Tav said, and Portia somehow knew that "the bloody idiot" was implied.

She pressed her palms into her eyes, waiting for Cheryl to bring the milk, or the earth to open and swallow her. She'd been in Scotland less than an hour and had managed to assault the man who would be her boss for the next six months—and herself in the process.

Project: New Portia was off to a fantastic start.